THE FAITHFUL DARK

Cate Baumer (she/her) is a fantasy writer who lived half her life in Japan but currently resides on an Appalachian mountaintop and is occasionally visited by foxes and bears. While she works as an international relocation consultant by day, she spends her nights crafting bittersweet stories set in lush and haunted worlds. *The Faithful Dark* is the first book in The Brilliant Soul duology and Cate's debut novel published by Hodderscape.

CATE BAUMER

THE FAITHFUL DARK

First published in Great Britain in 2026 by Hodderscape
An imprint of Hodder & Stoughton Limited
An Hachette UK company

The authorised representative in the EEA is Hachette Ireland, 8 Castlecourt Centre, Dublin 15, D15 XTP3, Ireland (email: info@hbgi.ie)

1

Maps and illustrations by Dewi Hargreaves

A CIP catalogue record for this title is available from the British Library

Hardback ISBN 978 1 399 75115 5
Trade Paperback ISBN 978 1 399 75116 2
ebook ISBN 978 1 399 75117 9

Typeset in Garamond Premier Pro by Hewer Text UK Ltd, Edinburgh
Printed and bound in the United States of America

Hodder & Stoughton policy is to use papers that are natural, renewable and recyclable products and made from wood grown in sustainable forests. The logging and manufacturing processes are expected to conform to the environmental regulations of the country of origin.

Hodder & Stoughton Limited
Carmelite House
50 Victoria Embankment
London EC4Y 0DZ

www.hodder.co.uk

For Halle, who was no help at all.

Content Notes

Religiously sanctioned torture, violence (no identity-based or sexual violence), animal death, character death, and alcohol and substance abuse.

Pronunciation Notes

Characters

Csilla: *Chi-la*
Mihály: *Mi-high*
Ilan: *Il-lan*
Abe: *Abuh*
Tamas: *Tam-ash*
Ágnes: *Ahg-nesh*
Erzsébet: *Er-jebet*

Angels

Arany: *Ah-ran-ye*
Ezüst: *Ehzusht*
Kosiv: *Koshiv*
Taáj: *Ta-ai*
Lajol: *Lai-ol*
Savir: *Shaveer*
Ignaz: *Ignahz*
Orsolya: *Orzo-lia*

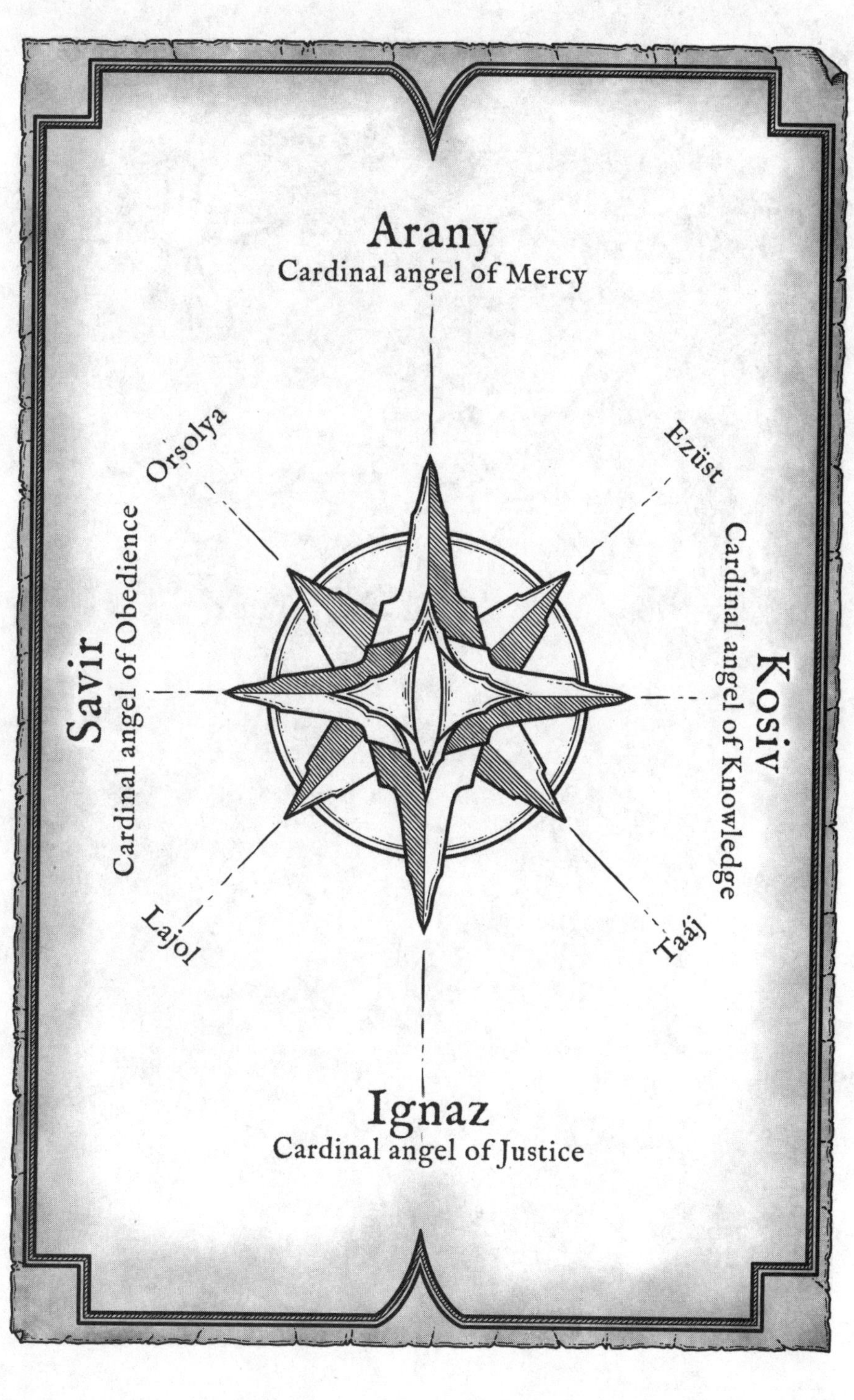
Arany
Cardinal angel of Mercy
Orsolya
Ezüst
Savir
Cardinal angel of Obedience
Kosiv
Cardinal angel of Knowledge
Lajol
Taáj
Ignaz
Cardinal angel of Justice

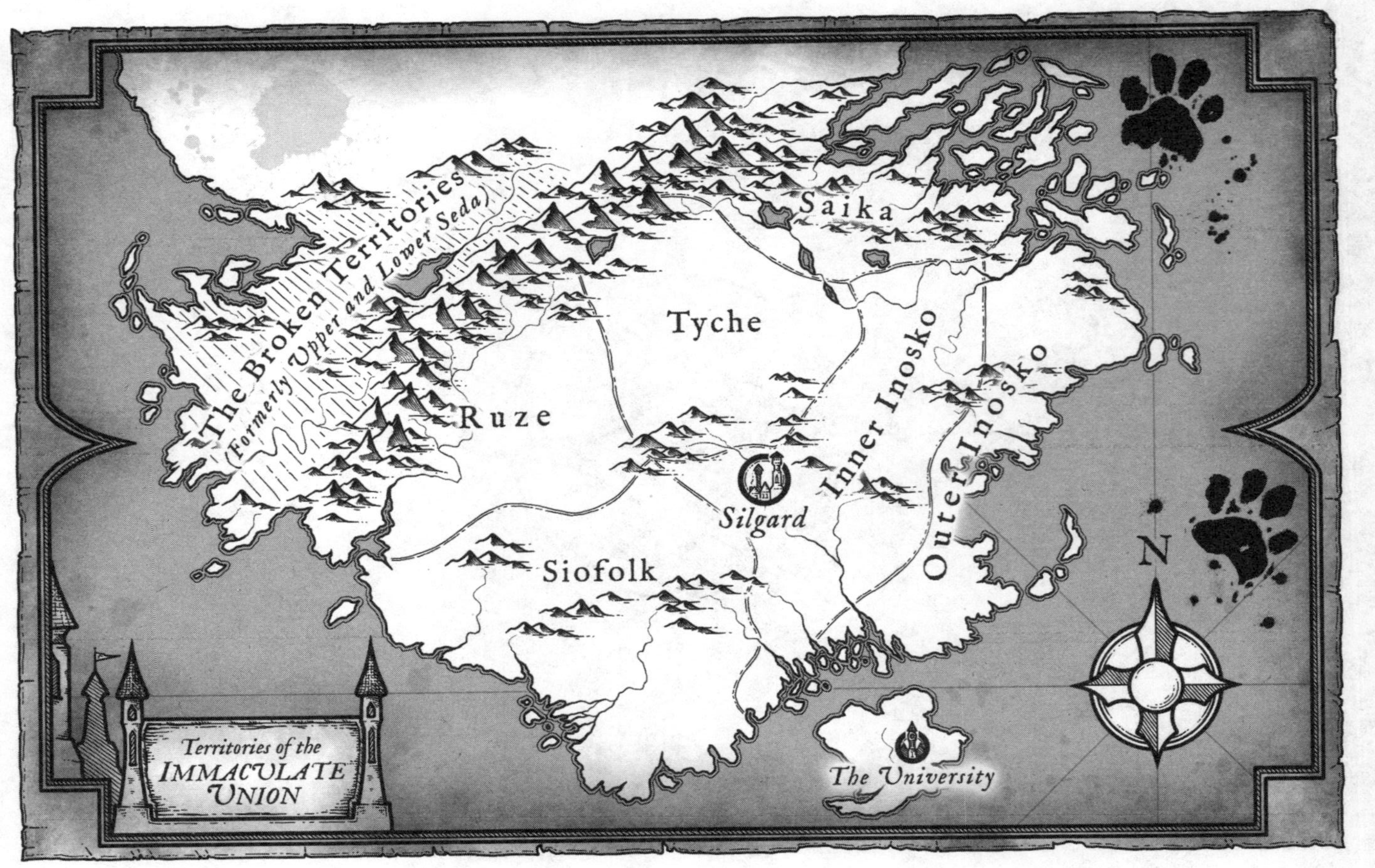
Territories of the
IMMACULATE
UNION
The Broken Territories
(Formerly Upper and Lower Seda)
Saika
Tyche
Ruze
Inner Inosko
Outer Inosko
Silgard
Siofolk
The University
N

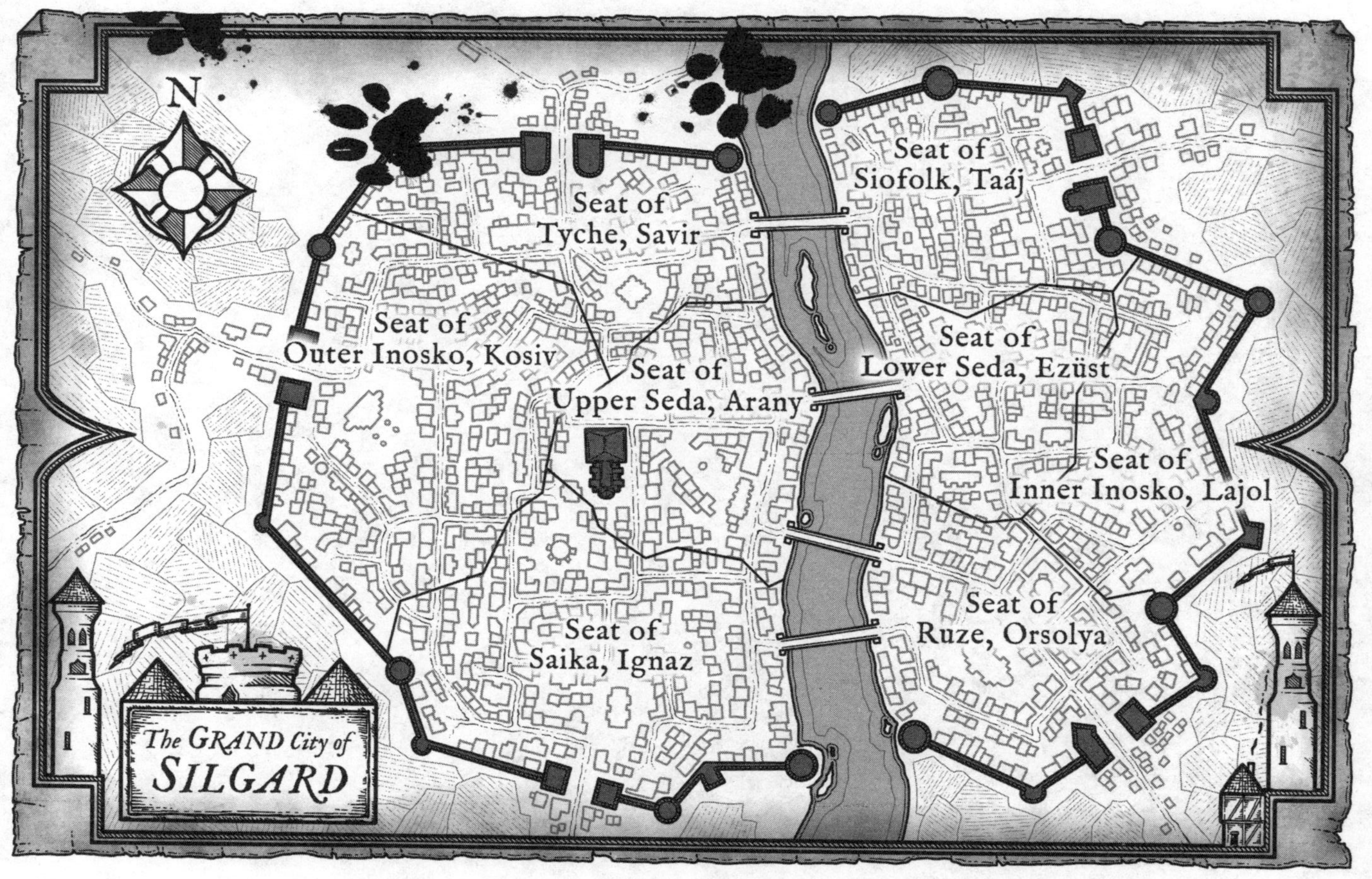
N
Seat of
Siofolk, Taáj
Seat of
Tyche, Savir
Seat of
Outer Inosko, Kosiv
Seat of
Upper Seda, Arany
Seat of
Lower Seda, Ezüst
Seat of
Inner Inosko, Lajol
Seat of
Ruze, Orsolya
Seat of
Saika, Ignaz
The GRAND City of
SILGARD

1

Csilla

THERE WAS an art to mercy. It was science, measured in the drops of poppy milk to ease pain, the days a child needed in the womb. It was faith, too. Everything was.

Csilla was as competent at tending the ill as anyone raised as a kindly hand of the Church, but faith was where she excelled. Faith that her service made a difference, despite its ceaseless demands.

Despite the fact that, no matter what she did, the Church would never care. Every time she touched a consecrated chalice or the iron mark of virtues worn by the Faithful and left it dull, she revealed the truth of herself: soulless, and darkly singular for it.

'How are you feeling?' Csilla asked, waving Elmere to the unsteady firelight of his hearth, hoping as always that her treatments had finally taken root and there would be no more work here, save a prayer of thanks. But dark-edged lesions still bloomed on his face and neck, and the wool over his elbows and knees had rubbed thin against his swollen joints. Bitter winter was hard on everyone in Silgard, but the old, sick and poor always suffered most.

Every day, new smoke carried the ashes of the dead through the air of the Brilliant City, from those delivered to their maker by illness, or hunger, or battlefront injuries that refused to heal as soldiers died cursing an absent god. It had been over three hundred years since They'd answered any prayers, and Their last response to humanity's transgressions and pain had been to remove Themselves entirely.

Then there were the other bodies dragged out of the city gates before dawn, bloodless corpses swaddled and bound with ink-smeared strips of knotted scripture.

It's not for you to worry about, dearest, Elder Ágnes had said when Csilla asked why they weren't being blessed, and washed and burned.

But worry was the only thing that came as easily to her as care.

The lines on Elmere's face deepened with a grimace. His teeth were loose against his thin lips.

'Better than I was.'

Csilla poured blessed water onto fresh linen and dabbed at the open wounds. They did look cleaner, free of pus or crusting edges.

'Surprised you're working alone,' Elmere continued, tilting his chin so she could continue her ministrations. 'They've finally accepted your vows? Do I owe you more deference now?'

But they could both see her overdress was a grim stained colour that could charitably be called off-white, not the deep grey worn for mercy work. Even a Curate, the lowest rank of clergy, would wear the colours of their order of virtue.

Csilla held up her palm, pale and unscarred by the Prelate's holy knife, and offered a smile she hoped looked less pained than it felt.

'Not yet. The fevers have everyone busy. Ágnes is just next door.'

'A treat for me, then,' Elmere laughed, and Csilla's smile turned more genuine, her cheeks flushing with the simple pleasure of being seen.

Her patients never minded who their care came from as long as it came with gentleness. Or if they did, they were polite enough not to mention it in her presence.

She pulled a bottle of distilled herbs mixed with just enough of their strongest syrup to blunt any pains from her leather sack, the final piece of today's mercy. The glass picked up the fire's glow, becoming almost a lantern as it bent light into the corners of the dim and dusty room.

'Don't drink it all at once,' she cautioned as he eyed the bottle and its liquid hope.

The poppy syrup was almost gone. There were too many suffering, too little in the stores, and no way to get more of the precious pods to milk until the warmer months. She'd exhausted every text they had, cut recipes down to the bone and shaved off further shards in hope of extending them, studied miracles and history and come up with nothing better than that people would die.

But fewer of them than otherwise if she kept to her work.

'I won't,' he promised, hands not stirring from his lap. Odd. Usually he poured a cup and they chatted while she boiled water for hot compresses and fixed up what she could to spare him trouble, sweeping rushes or mending oil-paper windows, and wishing she could give him better. It wasn't like the Church was lacking.

'You're feeling that well?' She grabbed the rough handle of his iron pot with both hands and heaved it up to the hook over the fire, breath short with the exertion. Being used to the work didn't make the pots any less heavy.

When she glanced back, Elmere's face was alight with a strange sincerity, rheumy eyes solemn and lips curved up.

'What?' Csilla asked, unable to keep the fondness from her voice. Elmere had been her patient since she was twelve, tolerant of gaping bandages and clumsy adolescent fingers as she learned the art of care. Eight years on, and he still sometimes slipped her pieces of rosewater candy on her way out, when he could afford them. 'You look like you have a secret.'

He touched his lips in acknowledgement, and her skin prickled.

'I went to see the Izir.' Elmere's voice slipped into reverence.

Csilla turned so quickly she bumped the pot, spilled water sizzling to faint mist in the flame. 'Oh?'

Izir were rare, descendants of the angels who walked the world of salt and blood before the Severing and those humans they had loved. There had been one in town for weeks – not that her endless work gave her leave to gawk. He certainly didn't come by the cathedral; blooded divinity had no need of intercession.

Elmere nodded, gesturing to his pocked skin. 'He heals, child.'

The lesions *weren't* healed, but if Elmere was feeling better, that was a true blessing.

'How?'

A hundred litanies crawled through her throat. Where there were blessings, there should be praise, and this was the closest that remained to miracles in the world.

The old man's laugh was a bark. 'Through Asten eternal. Virtues and vices, didn't the Church teach you anything?' She bit the inside of her cheek at his teasing as he continued. 'He heals with a touch, and he has the most marvellous voice. Makes one think of how Silgard must have been in its glory.'

There had been a time when the streets glowed with the divinity of those who walked on them, every footstep a benediction. Saints and angels had made this city the locus of the Faith, nestled safely in the centre of the territories of the Immaculate Union, its walls of stone inlaid with prayers to last until the material world fell to dust.

But that was when their god, Asten, still found the world worthy of notice. Now, when the walls cracked, they were repaired with nothing more than earthly mortar, and the only things that watched from on high were vigilant pigeons.

'One day we'll be gloried again,' she said, words tripping off her tongue as easily as song. 'Once every soul is Brilliant.'

It was the Church's most important charge. Asten may have left, but perfect obedience would lure Them back and wash the world clean, would allow the angels to return and bring a second golden age. It was only the fact that humans were a corrupted creation in the first place that made obedience so hard.

'He might get you a miracle too, you know.'

Elmere's voice was soft, but the words chafed as she bowed her head for a prayer to blessed Arany, an angel whose sacrifice had kept humanity's hope alive long centuries ago.

It was kind of him to say, but there was no miracle for something like her. Not even in a city built on one.

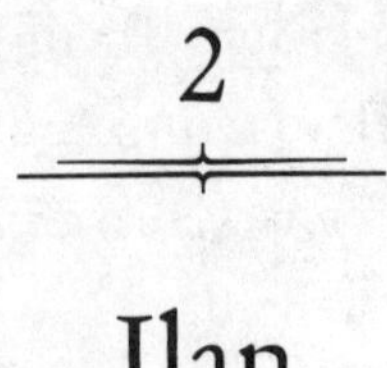

2

Ilan

THERE WAS little pleasure in burning a man when it produced such dismal results. The High Inquisitor scowled at the pinkened strips along the shaking merchant's forearm, skin that would soon shrivel to blisters.

'I've already told you everything,' the man gasped. 'The cheating I'll give you, but I didn't have anything to do with that girl's murder. Mercy. Please.'

Ilan's lips thinned at the impotent plea. He set the iron rod back in the fire, gaze lingering on the steady orange smoulder that gave the windowless room a smoke-tinged glow of golden holiness. He'd been sure of this lead. Multiple witnesses had testified they'd seen the man prowling Silgard's dank riverbank in the mornings, right where the latest death had been. The man himself had confessed to sabotaging his neighbour's eel traps so readily Ilan had been sure it was a ruse.

But he really was just that easily cowed, a cheat wanting to be the only option for serving eel pies when the city opened its doors to celebrate the Incarnate's return from the war front. Failure scored him as surely as the marks he'd left on the crook, and Ilan let his hand linger on the metal until the heat stalked back up it, ready to scald.

'Hold out your hand.'

The merchant uncurled his tense fingers, wincing as if expecting to have them broken.

Ilan fished a piece of consecrated glass from his pocket and placed it on the man's sweat-slick palm, murmuring a cleansing invocation.

The misshapen piece, broken off an older miracle and worn smooth by years of sinners' touches, glowed with soft light as it read the man's soul. The taint of guilty Shadow present before Ilan's care had been brushed away by the man's confession like the soil covering a buried gem. A small satisfaction eased the knot in Ilan's stomach. At least he'd set one part of the city right tonight.

He untied the ropes binding the man's forearms to the table and gestured to the burns.

'Find a mercy priest to tend to that before it blackens.'

With luck it would scar, a daily reminder of what Asten thought of swindlers, and save him work in the long run.

The man half-sank before he stood, his run out of the purification room more of a stumble. He was replaced in the doorway by a long-faced novitiate, one burn-reddened hand curled on the door frame.

'Yes?'

Ilan didn't bother to temper the sharpness in his voice. It was late, and the driving energy that came with his calling was fading. Chasing whispers and paranoid suspicions was long and haggard work, even before the physical acts. Bodies in pain, souls desperate for escape, were also closest to the divine, their confessions the most likely to save. But getting them there was exhausting and left tired grit behind his eyes.

The boy averted his gaze from the whips and ropes that dragged the misguided back onto the path, focusing instead on the floor.

'It's the latest corpse, Inquisitor. We're sending it out tonight.' His voice cut off as his teeth worried at his lower lip. 'No one wants to give her rites. They say she shouldn't have them.'

Of course. The congregational priests whose prime virtue was Obedience joined the Faith to cocoon themselves away from sin, not confront it, and it showed in the distance they put between themselves and his work even as they praised it. A thousand hymns and confessional comforts didn't do a darkened soul the good of one well-timed strike. And now that discomfort at reality was leaving a dead girl disrespected.

'Fine.'

If he couldn't yet give her justice, peace was the least he could offer. He followed the boy out and into colder and deeper parts of the cathedral, the stone halls narrowing to squeezed passages and a low slanting roof. It was a blessed thing the killer had decided to take up his sport in an icy season, but the hold still stank with the lingering sour of rotting bodies; the wine merchant the week before, and now this girl. The novice passed him a hand cloth doused in altar oils, but the sandalwood wasn't strong enough to keep the stench at bay, and Ilan's head throbbed.

'Has she at least been given a deliverance writ?' he asked as he approached the corpse.

The murdered girl – Kovács Lili – had lost any charm she had in life. Ilan slid her eyelids shut to cover the last bit of her empty stare and smoothed her pale blonde braids over the jagged rat bites on her ears. She was from the north; his mother used to plait his hair much the same. She could have been one of his sisters if he didn't look too closely. Or even Ilan himself, before he'd realised he was no one's daughter.

The boy stared at the body, face twisted in discomfort.

'Well?'

He finally bowed, and Ilan let the hesitation in it slide. 'No, Inquisitor.'

'We respect those delivered, no matter how they got here. You haven't even kept the vermin away.' He picked up the corpse's arm, turning to look at the palm where shallow cuts festered. She'd made a brave attempt to defend herself. 'Bring me paper.'

He inspected the blackened wounds with pursed lips as the boy scurried off, then traced his fingers along the carved flesh under her collarbones, turned into a macabre decoration of dribbled blood dried to black garnet and citrine-yellow pus. The script of this killing was in the language of the ether, the message a corrupted and Shadow-touched one he couldn't read, no matter how many times he traced the words peeled in her skin.

The bodies had begun appearing after the shortest days of winter. People still murdered even in Silgard; holy walls couldn't stop rash impulses and elements of jealousy or rage. This, however, was something new.

The Church had ruled the first death a singular event; unsettling, but within the realm of reason. The second, not two weeks later, raised eyebrows and pulled together late-hour meetings. The third, and the Church closed ranks, citing potential panic if word got out that someone was killing citizens and marking them as unholy.

Now they were on four, perhaps five, and he was no closer to finding out who was responsible.

Prelate Abe and his council had suggested sabotage from the broken territories or perhaps the Apostate cults springing up in the wake of war using dark imagery to terrorise. Madness was always a suspect, as was vendetta, though the killer had a wide reach, and there was no clear link between the victims save the manner of their deaths. The families all denied their loved ones had enemies or dark interests; death made a saint of everyone. There were never any witnesses.

The novitiate trotted back and passed over a crisp sheet of paper, the pale surface starkly bright in the flickering shadows of the room. It wasn't the vellum used for holy manuscripts or even the parchment of the Incarnate's letters and missives, but it was fine enough for something that would be ashes by the morning.

Ilan wrote the girl's name in a careful hand and inscribed an intercessory prayer beneath. If there were a particular saint or angel she wanted to lead her, there was no way of asking now, and any fresh blood that would have sealed the request had been emptied into the river to flavour the carp. He touched her cool forehead and penned in the name of Sainted Vasya. This girl was also a child of Saika, and their home territory's most beloved saint should be willing to lead her soul across, far as they were from her.

He folded the paper and placed it on Lili's chest, her arms too stiff to be bent to hold it. A memory flashed; another body with arms folded, and leather cuffs, and snow-heavy pine branches scratching at the windows as they prepared the body to burn. It was said to be a blessing for anyone to die in Silgard, in the sight of the spires of the grand cathedral and heart of the Church, but he'd wager she would have rather been delivered while looking at peaks and ice. For a too-brief moment, a sharp memory of the forest scent of Saika, wild and evergreen and seven years behind him, chased out the scent of death.

'Send a message to the Servants of the Road that we're done with the body and put her out,' he said. 'I'll let her parents know when I speak to them.'

He turned and left the disquiet of the cell-turned-morgue, but childish whispers chased him.

'—lost Asten's favour.'

Ilan turned, the snap of his boot heel on the stone enough to silence, but not to erase what he'd just heard. The two novices skulking behind Ilan bent together under his gaze. Likely shirking their duty.

'Did you have something to add?'

One of the boys was shaking his head, and the other put his back to the wall as if he could blend his oak brown robes into the grey stone.

That was the one who had spoken. Ilan grabbed his wrist, and though they were nearly the same height, the boy folded in on himself as if to protect his viscera, his already pale face a shade close to Lili's.

'No, Inquisitor.'

Ilan's reflection looked back at him in the gleam of widened, frightened eyes. He pulled out the blessed glass and forced it against the boy's skin, where it clouded with the grey stain of lies.

'Would you like to answer again?'

The boy jerked like a hooked pike, and his thrashing was equally futile. 'It's not what *I'm* saying! But you must have heard that the Seal is . . . It's weak.'

Of course it was weak: the city was too troubled for it to be otherwise. Ilan nodded at the glass, darkening by the second with the boy's fear.

'Our blessing remains.' There hadn't been so much as a stutter in the glass, or any of the powers of the Church. If the power of Arany's sacrifice was waning . . . well, he measured the city's balance of vice and virtue. He would know. 'We can't make any judgement beyond that.'

If the boy were wise, he would drop the matter.

He was still too much of a child to be wise.

'But it's been almost two months and so many people are dead, and the congregational priests are saying you're going to have a replacement, and if Asten really has called you—'

The force of Ilan's hand took the end of the sentence. Blood bloomed from a dry crack in the boy's lips, parted in shock from the smack.

Ilan made a loose gesture of blessing over the wound and dropped his wrist. Congregants called him the Holy Wolf for his viciousness.

What they seemed to forget was that creation itself had been an act of gloried violence. It was only right that a certain amount was still required to keep it pure.

'Apologies, Inquisitor,' the boy mumbled, tongue darting over the seeping red.

'Watch what rumours you listen to. All our souls are at risk – be thankful I just corrected yours.'

The boy bowed, and Ilan nodded.

There was silence as he left, but the disquiet in Ilan's mind echoed louder than any words.

A replacement. Unlikely. The Prelate would have warned him if things were truly bad enough to threaten his appointment. The Incarnate himself had named Ilan head of Silgard's Order of Justice, the High Inquisitor and steel hand that scoured away sin. No lesser power could undo that charge, and the only higher power was no longer speaking to Their creation.

Ilan straightened his cassock, touched the sharp silver four-point mark pinned to his collar. He would take evening prayers in his own chambers. And he would pray for the same thing he'd prayed for nightly for all these long weeks, as blood polluted consecrated stone.

Let me be Your justice, swift and holy.

He would show them all that *he* was Asten's chosen servant, brought here to purify with leather and steel. And he would show this monster, who had driven his city into froth-mouthed fear, what it meant to face the wrath of the divine.

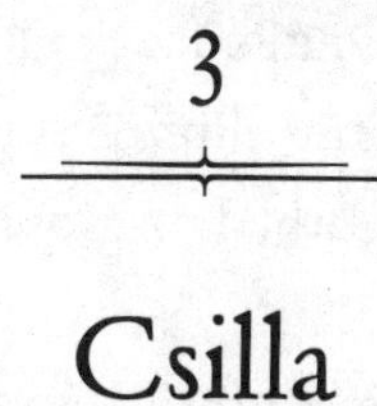

3

Csilla

CSILLA WALKED with small, sure steps that paused as she bowed her head to every wisp of holiness on the streets. The Eyes of Asten were carved on doors, illegible intercessions to saints baked into bricks along with the maker's fingerprints, infusing even the shadows with a certain hallowed air.

The fierce form of the angel Ignaz, cardinal embodiment of Justice, was pressed into an alcove, a fat black cat curled beside it. The silver-plated statue was clean of bird droppings, and she nodded approvingly at the resting feline as it opened a slit-pupiled eye.

'You're doing wonderful work for the Faith, cousin,' she told the cat, who yawned wide enough to show fang then shut its eye again. Well. Maybe he couldn't appreciate the praise, but it was worth giving all the same. Ignaz would certainly welcome the feline acting as judge and executioner to any pigeons or crows who sought to dirty her holy form or her protected district when she couldn't do it herself.

Bells echoed across high roofs, tolling the hour, and Csilla sucked in a breath. She'd meant to be back an hour ago, but extra minutes here or there, helping take down laundry or soothing a colicky baby, did tend to add up. She pulled her empty satchel to her chest and ran, dashing through a side street that would let her out near one of the bridges mostly used by merchants. Then if she cut through one of the open courtyards of the guild district, avoided the main thoroughfare and its horse-drawn cabs, and slipped through a back entrance, she could technically be on Cathedral grounds in time to help make dinner.

The city truly wasn't that confusing, much as pilgrims complained that the districts bled together and the door fronts didn't always face the expected direction. It was simply much like the divine itself: difficult to parse when in the thick of it, and best understood through long study and the occasional overview from on high. She'd had nearly twenty years, and plenty of time hanging out high cathedral windows, to take in the whole.

Her calculations were almost correct. It was only the wobble of a loose heel that slowed her. Shoes donated for charity had already walked a fair number of miles.

Csilla pulled the iron of the back gate closed with a sigh, adding 'mend a boot' to her list of tasks.

'Csilla. I've been waiting.'

The quiet voice drew Csilla up short and dispersed the mental calculation. Elder Ágnes, her face shadowed by the peak of her red hood covering the frost-rime white of her hair. The Head of the Mercy order must have been waiting for her arrival, and watching in feast day colours. Csilla bit her lip. Had she missed something?

'I'm sorry, Elder. There was just so much to do. I'm late for dinner, aren't I?'

Whoever she'd inconvenienced would no doubt be cross, and then she'd have to apologise for that. She sighed. Sometimes it seemed like her life was nothing but apologies.

Ágnes put a hand on her shoulder, urging her through the low door. 'Oh, don't worry about that. There's something else for you to do.'

‘Hm?’ Csilla let herself be led back to where she slept, a windowless side room of the cloisters crammed with three small beds for visiting penitents to share. They came and went. She never left. ‘What else could there possibly be?’ Not that she wouldn’t do it, if asked, but she was tired.

A set of grey robes lay on the bed, the sleeves and hems embroidered with a dance of red poppies and lined in matching scarlet. The uniform of the Church’s mercy priests, the inverted match of Ágnes’s colours. Her heart dropped.

‘Who died?’

She jumped to take the bundle before the older woman could reach for them. If there were empty clothes, it was because a body had left them. Ágnes was sick enough without handling the things of the dead. Illness had a tendency to creep, and the mercy priests were more often than not tending their own.

But the older woman shook her head, smile lines deepening around her heavy-lidded eyes.

‘They’re for you, dear.’

Csilla ran her fingers across the wool. The fabric was stiff with newness, not a single worn hem or stain.

‘For . . . me?’

Ágnes nodded, her smile soft. ‘The Prelate has decided it’s time. Change and come quickly.’

‘Now?’ There was baby spit in her hair, and she had a broken boot, and she still wasn’t entirely sure she hadn’t misheard.

The woman’s posture sharpened. ‘Unless our Lord has told you differently, yes, now.’

Csilla flushed. Elmere would be thrilled when she brought his next dose. ‘But . . .’

‘But?’ Ágnes’s face softened, stepping forward to take Csilla’s cheeks in her dry palms. ‘My sweet girl, this is your reward. Be happy.’

'I am!' The words came out too quick, too young, and Csilla folded her hands together, half in reverence and half to hide the tremble. 'I just never expected . . .'

She'd never expected anything. Hoped, yes. Prayed, often. Those were comforts. Expectations were what hurt.

But the wool was freshly dyed, the robe cut short for her scant height. Ágnes was dressed for celebration. The Prelate was waiting for *her*.

Ágnes ran a hand through Csilla's chestnut hair, untangling the wind-mussed curls with a mother's practiced grace.

'Quickly, Csilla.'

Csilla stripped her dirty overdress. Cold puckered her skin as she slid the new robes over her linens, breathing deep of the smell of wool unstained by human sweat.

She adjusted everything so it fell properly and knotted the apron with care. There was only one last piece.

In Ágnes's palm was an iron mark of four, the cross-shaped reminder of the cardinal virtues: Knowledge, Justice, Obedience, Mercy.

The metal glowed warm like a firefly at dusk, reacting to the consecration on it and the goodness in Ágnes's touch. The connection between the creative spark of the divine and the Brilliance of the human soul, still visible thanks to Arany's sacrifice.

Csilla kept her hands fisted at her side. If she touched it herself, she would break that fragile spell. Ágnes pinned it to her chest with a smile of pride.

The last thing Ágnes offered was a dark cloth, and Csilla bowed as it was wrapped over her eyes. Everyone, save the Prelate and the Incarnate, went to the heart of the cathedral blind.

They walked for long minutes before Ágnes stopped, and papery lips brushed Csilla's forehead. This close she could hear the rattle in the woman's lungs, a sharpness with each breath that dug into Csilla in matching agony.

'Whatever happens, remember that our job is to serve. Trust in the Church.'

Csilla furrowed her brow as a stronger arm took hers and she heard the slide of a door where she was fairly sure there shouldn't be one. Trust should go without saying. She served, and she trusted, even as she was walked into the depths.

The Seal was well hidden in the labyrinth below the cathedral, surrounded by centuries of tunnelling passages that stretched from the sacred heart and out of the city, now mostly stoppered with sinkholes and refuse. She'd learned the twists and corners of the structure like she'd learned her letters, and though this path was new and unfamiliar, the broken steps and cool damp air of the underground were old friends. Her fingers dragged along the water-eaten wall as she was led through and back around bends and curves and odd corners, brushing lichen and the splintering wayward roots tunnelling through the walls, occasionally catching on something that might have been bone. Before the orders came to save the land and burn the dead, Silgard had been built on the backs of the Faithful.

She'd crept below often in her childhood to search for blessed Arany's sacrifice, breath heavy as she made prayers that wouldn't be heard, and waited for the blossom of a miracle in the dark.

She'd never found the Seal, but today there would be a miracle. It wasn't Gellért's glass forest or Rozalia's perfect corpse, but a welcome for a soulless girl was miraculous enough.

The door to the sanctum groaned like a dying thing as it opened, and the cloth was removed from her eyes.

Elder Abe, Prelate of Silgard and second only to the Incarnate in Asten's eyes, ushered her into the prayer chamber, bony fingers pressing her lower back. In his other hand was a knife, its handle twined gold and silver, inlaid with a topaz eye ever-glowing with inner fire. Csilla pressed her palms together, eyes on the holy glitter of the blade in rushlights.

It was what she'd been waiting for.

The other orphans used to make a game of telling her there was a family who'd asked for her, and would help her comb her hair and offer her clean handkerchiefs, then laugh as she sat outside on the steps for hours. They'd bet sweets and chores on how long she'd wait, but even after she'd caught on, Csilla still went. There was always a chance that the next time they'd be telling the truth, and hope was stronger than the potential for humiliation.

Standing before the Prelate felt exactly the same.

'Csilla,' he greeted, inclining his head. His grey hair was clipped short, thinning to bald at the crown. 'Ágnes has you ready for your role, I see. It suits you.'

'Prelate.' She dipped low in response, her voice barely audible, the rest of her silently begging him to say why she was there and assure her thrumming heart that this wasn't another jest.

He wasn't wrong, though. The dove-grey wool, with its slaughter-red lining peeking out at her wrists and throat, did suit her. She might not have a soul, but she'd served the city too long for it not to live in that empty place inside her, moulding her to minister to its needs. Now anyone who saw her would think her a member of a mercy crew and know she was living shelter for their pain.

'I remember when they found you,' Abe said, and she tilted her head at the fresh wistfulness in his tone. Ordinarily it would please her, but at the moment it was a torture worse than anything the inquisitor could produce. Every second of uncertainty was a misery. 'At Arany's feet, in the snow. A baby who no one quite knew what to make of.'

Csilla shivered, as if the frost on her skin had lingered. She'd heard the story so many times it was practically a memory. A baby near-dead from cold at the statue's base, scalp weeping blood through crusting scabs and speckled with Arany's miraculous gold. A baby who left her baptism water cold and clear, whose touch never sparked the smallest reaction in anything from a consecrated threshold to a relic. No one had ever heard of anything like her, not evil, not good.

'And I thank you for your mercy in taking me in, Prelate.'

They could have done a hundred things with her – sent her to a farming family in need of extra hands, sent her to the ever-burning garden in the great northern forest of Wesp, said to be where creation broke and brought forth Shadow. They could have simply given her a large dose of tonic and rocked her over the veil with lullabies. But they let her live. Every thudding beat in her chest was a reminder that no matter how confusing her existence was, mercy had won.

The thousand flat eyes of the angels watched them from the stuccoed wall, flaking old paint like paper tears. Their golds and whites had dulled to a dead, smoky brown, expressions lost to time; had she not long ago memorised the eight-pointed star of their compass of virtues, she wouldn't have even been able to tell Arany from Lajol.

The Prelate beckoned her further into the chamber, light lost with each step.

Beckoned her to the Seal.

It was nothing like she'd pictured. It was said to sparkle like the endless dazzle of winter stars over Silgard. It was said to glow like the eyes of the angels, ever watchful over the humanity they loved.

What lay on the ground was a dim, foggy etching with charcoal flecks darkening what light still shone. She squinted, her eyes adjusting to see the lines that had been carved down in this deepest floor, the compass of angels and a circle embracing the whole. Little touches of light, each no bigger than a mote of dust, resembled the glowing sparks thrown off a tended hearth.

It was beautiful, but it wasn't what she'd had described to her, and not what the texts and prayers spoke of. The books told of how Arany created the Seal on her deathbed, linking each of the territories of the

Union to Silgard with her own blood and divinity. There should have been millions of lights, one for each soul in the Union, incandescent and gathered at the point of their home. But parts of the Seal had only the barest scattering of glow. Tarnished gold flickered across the darkened points like the frantic heart of a dying bird.

Her mouth went dry. She'd studied too long, done too much mercy work, not to recognise wasting when she saw it. And though it wasn't logical, as she watched the twisting sparks struggle to light what was shadowed, only to fade again, all she could think was: *pain*.

Abe moved behind her, fingers curling into her shoulders. 'The Church has found a use for you, Csilla. If you still wish to serve.'

'Has it always looked like that?'

The question was rude, she should stay silent and obedient, but perhaps she was wrong. Maybe this was what it was meant to look like, and it was only childish imagination that had made it more than it was in her mind.

The Prelate sighed, a sound that echoed from deep in his chest.

'No, child. No.'

She barely heard with the horror before her. If the Seal was dying, the power of the Church was, too.

'What's wrong with it?' This couldn't be everything.

The Prelate ignored her, hands still caged around her. 'Do you know the Izir who has graced our city of late? Nemes Mihály?'

She nodded, head ringing with the echo of Elmere's delighted ramblings about the healer.

'Do you want me to bring him here?' She did not mention her own silent, stumbling prayers to the Izir. Perhaps they thought he could heal whatever this was.

Abe cleared his throat, the words caught and gargling.

'Izir Mihály has been preaching heresy.'

'What?'

The words were so incongruous they were nonsense. The Izir were closer to Asten than anyone, with one divine ancestor who had never been touched by the corruption that came with the creation of humanity. The world may have lost the presence of the angels, but even the Severing couldn't steal the sacred blood of their children left behind or stop those children from having their own. Even diluted as it was, the power of their angelic forebearers still manifested once or twice in a generation, as remarkable and unpredictable as a falling star.

'He's been drawing worshipers from the Church.' Abe's voice thrummed with the fire of a sermon. 'Claiming to see the dead, saying there are paths to grace before judgement, a time when the fate of souls is malleable. It's just the kind of thing that appeals to the weak, false comfort that if they die in Shadow, it's not the end.' He gestured to the flickering Seal. 'We need the people's faith, now more than ever. He's brought doubt to our doorstep, and it's showing in service attendance. Anyone who trusts their soul to him . . .'

Would spend their eternity wrapped in nothing but hunger and self-flagellating misery, forever apart from the divine. Knowledge was one of the four virtues, but only if what was learned was true.

'I'd be happy to speak to him . . .'

It was a strange mission. Csilla swallowed a bleak laugh at the idea that she could convince anyone of anything. Her skirts were stained from years of kneeling outside during services. No one listened to her about what to serve for breakfast, much less theology.

'We've already tried.' Abe's voiced wavered with something she didn't understand.

Csilla tensed. 'But then, what—'

The priest reached into a pocket of his robes and pulled out a necklace. A bird skull on a chain, the beak replaced by one made of silver filigree. The bleached bone and polished metal were awful and lovely in one, the hollows of the eyes almost alive with the flickering shadows.

Abe snapped off the beak, revealing a stoppered vial nestled inside. It was far smaller and slimmer than the medicine bottles she took her patients, and whatever in it was clear, not the brown syrup that soothed coughs. He put it in Csilla's hand and closed her fingers around it, the glass still warm from his body heat.

'Perhaps in your reading you've come across Scorn's Friend. You always were a studious little thing.'

She was, and she knew the piece of death in her palm. *Poison.*

Her head dizzied, her face dampening with sweat despite the cellar cold.

'But I'm a servant of the Church.'

Mercy workers saved, protected. She clutched at the vial, metal digging into the flesh of her fingers. She'd been right to be shocked at her acceptance. It was a dream, and this was the second when the beautiful turned grotesque and the shock of the impossible shoved you back into waking.

There was no waking. Only strokes of fire and Shadow, the corroded magic, and the Prelate's unwavering gaze.

'You're not, though, are you? You wear our robes, speak our words, pray to our god.' His voice wasn't unkind, merely flat with truth. 'But you lack a soul. And that's why you're the only one who can do this. It's no sin for you. There's nothing of you to blacken.'

'But *murder . . .*'

No one stole the right of death from Asten. Even the worst crimes were punished by abandonment on the winter ice or in the forest ravines of the north, not execution. It may have led to death all the same, but it wasn't murder.

People die, she reminded herself, though her vision blurred. It was a mercy worker's job to know that, even more than carefully memorised prayers and the ratio of herbs to blessed water. It was a truth pressed into their hands every day as they folded endless bandages and soothed fevered skin.

Abe reached for her trembling arm. 'All you'll be doing is delivering him back to the arms of the divine and saving the city from apostasy. It's not murder, it's mercy. For all of Silgard. The Incarnate himself has signed the order. It will be secret, but it will not be unholy.'

If the Incarnate signed the order, why do you still think it's a sin? How could the Prelate stand in this place of light and ask something so dark? She shook her head, not trusting her voice, and the new fabric scratched around her throat.

Abe's grip tightened. 'If you won't do it, you can leave. You'll never pass a holiness test, child. Silgard has no place for you, and we've given you shelter long past what is owed by the tenants to care for orphans. An adult's duty is to take a role and contribute to order. If you won't serve, you're no use.'

Her mouth twisted in open shock. What was treating the city's ill, washing its dead, and giving a lap to its children if not being of use? It didn't matter if she wore the brown lining of a novice or the glowing white of a prelate or the hand-me-downs of no one at all, her work was good.

'I don't want to . . .'

'Asten doesn't ask what you want to do for Them, but what you will do for Them and for our eventual perfection.'

Csilla turned her gaze to the saints and martyrs watching the exchange. If she could pray for their strength and be answered, maybe this wouldn't feel so much like drowning.

'I don't understand . . .'

'Submission isn't meant to be light work. You don't need to understand to serve.'

He was right. It was selfish, presumptuous, for her to argue. She wasn't anything, and she was being offered a way to do good.

Even if it was no kind of good she would have ever elected to do.

'Alright.' She barely recognised the voice that came out of her, choked and small. 'I'll do it.'

If this really would protect the souls of the city, she had no choice.

Abe's smile, ordinarily so kind, curled her stomach. He beckoned her forward.

If she'd had a family, they would have bathed her in water infused with rosemary and mint and given her an equal dose of affection, sent her to her vows with a crown of poppies and her dowry in hand to offer at Asten's Eye.

Instead she shivered, unadorned and empty. Together they knelt before the tattered magic of the great Seal. She spread her fingers on the earth, taking a deep breath and taking heart with it. This was what every servant of the Church did, and she was fortunate to be able to do it over the remains of Arany herself. In other territories they made do with facsimiles and floors stained with wine and varnish to look like the martyred angel's resting place. They claimed the blood of the Faithful would always find its like, connecting the country in a web of consecration. It was a pretty idea, even if it sounded more idealistic than true.

Abe's chant caressed her to her bones. The sound grew as it echoed against the damp walls, as if the centuries of the worshippers were speaking through the paint in welcome. On the far side of the wall were portraits of the noose-necked last saint Angyalka and the star-crowned first Incarnate Imre; stand-ins for the kin she would never know. They would have to be enough.

'Csilla.'

She opened her eyes again and offered her palm. He took her smooth fingers in his weathered ones.

'Do you swear to serve in perfect and perpetual Obedience, to accept the Church as judge and Justice of this world, to full-heartedly seek knowledge of the divine and Their creation, and provide unfailing Mercy?'

'Yes,' she answered before he'd even finished. Before she had any more time to think about the terrible nature of her calling.

Abe brought the knife to her skin, drawing a thin line of red to well on the surface. Then he squeezed, letting a drop fall to the gritty earth. The Seal remained still, dashing a final, quiet hope. Her soulless blood didn't carry any spirit, couldn't do anything to strengthen the Faith.

The Prelate rubbed his thumb through the dirt, her blood, and whatever echoes of Arany's holiness remained. She closed her eyes as he smeared a warm line down her forehead.

Bled and marked for the Church.

Called to service, just like she'd always wanted.

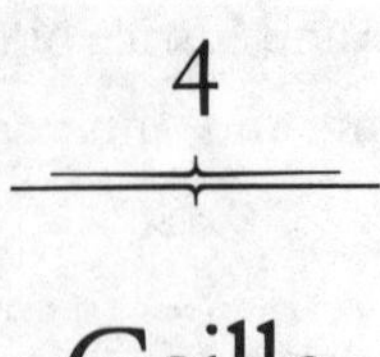

4

Csilla

THERE WERE three things everyone knew to be true of the Izir: he was beautiful, he was holy, and he never turned down wine. It had been easy enough to steal the bulb-shaped bottle now sloshing in her leather sack. If Csilla had a soul, she would have earned another black mark against her. And if she thought too hard about what was coming, she'd be drinking the wine.

He was a heretic, and he was keeping souls from salvation. That was what she had to keep reminding herself as she trudged to the farthest of the eight city districts. The Izir was a heretic, no matter who his ancestors were. Asten had given harder tasks to Their followers in ages past. The Prelate had said it himself, and her stinging palm reminded her of who she belonged to with every nervous twitch of her fingers. Obedience was a virtue: Obedience was submission.

The snow was thicker on this side of Silgard, and the roads darker, with many close-crammed houses that couldn't afford a door lantern. Just two days ago a body had been found pressed into the squelching mud of the riverbank. The thought of the girl lying dead in the night for hours chilled worse than the air, and Csilla said a quiet prayer that her departed soul was at peace, that she'd been good enough in life to join the Brilliance in the ether. She quickened her steps, touching the necklace to keep the chain from sawing at her.

In the square, orange fires burned in baskets set high on wooden pillars, flames flickering with each pass of breeze. The gathered crowd was a flock of ravens in the smoky light, all dark coats and anxious voices. A few specks of white and green – patterned kerchiefs, children's gowns – peeped here and there as the throng shifted, but everything else was navy and black, colours that wouldn't show soot or stain in the months when they couldn't be easily washed.

Snippets of conversation reached her ears, wants and wishes and fearful requests, some in languages she didn't speak. Anyone could petition to live in Silgard, as long as their soul was clean and they swore by the virtues. But these people, their faith so palpable it was almost a chorus, weren't here for Asten. Their praise and yearning were all gifts for the Izir.

'There is so much hope beyond what the Church offers you, cousins. There is comfort to be had, even in the unknowable. Death is not another Severing. The worlds here and there are not so far.'

The Izir's impassioned lilt carried even to the edges of the crowd where Csilla lurked as a flickering shadow, her shaking hands tight around the poison bottle. He spoke in the rhythm of liturgy, his tone as resonant as the bells that rang the hours. No wonder the crowd had gone pliant. Csilla paused after every step further into the throng, his words snagging the ever-present hollow in her chest and pulling her closer as surely as if he had her by the hand.

She wouldn't call it Shadow, but it was honey-sweet temptation. Csilla tried to block the words, keep her focus on the bone around her neck and the promise she had made. The city built by Asten's own angels was proof of the truth. And in the face of such undeniable, beautiful proof, who would sin?

But people did. Even now, they shoved each other, trying to be the closest to the blessed man. Their dark desires rolled off them easily, stirred by his presence. Greed. Wrath. Lust, in flushed cheeks and grasping hands.

The hard glass of the wine bottle bit into her ribs as she pressed it close.

'We're meant to relish this existence and learn, not cower. There is a reason Knowledge is counted among the virtues. I've seen proof that death is not the end.'

His words were met with raised hands and murmured prayers. The crowd began to shuffle forward for whispers, offerings, a final word. Idolatry.

The worshipers shifted as they recieved their final blessings and dispersed, and Csilla took her first full look at the man she was to kill. He was more simply dressed than she'd imagined – two buttons on his overcoat had been resewn badly, and his boots showed obvious scuffing. All of it was the simple black worn by priests who worked among the public, even his four-mark carved from obsidian. But he was as tall and had a face as finely formed as she'd expected, with light reddish-brown hair as sleek as summer fox fur. His beard was neatly trimmed, his eyes warm, and every inch of him seemed to glow from within, an aura that made her palms itch to press together in supplication, to touch her forehead to those damaged boots. No wonder there were at least a dozen stragglers eager for a few moments of personal attention.

A man with bloodshot eyes approached, and the Izir touched his face without hesitation, running his thumbs over the man's crusted lashes and murmuring something Csilla couldn't hear.

When the man opened his eyes again, they were clear and filled with adoration.

Csilla pressed a shaking hand to her lips, breathing awe. A miracle. Elmere had been right. This man could do *real* miracles.

And she was going to kill him.

He continued through the crowd dispensing touches of grace – a word to a person with a swollen knee, a brush of the forehead for a boy whose mother claimed he was filled with demons. Csilla frowned at that. There were no demons in Silgard, and if the woman needed the Izir to tell her so, she should never have been allowed to live in the Brilliant City.

The Izir must have known it, but he checked the boy for marks and blood anyway, reassuring the woman with a gentle hand that she and her child were well and the trouble was only earthly nightmares. The wrapped cloth she passed him bulged with tribute.

Then he was in front of Csilla, and she was all too aware of the jealous stares of the crowd.

'Are you here for a blessing?' His smile was kind, practiced, the face she'd seen on Ágnes as she rubbed the backs of small ones who wouldn't live through the night.

'I . . .' She couldn't give him poison where there were still people to see. 'I have something I want to discuss with you. It's very personal.'

Her cheeks burned at the accusing voices of those still waiting.

'Oh?' He stepped close, and she breathed in the spice of incense on his skin, and under that, something clean, like fresh water. 'And I see you've brought an offering.'

Her stomach dropped, and he reached out before Csilla could pull the bottle back. When his fingers brushed the glass, it glowed as bright as the glare of sun on morning snow.

Csilla winced, snatching it to her chest as a curse threatened to slide from her mouth. She'd been *sure* the bottle hadn't been through rites yet.

But all bottles were equally dull to her touch.

The Izir jerked his hand away. 'That's consecrated wine. Why is it dark?'

He was right. If it were held by any souled person, the bottle would be dusted with the pale golden sheen sparked by the latent connection between humanity and their creator.

'I . . .'

He gestured to the Eye of Asten melted into the glass, a sign of Church make. 'And it was stolen.'

Csilla's heart seized. She should have come up with a better plan. But when she looked into his eyes, there was no judgement there. He seemed . . . delighted.

She stepped back. People were never delighted to meet something like her.

'Well,' he said, looking her over more carefully as she shuffled her feet on the ground, willing them to sink and save her from this humiliating turn, 'it seems we do have something to discuss.'

She should have dropped the bottle and let it smash, run and been done with the whole business. But if she failed and lost her home in the Church, she'd be lost herself, and all these souls believing the Izir would be damned. Only the Church could lead them back to truth. The thought came with a note of sweetness more tantalising than even the heresy.

Once everyone was Brilliant, Asten would return and make the world perfect again, the way it was always meant to be.

A flutter of hesitation rose in her throat as the Izir smiled down at her, his face as radiant as a saint's vision.

She bowed, touching her still-aching palm to her chest. The Seal was weak, but the Church was strong, and she would be strong for it.

'If you would, Izir.'

Hopefully preaching made him thirsty.

5

Csilla

WITH THE city ringed by walls, the Faithful built towards heaven. The Izir's room was a converted attic in an upriver district, the window enlarged to the size of a door with a ladder leading up, and the whole thing clearly a newer make and more hastily wrought than the sturdier building below.

Csilla blanched. Not only did he expect her to follow him home, she had to climb into it?

'Sorry about this,' he called over his shoulder as he climbed, and she dodged the grit falling from his boots. 'I don't entertain many guests.'

From the knowing hunger in the crowd, she doubted that, but it didn't seem polite to say.

'You live up there?'

It was barely suitable for a poor apprentice, much less an Izir. Surely among all those ardent followers was someone who would have been honoured to host him in a home that actually had a door.

'Reminds me of where I grew up.' He pulled the shutters open then looked back, holding out a hand she didn't take. 'Be careful.'

With a deep breath she stepped up another too-thin rung, stomach lurching every time her eyes caught the dark stone of the ground below.

This is the worst idea you've ever had.

This is what you're meant to do.

Both thoughts were true.

At last she crawled through the window, breath as unsteady as her feet as she tumbled in. The Izir closed the shutters with a snap as she adjusted her skirts, and it took her eyes a moment to settle as everything washed pale yellow in the glow of the oil lamp he'd set burning. The room was even smaller than she'd expected, just a sagging straw-stuffed mattress over a hemp rope bedframe, a lamp, a travel sack. Green and brown glass bottles, lots of them, all empty and most toppled, and the lingering smell of brandy and smoke. The whole thing was claustrophobic, the slanted ceiling not tall enough for him to stand at full height.

'You climb that every day? It's dangerous.' The old ladder had rocked against the wall, and at least two rungs were splintered. 'But if you fall, I suppose you can fly . . .'

His laugh sent her shoulders up around her ears and heat to her cheeks.

'You believe that?' He let his outer cloak fall and his fingers found the top button of his jacket.

Csilla's stomach seized and her eyes darted to the window in quick calculation. He was standing between her and the only exit. The room was small, and he was large, and there was nowhere more than an arms-length away.

'Izir, please don't . . .' Her words choked as she backed up as far as she could. 'I only came here to *talk*.'

He couldn't have misunderstood.

Or maybe she was the one who had misunderstood. She touched her mark, the sharpness of each metal point. From the look of the crowd, he must have been used to people offering their bodies instead of just praise and spirits.

And she was darkly sure he wasn't used to being told no.

He turned, sliding one arm out of his jacket. The movement revealed the linen collar of his undershirt, but she lowered her eyes to avoid any glimpse of things best left covered.

'Do you see room for wings?'

Csilla's gaze fixed on her fingers as they clenched into ineffectual fists. But she glanced up, caught by the jest in his tone.

No, no room for wings.

'No wings, no extra eyes, no tail, nothing useful.' He slid his jacket back on quickly, muttering about the cold. 'And you can call me Mihály,' he continued. 'I'm not vain about my title.'

He raised an eyebrow at her little chuff of relief. He hadn't been trying to touch her, and she pretended she'd known it all along.

'Mr Nemes—'

'Mihály,' he stressed. 'I promise it's not a sin to call me by my given name. And what should I call you?'

'Csilla.' She bit her lip. 'Just Csilla.' Servants shed their family names when they joined the Church, but the admission she never had one to give up scratched at old loneliness.

'Well, that's lovely.' He smiled, and she warmed in spite of herself. 'And how old are you? You hardly look of age to be out and about at night.' There was a touch of condescension in his kind expression that stole the pleasure of being paid attention to.

She pulled herself up to her full height, unimpressive as it was.

'Twenty,' *probably*, 'though I hardly see why it matters.'

'Then why steal wine? Even in Silgard there's no shortage of friends willing to treat a pretty girl in the tavern. You look like you could use a good night.'

His wink set off a fresh wave of indignation that smothered the shock of the compliment. With her unwashed hair and work-worn hands, she wasn't pretty, and he was supposed to be *holy*. But though she'd just seen him heal with a divine touch, he spoke like any common man. He didn't even have a novice's reverence for the city.

But Izir were still mostly human, for all the touches of power on them. That mere humanity should have made her task easier, but instead her hands began to shake.

'You were right. It's an offering.' She rubbed her fingertips against her skirt, silently begging for intercession. If there were a time for their god to hear her, it was now.

'Just take it.'

If he took it, he'd take the damning choice away.

She hated how she wanted that loophole.

'People don't bring offerings unless they want blessings.' Mihály deftly pulled the quilt from his bed and folded it on the wooden floor, gesturing for her to sit on the faded red and green squares. The joviality leeched from his eyes. 'What have you heard?'

Csilla lowered herself onto the quilt, tucking her skirts tightly around her legs. Now she was sitting where the Izir slept, almost – not even the tiniest second-hand sin, but enough to send a fresh heat to her cheeks and worry across her skin.

He crouched down, forearms draped over his knees, perched like one of the loathsome stone demons that peered over the eaves of the cathedral, monstrous reminders of ever-lurking Shadow.

'Show me the wine again.'

Csilla swallowed and took the bottle from the sack, the surface still dark against her hand. Mihály reached out again, this time only a fingertip. Enough to spark the silver glisten on the glass.

'Why doesn't it react to you?' he asked, tapping the bottle and watching the light shimmer and dim under his touch like the wink of moonlight on water. Each little light was a needle prick in her heart.

'That's personal.' Csilla shifted, starting to stand again. Surely leaving the wine with him would be enough; by the number of bottles around he went through troughs of the stuff. 'I have to go.'

Another second and she would confess everything; the fresh rarity of his instant acceptance, like they were equals, had stripped what little resolve she had managed.

'Wait!' He lurched forward, hand outstretched, stopping a hair's breadth away from her arm.

She froze at the panic in his voice. There was a note in that one word more genuine than all the smiles and blessings she'd seen from him.

'I just want to know,' he continued. 'It's like you don't have a soul.'

Csilla swallowed. If he had any knowledge about what she was, she'd better find out before he was dead.

'And if I don't?'

'I'd say that's impossible.' But his slight smile widened, as if impossible was his favourite thing.

'The Church thought so, too. But here I am. They tried to come up with an answer, you know. I was studied extensively. No one ever made sense of it.' *Until now.*

She looked down at the floor, shame creeping up her neck. The Prelate had called this a use for her flaw. Her designated place in the grand design. And she wished she could reject it.

His tongue darted to skate his upper lip as he considered.

'Is that the blessing you came here for? You think I can miracle you a soul from the ether for the price of a bottle of stolen wine?' His brow arched, and he sat back with a thump that made her wince. 'I hate to disappoint you, but I have as little power to make souls as I do to fly. We Izir may have a touch of angel blood from those long years back, but we're still mostly human.'

She hadn't realised a small part of her had hoped for just that until the idea died at his words. She forced down the lump in her throat. It shouldn't even matter. She'd been given the one way she could serve, and it was with his death.

'My affinity is finding sickness and knowing what treats it, a remnant of Ezüst I'm told,' he continued. 'But I can't make a soul.'

He gave a shy smile that made her feel as if she should be the one apologising for pointing out his weakness, something small and haunted in his gaze.

Ezüst the healer sat between Mercy and Knowledge on the starry compass of virtues. There were ghostly impressions of handprints still visible on the wooden table where they prepared medicines that were said to be his. The connection softened her more than it should.

'Now that you've put it like that, I see that it's foolish. Just . . . drink the wine. You can keep it as payment for indulging me.'

Csilla looked down again, heart hammering. There was no way he wouldn't be able to read her guilt, even with her expression half-hidden by the shadows in the room. She felt cracked open, a split fruit ready to be picked through for what was good and useful, the rest thrown by the wayside. There was very little good at the moment.

'I didn't mean to upset you, truly. I'm glad you're here.' He stood and dusted off his hands. 'I'll make you tea and a snack if you'd like. I've got water left.'

She tried to protest, but he wouldn't listen, and her stomach argued that if she was going to kill him, his food would go to waste unless she ate it. The room was soon warm with the heat from their bodies and the wavering steam of the kettle. The tea he put in her hands was a deep rust-red, the aroma spiced and heady. Expensive.

'Another tribute,' he smiled. 'Go on, drink. I think she left some sweets with it.'

He rummaged around until he found a white handkerchief of soft linen, far too fine for wiping hands on. She turned it in her hands, stroking the fabric, and examined the two mottled doves embroidered in the corner. The Varga family. Csilla's warmth was replaced by a touch of despair. So even the wealthy were swayed by him now. No wonder the Church was worried.

Mihály picked up her hand and plopped two fried lumps of dough onto it.

'Ah, here. They're dry but should taste alright.'

Csilla's mouth watered as she bit into the dumpling, and she blinked in pleasant surprise at the centre of cherries stewed with enough sugar to take the edge off their sourness.

Still chewing, she offered the other one to Mihály, but he held up his hand.

'No, go ahead.'

She finished the first and choked down the second one quickly – half from hunger, half from embarrassment at the way he watched her. She washed it down with a swallow of tea, all too aware of the money on her tongue. Everything here had been paid for with heresy.

'I'm sorry, but I have so many questions,' he said. 'In all my studies I've never heard of anything like you. May I touch you?'

'You may not.'

She didn't have to leave her dignity with her morals. The Church couldn't ban touching, but she'd been warned since she was small about the dangers of too much contact. Bodies were Shadow-born, and skin had its own appetite. A good servant didn't stoke its cravings, not that she'd ever seen the appeal. At fourteen she'd asked Ágnes when she should expect such temptation to start, so she could be properly prepared. The woman had laughed and, upon realising Csilla was actually serious, informed her that it would be somewhere between any day now and never. So far it had been closer to never, but she wasn't going to let her guard down.

Mihály chuckled. 'Nothing indecent, I promise. Please.'

She hesitated, mind spinning rationalisations. She touched her patients when caring for them. Him being young and handsome, them being alone in a locked-away attic didn't make it any different. He might not even like women, or anyone. And it wasn't like he would find anything the Church had missed all the times they'd looked for demon marks. She offered her hand.

He took her by the wrist, tracing a word across her palm with a delicacy that sent a shiver across her skin. He was surely going to feel how her heart was racing.

'Hm.' He pursed his lips and dragged his fingertips over her skin again.

Her whole body lightened with hope, the soaring, beautiful ache of listening to the choir's hymns of praise, every note yearning for something lost before humanity had even finished forming.

It's not real. It's not real.

But it felt like it *could* be. She pushed herself up and away from him, wordless. If that brush of holiness was anything like what she was missing, she wished she'd never felt it at all.

'You are exceedingly healthy, but what happened on your scalp?' he asked.

She stiffened, touching her kerchief as embarrassment dragged back the truth of what she was.

'You can see those? The scars are from when I was a baby. Rat or cat bites.'

Unsightly as they were, they were all she had from before.

'Hmm.' Then he picked up her right hand, the one she hadn't offered, and peeled her fingers from the fresh scab of the slice from her vows. 'And I see you're from the Church. Or a very clumsy cook.'

Csilla gritted her teeth, unsure of the safest answer.

'Don't worry, you're not the only one.' He cradled her palm in his larger one, and Csilla went very still. 'Though I think you might be the first one who ran directly from vows to me. Does it hurt?'

'Of course,' Csilla said before recognising it for a lie.

It had hurt right up until he'd touched her. Now what had been an angry wound was a pale scar. She'd always healed quickly, but not instantly. She flexed her hand and found none of the tension that marred the grip of poorly healed clergy.

The pain was meant to remind the sworn of the gravity of their choice and the care required when using hands for holy work. Her stomach turned, threatening to reject the sweets and tea.

'I need to go.'

Mihály held up his hands, backing away. 'I'm sorry. I understand. I have scars myself.'

She raised an eyebrow. He appeared flawless from where she sat, even the shadows laying like adornment on his high cheekbones and soft lips.

'I want to show you my research,' he continued. 'I think you'll find it interesting. And I think you could be of great help to me.'

'Help?'

She tilted her head, the word catching her like a fish on a line. What help did he think she could possibly give him?

'I research souls.'

Her flare of interest only increased her agitation. Listening to any of this was pointless when she'd already as good as killed him. 'But you said you can't make one.'

'I can't,' he admitted. 'It's hard to explain here. As you may have guessed, it's not exactly in line with Silgard's . . . ethics.' He spoke quickly and settled on the final word as if it were a compromise.

Her brows drew together. Something more outlandish than what he was already preaching?

'You're an Apostate?'

There were pockets of them throughout the Immaculate Union, preaching corruptions of doctrine, making their own invocations and pretending they were the same as good work. They were little spots of blight doctored by the Servants of the Road.

'No, by the saints, though I certainly have a large enough flock.' He looked more amused than offended. 'I'll show you tomorrow if you'll let me. Trust me, it's something you'll want to see.'

A shiver of curiosity went through her. This was the closest she'd ever had to divinity speaking directly to her, filtered as it was.

But then the words hit.

'Tomorrow?'

It had to be today. She wouldn't have the guts to leave and come back, now that she'd sat in his home and spoken to him as a man and not a target. A warning sat in the back of her mouth, coming closer to escaping with every second she absorbed his kindness. She'd had so little in her life, she'd taken to it like drought-baked dirt welcoming rain.

'I'm sorry, but I have to go.'

'Surely you weren't thinking of walking back alone? The lamps will be dark by now.'

Arany's Seal was dark too. The reminder of the dying magic set her shoulders back.

He was damnedly right about the threat, but her part in Asten's plan for him was done. She could go back to the Church and no one would ever question her faith and place again.

That was what the pain in her hand had meant. What this new ache in her chest was. They were as good as words from above telling her it was time to return with her head held high.

And she didn't want to watch something so beautiful die.

'I'll be fine. I'm warm already. I was born in this city.' She stood, brushing off her skirts as she made a wall between them with her protests. 'If I don't go, they'll wonder where I am.' That was true enough.

His eyes narrowed. 'A girl was murdered by the river, and she wasn't the only body. Do you even know what the people are saying? There's a devil stalking the streets.'

She reflexively glanced outside at his words. Even an Izir shouldn't call ill luck so openly.

'You're the only trouble I've heard of. And this city is protected from devils.'

'I was speaking figuratively.' The teasing lilt to his voice died. 'You really don't know about the deaths?'

She had seen the strange bodies leaving the city, but that wasn't the same as knowing. She shook her head.

'I know there have been deaths, that's all. But people make bad choices, even in Silgard.'

'Some are saying the same person made the same bad choice four times.'

Csilla shook her head, keeping her gaze down so his worry wouldn't sway her. That she wasn't inclined to believe. Silgard was still a holy city, and people didn't plan to sin, even if their Shadow natures sometimes got the better of them.

'I'll be fine.' She would say it until it was true.

'At least join me for the wine. Sleep will come more easily to me, and if you're so convinced you have to leave, it'll keep you warm on your walk.'

He took the bottle again, and Csilla winced at the sudden shine. After a moment it dulled to a tarnished silver, and he popped off the cork.

Csilla's breath caught in her throat as he raised the bottle to his lips. There it was. Her truest moment of service.

'Stop!' She stepped forward, hands out and shaking.

He did, lowering the bottle and giving her a quizzical look. She squeezed her eyes shut to force back frustrated tears. She thought she'd be strong enough.

'It's . . . Don't drink it. Please.'

Her voice was dull even to her own ears. He'd shared his home and hospitality, and she couldn't let him die. Not even if it assured his place in the blessed ether and hers in the Brilliant City.

Asten would be as indifferent to her failure as to her life, but the Church elders, less so. She squeezed her eyes shut, haunted as she imagined Ágnes's disappointed face. All the good she could have done dissolved in a moment of weakness. All those people damned because she couldn't obey.

Shame filled her chest. She wasn't a good servant after all.

'What, is it poisoned?' His amused expression hardened with the realisation. 'You were going to poison me?'

Csilla spun and charged to the window. Wind slapped her face as she sat on the ledge, preparing to swing down.

'Who wants me dead? What's going on?' Mihály's voice rose as he reached for her.

The urge to run converged with pity in her chest at his stricken expression.

'The Church. You're not safe here, Izir.'

His hand caught the curve of her cheek, forcing her to look fully into his eyes, and she froze at the touch.

'And what will happen to you when you tell them you failed? Will you be safe?'

Csilla swallowed, unable to control her tremble at his concern, and the knowledge that he was right about the threat. She was hoping to not have to tell them anything.

'Stay here tonight, then come with me. It's not that far past the gates.' His eyes were shining, convincing, that lulling voice so tempting until the words themselves registered.

'Outside Silgard?' She jerked her head away. 'Be glad I warned you.'

'Oh, I am.' Mihály looked at the bottle. 'What is the poison?'

'Why?'

He swirled the contents, a black whirlpool in green glass. 'When you tell them, they might want details of how I met my demise.'

Csilla swallowed. 'Scorn's Friend.'

He snorted. 'I'd have thought I rated something more elegant than that. No nightlight tonic to send me gently to the evermore?'

What a bizarre man. 'I didn't have a say.' She twisted her hips further from him, closer to escape.

Mihály sighed. 'No matter. When that poison is administered, the throat closes first. It's useful in crowded spaces because the victim rarely has time to scream or gasp. The face will turn violet, and when they die there will be a large exhale as the muscles relax. There's no sweat or vomit.'

Csilla couldn't suppress her grimace as the angel-touched man described the grisly symptoms. He chuckled slightly.

'Now you know what to say if they ask. Though something tells me you have trouble with lies.'

She shivered at being read so truly.

The bottle still lit under his touch, and the expression on his face made her wonder if he was going to drink it anyway. Perhaps in addition to his powers he had Blessed Imre's incorruptible tongue, nullifying poison on the spot. Maybe this whole venture was damned from the outset.

Gritting her teeth, Csilla swung the rest of the way out of the window and went hand over foot down, palms searing on the rungs as she hurried.

'Csilla, please, *wait.* I'm not mad.'

One step, two, a crack . . .

Her foot skidded, and she tumbled.

Csilla screamed as she fell, grabbing at the ladder which came away with her.

'Csilla!'

Mihály's voice sounded far away as she hit snow slush, not quite deep or solid enough to cushion the impact of the ground. Was the black how dark it was, or was her vision going dim?

Pricks of candlelight and shadowed shapes appeared in neighbouring windows.

'Are you hurt? Can you come back up here? Put the ladder back, let me . . .'

His voice sounded like it was coming from much further away.

Dazed, Csilla stood and stumbled to the street, letting the dark take her, though Mihály's cries grew more and more insistent at her back.

It was foolish to have gone out without a lantern. Tears of pain and frustration pricked her eyes, and she tried to hold them back lest they freeze on her lids. She could barely see in front of her as it was, and her shoulder ached something terrible.

She was worse than a liar, the worst kind of hypocrite. She'd thought herself the perfect servant, but when finally given a true way to serve, she'd failed.

She pressed her cut palm to her cold lips, skin alight with the ghost of Mihály's touch. The Church had been right not to trust someone who Asten didn't even consider worthy of a soul.

A light and hoofbeats approached behind her. Csilla tried to step aside from whoever was so clearly hurrying past, but a voice called out.

'Stop.'

She knew that voice like she knew the evening prayer. The High Inquisitor. Ilan.

You've no need to be scared of him, she told herself as he rode close, lantern in hand. He was righteousness itself, lauded for the viciousness that served the Faith. But his work wasn't nearly far enough from the rooms used by the mercy crews, and she'd sewn up the backs and packed snow on the crushed fingers of those he purified with pain.

'Csilla.'

She turned her face upward at the address. The moonlight turned his expression more fierce than usual, the angle of his cheekbones like a stone carving, his long lashes casting shadows.

She hadn't even known he knew her name. She hadn't been officially clergy for more than a day, but she'd been there when he arrived from the north, with a retinue almost worthy of the Incarnate himself. He'd appeared a perfect priest of Justice even then, looking at everything with a gaze that said things were as they should be, and if they weren't, he would quickly make them so.

Ágnes had always had her thoughts about him, his youthful arrogance that should have been tempered with longer service before being given such a post, his relishing of the lash, his disinclination to consider the benefits of mercy. Csilla had only been grateful to be ignored for once. It made sense that she would be beneath his notice; she had no soul for him to save.

'Inquisitor.' She bowed as he nudged his horse forward, the animal's breath huffing pale clouds in the chill air.

'Why are you still out? Was that your scream?'

She froze. Shouldn't he know? Her task was a matter of Church justice.

'I had an accident. I'm going—' *Home*. She stuttered on the word. The cathedral had stopped being home the second she'd told Mihály not to drink.

The inquisitor muttered something that surely couldn't have been a curse.

'I'll take you. Too many bodies around lately.'

She wanted to refuse. Justice was one of the four sharp tenants of the Church, and she wore it on her breast with the rest of them, but the way he delivered it had never sat easy.

Still, it was a long, cold walk back and a much quicker ride, and he wasn't wrong about the bodies. She looked down at her scraped knuckles, her fingers numb from the fall. Ilan wouldn't have hesitated to carry out his orders. He would have served the Faith, no matter what.

She offered him her hand. 'Thank you.'

Ilan dropped his stirrups and helped her step up and slide onto the saddle in front of him. He shoved the lantern into her hand. 'Sit lightly.'

The black horse covered ground quickly and Csilla leaned forward, both in an attempt to sit lightly, as directed, and to avoid the stiffness and irritation radiating off Ilan. The horse, Vihar, was a friendly sort, even if his master was not. He always took an interest in her when she walked through the stables, even if his affection had been bought with apple scraps. She scratched his neck in silent thanks and he swivelled an ear in acknowledgement.

'I didn't think you'd be out this late,' Csilla said as the long seconds of quiet scratched at her. He should have been at prayers, but she wasn't one to correct him. 'Did you find anything? Mihály said . . .'

His sharp intake of breath that ate the end of her sentence told her it had been the wrong question.

'I thought we'd had a lead with that scream, but it was you. What were you even doing with that blasted Izir?'

He really didn't know, and her heart skipped at the incongruity. The Church was hiding her task even from their appointed Head of Justice.

'I . . . I was curious.' She twisted strands of Vihar's coarse mane around her fingers as she spoke the shallow lie, but it was simple enough it might not be questioned.

'I thought better of you than that.'

Her cheeks burned that he'd ever thought of her at all.

The cathedral was as central to the city as Silgard was to the Union, and Csilla gritted her teeth and gripped the front of the saddle as they moved into a high-stepping trot that carried them until they finally reached the broad courtyard. The clouds had blown away and the stars were out, their sparkle adding an extra layer of infinity as the gold-plated spires reached toward the silver speckle above.

In the centre of it all was the statue of Arany, the golden feathers of her eight wings and a dozen gold-dripping eyes alight from the ever-glowing candle fires at her feet. The shadow of her judgement was inescapable. She'd died so the world could still be good, and Csilla was leaving her legacy in tatters.

Ilan brought Vihar to a halt. 'You can let yourself in from here. And for all the saints, stay off the streets at night.'

Csilla slid off the horse and smiled as Vihar reached around to lip her hand in case the small miracle of a treat appeared. She clucked her tongue, about to tell the sweet thing that he had to wait for breakfast, just as she did.

The little warm feeling died as she realised Ilan was still staring at her, waiting for acknowledgement.

'I will.' It wasn't like she'd wanted to be out there anyway.

He nudged Vihar away, trotting hoofbeats echoing on the stone walls as they faded into the dark.

Arany's eyes followed her to the short steps to the entranceway. The shame of disobedience chafed, and the only thing stemming her rising desperation to apologise was that she wasn't sure who she should apologise to.

There was still light in the sanctuary hall, the tall glass windows lit with a ghostly glow and a crack of pale orange visible under the heavy doors. No doubt the Prelate was there, tending the ever-seeing Eye. He would ask what had happened, force her to take refuge in a lie or admit the truth and break herself.

Both were intolerable. Csilla crept away from the doorway, toward the darkness of her room. She could at least rest before facing punishment for ill-timed mercy.

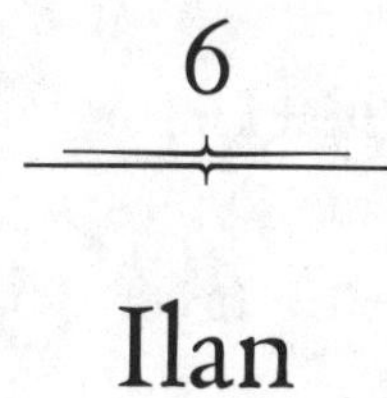

6

Ilan

ILAN TOUCHED each whip, clamp, and tool of confession lightly, every piece in its place and scrubbed clean. The unblemished leather was a sign of a meek city. Still, his fingers itched. For all his patrolling, the night had turned up nothing worse than a few citizens far enough in the bottle to tip to belligerence and Csilla, shaken and bleeding from her own clumsiness and bad decisions. But Csilla was none of his concern, and drunkenness was a sin that could easily be paid in coin. It was ill luck on his part that the current Incarnate had ruled gold as cleansing as blood for all but the worst sins or poorest sinners. A war was a costly thing, even a righteous one. When the large fought, the small under their control paid, be it the gentry taxing farmers or the Church taxing sinners. It was the way of things, and he had no right to complain just because it was boring.

Saints knew there was plenty else to keep his mind occupied. He couldn't close his eyes without seeing the gape-mouthed and mutilated bodies, and even though they'd done their best to keep the truth of the murders quiet, the city was half-mad with heresy he wasn't allowed to squash. The Izir's holy ancestors would scream. The angels themselves built the Church as a bridge to help flawed humanity approach the divine, and now their son was burning it and claiming the ashes revelation.

Even Csilla had gone to hear him out, and she wasn't the first from the Church to do so.

A steady drum beat driven by frustration and lack of sleep pounded behind his eyes.

'Inquisitor?'

One of the priests was in the doorway, her lined forehead further wrinkled with concern. Ilan drew his shoulders back, eyeing the goldenrod yellow at her throat and sleeves. Few congregational priests came to the torture room, though they were happy enough to send others there. Hearts of iron and stomachs of silk, the lot of them.

'Yes?'

'There's a problem. Out front.'

The worry in her voice shouldn't have excited him.

The Izir had six of the Faithful stopped on the street, distracting them from spending the morning in respectable prayer with promises that reeked of Shadow and children's tales.

The penitents scattered as Ilan approached, but the man didn't move. The subtle aura of the divine surrounded him like a perfume, calling hearts to trust and adulation. Even Ilan wasn't fully immune; as the Izir looked up, his golden-brown eyes widening, there was a pinch of a moment where Ilan thought perhaps he did deserve attention, if only for being so beautiful.

The smallest of moments, but no less irritating for being brief.

Ilan pointed down the street, past the cathedral walls to where refuse was dragged.

'If you won't keep your heresy out of our city, you can at least keep it away from our door.'

The Izir's lips quirked as he gestured to the statue in the courtyard, watching them with each of her carved and gleaming eyes. The gold seemed brighter for his presence.

'Am I not allowed to visit family? I have business here.'

'If you've come to repent, I'd be more than happy to help.'

Ilan's pulse quickened at the thought of dragging the Izir into the depths of the cathedral and flogging his ideas out of him. Fantasising about beating an angel was probably somewhere on the sin ledgers, the cleansing invocation set at an exorbitant price, but the thought of this man's handsome face cracking was deeply pleasing. One strike for every person who'd had the misfortune of hearing him would be enough to bring even this heretic back to rights. He'd wreck his throat begging for forgiveness.

'I'm sure you would!' The laugh in Mihály's tone was close enough to mockery that Ilan couldn't suppress a snarl. 'But I'm here for Csilla.'

Ilan's shoulders straightened.

'Last night she was running away from you.' Everyone had heard the Izir yelling after her. It was admirable of her to have run, really. Ilan had scolded half the city for panting after the angel.

'It was a misunderstanding. She fell out the window.'

As if that were better. Ilan shook his head.

'She wouldn't have fallen if she hadn't already been trying to leave. Now, unless you are here to renounce your heresy, go away. I have more pressing problems than you.'

Heresy could be rectified. Death, barring divine intervention, could not.

By the wry smile on the Izir's face, he knew the order was empty, and Ilan could sense claws beneath the gloves in the murmuring crowd. The city had little love for the person who kept their feet on the path of righteousness with iron shoes. Far easier to follow something offering hope that didn't require sacrifice.

The Izir scratched at his beard, then shrugged. 'You know if I stand here and tell you no, there isn't a damned thing you can do about it?'

Perhaps flogging wasn't the right path. Cutting out his tongue would be far more useful.

'If she'd wanted you, she would have stayed.'

The statement troubled him as soon as it left his lips. He could understand Csilla's desires, but why would the Izir want her? Csilla didn't have a soul for him to sway.

'I can help her.'

Again with his damned self-assurance.

'She doesn't need you.' Ilan had a marrow-deep understanding of what it was to yearn for a miracle, but this Izir would be a sorry place for her to put her faith. 'You have every right to be here' – it pained to concede even that point – 'but not even your holy blood gives you the right to force her to speak to you.'

Something flashed in the other man's eyes. 'A little late for the Church to be talking about rights, don't you think?'

Genuine anger simmered through Ilan's irritation. 'Says the heretic.'

The Izir bent close, warm lips brushing Ilan's ear, and Ilan's hand tightened on the hilt of his cane, eager to draw the blade inside. The Church frowned upon carrying weapons that were too obvious in the city; he'd managed a compromise by which he simply didn't tell anyone, and they didn't ask.

'Says the one who wanted to have me killed.'

Confusion warred with violent instinct, and for a panicked second Ilan feared the Izir could read minds.

'You're deluded.'

The other man turned his head slightly, dark mirth in his eyes.

'Feigning shock is almost a lie, Inquisitor. She came to me on your orders, didn't she? You baited a trap with a pretty thing and poison. I always thought your methods were more straightforward than that.'

'I have no idea what you're talking about.' Ilan slid the blade out of the cane and let it rest at his side. He couldn't strike the Izir, but he was going to make quite sure the consecrated ground wasn't sullied with so much as one of his footsteps while he made such accusations.

'Really?' the Izir laughed, still close enough for his breath to warm Ilan's skin. 'Then the Church thinks very little of you.'

Ilan's lip curled, not letting the doubt seep through. The Izir couldn't have known exactly which nerve he'd managed to strike.

'If what you're saying is true, you're foolish to be here.' A smart grouse took a missed shot as a lucky lesson and quickly flew out of reach. It didn't roost on the hunter's stoop.

Mihály stepped back, looking over Ilan's shoulder as if he could see through the stone and glass to whatever corner Csilla had tucked herself in.

'She's worth the risk. And what are you going to do to me in daylight? Are you that sure of yourself?'

The spectators stepped closer, straining to hear the conversation, waiting to see what their idol would do.

The Church would lose these six no matter what he did, Ilan realised with a hardness in the pit of his stomach. They'd come to pray in Brilliance and would leave in the false light of heretical promises with gossip on their lips.

He waited for the Izir to push further, to give him a true excuse to strike.

'I will not let you cross this courtyard until you've renounced your heresy and made a proper confession.' More words he'd have to bark, not allowed to bite. The Izir was right that, should he decide to stride on in, there was nothing Ilan could do.

But the Izir paused, looking between Ilan and the spires, something calculating in his gaze.

'Fine,' he conceded. 'I'm not in the mood to get stung today. She'll come back to me.' He turned and locked gazes with Ilan. 'And I'd stake my blessing that you'll be the one that forces her to.' Then he leaned forward again, voice low and filled with sharpness like a scattering of broken glass. 'Watch yourself, Inquisitor. If there's one thing Asten hates more than heresy, it's hypocrites. And don't you have more dangerous things to catch than me?'

'You're the only threat to the Church.'

But that wasn't quite true. Murders were a threat to the people. If the dark markings he'd seen on the bodies were real, they were a bigger threat to the Faith. The only thing that could erase the power of divinity were works of Shadow.

But they still had divinity on their side. His glass still worked. His ministrations still absolved. They could still see how their faith purified.

Nothing in the Izir's face gave away whether the secrets the bodies carried had leaked. He could only be referring to the fact of mortal deaths.

'I'm not a threat to you. I simply think about things differently.' Mihály drew back, voice still low. 'But if you'd like me to be, I could certainly tell my followers what the Church tried. Now let us go in peace.'

The sharp smugness in his face evaporated as he turned to his waiting followers, his smile again luminous as he was embraced by their raised arms and grateful sighs.

The Church couldn't compete with such direct intercession.

Ilan watched a moment longer, sweat on his back and breath shallow. He then turned and strode back to the cathedral, bypassing the airy light of the sanctuary and heading straight to the Prelate's office in one of the small side chapels.

The young attendant dozing outside startled as Ilan pushed past, shoving open the door without knocking.

Prelate Abe was at his desk with an open copy of the writ before him and a letter in one liver-spotted hand, the translucent wax of the Incarnate's seal crumbling on the edges of the paper. The Prelate tilted his head in admonishment, but Ilan spoke before he could be scolded.

'The Izir was at the gates. He was looking for Csilla. He implied that she tried to kill him.'

The staccato words sounded all the more ridiculous leaving his mouth. He'd once seen Csilla carrying a mouse in her skirts, protecting it from the cats, cats who took more of her dinner than she did with her worry over their care. Soul or no, she was a perfect reflection of steady Mercy.

Abe paled.

Ilan's heartbeat quickened. He'd seen that look of guilt on hundreds of faces, and it didn't belong here.

'Thank you for telling me.'

Abe pushed away from his desk and reached for his knife. The blade gleamed in the light thrown by the stained glass behind them, the halo of Blessed Imre consecrating the metal in pale yellow and milk white.

His reply was far from a denial of the accusation.

'Is there any truth to what the Izir was saying?'

Abe's hand spread on the open letter as if performing benediction. 'We have permission to root out evil in the city. It would solve one problem.'

'By sending a girl to kill . . .' He couldn't even finish the sentence. There were already unholy deaths in the city. Adding a holy one to the body count didn't seem helpful.

'She clearly didn't.' The Prelate's words dripped with blame. 'Or perhaps there's another explanation. We can be charitable.'

He didn't sound like he intended to be. Ilan opened his mouth, but his words were stilled by Abe's raised hand.

'This was a direct order from the Incarnate, a way the girl's flaw could be useful in protecting the Faith. Are you going to argue?'

'Of course not.' The answer left his mouth automatically. Asten spoke directly to the Incarnate. If Ilan found it unsettling, it was his own weakness, and one he'd do well to carve out at the first opportunity. 'I only wish you'd told me. I'd have done it. I'll still do it.'

He could set the whole thing to rights, taking up the holy charge where Csilla had failed if they'd trusted him. Old insecurities threatened to rise like sour bile. He would have succeeded. He would have enjoyed it. But by the Prelate's face, he wasn't going to be given a chance.

Abe smiled with clamped teeth.

'He'll be on alert now if he hasn't already made plans to leave, and you're far too well known around the city to get near him without notice. Killing him openly will just make him a martyr and rally his followers.'

He wasn't going to leave. Not with his interest in Csilla. 'But the Incarnate ordered . . .'

'He'll be here soon enough, and may holy inspiration lead him to a better way to manage it. But you can come and witness for us now.'

'What, you're going to kill her instead?' He couldn't picture Abe putting the blade to Csilla's throat, the blood spray of a butchered lamb painting the pearl white of his robes.

The older man swallowed, hesitation in his eyes.

'No, there's been no order for that. But if she refuses to serve, she can't stay, and we don't want word of this . . . mess . . . reaching those already drawing away from us. We'll take her tongue. Her hands, too, if you think she'd survive it.'

'She wouldn't.'

There was nothing righteous about mutilating a girl with no soul to save to cover a failure. But he wouldn't stand against the Faith's judgement; if they wanted him to punish her, he would. The fact that they hadn't asked him to take on the task in the first place only showed he still had more to prove. Those sworn to the Faith were more than servants. They were tools, shaping the world into something Asten could love again. That was more important than any one life.

He wouldn't think about how she shook tucked in front of him on Vihar, her small hands and their years of thankless work.

'If that is Asten's will, so be it.'

He'd borrow a little of her kindness and make the cuts as clean as possible.

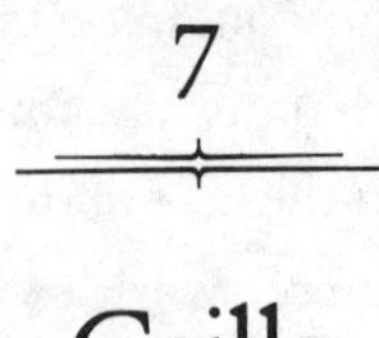

7

Csilla

THE SLICE-*THUNK* of knife through onion was repetitive enough to be soothing and quick enough to distract. Kitchen preparations were hardly Csilla's favourite duty, but today she was grateful. She could be alone, with only the cat twining around her feet waiting for her generosity, and any watering eyes could be blamed on the onion sting.

Had Mihály run?

It was the only question that mattered. If he'd been wise and left the city, she might have a prayer of staying. She would have at least gotten the trouble out, and that had been the result they'd wanted. Even if every second of her continued service was a lie.

The cat, Erzsébet, batted at her skirt hem, catching a dangling string and rolling, fiercely defeating the cloth. As Csilla glanced down with a sigh for the new fabric now fraying, the cat gave a hungry and hopeful yowl.

'You can't even eat these. Bad for cats,' Csilla cautioned, leaning over to scratch the tabby between her ears and earning a swat at her hand. At least Erzsébet pulled her claws this time.

When she looked up, Ágnes was in the doorway.

Csilla's smile fell at the sorrow in Ágnes's expression. The woman had aged a dozen years in the span of as many hours.

'Oh, my Csilla.'

All the weight of the world was in those soft notes. Csilla's throat closed, and she set her knife down.

'Show me your hand.' Ágnes gestured, and Csilla had the immediate urge to shove it in her apron pocket like a child insisting her fist wasn't full of sweets. But she wasn't a child, and she couldn't lie. She uncurled her fingers one by one and offered her palm.

The truth of where she'd been and who she'd let touch her was undeniable on her skin.

'So it's true.' Ágnes's voice quivered.

Csilla's breath quickened as apologies, excuses and confessions all struggled to come out at once. *I showed mercy. I made a kind judgement.* She needed Ágnes to see how well she'd paid attention to everything she'd been taught, but her nerves failed, and she stayed silent, back pressed against the counter.

'I don't blame you,' Ágnes said as she squeezed the blasphemous hand, the words so quiet it was as if she were afraid of even their god overhearing. 'But I'd hoped they were wrong.'

'They?'

For a dizzy moment Csilla thought she was referring to Blessed Asten. Had her weakness been so wicked They'd sent Ágnes a personal vision to torment her? But Asten could never be wrong.

Ágnes didn't let her go. 'The Church knows you didn't do it.'

How? The question scratched, but it was smothered by the older woman's sudden cough. Sharp worry seized Csilla, and she swallowed down the lump in her throat.

'Mihály heals. If you talk to him . . .'

Ágnes caught her breath.

'Mihály? You speak of him like a friend now?' The disappointment in her tone was worse than any childhood slap. 'We taught you Mercy, but perhaps you drank too deeply. Obedience is an equal virtue. As is Justice.'

Everything in creation was balanced. Even Mercy had counterweights.

Csilla's answer was cut off as Prelate Abe and Ilan entered. Her eyebrows knitted together at the grim procession. Of course the Inquisitor had been the one to turn her in. He should have taken her directly to the gates and thrown her out if this was how it was going to end. Why even pretend to care whether she returned safely? Why pretend he hadn't known?

'Csilla,' Abe said, and she stepped into the cat, who gave an indignant hiss that nearly made her laugh; Erzsébet wouldn't understand the gravity. She looked from face to face – sorrowful, judgemental, indifferent. 'The Izir showed up at our gates asking about you. How is that, assuming you did the task we entrusted to you?'

Mihály. Here. Even after what she'd done, he'd come for her. The thought gave her a kernel of heart. He'd known her an hour and offered her more grace than those who had raised her.

'Was there some intervention?' the Prelate continued. 'A reason it didn't work, perhaps?'

He was trying to excuse her, Ágnes nodding at the gentle question. It was kind, but futile.

'I gave him a tainted bottle.' She was always careful with her words, but she could never resist adding a little extra truth to lay herself bare. 'After telling him it was poisoned.'

'*Csilla.*' Ágnes sagged against the countertop, and Csilla blinked away new tears. It was horrible enough that her only family had to hurt, but it was hot-iron agony to be the cause of the pain. She should shut her mouth to anything except apologies, and pray they were enough of a balm.

But there were more truths she had to say, lest they choke her where she stood.

'The taking of a life is reserved for Asten and Asten alone. I won't make myself a murderess or him a martyr.' Her voice shook, but the words made it out. She loved the Church, and the Church was wrong to ask for a death, and both those things could be true even if it ripped her apart inside.

'The Incarnate speaks for Asten and Their will. Do you deny it?' With every word Abe closed the space between them.

'No.' But she'd never met the Incarnate directly, only seen him in his coat of dazzling silver riding far from the people he guided. She'd felt Mihály's power on her skin.

'Then you admit you think yourself above him?'

Prelate Abe was close enough now to fill her vision, and the waft of sandalwood clinging to his robes mixing with the kitchen scents curled her stomach. It was the smell of a place of comfort, even as he shifted his knife.

'Of course not!' Csilla's voice coloured in despair. 'I don't understand why you're acting like I've done some horrible thing when all I did was choose not to kill someone.'

She didn't want to be disobedient, but they had to understand that it was too much to ask. No matter how they justified it, it was wrong. If it hadn't been, one of them would have gone instead. There would have been no question of sin or glory.

The Prelate's eyes darkened. 'You didn't just fail, then. You refused to protect the Church.'

The truth of that slid between her ribs, hitting vital spots.

'Then I was weak, and I'm sorry.' She glanced towards the inquisitor standing at attention in the doorway, his face a mask. He no doubt already had an appropriate consequence in mind. Hopefully she came out of it with all her fingers. 'If you're going to punish me, fine, please at least wait until I've finished here. People are hungry.' Others shouldn't have to suffer for her failure.

Abe cleared his throat. 'There's no sense in cleaning your soul when you don't have one.'

The words dropped like stones in still water. They would kill her.

'Send me to the front.'

Even as the words left her mouth, she knew the hope was fool's gold. More and more people had been conscripted for the holy task of bringing the broken territories back into the fold, ensuring the Union's borders spread the breadth of the land in hopes that it would coax Asten into a full return. A place in the war was a common punishment, one that came with the promise of inherent salvation in taking blows for the mission. And where there were injured, there was a need for nursing.

She would gladly accept that. It would be a gift.

'No. You will never represent the Faith again, not even on the battlefield. You'll leave with no tongue to speak of what happened and fewer fingers to sign and write.'

Fear drenched Csilla. She'd live on charity, if she managed to live at all. She'd seen wounds full of gangrene and people who starved after that kind of sentence.

'Prelate, please.' It was Ágnes who stepped in front of her. 'Her life will be hard enough. No one will believe anything she says regardless.'

'Of course a mercy worker would think so.' He turned to Ilan. 'Inquisitor. Give me your honest opinion of our justice.'

Csilla met Ilan's pale blue eyes. He wouldn't be swayed by pleading, but she could at least keep her chin up and hope.

'I told you I'd do what was asked.'

Of course he wouldn't speak for her. He was probably looking forward to hearing her scream.

'I know we have your loyalty, Ilan. I asked for your honesty. Our Head of Mercy has asked for her virtue to reign in this judgement. As Head of Obedience, I disagree. I see no reason to call for Knowledge, but I will let Justice be the deciding vote.'

Ilan's eyes didn't leave Csilla, but there was a distance to his gaze that had her doubt he was seeing her at all. Whatever he was thinking, it was a private war in which she was a piece, not a person.

After too-long seconds, he stepped back and crossed his arms.

'Honestly? I'd rather we bring the Izir here directly. Punish the source of the crime not your own mis . . .' He closed his mouth and took a moment as Csilla gaped and the Prelate inclined his head in silent warning. 'She failed at an unfair task. But, again, I defer to the will of the divine.'

The Prelate looked between his Head of Justice and the Head of Mercy, then at Csilla herself. Her first instinct, trained when she was small and unloved, was to smile and placate, and by his blink of surprise, she hadn't quite smothered it. Not many smiled in the face of execution.

'Very well. We will only take back your place.'

Perhaps there was the smallest note of relief in the Prelate's voice; Csilla herself was too relieved to notice.

'And I thank you for that,' Ágnes said quietly as she moved to put an arm across Csilla's chest and laid her head against Csilla's own. 'Be brave.'

Her arms had no strength to hold, but Csilla stood frozen anyway, the realisation of what Abe was about to do finally landing.

He was going to cross the scar she'd been so proud to bear and show the world she was no longer of the Church. Every protest died in her throat as her pulse echoed with the flicker of firelight on the blade.

'This is a kindness you should remember when you think of the Faith.' Abe's voice was soft as he took her hand and pressed it against the wooden counter. 'We could have mutilated you so your soulless tongue couldn't speak against the Church or sent you to the North to starve.'

She nodded. This pain would be a goodness. She would repeat it over and over until she believed it.

'Stay still,' Ágnes said. It was an order she'd heard a thousand times, fussing as a child, mind and feet wandering during lectures. She'd never heard it with tears behind it before.

Abe pulled the knife vertically across her palm and a thin line of blood split where it bisected the fresh scar, white at the corners of her vision.

In the doorway, the inquisitor watched with narrow eyes, making no reaction to Csilla's gagging cry of pain.

She'd been accepted for less than one day. The humiliation was worse than the cut. Abe claimed he was showing her kindness, but she'd find no warmth anywhere.

Ágnes led her out of the kitchens by her uninjured hand, and for a brief second Csilla wanted nothing more than to be a child again, warmed by the belief that everything would be right in her world as long as she was good.

But she hadn't been good enough, and there was no one to blame but herself.

'I'll prepare some things for you. We won't throw you out empty-handed.'

The gratitude was warm until the finality of it scalded.

'I'm sorry to be such a disappointment.'

She'd grown up telling herself if she were better, quieter, the first to offer comfort, the one who knew every prayer, everything would be alright. That the Faith served Asten, and everyone had a place, and hers was at Ágnes's side in service.

'I understand your choice,' Ágnes replied as she led her up twisted stairs towards her own rooms.

But she didn't deny that Csilla was a disappointment.

'It's not fair!' Csilla clenched her hands until she felt the slice of fingernails into her palm, digging at the fresh wound and not caring how it hurt. 'I've done nothing but serve since I was a child. I've cared for the people of this city, cared for our people—' The end of her sentence was lost in memories of other wounds, other tears, and the comfort she'd tried to offer.

Ágnes sighed. 'It's up to a higher judgement than ours. The rules are to show us . . .'

'Show mercy to souls in need, keep them safe and whole so they can be guided to Brilliance. Isn't that what we're taught?' The tears were coming faster now, her words interrupted only by tiny gasps.

'*Souls*, Csilla.' Ágnes shook her head. 'All my prayers weren't good enough for a miracle. Perhaps I'm the one who should have been better.'

The resignation in her tone stilled Csilla's heart. The elderly woman led her to a window where the light was good and wrapped oil-soaked cotton and linen over the bleeding hand. Csilla almost stopped her, but she didn't have the strength to advocate for saving the supplies for those worse off, and her selfish heart craved that last bit of care.

'But I don't know anything but here.'

Worse, there was nowhere in the Immaculate Union that would fully trust her, especially now, and nowhere on the continent that wouldn't belong to the Union soon enough. The edges of the wall that protected the sanctity of the city teased her eyes, rising just above rooftops and smoke to divide the Brilliant City from a world that tried its best to fall to Shadow.

Each roof was a story of the lives inside, people she'd fed, babies she'd watched delivered – some red and squalling, some grey and silent – old and young hands she'd held as the bodies of their loved ones were taken for burning.

There might be work outside the city, but this was the only work that mattered.

'Perhaps someone will take you in,' Ágnes suggested, a sigh in the words. 'At least then you wouldn't be far.'

Csilla closed her eyes and let her lids grow heavy. There was a better chance of Asten returning this second than finding someone willing to take responsibility for a cross-marked soulless girl in the holiest city of the Union.

Except perhaps Mihály. The memory of his warm-honey gaze crept over her.

He had come back for her. He'd tried to warn her.

'I'll be sleeping on the streets.' A sharp thought prodded her. 'The Izir told me something curious. He said there was a killer in the city.' There were dangers on the streets she was being banished to.

Ágnes's eyes narrowed. 'Don't listen to a thing that man says, Csilla. Yes, there have been deaths.' She drew a shaking breath. 'But they are being handled. Panicking and making more of it than what it is, that's the type of thing that drives people to heresy.'

'But sending the bodies outside . . . and I saw the dying Seal.' There was no pretty way to excuse that.

Ágnes took her hand. 'Yes, the Seal is suffering with the fear and lack of faith in the city, and wild rumours will only make it worse. Don't add to it any more than you already have. Please.'

Csilla clenched her teeth and nodded, though the rebuke hurt. Ágnes had been so quick to accept Csilla's role in the Church and now was treating her like a child again.

'Rest. They won't begrudge me one night. I'll sit a vigil for you and see you off in the morning.'

The woman could sit a year's worth of vigils and it wouldn't change anything.

'You don't have to.'

Ágnes touched Csilla's head lightly and turned towards the door.

'I want to.'

Csilla nodded, all further protests wrapping up inside herself. If there was one thing she knew about prayer, it was that it wasn't always for the sake of the person being prayed for.

Her eyes fell again to her bandaged palm, drops of red seeping through. If only there were a way to convince the Faith she wasn't worthless. She couldn't even comfort Ágnes, so clearly shaken. The fear wasn't just outside. The Church was walking the line of its own tenets to get to the heart of it.

A frantic idea took flutter inside. Mihály knew about magic and souls, might know something of the trouble with the Seal and the fear eroding it. And right now, he was one of the most connected men in the city, with followers who would give him information. She nodded to herself, each motion deliberate and steadying. The Church would never work with a heretic, but, soulless and outcast, she could. She could help the city. She could help herself.

Csilla fretted and dozed until well past the midnight bells, only getting up when it was safer to wander. Stained-glass windows and the milky white candles below them illuminated the hallways, the cold eyes of angels and saints and Blessed Asten in all Their aspects heavy on her. She couldn't even lower her gaze to escape; the glass cast coloured flecks underfoot and she walked on ripples of sanctified light.

Behind her came the quick padding of a cat, and Csilla paused to let her catch up. At least someone cared enough to check on her.

She approached the cathedral library as if the door itself might have teeth, but the latch was plain iron, worn down with years of finger pressure. She slid it out and pushed, only to find there was no give. Csilla pursed her lips. She'd meant to see if she could find anything about the Seal, the deaths, or even the strange theories Mihály seemed to have, but someone had it bolted from the inside.

She stiffened and pressed her ear to the door, but the thick wood muffled any sounds, and the only thing she caught was the echo of a cough. Maybe she could hide in an alcove and wait for whoever it was to emerge. Depending on exactly what they were researching, it could be hours. It wasn't unheard of for particularly deep studies to take days. The head archivist once took his meals inside for a month.

Erzsébet chirped before giving a pleased meow as she rubbed against Csilla's legs, ignoring the fingers that tried to hush her. She meowed again, louder, waiting for a response with no care for the secrecy of the mission, only protest that she wasn't being included.

There was no reasoning with cats.

Csilla picked her up to stop her fussing, letting their foreheads bump together.

'We have to be quiet,' she whispered, snuggling the cat against her chest, wincing as kneading claws dug into the fabric of her overdress.

Maybe Mihály liked cats. If she could sneak Erzsébet out, at least she'd have one friend in wherever her new home was to be.

Erzsébet meowed loudly with fresh insult at whatever it was about being gently held that offended cats, mouth wide enough to show little fangs and pink tongue, and before Csilla could shush her again, the door opened.

Ilan. Looking even more worse for wear than perhaps she was, his eyes rimmed in bruise-like dark and his skin wax pale.

Csilla froze. There wasn't anywhere to run, or any way to pretend she hadn't been trying to get in.

The inquisitor leaned against the door frame, annoyance giving way to momentary surprise.

'You're supposed to be gone.' His voice dripped with exhaustion.

You're supposed to be asleep.

'I will be, in the morning. I just wanted to look at something.' Not a lie, at least.

'What could you possibly need in here?'

'I . . .' Erzsébet squeezed out of the sudden constriction of Csilla's clenching arms and leaped to the floor with an all-over shake. 'My own records. I should copy down my birth record if I'm to live elsewhere.' That was also true, even if it wasn't what she intended to do.

The single sheet in the book of orphans would say the same thing it did every time she'd looked: date found, name given, no family, adopted or otherwise, perhaps a note of her vows, then a blot over them if they'd been quick in their updates. The one small notation of her existence in all the Union's history, only to be edited if she married or had children, was reinstated, or died. Only one of those things was looking likely at the moment.

The inquisitor rubbed the bridge of his nose.

'Very well.'

But instead of leaving her to it, he stepped back in. Hopefully her smile looked grateful instead of concerned. It felt more like a grimace as she passed him.

The cathedral library was second only to the University stacks in its collection of knowledge, possibly also its size. Wall-length windows were partially hidden by the shelving that stretched up to the level of the clerestory, the wood further blocking what light could come through the grime on glass too tall and awkwardly placed to clean regularly.

Ilan had gone to sit at one of the quill-knife-scratched tables, bent over something she couldn't read, everything soft and hazy in the candlelight and dust. Erzsébet took the opportunity to steal into his lap, a paw occasionally tapping at the papers he was sorting, brushed back by a surprisingly gentle hand.

The little traitor was purring. Csilla glared, but the cat showed no remorse.

Fine, it was probably easier to search without her underfoot anyway. Csilla thumbed through bound texts on the pretence of a search, silently willing him to leave. There were a few volumes that looked very interesting and would open a tribunal of questions if she were caught looking.

Ilan didn't move. He muttered to himself, he made notes, he occasionally shifted and clucked as the disloyal cat attempted to capture his attention with a headbutt to his face, but he didn't leave or look at Csilla. She stepped lightly around the room, trying to pretend she was simply confused, when her eyes fell on his work and she couldn't stop a gasp. It was what she wanted to see, but so much more horrific than she could have imagined.

There was a sketch of a girl's body, exquisitely rendered and grotesquely intimate, and across her chest there were carved symbols, not wholly unfamiliar. Beneath the paper were older works, notes of demons and the hero priests and saints who vanquished them, Ilan's notations fresh over the yellowed pages with their browning letters.

She brushed her wrist where Mihály had touched her as if some holiness lingered.

'Shadow script?'

The words escaped before she could help it. Mihály had been right. There was something dark here. No one in Silgard would risk those corrupted words. There were knives that killed a body, and there were words that destroyed a soul.

'You know it?'

There was a measured note in his voice as he turned, gaze suddenly sharp and pinning, and she stepped back until her shoulders hit the stacks.

'I've seen it.' Not like this, not written on flesh. 'When I was little they thought I might be . . .' She flushed to say it. 'A demon, or something adjacent. They tried to make me read.'

She'd been made to kneel on stone until her knees bruised, offered book after book until she'd ruined pages with frustrated snot and tears and earned a cuff on the back of her head. Even now she curled in on herself at the memory, forcing it back with a shove.

'Could you?' His eyes swept her as if he could possibly see something the scholar priests had missed.

'Of course not!' The words were hot with the shame that still squeezed her chest at the memory.

'Useless, then.' He leaned back in the chair, Erzsébet jumping to the floor at the sudden shift.

It wasn't like she was ever anything else.

'Is it real?' The words fluttered as they left her lips. Real, as in not a copy made by someone who had studied the imperfect remains from before the Severing. Real, as in written in the hand of a demon itself.

Ilan didn't answer but instead raised a hand to beckon her closer, pushing the papers slightly to the side. There were three other bodies.

'Saints preserve,' Csilla whispered, brushing her mark as a ward, though the paper couldn't hurt her.

'Does it look familiar at all? From what they showed you before.'

It was a simple question, but still unfamiliar enough to throw her, and she stalled. Every line he'd drawn was once part of a breathing person.

He looked back, a pale eyebrow arched. 'I don't remember taking your tongue.'

Csilla forced herself to step to his shoulder and look.

'They're . . . different. All complete, for one thing.'

The examples of Shadow invocations she'd been brought had all been broken, lost to time, or even for those not, a syllable here or there purposefully left blank or reversed to avoid any accidental workings.

'Complete or correct?'

She flinched at the way his tone snapped like the crack of one of his whips.

'That I wouldn't know. But the scholars never brought full lines.' She reached over him, finger hovering just above the inked marks. 'Whoever did this writes it well.' Even on flesh.

'Well enough to curse us. Not that any of those supposed scholars have been dispatched to confirm it.' The frustration in his voice was dangerously close to soul-blotting anger.

'And this all happened in Silgard?'

A cold shiver passed over her scars. His eyes flicked in hesitation, then he nodded.

'It's no secret we've found bodies.'

This was so much more than bodies. If any word had leaked, it was no wonder the people were afraid, and that the Seal was suffering.

'You think they're related? That there's a demon?'

Her words became hushed. The demons had all been imprisoned after the Severing, and even before, the Shadow-born creatures struggled to raise physical form for long and had to borrow skins to work in a world that still held too much of the divine for their comfort. Those possessed by them could never hide from Asten's Eye; the testing glass would read their soul and show them for what they were the moment they tried to enter. There couldn't be one here.

He didn't answer, only closed his eyes.

'Finish what you came for and go. Don't touch anything else, and I'll pretend I never saw you.'

He went to stack the papers and books together, clumsy with exhaustion, and she raised her hand.

'I'll clean up here. You can start fresh tomorrow. Please, rest. I owe you.' Let him think it was repayment for his kindness in not asking for harsher punishment and for talking to her at all. And it was, in part. 'I've already seen it all, anyway.'

Ilan snorted. 'You don't owe me a thing. My honesty was for my own sake, not yours.'

She hadn't expected any less. 'That doesn't mean I'm not grateful.'

He met her gaze then, cool and steady, and rose.

'Stack everything together and put it over there. Don't get anything out of order.'

He inclined his head to a corner that held nothing more interesting than construction orders from two decades back. No one would bother anything there.

She held her breath and counted to thirty after the door closed behind him.

A horrified fascination overcame her as she sank into the seat with the stack of papers, ignoring Erzsébet's biting and pulling at her bootlaces. Four victims. The unholy details burned themselves in her mind as her stomach twisted further with each page of etched brutality. The killings were scattered across the city, the dead with nothing in common but their misfortune and families left to mourn them.

No wonder the Church had been so keen to see Mihály dead. If people were already turning away from the Church under his influence, they would be that much closer to damnation if death came to them before they could make right. His spark of divinity couldn't counter this. And if the lack of faith was the reason the Seal was faltering, letting all this out would be its death knell.

In all the horror, there was hope. If she saved the city from something worse than heresy, they'd have to take her back. She could make up for all her wrongs and perhaps show the Church one of theirs as well.

She shuffled through the papers, looking for a blank piece. There was no way around the fact that her investigation would have to start with one small sin.

A piece towards the bottom only had a few scrawled street names, and she pulled it from the pile and began to copy out the names of the victims, and the details as far as she understood. She couldn't bring herself to replicate the Shadow script, but names would give her a good place to start.

Erzsébet was less pleased, pacing across the table and causing Csilla to scatter blooms of ink where she tried to wave the cat off. When she was finished, she had her names, but there was also a mess, and a little black paw print in signature.

She blew on the paper to dry, eyes on the lightening sky outside. At least she'd be gone before Ilan realised what she'd stolen.

8

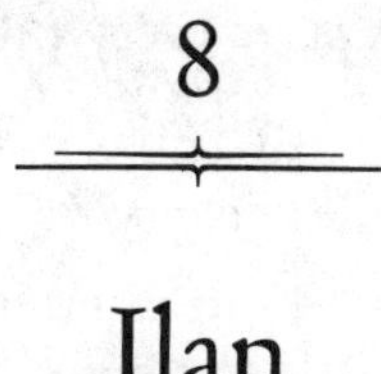

Ilan

'OUR LILI was a righteous girl.'

The murdered girl's father was sweating, though in the early morning air their home was cold enough their breath was visible and the mother had an extra shawl draped across her shoulders. Ilan made a note, though it meant very little. The citizens of Silgard often squirmed and sweated before him. Gratifying as the fear was, it made getting information slow.

At least he'd gotten a few hours of sleep after leaving Csilla. Few people would trust you if you were yawning during an interrogation.

'Please, Inquisitor,' the mother said, placing a hand on her husband's back. 'We have to prepare her. We've readied her place in the . . .' The woman choked on the last word, eyes unable to meet his. 'They won't even let us see her body, much less sit for her. She was loved. People need to see that.'

Ilan cleared his throat. 'She can't be interred inside the city, I'm afraid.'

They didn't need to see the obscene wounds on what they doubtless remembered as perfect skin or spread the secret of what those wounds actually were. None of the victims' families had been allowed to see what the killer had made of their loved ones.

'She's already been put out for the Servants of the Road.'

The travelling priests swept up everything too far from the provincial Church seats to warrant congregational involvement or theologically messy deaths with bodies no city would claim. They would burn her without ceremony, but they would treat her with respect.

The father's fists clenched, his wife's face now the bloodless white of a scar. Ilan held up a hand.

'I sent her with a writ. Vasya will see her soul to Asten if she's earned it.' He could at least give them that comfort.

'We can't even send her back to Saika?' The mother's accent slipped through in her anguish, tugging an irksome note of sympathy in him. He knew as well as they did how long that road was. No one would be willing to carry a desecrated corpse through the eastern wilds and the endless mud that would come with the spring thaw or even hold ashes that long. 'Somewhere family could visit her remains, even if she can't be here . . .'

'I'm sure her soul is at peace with the eternal,' he said.

He hoped it was true. The one blessing in all this was that even the defiled spirits seemed to be passing on, no matter what the Izir was preaching about lingering souls and ghosts.

'The body is only a vessel, after all. And she's already gone.'

That was why he'd waited to speak with them. Any questioning that spent the whole time debating where to put the body would be a waste of everyone's time.

The mother murmured a prayer, a balm for grief, but the words were slow in her mouth. The father's eyes were still wary.

Ilan leaned forward, pressure with nowhere for them to run. 'I need to know if you saw anything suspicious in the days before her death. Was she meeting anyone new? Did she mention being followed, or seeing anything strange?'

The woman gave a little shake of her head, the man rubbing at his knuckles.

Ilan narrowed his eyes. 'Think carefully.'

The two sat silent, breath heavy. That was fine. He'd set the temperature to one he was well used to; he could sit here as long as it took for them to boil and crack.

The father leaned forward first.

'She—'

'*Karlos*.' His wife grabbed his sleeve.

Ilan raised an eyebrow. 'If there's something I should know, say it. She's dead. There's nothing that can stain her now. All we can do is try to give her justice.'

The mother's hand dropped back to her lap. Her husband continued.

'Lili had come to resent going to service.' He spoke slowly and with struggle, as if the words were being fished from his throat. 'She was going to see the Izir. I worried for her soul, whether she'd even be allowed to stay in the city.'

The Izir. Just one more wretched thing in the middle of an already wretched business.

'Why was she visiting him?' It didn't reflect well on her, worse on them for letting her stray. 'Was she ill? Or perhaps . . . other interests?' She would hardly have been the first to lust after the angel.

The man's eyebrows drew together.

'It began after that first body was found. She couldn't sleep for worry and nightmares – she was always a sensitive girl.' Now his words were tripping over themselves in eagerness to be done talking. 'She said his prayers and tonics helped, stopped her from pacing all night at least. But I don't think she believed his heresies – she was desperate. She'd even talked about joining the Church, so it doesn't make sense. She couldn't have believed him. She just liked that he was divine. That he was a comfort.' The man's voice rose with every anguished word.

'What sort of nightmares?' Ilan asked. They'd been careful not to let word of the marks on the bodies slip to the public. Novitiates, however, were young and gossip-prone.

The parents shook their heads. 'She never said, not specifically.'

He made a note anyway. 'If she was scared of going out at night, what was she doing by the river? A lover, perhaps?'

The fetid riverside would be a strange choice for a romantic encounter, but perhaps a fisher or trader had caught her eye. A love-struck girl might have thought it a chance to sin in the open without being caught, and family often elected to be naive when children grew up.

The couple's eyes met, but the mother spoke first. 'No one that we know of. We didn't even hear her go out.'

His lips thinned. More intangible testimony instead of evidence.

'Perhaps you should have also urged her more strongly to be cautious.' Ilan reached beneath his vestment cloak. 'A memento to burn, if you like.'

He placed one of the girl's blonde braids on the table, where it lay curled and frayed like a strip of pelt, and averted his gaze as the woman broke into gasping sobs.

The father stared down at the twined hair, skin as ashen as the salt white in his beard.

'Why isn't the Church doing more?' he asked, voice grave and flat. 'We've been terrorised for weeks, and the Prelate hasn't said a blasted thing.'

Ilan tilted his head. 'Excuse me?'

The fear was gone from the man's eyes, replaced by a cavernous anger as he half-rose, fingertips pressing into the table.

'You relish punishing those who sin, but what are you doing to prevent these crimes from happening in the first place? If prayer was going to work, the city would be free already. Say what you want about the Izir, but at least he's on the streets and not hiding in the cathedral. He's offering what comfort he can.'

'Karlos!' The man's wife pressed her palms on the table and bowed her head until it nearly touched the surface.

It had been a long time since Ilan had seen quite that much deference.

Then again, these people were from Saika, for all they currently lived across the river in a district that had once been linked to Siofolk. He didn't know when this family had left the northern territory, but if they'd seen his arrival they would know his background. They may have seen him in clothing far more decorated than what he now wore, or known his family. Perhaps owed his father.

It was on the tip of his tongue to ask, but it was a poor impulse. A servant of the Church had one home, and it was the one currently being threatened.

'And what would you have me do?' Ilan's lip curled. 'I have the census of everyone in the city. Would you like me to call them in, one by one, and pull out their fingernails until I get a confession?'

They'd already tested the population against the glass, a production of weeks and disruption. They'd found all manner of minor blasphemies and a few horrors, but nothing close to this level of sin.

'If that's what it takes.'

The man's chin was set. Grief had snatched the colour from his world, rendered it black and white, illuminated only with flashes of pain. He'd seen it in the Church, among those who thought taking vows after tragedy would bring some meaning to their loss. He'd seen it in his own home, with two siblings delivered before he'd turned fifteen and his mother reduced to a ghost herself for years.

But there was a reason Justice and Knowledge were equal among the virtues. Ilan himself had considered putting more pressure on the interrogations, and just as quickly dismissed it. He wasn't going to scar a city of the devout in the hope some rumour of smoke turned out to be fire. The Izir was making enough people question the Church as it was; any more and it would spill over into outright anger at the Faith.

He'd been raised on politics and stories of what happened when the hungry turned hateful against those guiding them. In the dark years between the Severing and the Union, the territories had been in constant fear-stoked uprising, and trust had only slowly been rebuilt in the three hundred years since they'd come to a sort of order. Managing a population for their own good was delicate work.

But this man didn't need to know that. Ilan let teeth show with his smile.

'Then why don't I start with you?' Let the man look his call to violence in the mirror. By the way his lip curled, he found the reflection sickening.

'My daughter is dead. You can't think I killed her.' He was standing upright now, backing up to put a cowardly step of space between himself and the inquisitor.

'You would be surprised. But I don't think these murders are a family matter.'

The older man leaned back and stared at the ceiling, retreating into the shroud of impotent anger, and his wife saw Ilan out with a bowed head and breathy prayers to their shared saint.

When he shut the door, he paused to place his hand on it and say a prayer of solace, one he'd learned from his own mother in the endless nights of deep winter. These people would need strength.

Murders happened in Silgard, but never in such isolation. There was always a thread – jealousy or anger, or greed, and he wasn't lying when he said it was kin killing kin more often than not. The only connection here was spilled blood, the writing on the bodies, and the way the killer never surfaced.

Thoughts he had tried to suppress leaked to the surface like smoke finding hairsbreadth cracks in a sealed door.

Ilan would have bet his own soul that there could never be a demon in Silgard. The city was warded, the people striving for good, and creatures of Shadow required invitation.

But this was the city of miracles, and not everything miraculous was good.

'Prelate, a word.'

The man stood before the glowing gold-wrought Eye at the front of the sanctuary hall, but he shifted to let Ilan take a spot at his side. This close, the fire inside was warming, then scalding, turning the gilt molten.

'A helpful one, I hope.'

Ilan wouldn't go that far. 'A concerned one. I spoke with the parents of the latest victim. There was nothing overly suspicious in the girl's life.' Not that he had expected them to say anything else.

The Prelate's soft sigh stirred the ash on the air. 'Unlucky, then. Wrong place, wrong time.'

'Very strange for the place and time to have been by the river at night, don't you think? Almost like there was some influence. Haven't you considered . . .' It felt blasphemous to be the first to suggest it, but he couldn't do otherwise. 'Have you considered that this truly is Shadow work? A broken ward, Sotir, something . . .'

Something that hadn't been seen since the Severing.

Abe stared into the flame, not even acknowledging the possibility with his gaze.

'Arany still weeps. There is no proof this is anything more than a human killer with a taste for the macabre. The bodies smell like bodies. The wounds don't smoke or release evil.'

Because whatever made them is gone.

'The Seal . . .'

The moment he'd first bled for the Faith on the mock seal in Saika was still one he saw when he closed his eyes, the presence of Asten's power and the sure knowledge of his purpose crystalised into a single perfect moment.

And when he'd offered his blood to Silgard before he'd taken his post, the answering shine had been whiter than glare on a snowy peak. Prelate Abe had kissed both his cheeks and told him the Church had never seen someone so blessed.

But when he went down with Prelate Abe weeks ago, it had been flickering and dull. He'd offered to bleed again and the Prelate had only shaken his head, showing his own hand covered in small scabs. There was no power in their sacrifices.

'The Seal is fading because the people's faith is weak. If they trust the Church to protect them, all will be well.'

It would be easier to believe that.

Abe turned and his hand found Ilan's shoulder, fingers pressing to prevent Ilan's instinctive flinch.

'You're wise to consider all ideas, Ilan, but a lack of focus will lead to failure. If it were truly a work of Shadow, the Incarnate would have returned already.' The older man's lips pressed into a cutting line. 'As it is, he has been delayed.'

'Again?' They'd been sure he'd arrive before the spring. Pilgrims and merchants had already started appearing in the city, hoping to participate in the celebration of his homecoming, or at least capitalise on it.

'Again. But he is sending us help.'

'We don't need help. We need *him*.'

The Incarnate was the one person the divine still deigned to speak with.

The Prelate sighed. 'We will be obedient and grateful for what we are sent. And you will drop that train of thought. I wouldn't be surprised if spiritual dissent is part of what our killer is after with these mock-Shadow deaths. We have to be united, and strong.'

Ilan murmured respect. He would be obedient; it was a tenet. But there was nothing in scripture that said he had to be grateful, and he was hardly going to stop thinking.

He waited until he was out of sight to pinch the bridge of his nose and try to stave off a headache. He would add a few notes to Lili's file, then check who the junior inquisitors had rounded up. And look at the old records and their descriptions of older magic again.

It was blasphemous to think it, but all creation was a selfish act in a way, and the very act had birthed dark demiurge with god-sprinkled humanity. The Severing had cut the world off from the extremes of the ether, but the remnants Arany's sacrifice had preserved still stained. The Izir and his sham of Brilliance. The demons that the Servants of the Road kept sleeping in their tarry prisons. They weren't so far from Silgard, and the wards the Church trusted in were old and maintained by the Faith that even Abe admitted was weakening.

The floor outside the library was dotted with little smears of black cat prints. A sinking feeling overtook him as he opened the door.

Everything looked neat enough, and the stack was where he told Csilla to put it, but as he approached his work it was clear that it was a facade. There were fingerprints and ink dots and one very suspicious paw print, and as he shuffled through the papers, one was missing.

His brows drew together. The paper was replaceable, the information less so. She was probably going to take it to the stupid Izir, the person in Silgard least likely to keep their mouth shut. She was going to spook the killer, no matter who or what it was, even further into the dark.

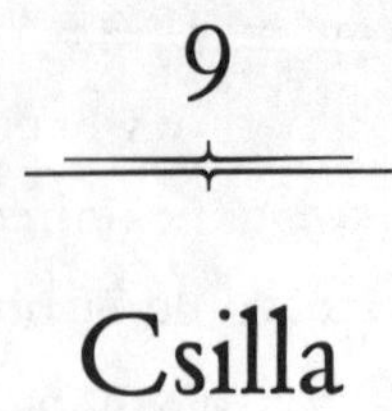

9

Csilla

THE DAY was rudely bright. Snow had melted into puddles in the street too large to avoid, dampening her hem. She hiked her skirts up, trying to keep her dress out of the slush, suddenly conscious of the value of the fabric. Her clothes had rarely been nice and never new, but if she stained or tore something beyond repair, it would be dear to replace now.

Everything in her told her to look back. But what had been safety was now locked from her. She had to look ahead. And she had to be careful. Even when working alone, the knowledge she had a home to return to and people who knew and cared where she was had been a comfort as tangible and unnoticed as the fit of perfectly broken-in shoes. Stripped of it, every step was cold and aching.

There were eight districts in Silgard, with the cathedral at its heart, once divided to provide a seat to every angel and the representatives of their respective territories. Now the lines bled and the grand governing houses only sheltered the secular nobility when they saw fit to make pilgrimage. With the Incarnate returning, some were no doubt preparing for just that, and there'd be no chance of hiding in an empty outbuilding to save her coins.

First, to find Mihály. Maybe he could even convince one of his followers to give her a place to stay. They seemed willing enough to do anything for him.

She picked up speed, brushing past women on their way to and from shopping at the streetside market stalls, nearly stepping into the road as a carriage clipped past. She couldn't move back fast enough to avoid being splattered with grey water and barely got her arms up in time to defend against flecks of gravel that shot out from beneath the horses' hooves. The driver never slowed, yelling an insult to her mother as he passed.

Well, the insult was a black mark on him and nothing to her. Csilla had no idea who her mother was. She shook her skirts off as best she could and picked up her pace again. The alley looked more open in the bright light – all the easier to see that the ladder on the side of the house was gone.

'Izir!' Csilla called, but her voice didn't carry. She scuffed her boot against the ground, seeking a rock to toss at the window, but there was only cobblestone and grit under the slush.

She hefted the weight of her bag again. The cheapest coins were thick iron grots, heavy and rough. She pulled one from her bag and threw it.

It hit under the window with a clank on the stone facade, then fell back. It left a pierced hole in the grey snowmelt banked against the house below. Csilla fished it out of the snow, ignoring the cold on her fingers. Steadying herself, she took better aim and threw again.

This time it hit the shutters with a satisfying crack, but the wood panel chipped under the assault, a flake of green drifting to the ground. Csilla gaped at the pale wood revealed by the damage. She hadn't meant to hurt anything.

She startled at the creak of a tight-hinge door swinging open, and from around the front marched a middle-aged woman, face red beneath her kerchief.

'What are you doing to my house, girl? All the commotion last night, and now throwing . . .'

She paused when she saw what Csilla was holding.

'Throwing coins! Oh Great Asten above, deliver us from madwomen.' She threw her hands up, eyes rolling towards the sky, and Csilla shrunk back. 'I suppose you're looking for the Izir,' the woman continued. 'He's gone, came down the trap door in a hurry last night and took off. Scared my wife half to death.'

'Gone? For good?'

Her stomach dropped. She'd told him to go herself, and it shouldn't have been a surprise, but he was her only lifeline. *At least he's safe*, she told herself. That was the most important thing. She had to be cheered by having saved a life, even if her feet were freezing and she wasn't sure where her meals would be coming from.

The woman waved her hand. 'He's always coming in and out at odd hours, might be gone, might not be.' Her face shifted, eyes narrowing with hawk-like focus. 'What did you want with him?'

That was a very long story that wouldn't make her come out any better in the telling of it.

'I . . . I'll just wait here and see if he comes back. And I'll pay for that.' She gestured to the chipped wood, hoping it wasn't all the coins she had.

The little sack Ágnes slipped to her had felt like riches when she'd first held it, but now she could feel how quickly money slipped away and how hard it would be to replenish. She touched her iron mark again. Those calculations had never crossed her mind when she belonged to the Church. Asten provided for those who served Them so they could focus on more important work.

'Don't worry about that, just get on. His people are like pigeons. One starts strutting around thinking there's food and the whole flock shows up squawking.'

She waved Csilla away like one of the birds, and Csilla stepped back.

'Do you have any idea where he is?'

The woman looked over her worn clothes, the money sack in her fingers all too clearly all she had in the world, and her face softened.

'Try the cemetery. When he doesn't come home, he's talking to ghosts.'

The dead had their own sanctuary. The limited space available to cemeteries within the walls of Silgard had led to the soaring limestone and marble towers that interred ashes. When Csilla stepped into the cemetery, it was as if the rest of the city had been sucked away and this was an empty quarter where only the delivered were welcome.

Mihály's black coat was stark against the white of the tomb. He lay with his forehead on the stone as still as if he'd been carved from it. His lips weren't moving. Odd, to be in a cemetery and offering no prayers.

'Izir . . . Mihály?' she said softly as she approached.

He lifted his head to look at the tomb, face momentarily brightening, then over at her, a strange disappointment flickering over his face.

'Csilla?' His confusion softened into a wan smile. He looked disappointed that it was only her speaking. Perhaps his ghosts talked back. 'I knew you'd find me. Or have you come to kill me again? It's a very convenient location.'

Was that a joke? When she didn't reply, he rubbed his eyes and looked at the cloud-dusted sky, face surprised.

'What time is it?'

'After lunch, I think.' She was so wrapped up in her head she hadn't heard any bells. 'Are you alright?'

He gave a little shake of his head and straightened, placing one hand on the marble wall.

'Fine. Perfectly fine.' He tilted his head, looking down at her in a way that made her stomach squirm.

'I'm not here to kill you,' she said as he opened his mouth again. 'I need your help.'

His hand pressed harder against the stone.

'I spared your life,' she continued. 'And I warned you to leave, even if you didn't. You have to help.'

'Not even the priests dare command Asten's chosen.' But there was a slight smile on his lips and a sweetness to his voice that called her to step closer. 'Go back to the Church. You belong there. Or maybe in the seat of the Incarnate if you're so bold?'

She cringed at his words. She was being terrible and didn't even have a Shadow soul to blame for her rashness. But this was the only door open to her. She stood up straighter and tried again.

'They won't have me.' The wind picked up, plucking at her cloak, and for a moment she froze. The touch was too much like spectral fingers.

'That is a problem.' He was looking back at the stone now, a long finger trailing the cold surface.

'So *help* me.' She couldn't keep the pleading out of her voice. 'You said you wanted to show me your research.' That had to be true. If not, there wasn't even one person left in the city who needed her. 'I'll go with you. I'm ready now.'

Well, maybe not ready. Just willing, for a lack of options.

'You've come here asking my help, but only on your terms? Cheeky.' He reached out and tapped her nose, laughed when she started and blushed. 'Well then. Tell me, Csilla. What do you want me to do for you?'

His eyes were still indulgent, amused. She held his gaze, waiting for the moment the patronising would stop.

'There's a killer in Silgard.'

'So I've heard. So I told you, in fact.' His smile turned cutting. 'Is that what the Church was getting at? They say I encourage disobedience. Make it so people don't mind sinning quite so much.'

'You do . . .'

It wouldn't be much of a stretch to think someone who listened to rumours that dead souls weren't lost wouldn't feel as much guilt about killing. Or that the kind of person who was interested in heresy would also study demons.

He put a finger under her chin, raised her gaze to meet his as the point of contact burned.

'I give people hope, Csilla.'

She swallowed. She couldn't fault him for that. 'But this isn't about you and the Church. I want to catch them. The killer.'

Something glittered in Mihály's eyes. 'You think that's going to make the Church care about you?'

Tears pricked her throat, and she wasn't even sure why. She didn't blame him for the doubt in his voice. She barely had any faith in herself. But she also didn't have a choice. It was going to take an amazing good for the Church to open its arms to her again. Something like saving the city.

'It might. And I do need help. You hear more from the people than I do. You know more than I do. And I didn't kill you.' It couldn't hurt to remind him.

He stood silent for a moment, filling the whole of her vision.

'I do want you to see what I do,' he said, voice softer. 'And I think it will benefit both of us.'

'And you'll help me?' It came out as a plea. He still hadn't agreed to anything.

He placed a hand on her head, the way priests gave benediction to the small.

'That very much depends on you.'

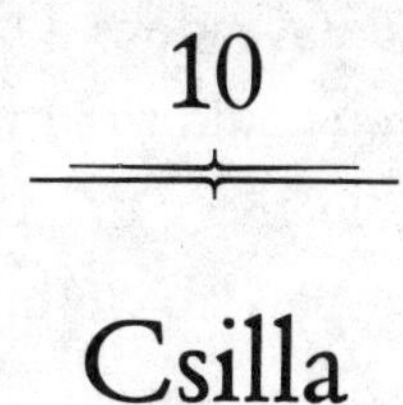

10

Csilla

CSILLA'S FEET stilled as they approached the city gate and she touched her mark of virtues, measuring the distance between her faith and Mihály's ideas.

'Why so pale?' Mihály said, an amused glint in his eyes. 'The gates of Silgard don't open directly into oblivion, regardless of what the self-righteous here think.'

She wasn't naive enough to think so. The land outside the city was still under the banner of the Immaculate Union, bound to the same practices and laws. But people were only there because they weren't good enough to be here. And surely Mihály would realise what he was asking of her.

'If I go, they won't let me back in.' That was what she'd been told and what the finality in Elder Abe's eyes had promised. She was no demon, but anyone let into the city had to be proven pure. She was nothing, pure or otherwise.

'Then it's very lucky you'll be travelling with me.'

He gave a smile that would be impossible to argue with, and it lit a flicker of confidence in her, even as the iron gate swung closed behind them with a crash. She should have taken some holy water or dirt from the cathedral grounds, a small physical token of where she belonged.

Csilla turned her head one way and then the other, drinking in the frightening expanse of land unshadowed by walls. There was almost nowhere inside the gates you could run full out and not risk hitting brick or body or both. Even the indulgent gardens kept by those wealthy enough to devote space to nothing more productive than beauty weren't so large.

'How far is it?' she asked, eyeing the dark woods in front of them, breathing deep of the unpolluted scents of dirt and dry grass.

The area directly around the city was cleared to make it easy for farmers and loggers to move in their goods, but the bare trees ahead had stripped silver branches with peeling bark that clawed what light there was out of the sky. It wasn't all grim, however. On the branches that stretched towards the clouds there were buds that promised spring, same as there were on the weeds that forced their way through cracks in city stone.

It didn't feel any different, standing on ground that wasn't blessed.

But the knowledge of it made all the difference in the world.

'Not far. Maybe an hour?'

An hour? An hour with his long legs was far more with hers. Her feet pre-emptively ached.

She hummed, sang, and answered Mihály's questions about growing up in the Church to pass the time. She kept her own questions to herself lest he take offence and leave her in the woods. There was no sign of travellers or any bandits, but every twig snap and rustle made her start until she relaxed to the beauty in the winter-ravaged wood. The vast, cool peace was how she had always imagined the eternal to be, and a part of her wanted to step off the road and sink into the quiet tangle of the briars.

If it weren't for the wheel-rutted road that spoke of pilgrims and trade, it would have been as if they were the only two people to exist. She'd always been surrounded by voices and steps; the whispers of the other children in mercy care, the comings and goings of clergy doing both the sacred and mundane work of life, the never-empty streets of Silgard. But here the woods swallowed everything. Even the birds' calls came and fell away as quickly as a breeze.

She paused to sweep her eyes up a tangle of dried vines, some thicker than her wrist, so entwined around the trunk and branches of a tree it looked to be choking it. Similar vines tried to climb the bell-tower, only to be pulled down year after year before they could spread past the reach of the gardeners. These had been allowed to embrace their cycle of dormancy and rebirth, and she hadn't known they could grow so large.

'You'll catch flies in your mouth if you keep staring like that,' Mihály teased, and she scowled, which did at least close her mouth. 'You really haven't been outside before? You've never seen a tree?'

'You know we have trees in Silgard.' But not many, and not tall.

Csilla had always been told how lucky she was to have been born – and given a graced childhood – in the holy city. The words had been a comfort when she was sharing a bed with two other girls and their sharp elbows or when she was last in line for what was left of breakfast. But the forest had its charms, and the unplanned lines and curves of leaves and trunks were softer on the eyes than angled stone. Even the birds seemed happier than the fat crows and ever-moulting pigeons who had thrown their lots in with civilisation, and their rosy breasts and warm brown wings in the bare trees were as pretty as any festival decor. The world hadn't been made in brick and mortar but wood and earth and flesh. This was as close to paradise as one could visit – nature before the creation of humanity soured it.

She was so busy with her gaping that she nearly walked into the dark slash on the road. A black scorch marked the dirt, angry like bubbling tar.

'What's that?'

Mihály walked over it like it wasn't even there. She blinked for a half-second, wondering if she was hallucinating.

He turned, eyebrow raised. 'A tarry prison. You haven't seen a sealed demon before? Of course not, blessed thing that you are. Take a look. That was Asten's will, after all, when They left us.'

Csilla flinched at the mention of the Severing. The world had gone dark for three days, and then no more angels or demons walked among them.

'There's a demon in there?'

The damaged surface of the road was glassy, but as she peered over, she couldn't see her reflection. The black sucked in every hint of light and colour that touched it. It wasn't so much looking into darkness as it was looking into a hollow nothing, and a deep, animal terror crawled up in her.

It was said that the birth of humanity was a crisis that became the world. That when the angels urged Asten to make just a little more, to make companions so they could be to this new creation as Asten was to them, that the selfish seed in that urge brought forth creatures of hungry Shadow along with humanity, equal parts dark and divine. That somewhere in the north was a burning garden that was never extinguished, that was the childbed of evil. Here was proof. Not burning, but dark enough to take her breath away.

'It's perfectly safe. The Servants of the Road take care of them, and if one popped out right now, I'd banish it for you.' He tapped it with his foot, and she cringed, imagining Shadow-born flesh reaching through, inhuman hands grasping his ankle.

There were hundreds of years between her and the creature trapped in there, and it suddenly didn't seem enough.

'You could do that? Banish a demon?' The notes she carried and what she'd seen Ilan researching burned hot in her mind.

He tilted his head and looked thoughtful, scratching at his beard.

'Maybe? I've never tried, but I suppose I'm holy enough.'

That was an endorsement she had no desire to test. Csilla stepped carefully around the edge of the tainted ground, but as they made their way further down the road, she kept glancing back over her shoulder. No matter how far they walked, the black spot lingered on the horizon.

'Here we are,' he said as they approached an old logger's stead, the trees around it stunted and young compared to the greater forest.

There was a solid-looking, if small, house with broken windows covered in faded and drooping cloth, a wide and sagging porch and a thick-planked barn much larger than the living space. The well was covered, but freshly split logs in the woodshed showed the lot hadn't been abandoned. Everything else was dire. The roof had a recent patch that was just a board laid across at an awkward angle. A gust would send it careening.

'Who lived here before?'

The porch boards looked so worn Csilla was sure her foot would plunge through. Winter damp had left them spongy in places, and it was a wonder Mihály hadn't broken the whole thing with his weight.

'The family here had plague, I think,' Mihály said without the slightest hint of concern. 'I found it on my way to the city last year, thought it might be useful. Space is quite the commodity in Silgard.'

Csilla shuddered, remembering the last outbreak. Mothers with aprons dotted with bloody phlegm begging sanctuary for fevered children, delirious victims claiming to see angels with hundreds of eyes or demons with the foaming-mouthed heads of rabid animals. The cracks left in the Faith made the city ripe for a preacher like Mihály who could offer hope. With the Incarnate away for longer and longer stretches, people were starved for a connection to the divine.

'Don't be afraid,' he continued. 'I'm here all the time, and I've never gotten sick.'

Mihály's nonchalant tone made her skin tighten. He hadn't been through the worst of it. The miasma of illness could be stirred with the dust at their feet, or soaked into the wood like mould spores, or carried in her clothes to people who might not be blessed with her health. He should know that.

He led her to the barn. Inside was dim, even with the doors open. A few lamps hung from rafters – clearly salvaged, no two matching – carefully positioned away from anything that could catch fire. Mihály lit the oil with a long starter stick.

As the fire flicked, doves flew from their roost, and Csilla startled at the grey storm of wings and the dust they cast down.

The light revealed a long table covered in tarp cloth that looked like it had once served as part of the barn floor. Brown could have been the original colour of the cloth or just as easily manure residue. He paused, hand light and hesitant on the wood.

'I'm sorry, this isn't the kind of thing a delicate girl should see.'

Csilla gave a little huff. He didn't know the work the mercy crews did if he thought her delicate. And she was still the girl who'd at least *considered* killing him.

But when he pulled back the cloth, her hands flew to her mouth to prevent a scream.

The table was covered in animal corpses.

There were squirrels, their bushy tails frozen in unmoving question marks, a few with open stomachs revealing lines of dried intestines, looking like draped paper cutouts. Little chipmunks lined up in a row, black eyes shrivelled in their balding heads and sinking into the sockets. Tufts of brown fur were scattered around their paws, some of it with skin still attached.

A fox with one mangled leg stood with the limb drawn up as if his black-tipped paw still caused him pain, and the white bone and tendon poked through black congealed clots around the wound of whatever trap had felled him. At least a dozen doves with wrung necks were laid out like game in a butcher shop. No wonder the roosting birds had panicked.

His grotesque collection wasn't limited to warm-blooded creatures. There was a blacksnake, a dried-out toad, and even a handful of small river fish with brown and flaking scales. Perhaps the flies lying around were part of the design and not eager opportunists drawn by the gore.

'You . . .' She had to pause for a breath. 'You killed all these?'

A small voice in the back of her mind began to murmur. What would his followers say if they knew the man offering them so much hope of life spent his time like this?

Her feet tensed in her boots, ready to run.

Mihály stared at the bleak menagerie, his expression unreadable. 'I find those that are already sick or hurt. I don't go around killing things for death's own sake. In most cases, it's a mercy.'

Csilla grimaced. 'What do you *do* with them?' She forced herself to walk over. The creatures were beyond help, but they deserved the respect of being seen.

Oh, there were *kittens*. Tiny, with brown and white patches, looking so much like her Erzsébet it cracked the centre of her heart and sent the pieces to her lurching stomach. She longed to be back in bed with her cat snuggled close, timing her breath to the rhythmic purrs. Enjoying what life she had, not staring at this panoply of death. She missed the cathedral with a seizing homesickness, and she grabbed her mark of virtues. When she'd had a question, she only had to ask Ágnes and be given the correct answer. She didn't have to confront so much awfulness on her own.

'I study them,' Mihály said. 'I study the bodies. And I study their souls.'

'Study their . . . How?' She reached out and stroked the head of one of the kittens with a fingertip, the fur now dry and patchy. They couldn't have lived long. She had to believe they hadn't lived long, that they hadn't suffered.

Mihály's cheek twitched, and for a moment it looked like he wanted to stop the words.

'I can see souls when they leave the body. Hear them, if they stay around. Call them, direct them, if they want to come back.'

Direct them? Did his heresy have some truth to it? She tried to quiet her thoughts with recitations of Faith. People were born with split souls, theirs to do with what they liked. If they obeyed the tenets of the Church and remembered the Brilliance within them, they would rejoin Asten's peace after their mortal trial ended. And if they followed the corruption of the Shadow, their soul would never join Asten eternal. They would spend eternity knowing nothing but loneliness and all the sorrow that came with regret.

There were ghosts, but they were said to be born of trauma, souls that refused to let themselves be escorted beyond the ether. They weren't anything to speak of gently, and some didn't even believe they were real. They couldn't, shouldn't, be created on purpose.

'That's the province of Asten.' She could hear Ágnes's own instructional sharpness in her tone, and she straightened from muscle memory. Though, if Ágnes had been here, she would have no doubt been dragging Csilla away.

'And They gave me this gift.' Mihály raised his hand in oath. 'The purest way to worship is to fully understand creation, to never stop trying to see what They have truly given us. That's why Knowledge is counted among the virtues. And our souls are Their most perfect creation, as eternal as They are.'

'Yet They corrupted Themselves in the making of them.' Shadow had only come about in the creation of humankind. Even an Izir shouldn't forget that.

A sad, sick meow echoed from somewhere in a dusty corner, pulling her from the argument. A thin cat shook against the clapboard wall. She was so dark, knotted and thin, she nearly blended in with the shadows.

'That's the mother of those dead kittens,' Mihály sighed. 'Skittish thing.'

Csilla scowled and walked diagonally towards the wall, giving the cat a wide berth. Then she crouched, held out her hand, and waited. She tried not to think about the man staring at her, watching as if she were another experiment.

Gingerly, the cat stepped forward. She was a skeleton – not many mice around this time of year, and she was clearly too weak to hop on the table and fight the tarp for what Mihály had laid out. She might not even be able to chew bones.

The pink nose touched Csilla's fingertips, and Csilla stroked the ridges of her spine, trying not to even breathe. When she got close, Csilla snatched her up in her cloak. The cat yowled but didn't fight. She didn't have the strength to.

'I'm sorry, I'm sorry, sweet thing. I'm going to help you.' Her own breath quickened with the cat's panicked panting.

She turned back to Mihály, revulsion churning. She thought she could still help the Church by finding the killer, or at least help herself to Mihály's knowledge. But this was more than she could stand. She wasn't lying when she said she wasn't delicate; she'd treated festering wounds and wrung chicken necks, walked hours in freezing sleet delivering medicines. The difference was, that was all in the service of life. There was no life here.

'I'm going back now.' Her shoulders shook with anger, but it was all directed at herself for daring to expect something better. 'Forget I ever came to you.'

He arched an eyebrow. '*You* came looking for *me*. You believed I could help you.'

She cringed at the reminder as he continued.

'And I can do more for you than you even know if you stay with me.' The sweetness was back in his voice, softening her again despite her instincts. 'The Church has turned its back on its own tenant – I have knowledge they wouldn't ever admit to. That is why I preach. It's a light, meant to uncover. Not darkness.'

'What do you mean?' Csilla looked back at the table, all the stiff and dried-out corpses, their frozen yawns uncomfortably close to screams. 'You said your powers don't create souls, and you hardly seem inclined to help me help the Church.'

'Create? No. But with the right vessel, I can move one.' He stepped in close and drew a finger across her cheek. 'Do you know what that would mean for people? How much hope there is in the idea of rebirth?'

She jerked back, the sudden familiarity a jolt.

'I wasn't prepared before, and animals have a fragile essence. No Shadow, of course, but not quite Brilliance either. And moving a soul into a creature that already has one never ends well. But you, empty but not dead—'

'Do it, then.' Her heart hammered, and the cat squirmed. 'If you can prove you're right using me, you can leave them alone.'

He took a deep breath, closing his eyes for a moment. 'First, we need the soul. And a lot of blood to carry it.'

Her throat seized, dry and closing. 'Whose blood?'

'And that is where our interests align. I agree the killer needs to be caught.'

Her heartbeat thudded in her throat as pieces slid together. 'You want to give me the murderer's soul?'

Mihály shook his head. 'We could, if it comes to that, but what we need is his blood. Trust me, it's better if we use someone else's. It's hard to work miracles with an open vein.'

'You know something about it, then?' Her voice was so quiet she wasn't sure he could hear her. But his lips thinned, and he rolled up his sleeve. Along the river of his vein was the raised pale flesh of a scar at his wrist. By the thickness, the cut that had made it had been deep, and she instinctively reached for it even though it was long healed.

Magic that came from the body was powerful. There was a reason the Church used it in vows, and spilled blood was prayed over and cut hair was burned. That power made it easy to turn dark.

'But you're an Izir.'

'Which is why I can't work Shadow magic.' His tone was even, and the Brilliance of his soul showed in his smile, melting her doubt. 'Asten intended for us to have these physical forms, no matter what went wrong in the making of them. Let me help you. And you will help me.'

Her entire being curled with want at his promises, rich with power and more than she'd ever dared hope for. 'But we still need a human soul.' Her voice was nothing but a whisper.

'I have one in mind. A kind one, don't worry.' His eyes were lit with a look she recognised. Hope, undercut with desperation.

He talks to ghosts. He said he calls them.

The idea of rebirth.

'What—'

'You'll still be you,' he promised, eyes earnest. 'Just . . . just more. I know I can do it.'

She looked again at the scar visible from under his shirtsleeves, a stark warning on his skin. She believed him. That didn't mean it was safe.

'What if you can't?'

Offence flashed over his face, and then he softened.

'Then at least we've caught the killer. You can stay, the faithful girl who delivered them from a monster. I'm no worse off. I've failed before. I can handle it.'

She could save everyone and be saved in turn. She wanted so badly for it to be true, even as her eyes flicked back to the corpses. *Graced Rozalia*, her mind whispered, conjuring images of the miracle of preservation, the perfect corpse said to still rest somewhere in the deep passages of the cathedral, the knowledge of her lost but the miracle never forgotten. There was precedent for miracles requiring death.

Mihály placed his hands over her free one, pressing her palm as if praying through her skin.

'Asten brought us together for a reason. I'm the only person who can help you. And you are the only one who can prove I'm no heretic. This is real.'

She swallowed. Their meeting did have an uncomfortable ring of fate. The Church taught there was nothing without purpose.

'If you can't trust me,' Mihály continued. 'Trust Them. You made the right choice in coming here.'

'I have faith in Them,' she answered. But she'd never had a reason to spare much faith on herself, and doubt was a worm gnawing at the hope trying to root.

'And me?'

He brushed his fingers over the mark on her cloak, and a starry silver glitter danced on the surface. He was right – he was chosen. Trusting in one meant trusting in the other and that's what she had been raised to do. She closed her eyes, blocking out the dim and stinking barn, the ruined creatures, everything but the warmth of the man in front of her.

'Yes.'

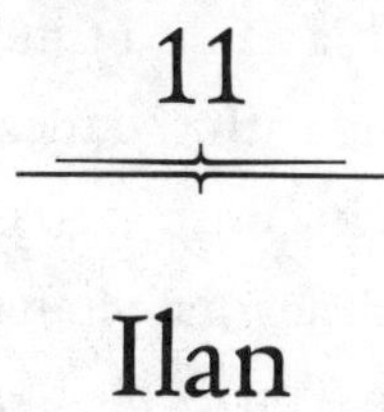

11

Ilan

NOTHING GOOD ever came of sudden meetings. He'd been planning to track down Csilla and question her about her little act of theft, but the muster bells ringing urgent summons stopped his feet, and the eyes of the other priests forced him to follow into the chapter house. There wouldn't be a way to explain where he was going without the galling admission that a combination of exhaustion and misguided pity had resulted in what could be the largest leak in their investigation.

There were far too many clergy gathered in the dim room. Ordinarily the chapter house held a half-dozen members or so as their committees debated the daily workings of keeping order: food, supplies, sanitation, changes to service. All necessary tasks, but none requiring so many hands for approval.

Prelate Abe stood before them with a broad, dark-haired man dressed in the cream and silver cassock of the Incarnate's service, though the hem hung above his ankles and black soil crumbled from beneath his boots with each step. Ilan frowned at the little clumps dotting the stone floor. The roads were damp this fickle time of year, but a wiser servant would have changed shoes before creating more work for his fellow Faithful. They didn't wear road boots to service.

'Sandor has come to us at a fortunate time,' the Prelate said.

The stranger nodded at his name, raising a heavy hand in greeting. A gold and ivory signet ring with the Incarnate's mark decorated his small finger, oddly delicate in contrast to the thick joint.

'He has been sent by the Incarnate in response to the troubles.'

So this was their stand-in. Ilan let out a sharp breath as others raised their voices in praise. He, the Prelate, and others had all written to the Incarnate, urging him to hasten his return to the Brilliant City. War and taxes and council would mean little if the Church lost its power.

But the Incarnate didn't come, and the stranger looked to be a poor substitute.

'Indeed. He apologises for his delay; one man can travel more quickly than his convoy, and there has been far more . . . trouble than anticipated.' The man addressed them in a rolling voice that carried easily through the murmurs. 'I would like for the High Inquisitor to come and tell me what we know so far.'

'You've gotten my letters, no doubt?' This man should already know everything. Everything Ilan had been allowed to write, anyway.

'Things get missed. The further out you go, the worse the roads are. And what has arrived is still with His Divinity.'

Ilan hoped there were letters missed, waylaid by a lame horse or a late-season freeze. If the Incarnate didn't know how bad it was, his absence could be excused. Even the Incarnate couldn't always count on the voice of Asten to speak clearly.

He scratched his tongue against clenched teeth as he walked past the muttering servants to the front of the room, their eyes like poking sticks.

'There have been four deaths, all marked with demonic symbols.' Ilan kept his tone neutral, but the quiet voices grew into a buzz like flies that needed swatting. 'I asked for a script expert. Would I be right in assuming that's you?'

Someone in the back made a noise of dismissal. A knifepoint of a headache began to form over his right eye.

'Unfortunately, no. Have you had any leads that aren't speculation?' Sandor said the word like it was blasphemy.

The blade dug deeper.

'None that have gone anywhere. The killer . . .' The killer was smoke or spirit, fading in an instant and impossible to grasp. 'No one has confessed to seeing him. I believe we might be dealing with something that slipped past the wards.'

If this man were meant to stand in for the Incarnate, he had little to lose from speaking plainly. Dancing around the issue had only left them leadless and sore.

The Prelate turned.

'Ilan.'

Ilan stiffened at the plainness of his name here in front of the gathered clergy. It was a mark of the equality of the Faithful to make no distinction between each other aside from that earned through service. Inquisitor was a role he'd earned with every sin he'd scourged. The Prelate should acknowledge it.

'Perhaps either you've been working too hard, or we've lost more of our power than we thought, but you've yet to come up with anything useful.' Prelate Abe clasped his arm, as if worried about a strike. He wasn't wrong to be. 'Either way, Sandor will take charge of judicial matters for the time being. Ilan, you are hereby relieved of your duties as High Inquisitor and will act under Sandor, who will report directly to the Incarnate.'

Ilan's mouth fell open soundlessly. He would have rather taken two hundred lashes.

'Prelate, with respect—'

'With *respect*, you will hold your tongue. This is more important than your pride.' He gestured to the tiled floor, glazed red echoing the fading blood and power rolling below. 'You have done your best, but we need fresh eyes. You know what's at stake.'

Ilan swallowed hard, an unfamiliar fear skittering down his back. Arany's sacrifice was what let the Church still see Asten's hope for his creation made manifest, reflected in consecrated glass and water and stone. The weak would never keep faith without visible proof of sin or power, and Asten would stay beyond their reach.

If Sandor had been sent by the Incarnate, it was Their divine will. Ilan's place was not to doubt, certainly not resent, even if forcing his temper to heel made his shoulders shake.

Sandor smiled and clapped him companionably on the back, and it took all Ilan's willpower not to return the gesture with a blow.

'Come now, won't it be a relief to have the responsibility lifted from your shoulders? I will still be relying on you.'

Ilan gave the smallest possible nod. He would bear the humiliation for the sake of his city, acrid as the flavour was.

Abe nodded. 'Now, Ilan, go with Sandor and show him what there is to see thus far.'

None of the seated servants would meet Ilan's gaze as he passed, and his hard steps echoed in the rounded chamber.

'I'm surprised you haven't yet brought the man in to hang,' Sandor said when they were alone in the corridor. Though they had plenty of space and Ilan took up far less of it, the larger man insisted on walking right beside him, occasionally jostling his arm. 'You have quite a reputation for keeping the city spotless. Hard to believe you've only been at it, what, three years?'

There was a needling note to the question, though when Ilan glanced at the man, his eyes were still straight ahead.

'A little more than four now, I believe.'

He'd been twenty-one when he entered the great city for the first time and had been granted his rank two years later. The results had quieted even the loudest tongues wagging that he hadn't truly earned it.

'Humans crave order as much as they resist it. I simply put things right. I'm blessed to have such a calling.' He moved to the side and was followed, sped up and was matched. They danced step in step as his irritation rose. 'And how fares the Incarnate?'

'Things are progressing well. Asten's return is closer each day.' Sandor emphasised the words with another bump, and Ilan watched his steps, thinking how easy it would be to jut out his foot just so, and send the man sprawling to the floor in the dapple of stained-glass light. Just another accident, as Sandor would surely say all his ridiculous goat-like butting was. 'No doubt the broken territories will be welcomed back to our fold by the end of the year.'

That was a far more generous assessment than the rumours said. The plan to bring the entirety of the continent back into the Union was on its second generation and seemed more of a drudge than holy war. Seda had decided Asten's decision to abandon the world was enough reason to abandon Their Church, and in Ilan's opinion, good riddance. The Church and governing classes alike were bleeding money into the campaign. If an entire region wished to declare themselves damned, so be it.

'I'll pray for his success,' is what he said instead. It would serve everyone for the whole matter to end, one way or the other. 'He can only do so much from afar. Like send orders for murder.'

It was a sharp and graceless stab, but would show him how much the Incarnate trusted the man he had sent.

Sandor's steps didn't falter. 'The matter of the heretic, I take it? The one who didn't die?'

So he did know.

'Who wasn't killed,' Ilan corrected. 'The girl they sent failed.' Refused. 'I offered to handle the matter myself, but the Prelate thought it best to wait for the Incarnate's direction. He was worried about retaliation from the Izir's followers.'

The other man made a small *hmm*. 'He was right to. And as I rode through the city, it was quiet. Has the heretic spoken since the attempt?'

He'd spoken to Ilan, which had been unwelcome and extremely annoying, but not what Sandor meant. There'd been no gatherings last night that he'd been made aware of. 'No.'

'Then he was silenced, as Asten willed him to be. The Incarnate's order was wise, and the result was achieved without sin. If he stops speaking, the people will have to have something – they'll come back, whether it be from fear or for nourishment. We do not always know why Asten orders what They do, but this was clearly what was meant to be.'

'Clearly.'

Hopefully his rolled eyes would be mistaken for heavenward praise. Something about the easy dismissal still didn't sit well with him, even when he tried to push it away as his own desires being thwarted.

Sandor made a sound of assent that ignored Ilan's tone. 'If it becomes a problem again, we will address it again, but for now I would love to see where the more passionate side of your work takes place. I suppose now those duties will be mine, too.'

Ilan inclined his head. If the man had the stomach for torture, at least he might be useful.

'Of course.'

The main inquisitorial room was dim, even with the door propped to steal a little of the hall's window light, but every hook, table and instrument had been laid out to Ilan's specifications. Something Ilan couldn't read flashed over Sandor's face as he took in the sight of the ropes and stretched leather straps that hung expectantly along the wall, waiting for wrists and necks.

'They say you've been zealous in your punishments,' Sandor said, reaching out to shake the knotted rope tails of a cat whip. 'The

Church allows redemption through coin and service. Why choose this?'

Ilan shrugged. It was a common question, though people rarely liked his answer.

'We have the same rich sinners paying off indiscretions every week. Write something on a man's flesh, and he will remember it long enough to save his soul.'

As the words left his mouth, he remembered Lili and the weeping marks on the bodies before her. A momentary revulsion climbed his throat, and he quieted it with a prayer. When scars were made here, they were redemption.

'Noble of you to take on the sacrifice of such disturbing work.'

'Holy work,' corrected Ilan. There was no reason to defend the rest. No one sniped when a knowledge priest enjoyed teaching or a mercy priest found peace in comforting the dying. A talent for pain was an equally useful blessing. There were even those who crawled to him voluntarily, submitting to purging before they were consumed by sin.

Ilan ran a finger down the soft leather strap of a flogger. All gifts had their uses to the Faith.

Sandor picked up a small pair of iron shears, the kind heated to neatly sever fingers and tongues, and Ilan smiled. That tool had stopped many a heresy from entering the world.

'They cauterise as they cut. Quick and far less bloody.'

Sandor dropped them with a dull clank that did nothing for Ilan's headache. 'You praise the blades' mercy?'

'Mercy *is* one of the prime virtues.' He took private victory in Sandor's grimace. 'If not the tools, maybe the paperwork is one of your strengths?'

Ilan gestured to the back of the room, where a sheave of paper sat, fresh-drawn victim portraits and older references. Beneath lay the ruined sheets, paper dark and rippled with dry ink.

'It's not my strength you need to worry about, it's the Seal's.' Sandor's gaze fell on one of the smudged sheets. 'A compendium of demons?' He scratched a long fingernail down the list of unholy names and the places that marked their banishment. 'You really think the city is so far gone we've let a demon in.'

Ilan swallowed. 'The victims have all been marked with Shadow script. The Seal is reacting. There's clearly an evil presence.'

Sandor paused and looked him over – a long, appraising stare. The kind Ilan was used to giving, and loathed being on the other side of. 'The problem is sin. An abundance of mortal evil, here in our most holy city.'

Something in the man's posture, the slant of his gaze as it darted off the paper again, rubbed at Ilan with a niggling friction. He wasn't saying everything.

But when he raised his hand to wipe at his brow, Ilan saw the ring again. Sandor didn't need to say everything. He had spoken to the Incarnate more recently, accepted a direct charge for the Faith. Ilan could ask him question after question, and he would never be required to answer.

'So put all thoughts of the script aside.' Sandor set a heavy hand on Ilan's carefully illustrated work. 'The killer clearly means it as a distraction, and it's working. Their tactic has you wrapped up in stores of Knowledge, ignoring Justice. You were led astray from your purview, Ilan.'

He smiled then, though there was nothing kind in it. 'That is why I am here.'

The irritating smirk of the Izir flickered in Ilan's mind. 'No. But a demon or Sotir . . .'

'No Sotir have been born in a century and any child of the Union can tell you why.'

Because they and every soul who shared dark blood were slaughtered. There were murals devoted to the holy sacrifice of those dying so there was no chance the curse could spring up in future generations.

'If demons can enter Silgard, the city is already lost,' Sandor continued.

The truth of that stung like the kiss of a lash.

Sandor continued. 'This is someone who knows of Shadow work, but only that. I'm shocked the faith of the former High Inquisitor is so weak.'

He slapped his hand down on the stack, dislodging the buried papers. 'Even the records are trash. If you thought this so important, you would have been more careful, no?'

Ilan's frown deepened, the indignance of being rightly chastised fading with suspicion. He recognised something in that tone. The swagger of someone bluffing their way around doubts so they wouldn't be questioned.

It was how he became who he was, from when he was eleven and informed his parents he would no longer be answering to the name they'd given him, to seven years later, when he offered back his title to join the priesthood. He'd learned to speak like he was comfortable long before he was, claiming the words for what he wanted until experience gave them confidence and weight.

Sandor spoke with authority, but there was a quickness, a weakness behind it that a man serving the Incarnate should have been purged of long ago.

'My faith in the Church remains,' Ilan said, pushing the papers away from Sandor. 'You, I don't know yet. Where in the front were you serving?'

If Sandor would push, Ilan could push back. They would see whose footing was secure.

'Banksa. Would you like our list of stops? The names of the men who died in our convoy so you can check them against service records?' Sandor's gaze purposefully fell back on the pile of notes.

'I respect that an inquisitor is meant to be suspicious,' he continued, 'but if you don't want to work with me, perhaps you'd like to join the congregational priests? There is always other work for the Faithful.'

Leading sermons and taking confession, endless talking and administrative counsel . . . It was important work, but Ilan never had been one for tedium. Or talking.

'That won't be necessary, Sandor.'

'Inquisitor,' the man corrected. 'Don't worry, I'll give you time to get used to it.'

Ilan bowed, but his skin prickled with anger and lingering shame. There was no denying that he hadn't caught the killer. Underneath his quick-flaring anger was that unavoidable truth.

'I'm even going to give you a present, Ilan,' Sandor continued in a jovial tone. 'We are going to have to take stricter measures. You wait for evidence of sin before bringing people in – I think they'll be more encouraged to confess if we act first. We have some changes to make; we'll set a curfew and stricter watches and begin working our way through the city. You can handle the interrogations as you like.'

The man genuinely looked as if he thought this would be welcome news. Ilan frowned. 'The Prelate and I have had this discussion and decided against it. Not everyone here is a sinner.'

Silgard's citizens were still his to protect, and even the pain he gave was a part of that protection.

'No, but anyone could be,' Sandor said, gravel in his tone. 'That's why Asten left. Bring them all in.'

12

Csilla

THAT NIGHT Mihály had talked, and she'd listened until his words made sense through the pounding of her head and the heaviness in her bones. She nodded and dozed until the blanched moonlight over the trees was replaced by the shell pink of morning and the unfamiliar sounds of woodland creatures rousing.

He showed her more of his talents, including healing the blisters on her heels with a ticklish touch, laughing as she cringed at the sensation even as she was awed by the power. Twinned Brilliant and Shadow natures warred within every person, though she had neither. And when Asten's wisdom refracted to create the flawed creatures that were humans, perhaps there was something of Their grace present in even her flesh. In the blood. In Mihály's ability to heal.

A soul didn't make you alive – she was proof enough of that – but surely something in her would change when she had one. Mihály promised the dark spaces within her would become golden when Asten heard her. With a tangible connection to all of creation and him by her side, she'd never be lonely again. She'd be beloved by the city when she saved both it and the Seal.

He spun wondrous things, and what's more, he clearly believed them. Any doubts she had in him were her own weakness, not his.

‘What if the Church won’t let you back in the city? Or me?’ She touched her mark at the memory of the poison. At least the sin of almost murdering him wouldn’t stain her new soul. ‘I’m sure they’re being careful.’

He kept one hand on her back as he locked the door behind them. ‘And admit they wanted me gone? The people would protest. I won’t say a word of fresh heresy inside the gates, and you’re going to help me prove I had nothing to do with it.’ He smiled at her with such devoted attention she wanted to pull her headscarf further over her face with fresh embarrassment. ‘You’ll be safe with me.’

With Asten’s grace on him, that should be true.

Mihály hummed to himself, off-key, as they walked the long road towards the city. Csilla scowled at his back. Weren’t angels supposed to be good at music?

‘Hurry up, Csilla,’ he called and she sighed, doubling her pace.

‘Do you really walk this way every day?’ She wasn’t used to walking so far or on wagon-rutted ground. Fresh blisters were starting to form where he’d just finished healing them.

‘Not every day,’ he conceded. ‘I do sleep in town after preaching. But I like the walk. It clears my head.’

Maybe that was what he needed. She’d heard glass clinking and liquids being poured long after she’d laid down to try to catch scant hours of sleep. The only damage it seemed to have done, though, was a little puffiness around his eyes. He looked irritatingly rested and pleasant for someone who’d had less sleep and more drink than she had.

‘Do you need me to carry you?’ He paused, offering an arm, and she had a sudden and terrible vision of him slinging her over his broad shoulder like a sack of potatoes, humming all the while. ‘Or we can wait for a wagon. Lately there’s always someone coming along who will let me catch a ride.’

Of course. Did he not realise his very existence was charmed? She stomped back in step with him.

Ahead was the arching stone of the gates, with all the relief and dread they signified. She was going back to what she knew.

What she thought she'd known. She glanced at Mihály.

'Halt there,' the guard said, approaching. 'Izir, good morning.'

The man saluted, and Mihály nodded in return. The guard didn't look suspicious at all, his smile genuine, and after a moment, Csilla recognised him. He'd been in the crowd that night she'd brought the wine that had started this. No wonder Mihály didn't have trouble getting in and out of the city.

'Must we?' he said as the man presented a small, polished piece of glass, smooth as a tumbled river stone. She still smiled to see the little piece, one of thousands of shards taken from the miracle forest of Gellért. When he was lost, Asten turned all the trees to glass so he might find his way. Now that same glass, shattered and dispersed, was a signpost directing every sinner back to the light. In the old days, miracles were tangible – the creative force of the divine, momentarily held in human hands.

Just like her healed hand and feet.

'If you would, Izir.'

Mihály shrugged and held out his hand.

Why was the man closing his eyes?

Mihály touched the glass, and Csilla winced as it flared white, then settled to a silvery sheen that faded as he removed his hand.

'And you, miss?'

Csilla kept her hands at her sides, though her curled fingers tapped against her palms.

'You let me out yesterday morning, don't you remember? I live here.'

The man gave a little laugh. 'And who knows what you were up to while you were away. No offence.' His smile was much warmer than Csilla's strained one.

She reached out and pressed her index finger to the glass, a divot worn down by the fingerprints of thousands.

No reaction.

The guard frowned. 'I've never seen that before. Try the other one, and I'll turn it over.'

Csilla hesitated. He would see her cut palm, and know her shame.

'It won't help,' Mihály said, gently moving in front of Csilla in a protective gesture that warmed her. 'But she's no demon. She's working with me.'

'I'm not supposed to . . . I mean, we have to be careful.' The man's lips were pressed white-thin. 'We have rules. Especially now.'

Csilla's heart lodged in her throat as anger bloomed in her chest. She'd told Mihály this would happen. This was her home. She could see the spires of the cathedral from where they were standing, smell the muck of the river on the breeze. It was choking after the crisp pine of the forest, but it was hers, and though she'd never voiced it, in her bones she'd thought the city knew it, too.

That bit of hope fizzled, the blackened end of a snuffed match.

'You're not supposed to let anyone with a Shadowed soul through. And did the glass turn black?'

'Well, no . . .' The guard removed his glove and touched the glass himself, brow furrowing all the more as it glowed pale gold, with a hint of greying around the bottom, like wisps of incense smoke. He needed to say a few prayers and perhaps make a confession, but the problem wasn't the glass.

'Then let us pass. Helping me is a blessing to you. Look for yourself.'

Mihály walked through the gate, beckoning for Csilla to follow. As she stepped over the rune-marked entrance, the dim spots in the glass on the guard's hand vanished, his kindness to Mihály instantly reflected in the state of his soul.

They were back in Silgard. The clack of her steps on the cobblestone hadn't changed, but somehow everything else had.

They were swiftly turned away from every type of lodging. Being an Izir didn't stop the raised eyebrows and suspicious eyes when it became clear Mihály was asking for himself and a woman not sworn to him, and Csilla refused to play along and pretend to be his wife to get a room. He may have felt secure enough to ignore custom and talk his way around rites and lie, but there had to be some kind of propriety in all this. Every time he got too close or turned those sincere eyes onto her, it was like the thin squeeze of apron strings being tightened and she wasn't sure how many 'no's she had left in her.

'Let's say you're my ward, then,' he sighed as they stood outside of the fifth building that had refused them. 'You're short enough to pass for a child if no one looks too closely, and you're already an orphan. I'll tell them you're . . .' He paused and looked her up and down, and she crossed her arms over her chest, not that there was much to cover. 'Fourteen?'

'That is just going to make you look *worse*.'

The blisters were back to full-on wounds now, Csilla's stomach was protesting the lack of lunch and her bladder was aching. Her miserable body begged her to give in and make it easy. The city wasn't so large that there were endless options. If they couldn't rent somewhere legitimate, they were going to end up in that tomb Mihály was so fond of, snuggling with the ashes of the dead.

'Can't we go back to the place you were leasing before? We're wasting time.'

He snorted. 'You were up there – there was barely room for me. We need at least room for three of us.'

'Three . . . ?' Her voice trailed off as she caught his meaning. Somewhere large enough for slaughter and magic.

'I do know someone who would help,' he conceded. 'But you'll absolutely have to pretend to be my ward.' He sighed. 'Maybe we should look somewhere further downriver. The rooms are cheaper, though I hate the smells by the pig yards.'

'Mihály,' Csilla groaned. 'If you know someone, why aren't we there already?'

He scratched at his chin and shifted their bags. 'I don't mind being seen,' he conceded, 'but there's a world between that and having one's presence flaunted.'

The house was not as large as the cathedral sanctuary, but that was the only mark one could say against its grandeur. Csilla couldn't keep her lips together as she stared at the carved flowers and doves over the lintel, grace and movement etched in flecked granite.

Mihály rapped on the door twice, and a servant in a starched green frock, a world cleaner than they were, answered. Csilla drew herself up, but since she was still only chest-height to Mihály, it barely made a difference. From over the servant's shoulder, the sparkle of the lamps in the entryway set the dark wood of the banisters aglow, as polished as the golden holder of the Eye of Asten itself.

Mihály gave the man a charming smile. 'Is the lady in? Tell her it's Mihály.'

The servant looked them over for a moment; a quick scan of Csilla, a longer look at Mihály.

'One moment,' he said, shutting the door.

'This is your friend?' Csilla said, voice still half-hushed in awe. The widow Varga was well known across the city for both her wealth and tragedy, losing both her husband and daughter in the span of a month not even a year prior. 'Mercies, why were you living in an attic when you could be here?'

Mihály was about to speak when the door opened again to reveal an older woman, her shoulders draped in silver fur from foxes that were rare everywhere but the farthest North and the heady scent of rosewater cream radiating from her skin. Despite the lines on her face and the thinness of her greying hair, she was a handsome woman, even more so up close than when parading into the cathedral on service days.

Csilla's mind flitted back to Ágnes, her ashen skin and cough. This is what she should look like – with years of life still ahead.

'Misi, oh my dear, do come in. You don't even need to knock, you know.' She reached over to brush overgrown strands of hair out of his eyes, letting her palm linger on his cheek before her eyes slid to Csilla. 'Who is this?'

'Csilla, a ward I've taken in as a new assistant. She's very bright.'

Csilla smiled faintly at the compliment, though she knew it was a lie to make her presence go down more easily. It was at least better than wife.

The woman's expression pinched, taking Csilla in feet to crown.

'A very self-serving sort of charity.'

They were going to be turned away again, and Csilla would scream. She clasped her hands politely instead, squeezing until her fingers numbed.

Mihály waved his hand.

'She's my student. Please don't misunderstand. Everyone else in the city seems to.'

Csilla dipped forward, smiling through her worry, putting on the face any orphan learned to give in front of prospective homes. A look that asked to be taken in and promised no trouble at all.

'It's a pleasure to meet you, Madame Varga.' She tried to make it sound like it truly was.

'Well, I suppose you can both come in.' The widow glanced at what Mihály was carrying. 'And your bags?'

'I'm afraid I have to ask a favour. We are lacking in accommodation at the moment.' There was a slight catch as each word left Mihály's lips.

The woman's eyes lit, a pink flush coming to her cheeks that took ten years off her face.

'Of course, Misi, of course. You should have come when I asked you the first time. It's not a *favour* to help your family.'

Family? Csilla mouthed, but the woman pulled a string that sent a brassy chime echoing through the house. The noise only punctuated the draughty silence in which it rang.

The servant appeared again, and Madame Varga raised a ringed hand.

'Set them up in suites. Misi, would you like to stay in—'

'A guest room will be more than enough.' His voice cut so quickly that Csilla jumped. 'I've no wish to disturb anything. But if you could provide something for Csilla?'

Her eyes softened, and she touched his cheek again. 'Fine. It's been too long since I've had guests. No one visits this cursed house.' Her tone was light to the point of cracking.

Csilla shifted her eyes away even as curiosity gnawed at her. There were clearly threads between them, but she couldn't gauge how tightly they were woven.

They were placed in suites at the opposite end of a wing that had been disused for some time, judging by the marks that their feet left in the dust. A pang of sympathy twinged in her. As large as it was, the cathedral had never felt as empty as this.

'I'll send my girl over to clean up while we have tea,' Madame Varga had said, and Csilla looked around the spacious room she'd been placed in. If they failed and she had to leave the city, perhaps she could find work in a grand house like this, polishing the silver flowers that held up thick ribbon-tied curtains and floorboards of dark mahogany that gleamed like cut stones.

A knock on the door drew her up short. She opened it to see a young woman with a pale blue dress draped over one arm, gauzy fabric trailing, and a pitcher in the other.

'The Izir asked me to find you something. This belonged to the mistress's daughter when she was younger. It might fit with a bit of adjusting.'

Csilla bit her lip and took the dress. She'd never touched material so fine, with gold embroidery along the neckline and hem, the waist apron tied with a girlish sash of white.

She'd also never dreamed she'd be having someone else help her get dressed, and she was sure she was red from hairline to toes as the maid began removing her clothing.

'I'll do it myself,' she said as she slipped off the rest of her outer dress down to her chemise, thin enough to see the skin beneath. For an instant she was back in the dusty Church hall, young and naked and cold. The click of the door as the girl left barely registered.

She picked up the pitcher for a welcome drink when the smell of vinegar and herbs hit her nose and she saw the sponge floating on top. Of course, the lady of the house expected her to be clean. At least the maid had left before seeing Csilla try to drink bathwater.

Once refreshed and redressed, Csilla spun, the fabric lifting in the luxury of space. This was a dress made for swaying entrances and graceful dancing. Csilla's heart pained as she brushed down the skirts. She'd always worn charity clothes, and it was likely some of the original owners were ash, but it was entirely different when she knew where the girl this had been commissioned for was buried. The widow's whole family had been touched by death.

The hallway swallowed her as she made her way towards the sound of voices. Mihály and the older woman were in a sitting room, both looking up as she entered.

Mihály paled, but Madame Varga's eyes hardened.

'Is something wrong?' Had she spilled something, or stepped on a hem?

Mihály stood to take her arm, face softening. His golden-brown eyes took on a hint of reverence.

'Sorry. You look very nice.' He reached out as if he were about to brush his fingers over her uncovered curls but held back at her flinch. 'It suits you.'

She smiled, but only out of habit. Physical beauty was hardly something the Church saw fit to praise, and she wasn't sure she liked it.

He moved her to a lounge plush enough that it dimpled under her, and an assortment of foods on the low table welcomed them.

Csilla brightened at the food, mouth already watering. Mihály seemed to think enough cordial made a breakfast in itself; if there'd been food at the cabin, he hadn't offered.

'I apologise for the meagreness of all this. I don't often entertain, and my food needs are simple enough that I don't even have a designated cook on staff.'

Madame Varga gave a little laugh as if it were the most ridiculous thing that could be imagined. Csilla placed her hands in her lap and crossed her feet at the ankles, eyeing the pickled vegetables and ham beside cups of a weakly distilled herbal concoction. If only one of them would reach for the food so she could eat. Or at least speak and crack the awful tension that settled around like the dust of the hallway. Mihály's enthusiasm for talking had burned up the hours of the night, and now he'd turned stoic.

She waited, looking on as they watched each other, and finally gave up on being saved.

'Your house is lovely, Madame,' Csilla said to break the silence.

Instead of smiling at the compliment, the woman grimaced.

'What happened to the clock?' Mihály looked around the room as if seeing it for the first time, then grabbed a cup and drained it.

Madame Varga waved the question away. 'It's costly to maintain a household alone, and you would know all about it if you'd bothered to call on me once in all the weeks you've been here, or give me more than a word when I come to you. You refused all my offers to talk to the University about taking you back, to provide you a home if you won't go.'

'Give your charity to the Church, Madame. I wouldn't be here if it weren't for the difficulty of finding lodging with Csilla in tow.'

Csilla lowered her eyes at the truth of that, a finger sliding around the silver-plated rim of the cup.

'No, you wouldn't, would you?' She rested a hand on his knee and turned to Csilla. 'How old are you, child?'

'Twenty. Not a child.' Though she was starting to feel like one. She didn't know enough about the world outside Church life. Not even enough to sit here and take tea without feeling like her heart was going to break through her ribs with nervous pounding.

Mihály's eyes flashed as the truth slid off her tongue.

'Old enough to have a vocation, then. Or be a bride.' She raised an eyebrow at Csilla, her hand not leaving Mihály. 'Oh, eat if you like. You're staring at the food like a yard dog.'

Csilla grabbed a hard roll stuffed with potato and ham before Madame Varga had even finished the sentence and took an over-large bite, realising seconds too late she was probably being rude and had just been insulted besides. The old bread scratched as it went down.

'I've no desire to wed. I only wish to be of service.' She lowered her eyes. Anything to disarm the woman's suspicious glare. 'I came from the Church.'

It was the wrong thing to say. 'A Church ward. What use can she possibly be to you, Misi? Be honest with me.'

'I have been! I wasn't going to let her waste away on a mercy crew. As I told you before, I fully intend to continue my research to help Ev . . . to help others like Evie. And who better to help than someone raised among treatment and medicines?'

Csilla took another large bite of food to avoid a retort. If her chewing was sharp, he didn't notice. The older woman's face softened a fraction, though she didn't move her hand away from Mihály. He patted it.

'Perhaps Csilla would like to look through Evie's books, if you've kept them. It would be a great help.'

Evie, that was it. Her daughter's name had been Evaline. Csilla rubbed the fabric of the skirts again, trying to ease the sudden goosebumps on her skin. The woman had paid good money to have the girl remembered in prayer, and she'd heard the name chanted in memorial for weeks. She clearly remembered her at home as well, keeping her things like treasured relics. No wonder her gaze was icy as she looked at Csilla; Csilla was desecrating an altar, and only Mihály seemed to be comfortable with the situation.

Madame Varga took a sip of her cordial, but her head was held a little too stiffly, her sip a little too quick for the nonchalance of her pose. 'I'll see if there's anything of interest.'

Csilla could hear the *no*.

Mihály gave an accepting half-shrug. 'Csilla, pick up something to take if you like, but we have a project to work on, don't we?'

'Far be it from me to keep you.' Madame Varga rose, bending to drop a kiss on Mihály's head. His cheek flexed, but he didn't move away. 'Please, sit and eat. I'll have a look at what could be repurposed for . . . your friend.'

'My gratitude.'

When they were alone again, Mihály finally seemed to relax, picking up a baked cracker sprinkled with small seeds. It cracked against his teeth.

'Well now. That went better than I thought it would.'

'What did you expect?' She, for one, had anticipated a bit more welcome. But she wasn't a member of the Church anymore. Even someone who may have invited a mercy crew in under other circumstances would balk at her now.

'More argument about you, honestly. She's always been fond of me.'

'And yet you chose to stay in an attic?'

'Fondness very quickly turns to hovering. I'm sure you understand why I need privacy for my work.'

She pressed her lips together, thinking of all the dead eyes in his cabin.

'You studied, correct?'

'Very much correct. I had pen calluses for years.' He examined his hand before pouring fresh tea into her near-empty cup, a little gesture that flustered her. Then he reached into his pocket for a bottle and doctored his own drink before taking a sip, eyes darting to the doorway as he did so. No doubt the lady of the house wouldn't have approved; she and Csilla had that in common.

'Did you study anything about Shadow scripts? Demonology? Would there be anything about that in the books here?'

'And they call me the heretic?' He sat back with a thoughtful stroke of his beard. 'I was more interested in the lives of the angels, if you can imagine, as well as practical healing and such that made use of my gift. I told you what I do isn't—'

'It's the murders.' Just thinking about what she'd seen put a greasy feeling on her skin.

He scanned her face as if looking for a clue that she was joking. 'What do you mean?'

His voice held the same note it had when he'd realised Csilla was something strange, the taste of hidden knowledge setting off a burning thirst.

Csilla wrapped her arms around herself. 'Someone is covering them with demon marks, so it must be someone who studied.'

'Or a demon.'

Now she was the one unsure if he was joking.

'Or that. Though I don't see how.' The words fell sharply into her stomach. 'Four deaths so far, all marked up. Here, I have names.'

She pulled the stolen paper with the notes on it, and frowned to see how it had smeared. She hadn't had time to let it dry well, and he'd been too wrapped up in his own voice for her to show him before. But now they were both committed, for better or worse.

'Have you heard anything like this from the people who come to you?'

Mihály scanned her writing without recognition.

'Just that they're scared. They ask for intercessions I can't give, prayers to spare them and their loved ones. But there is someone who might know more.'

'Close?'

'Not far. But we can rest a little longer if you need. I know I put you out.'

He offered his hand, clearly expecting hers to follow. It wouldn't be so bad, perhaps, to offer him the comfort, though he seemed to think he was offering it to her.

Waiting any longer would make it more awkward. She put her palm lightly against his, though with the alertness of a bird ready to take flight. His thumb brushed the back of her knuckles, and she stiffened, now caught as his fingers closed.

'Your hands are quite cold. I'll buy you some gloves.'

He took another sip of tea as if this were ordinary. Perhaps for him it was. And yes, her hands were cold, because she was sure all the heat in her had fled to her cheeks.

'We have the victims' names.' She spoke because even the terrible business of the murders seemed better to focus on than the gentle warmth of his hand around hers. 'And I know roughly where and when they were killed. That's somewhere to start.'

'And you think we'll be able to find some clue the inquisitors missed?'

'I think people will be more willing to talk to you.' It was true, though it seemed blasphemous to say.

'Or to you.' Mihály smiled. 'You have a very calming presence. Has anyone told you that?'

She glanced down, freshly flustered. 'Not in so many words.'

'The Church was very foolish to let you go.'

He gave her hand a squeeze and withdrew before she even realised she'd started to welcome it.

13

Csilla

WALKING WITH Mihály in the evening air, dressed in more borrowed finery and a coat of wool with soft fur around her throat and wrists, was like walking through a new city. He drew light wherever he went, illuminating her to the eyes of the people whether she wanted it or not. She'd never been one to be envied, but now people watched as he slowed his steps to match hers or stopped to convince a street vendor to give Csilla a taste of whatever was on offer, sometimes from his hand to her lips, smothering any objection. It was difficult to form questions while reeling from the fact that his finger had almost been in her mouth.

And no one ignored her.

They came to a row of shed houses, pressed one against the other, what had once been something larger pressed and portioned to fit in more of the Faithful. He knocked on the door, and his posture shifted. He drew himself up, folded his hands, and Csilla did likewise.

The door was opened by an older man, his thin nose pinched by wire-rim glasses and his beard shot through with goose-feather grey. His face softened in recognition, but a flutter of hesitation shot over his features as he noticed Csilla.

She smiled anyway. It didn't help.

'I was waiting for you. You alone.' He raised an eyebrow. 'I recognise you, girl. You were there in the square.'

The night she'd chosen to disobey.

The man leaned on the doorway, blocking any view of the interior. 'Misi, you usually don't indulge your lovesick little doves.'

Mihály raised his hand in a placating gesture before Csilla could interject.

'Please, let us in before you start making assumptions.'

It was at least warmer inside as they stepped into a single large room serving as both a kitchen and sitting area, a ladder leading to a loft above. Coughs sounded from the house next door where wall pressed against wall.

'My name is Csilla.'

She might as well make this a little less awkward. A slight echo bounced off the high beams; save the table and a few wooden chests, the room was unfurnished. Perhaps he was new to Silgard. The room held things, but their haphazard placement and the lack of even a personal icon or homespun cloth gave it the air of being a mere house, no one's home.

'Herre Tamas,' the older man introduced himself. 'Sit.'

'My mentor. He was my instructor at the University,' Mihály explained, and Csilla's eyes widened. Her expression earned a laugh from Tamas.

'Oh, believe me, the pupil has far exceeded the teacher. I take no responsibility for him.'

There was a fond note of complaint as he shifted a few papers heaped with powders and tiny tinctures in amber bottles, the kind she'd seen Mihály use for his tea, and the tablecloth was soaked in places with drops of greasy oils.

'How are your spells, Misi? I've got something else for you to try.' He held up a small bottle, brown glass glowing amber in the firelight. 'In moderation.'

Mihály examined it, then slipped it into his pocket. 'I appreciate it.'

Csilla frowned. Something else to be on the lookout for. She'd seen various kinds of 'spells' – shaking fits, catatonias, ravings. Though, by the pungency of the treatment, she wondered if any supposed affliction was simply the tremors of someone kept too long off their spirits.

'So what are you doing with this strange little bird? I saw you with that wine, child,' he said before Csilla could jump in. 'You think he can help you?'

The tone of his voice twisted her hope into a pitiful thing, like he thought her a child as well, sure she could get a miracle. How much did he know of what Mihály did well away from the Eye of Asten?

'I—'

'What do you know about demons?' Mihály cut in. 'You were a Servant of the Road; you tended seals and wards.'

This man had also left the Church. Now that she was looking, the old cut scars of his palm were visible, though long since faded into other wrinkles.

'Getting right to the point, eh? You've been speaking to the refugees? They know more of broken seals than I do.'

'Refugees?' Csilla frowned. There had been more people coming to the city, but refugees and war orphans were tended closer to the lines. Silgard was at the centre of all but particularly close to none. 'I noticed more people, but I thought . . .'

'Thought they were coming to welcome the Incarnate back from his holy campaign?' There was a wry twist to the man's lips. 'Maybe he will have vanquished all the Shadow breaking free before he returns. May Asten's will prevail.'

Csilla reached for a mark that was no longer there, her hand brushing gauzy fabric and a jeweled brooch instead of the iron now folded among her old clothes and tucked in a drawer.

'All the more reason to keep the city safe.' She swallowed and swiped a finger over her knuckles instead. Children learned the four points of their finger joints could stand in to remind them of the virtues.

Mihály put a hand on her shoulder, though it felt more like being pushed into acting as a shield than serving as comfort. 'Csilla has asked for my help in catching the killer.'

Tamas stiffened, heavy brows drawing together. 'You have no business with that.'

'Do I not? This is my home, too.'

The man shook his head. 'Don't get involved. You're too valuable . . .'

'More valuable than anyone else in the city?' There was no vanity in his tone.

'Honestly, yes. And I don't see what either of you get out of this. Unless . . .' He turned to Csilla, about to speak, when Mihály cut him off.

'She's agreed to help me, and I'll help her.'

The older man let out a woofing breath. 'Oh no. You leave the poor girl and whatever soft-hearted pity she has for your distress alone.'

'Sir.' Csilla's fingers rubbed nervously together, though she tried to keep them still. 'I don't have many options, and he is helping me . . .'

'Did he tell you why he came to this city in the first place?' The man leaned back, crossing his arms over his thin chest. At this angle the light caught his glasses, hiding his eyes.

'To preach, I assume.'

Tamas's laugh caught her by the throat. 'What a dear thing you are. Church-raised?'

Her little nod felt like a confession. Tamas may have left the Church, but the judgemental look she knew from growing up was still stamped on his face.

'Misi is here because he was expelled.'

The Izir's face was dark, but he didn't protest. Csilla turned, her mouth dry. The little dead things in his barn . . . it wasn't the first time he'd tried to change the world with blood. He'd shown her as much.

'He has always been the first to try things he shouldn't, and he went too far. He came out of his experiment thinking that despite the . . . mistake . . . he could still get what he wants, that it was everyone else who was wrong. And if *you* are now what he wants, you'd be smart to run.'

Something small knotted in the pit of Csilla's stomach. Tamas said run, but there was nowhere to go. Silgard was her home.

'Do you think he can give me a soul?' That was what she needed to focus on. Saving the city and herself so she could go back to saving others.

Tamas paused, and Csilla's hopes dangled on the filament of the second. It wasn't a yes. But it wasn't a no.

He reached for a pipe, hands fumbling with the tobacco tin.

'This is dangerous stuff.'

Of course it was. Csilla rubbed her scarred palm. All power was dangerous, no matter how Brilliant. Humans were not gods. Even the best of them, standing next to her and murmuring placating words, was no more than a sliver of an angel.

'But do you?' She wanted Tamas to say yes, and she wanted him to say no. She was strung across the chasm of what Mihály wanted of her and the marrow-deep desire for a way to serve openly.

'No.'

Her heart sank with the simple word.

'I can.' Mihály's hand pressed harder on the ridge of her shoulder, thumb digging in. 'I've learned from my mistakes. And I wasn't entirely wrong—'

'Mihály.' The soft tones of the nickname were replaced with clipped irritation. 'May I speak to you in private?'

Csilla glanced around for a place to slip to, but there was nowhere. She smiled as if it didn't matter and returned to the stoop. The night was turning grey-violet, the icy breeze chilled the skin still exposed to the air. Csilla pressed her ear to the door, but their voices had dropped to a muffle. When the door swung back open, she nearly fell.

'You can think what you like,' Mihály spat, a flush on his skin. 'Come on, Csilla. He's only going to try to convince you that it's better not to meddle in things. Apparently when you're old you stop caring to learn.'

Csilla frowned at the honest sharpness in his tone. His sweet words to her seemed practiced in comparison.

'No need to attack, Misi. You're clearly tired.' Tamas reached out to turn Mihály's face one way, then another, picked a few stray hairs off his coat. 'Send her on and stay with me a while. We can bleed you if you're hot, give you something if you're cold. You're no good to anyone ill.'

It was kind of him to still care. She thought of Ágnes and her endless patience.

Mihály brushed his hand aside.

Tamas's face took on a resigned air. 'If you won't think of her, think of Evaline . . .'

Csilla couldn't help but shiver at the name. Of course he would have known her; they'd both been at school.

'I do.' There was a snarl there, that of an animal with a fresh wound. 'Every day.'

It hurt to see, and Csilla stepped up to at least draw this to a close and soothe that pain.

'Thank you, sir. I'll go home.' It wasn't a lie. She hadn't said when.

'Good to see one of you has sense.' Tamas glowered and muttered old blessings at their back.

'Let's go get some food, shall we?' Mihály's tone was light, putting the conversation behind them, and it stoppered Csilla's questions. 'That was a worthless stop. I know somewhere that will cheer you up.'

He seemed to need the cheering more. Csilla trailed a few steps behind, glancing over her shoulder and searching for movement in the shadows.

At least she was safer with Mihály than alone. She followed as the Izir guided her down streets where the stones were bleached white and scrubbed clean, the buildings marked with Eyes that were gilded and not merely carved. In daylight it would have been beautiful. In the dark the gilt threw shadows.

It was slow going, people of all types stopping Mihály for a word. He paused for each of them, speaking softly, and her heart warmed even as she worried that the Church would serve them better.

A freckle-cheeked woman with a suckling child bowed over his hand, asking for her husband's safe return from the front, and then he embraced another whose words Csilla couldn't make out as they spoke against his shoulder. What if she told these people everything she now knew?

She held her tongue. Whatever it was based in, the comfort he offered set people at ease, and there was honesty in that. And when they asked him to preach, he politely refused, with an expectant look at Csilla as he waited for acknowledgement that he was refusing to speak heresy at her behest, like a pup waiting for praise for correctly sitting. She settled for patting his arm, and he preened.

They stopped in front of a white-porched building with lanterns blazing in every thick-glassed window. A few small carriages, their ponies bored and stamping, lined the front waiting to cart away those drunk or stumbling out desperate for privacy. This was one of the dining clubs for the wealthy in the city, a place she'd only passed by.

'I don't think I belong there.' She didn't want to belong there. It was one thing to indulge a little in private, with proper knowledge of one's guilt. It was another to search for a way to flaunt while still under the cathedral spires, especially when there was work to do.

Mihály sighed. 'Csilla, you're not dressed like a church mouse anymore. No one will try to kick you out. You're very pretty, I promise.'

She frowned. Her hesitation wasn't embarrassment, and his attempt at a compliment wasn't pleasing in the least. The only reason she looked fit to join was because a girl who was now ashes had no use for gowns.

'There are sinful people in there,' she said, knowing she sounded like a child and hating it. But she'd heard the confessions and seen the sin ledgers of the kind of people who held membership. Luxury wasn't outlawed, but it was heavily taxed, and those who could afford to think about such comforts in Silgard could also afford to have cares outside the Church.

'There are people in there,' he corrected her. 'And isn't it vain to think yourself better than them?'

That bit. Her job was to care, not judge.

Politeness dictated Mihály hold the door, and Csilla found herself the first to step through onto the veined marble floor of the lobby. A man in a dark burgundy waistcoat gave her a pinched look. 'Are you one of ours?'

'No?' And she didn't particularly want to be. She could taste the oily perfumes and ashy tobacco in the air, souring the luscious smells of cooking fat wafting from somewhere beyond. At least her stomach was happy to be here.

Mihály stepped up behind her.

'Do I need to be?' the Izir asked. He slipped an arm around Csilla, and the man paled and bowed.

'Of course not, Izir. Are you here to dine? Or perhaps for the lounge? Though your girl . . .'

She wrinkled her nose at his last words.

'We are here to dine, and of course Csilla will be welcome.'

'Very good, sir.' The man looked visibly relieved as he escorted them through a hallway.

Beyond the open doors leading to the dining hall were smaller lounges with gaming tables and men shrouded by pipe haze, their heavy eyes turning to glance between Mihály and rolling ivories as they passed. The dining room was blessedly less smoky, but looked onto a grim garden, all spindly brown bush twigs and dry grass. They were seated next to the courtyard window, so close the cold seeped through the glass. Csilla started as a second servant appeared with a fur to drape over her lap. For a moment she wondered how the woman had known she'd shivered, but with the placement they'd been given, everyone could see them. And they were looking their fill, with curious eyes and curved-lip whispers pointed their way.

The people here *must* be good, she told herself. They were staying in Silgard, after all.

But even in Silgard, you could cleanse your soul with money. And there was so much money here the air seemed rotten with it.

'Is there anything you don't eat?'

Mihály scanned the menu. There wasn't a choice, really. The handwritten paper outlined what the chef would prepare that day. Still, the list stretched halfway down Csilla's forearm. Who needed to eat so much?

'If there's anything you like you don't see, I'll have it made,' he continued, stroking his beard and muttering something about a dearth of quail eggs, the paucity of the season.

The luxury of that comment was so foreign he might as well have been speaking another language. He went on, describing each treat and offering. Csilla nodded, pretending she understood while her heart pounded loud enough to muffle his words. His concern was overly sweet and smothering. Too much like courting. He'd denied any interest to both Madame Varga and his mentor, but this didn't seem like the kind of environment in which he'd practice self-control.

'I like everything, but I don't know that even I can eat all this.'

She looked down the list again to avoid meeting his eyes. Sauced winter pheasant. Three kinds of roasted turnip soups. Four kinds of dumplings, savoury and sweet, one for each course. A few things she couldn't even identify. And then there were the drinks, a dizzying tour of the continent in spirits that was even longer than the food list. 'How much does this cost?'

He waved off the question. 'What use is money and education if it doesn't get you a taste of the finer things?'

He spoke like someone who hadn't always had them. Before she could ask, he continued.

'And they do give whatever isn't used to the poor or the pigs. It doesn't go to waste.'

That was some comfort. But Mihály should know that it wasn't his money or education that had the doors opening or the best table being pulled out.

Csilla leaned back as a carafe of fruit brandy and two glasses were brought to them.

'We'll take a bottle, but we only need one . . .' Mihály started.

But Csilla grabbed her own glass and cut him off with a thank you to the staff. Perhaps it would ease her nerves.

'You drink?' he asked, pouring her a half glass of the pale drink that glimmered like a jewel. The syrupy scent stung her nose and took her back to the poison, when things had at least made a horrid kind of sense.

'No,' she admitted as she picked it up. There was wine in the cathedral stores, sacramental and ordinary, but no one ever offered either to her. But everyone else here was drinking. She could at least try to fit in.

'To health and holiness.'

They clinked their glasses together, and Csilla took a small sip. It was sharp, with a slight linger of apricot that brightened on her tongue even as it burned.

When she looked up, Mihály had his hand resting on his chin, half-smiling at her. She turned her attention back to the brandy, took a gulp, and choked. Her dining companion said nothing, only passed her a linen napkin. Csilla was grateful when the bread was served and she could absorb the taste with dark rye.

More and more people were coming in, spotted furs and tall hats. Csilla recognised a few from their parading into the cathedral, others were looking around like they'd never seen the room. Early pilgrims come to greet the Incarnate's return, then. *Or refugees*. Wealth didn't protect people from Shadow, though perhaps it guarded them from other things. There'd been no murders on the finely maintained streets of this district.

Yet another reason they shouldn't be wasting their time here, even if the bread was fresh and the wine plentiful. It was a mockery to sit here and feast while evil went unchecked.

Mihály's foot brushed her ankle under the table, and she jumped, rattling the drink again.

'You look very dour for someone dressed so prettily. Smile, will you?'

She tried, but the stretch of her cheeks hurt. 'I'm thinking. We don't even have a plan—'

'Exactly.' He nudged her again, toe skimming her calf as she stared. 'I'm no ascetic. I refuse to sit in the dark wearing haircloth and wait for a revelation when I might as well do it with an elegant dinner and charming company.'

Csilla examined the surface of the brandy, the colour close to the magic stirred by souls. The dinner was certainly elegant, but she knew she was lacking in charm. She wasn't even sure how she would put on a show of it.

She took another sip. Maybe it would help. 'So you were expelled?'

Mihály winced as his own drink went down wrong and he snatched the napkin back.

'So much for the charming company. But yes. My ideas weren't any more popular at school than they are with the Church. It's their loss.'

'And you knew Evaline at school? And that's how you know Madame Varga. And Tamas.'

He nodded, though his eyes stayed on his glass. 'Yes, Tamas quickly took me under his wing when I entered school, though I think he may have just wanted the distinction of being my mentor. Evie was two years below me. I was her tutor, at first. Her mother was always a great help to my accounts.'

So there was a time when he was fine with Madame Varga's charity. Csilla pressed her lips together. She was hardly one to judge.

A young man in a dark coat beckoned to Mihály from across the room, and Mihály raised his hand in an answering wave.

'Another admirer?' Csilla asked, grateful for the distraction. Her questions had dragged a gloomy cloud over what was already an awkward meal.

'Don't worry about it.'

'No. Why don't you go talk to him.' She pushed away from the table and stood. She didn't belong here. She wanted to think. To be alone. 'You can ask them if they know anything. I'd rather just go . . .'

There was no home. There was a Church who didn't want her and a fine and draughty house she didn't know.

'I'll go with you, then.' A desperation had lit in his eyes, and she flinched.

'I'm just tired. I'm not running away. This has been a lot for me.' Her eyes dropped at the intensity of his expression. No one had ever cared that much about where she was. 'Please, stay and enjoy yourself. I'm sure you'll have more fun if I'm not here falling asleep into my soup.'

He studied her for a moment, then nodded.

'Here.' He fished coins out of his pocket. 'Take a cab. Any of them will know the Varga house.'

'Thank you,' she said, though her first instinct was to refuse. Her feet had always served her well.

But when she stepped into the night, the idea of the claustrophobia of the little box cabs set her head pounding.

She could wait out here. It wasn't too bad – except her hands were cold. He'd forgotten to buy her the gloves he'd promised. Impatient horses pawed at the cobblestones, every breath frosted.

Through the windows she could see Mihály, who had moved to watch her, morose and betrayed as he sipped. Maybe he really did want her company, and she was the one being petty by choosing to sit alone where he could still see.

His own fault for wanting to spend the evening on dining or cards or smoking or any of the things that weren't quite sin, but were still ill-advised. There were plenty of people approaching him; it was hardly like he would spend the evening lacking companionship.

'Are you waiting for a ride, miss?' a coachwoman called. 'Do you need me to get something? It's easy to freeze after drinking.'

She could protest that she hadn't been drinking, at least not enough to matter. But she should be kind and at least move out of Mihály's line of sight and let him get on with more pleasant things than sulking. She climbed up into the covered cart with a final, guilty glance over her shoulder and a wave he didn't return.

The coachwoman opened the top hatch. 'Where to, miss?'

'Could we just . . . ride around a bit?' The only thing waiting for her at the house would be Madame Varga's pointed questions.

'It's your money.' The woman accepted the coins with a dark-gloved hand.

The clack of the horse's hooves created a pleasing rhythm, and she stared at the black ceiling of the cab, dozing and coming to over and over in exhaustion. The reflection out of the corner of her eye was depressing – a young woman, brown hair mussed, sprawled in the back of a cart that was both too much and not enough like a confessional booth, wasting money by the hoof beat. *And that's you.*

She'd barely left the safety of the Church, and now this.

Mihály was right – they had no plan. It was easier to think without him hovering, no unexpected touches or offhandedly flirtatious remarks to derail her thoughts. They'd start by asking the kin of the victims for any details that may have been missed by the Church, and perhaps Mihály could send word to scholars more willing to help. Surely he still had some well-connected friends despite the expulsion.

She stood, jostling at the bounce of wheel on stone, and opened the top door again.

'Can I ask you something?'

The woman pulled the horse to a stop. 'Ready to give me a destination, miss? Your fare is running out, and I'll have plenty of others clamouring for a ride soon enough. There's a curfew set, you know.'

Csilla gave an apologetic shake of her head that the woman couldn't see. 'I just . . . I imagine you see a lot of the city. You know that people have been killed . . .'

'Nothing anywhere close to this district, miss. You're perfectly safe.' The clip of the woman's voice was clear; she wanted direction, not discussion.

She needed to go back before the coachwoman dumped her at the far corner of the district and she compounded the waste of money with a long walk. She had promised to stay off the streets at night, what felt like a long time ago, when she was a different person.

'I'm ready now. Take me to . . .'

Before she could finish, a woman with a child too large to be carried in her arms, and another girl trailing them, caught her eye, the woman's stumbling and upward glances showing she didn't know where she was. Csilla opened the door and slid out as the driver exclaimed a curse of surprise.

'Do you need help?'

'On our way to a mercy hall,' the woman said. 'He's burning up, and the one in our district is full. But we'll manage.'

The coachwoman offered a prayer, but not her hand to help. Csilla motioned for them to join her. Unless things had changed very much in the two days since she left the Church, there wouldn't be any more room at the next nearest mercy hall. They would be given medicine if there was some to spare, but they would be turned away and even further from their lodging.

'Take us back. Is there enough on the fare for that?' Mihály could be useful in this if he wasn't too drunk. A little part of her was also pleased at the chance to alleviate the guilt of leaving him to dine alone.

'Not a problem of money,' the coachwoman said with narrow brows. 'The charity is a credit to your soul, but I don't need the air in my box tainted.'

'Surely you won't blacken your soul by refusing mercy.'

The woman sighed and gestured to the door. 'I'll be keeping the excess fare.'

The mother hesitated but passed the child over with exhausted arms. There was a high flush on his freckled cheeks, and heat radiated from him like a furnace. At least she felt like herself again as she made soothing noises to the child and felt him relax.

'It's dangerous to be out at night,' Csilla cautioned, adjusting the boy to rest on her shoulder. 'You must have heard what's been happening.'

'It can't be worse than Ruze.' The woman reached out to smooth the boy's sweaty hair as he quietly groaned.

'Is that where the illness is?' Ruze was a week's ride away, but there'd been no call for extra hands or supplies from their parishes.

'If only.' Her eyes were steely. 'Has the news truly not reached Silgard?'

'It hasn't reached me,' Csilla answered.

The woman pulled her daughter close. 'There was a creature sealed in our woods after the Severing, and it awoke.'

'Awoke?'

She shifted her daughter into her lap and put a hand over the upturned ear. 'Awoke and took a body. Took a girl, then killed her mother. Only one of our priests could work a banishment. Everyone else was powerless.'

Csilla clutched the boy tighter in horror. 'Have they sent—'

'They've sent no one, that I know of. Our bishop said the fact that only one priest could claim the glory meant it was no real demon at all. But the old black mark is gone. My brother went and looked. That's why we're here.'

She didn't want to ask, but she had to. 'The body of the mother . . . Was it . . . defiled in any way? Did you see it?'

'Unfortunately I did. But she was just dead.' The woman blinked like she wanted to cry, but that well was dry and filled in. 'At least in Silgard there's none of that. People are good, and if not good, at least human.'

That's what everyone new to the city would think.

The cart slowed again as they returned, but the hoofbeats turned quick and nervous. Csilla slid back the panel. The dim glow of lights showed nothing without the ability to look ahead.

'What is it?'

'Looks like everyone is on the streets, the blackcoats too. Maybe a fire?'

Or murder. The woman was still looking at her with hope. Csilla's fingers danced over the brooch pinned to her dress. The sapphires were probably real.

Before she could think too much about how she was robbing both an old woman and the dead, she pulled it off and passed it up through the roof slot. 'Take them to the mercy hall by the merchants' guild.' She touched the woman's knee. 'Ask for Katherina if they won't let you in. And if they have to send you back, this should pay for that, too.'

The mother thanked her for doing so much, but it didn't warm her when she knew she couldn't do nearly enough.

Csilla opened the door and hurried into the throng, searching for Mihály. He should have stood well above the crowd, but there was no sign of him. The people she passed were pressed tight together, faces worried, and when she reached out to touch an arm, the person jumped like she was scalding.

'What happened?'

The man drew his finger across his throat like a blade.

Csilla swayed on her feet. So close. 'Inside?'

Where was Mihály?

'No, out the back and a ways down. It was Janos.'

The name meant nothing to her, but her heart ached all the same.

'Did you see the Izir?'

'Oh, you're the girl who was with him.' The man looked her over with fresh eyes. 'He left not long after you did, said he was going home. Lucky he did. The rest of us have to freeze out here until we get permission to leave from the priests.'

He was no doubt waiting for her now, disappointed. She sighed, taking a measured breath to release her frustration, when a familiar figure caught her eye. The rhythm of Ilan's sure-footed steps coming towards her echoed in her chest, and fear closed her throat. The iron in his gaze was the weight of every right thing she'd given up, everything Mihály had told her. He would only have to touch a weak spot, and she would confess everything.

He was famously good at finding weak spots, and she was already thin-skinned with guilt.

She smiled through her shaking. He'd been kind to her once. More than that, really. He kept the Church's tenants even when they contradicted his nature.

Ilan eyed her gown and its embroidered vinework and her pearl-beaded slippers.

'What are you doing here?'

'The Izir brought me. But I left before anything happened.'

A fresh light entered Ilan's pale eyes. 'And yet you're here.'

He slipped a leather cuff over her wrist and snapped the leash tight.

14

Csilla

THE CHILL of the cathedral's cell leeched through every bit of her shoes and clothing, the floor sharp with chips of crumbled stone.

Csilla kept her knees up to her chest as she shivered against the damp. The space had a hollow carved out for lamp oil and holy books, a crusted drainage hole on the other side, and was otherwise bare. Somewhere in the walls and beneath the floors was the labyrinth of tunnels for ferrying holy relics and keeping the Seal of Silgard safe. In a more peaceful time, this was one of the cells where the Faithful went when they wished to give up the world in its entirety, but now it had been partially converted to house the Church's enemies, and the cells were full of people awaiting their turn for a whipping or for their family to gather enough money to pay off their sins. She'd heard that Mihály's theories inspired petty crimes as people lost faith in the Church, but this seemed far beyond people testing the limits of what they judged a sin.

She put her forehead down on her knees, surrendering to the dark and praying for calm for her roiling stomach. The Church would forget about her and leave her to dissolve like the water-eaten cracks in the wall. And that would be if she were lucky.

It was hard to believe this squalid and freezing room was part of the place she'd once called home. That somewhere above her Ágnes was likely in prayer, and the others in the mercy crew were folding bandages and laughing among themselves. That Erzebet was no doubt curled on Csilla's bed, pleased to have the whole of it for herself.

The scrape of a door opening had her on her feet, face pressed against the flaking iron of the bars. Grunting. The thud of boots. A wet, rough slap of flesh on stone.

They were dragging in an unconscious man.

No. Even the unconscious had some movement – the twitch of an eyelid or breath at their lips.

This was a body. The light of their torches highlighted the trail of blood streaking the floor. The man yanked Csilla's door open and deposited the corpse with a squashed thud too much like the delivery of a pig carcass to the kitchens.

What once was a man was now all fish-belly white flesh and smears of copper.

'We thought a mercy girl wouldn't mind. Everywhere else is full.'

They'd never been full before. But she had no time to reflect on that.

The victim was face down splayed on the stone, mole-dotted skin on depraved display. She touched her heart. They could have at least given him a blanket for dignity, and she didn't even have a cape to offer him.

The marks along his back were still smeared, hard to see in the dim light. Corpses had never bothered her – she'd worked with the mercy crews since she could toddle, and flesh was flesh. But as she touched the sliced skin, a pulsing shiver worked its way up her spine and set her scars burning. She traced the cuts the same way the scholars had made her trace their books. That had only been finger over paper. Now on this fresh human velum, her fingers froze. The cooling body couldn't explain the sudden frostbite twinge that shot through her fingertips. Crusted blood scraped away from the thin lines of the wounds under her probing.

She moved to the crushed column of the victim's throat, her small hands where the murderer's had been, a whispered prayer to the hanged saint Angyalka on her lips. Angyalka had lived and was blessed with the visions that led to the naming of the first Incarnate, even though the bruises never faded. The blotchy purple under her palms was still swollen, blood congealed under the skin like a sausage in the casing.

She stiffened as footsteps sounded in the hall and the cell door swing open, a moment later her shoulders were seized by skeletal fingers.

Ágnes.

'What are you doing?' she hissed. 'There's nothing that can be done for the man now.'

'I wanted to see.'

She turned to look Ágnes in the face, and sharply drew in a breath. She looked so much worse than she had just days before. There were bluish bruises shading her skin, and her eyelids drooped. But Csilla's gasp was too quiet, and the older woman continued, though her voice grew more hoarse with every word.

'See? And touch?' She shook Csilla's limp hand, and the sting in the scold sent her gaze to the floor. 'Is this what you've gotten from being with the Izir?'

'He's stopped preaching heresy,' Csilla said, looking down. Easier to face the entire inquest branch of the clergy than the woman who raised her. 'I'm on holy business.'

If it involved Mihály it had to be holy, no matter what it looked like.

She raised her eyes, a tiny grain of confidence rooting in her purpose. 'I'm trying to save the city.'

The matter of her own soul aside, Ágnes had to understand that she was trying to do something good. That she *was* good.

The woman's spasming cough shook her like a crumpled fall leaf. Csilla put an arm around her.

'You're worse. I'll get something that can help you. Mihály—'

Ágnes waved her hand. 'No.'

Csilla held Ágnes's shoulders as she coughed again, so frail there was practically no weight against Csilla at all. How could this be the woman who'd carried her around on her hip until she came waist-high and was far too old for such babying?

The new steps in the hallway were heavier.

Ilan emerged and leaned on the doorway, scowling, his collar and hems stark for their lack of decoration. He looked like any other priest, save the crackling anger in his stare. 'Csilla. And Elder Ágnes. Are you not late for prayer?'

'Aren't you?' she asked, standing and smoothing her skirt. Csilla's heart ached to see that Ágnes stood in front of her, still trying to offer some protection in her frailty. Too many of her few and precious breaths were being spent defending Csilla.

'I have to question her. Only questions for the moment.' He held out his hands as if the lack of a whip assured Csilla's safety.

The woman nodded, but her eyes didn't leave Ilan as she left. As if reminding him that whatever he did, it would be seen. If not by her, then by the divine.

'What are you planning?' Ilan leaned against the iron bars, blocking the door. As if there were any way she would run.

'Me?' How did he know they were planning something? Csilla shrunk under his dissecting gaze. Perhaps it had been foolish to think the Church wouldn't know. Asten's eyes were stamped throughout the city, seeing everything. Maybe that was more tangible than she'd realised. 'I'm just trying to help.'

It sounded pointless falling from her lips and even worse when reflected in his expression.

'How was stealing my notes helping?'

Of course he would have noticed. He continued before she could conjure another pale defence.

'And you didn't kill the heretic. How long have you been working together? Since before I even found you in the street?'

'You think this is some kind of conspiracy?' Her exhalation was a brittle laugh. 'I didn't kill him because I'm not as good as you, I suppose. And as for your work, I just needed information. Not for anything bad.'

'Why?'

He didn't sound like he believed her. Her breathing quickened. She knew what happened when he didn't believe someone – screams and burns and blood. He reached for the cell lock, fingertips scraping the iron.

'Ilan, what is the meaning of this?' A new priest was behind Ilan, arms crossed, and Csilla had never been so glad to see a member of the Faith. Then she blinked, looking between the stranger and Ilan. It was this new man who wore the High Inquisitor's robes, and Ilan was in the plainer garb of an ordinary justice priest.

'This is the last of them?' The stranger tilted his head. 'Good. Question her and be done with it. No need to toy with her like a cat.'

Csilla pulled her hands to her chest as if that could spare them from the ropes. Ilan didn't take his eyes from her, pinning her as surely as with iron.

'I know this girl, and I know she hasn't killed anyone.'

Csilla shivered at the slither in his voice; he called her innocent, but there was no exoneration there.

'Then she has something to say about someone else?' The man's expression lightened. 'Come, then, girl, out with it. Who should we be bringing in for iron shoes tonight?'

‘I – no one!’ Csilla stuttered. ‘I don’t know who the murderer is.’

‘You won’t give us a name, any person who might have information? It will be a blessing on your soul.’

She winced as he continued.

‘Surely you must have some little sin you wish to clear. And we have ways if you don’t wish to talk.’ He delivered the threat with no change to cadence, so smooth it almost slid right past her.

Torturing people for information? She chilled at the thought. The Church was there to protect the Faithful, and if it hurt them it was only in the name of salvation. Her eyes flickered to Ilan, but he remained in stony silence – no mention of the torture. Not even of the fact that there was no way to view her sins.

And she certainly had sins now. She shook her head.

The large man reached past Ilan, taking the key and freeing her.

‘Well then, we’re done here. And you,’ he said, eyes back on Csilla, ‘you’re always welcome to return with better information.’

Ilan’s fingers tightened around the bar, and his face took on a terrifying calm. ‘Come then, Csilla. I’ll take you home.’

He walked her out through the courtyard in tense silence.

‘I’m staying with the widow Varga.’ Csilla tried to fill the cold morning air with chatter, if only to stop Ilan from asking the questions he clearly wanted to. ‘She was very kind to take me in.’

Her head pounded, and she realised too late she should have asked for water while she was still in the cell. Mercy would have had them give it to her. He only answered with a considering *hmm*, not looking at her. Even she wasn’t naive enough to think he’d forgotten the wrong she’d done. But maybe, if she was quick, she could stall it long enough to cross a friendlier threshold before being questioned. Use Mihály as her shield.

Mihály, who hadn’t come for her, even though he must have guessed. She had to soothe that anger, lull it into something harmless, before going back to him.

'You know, I can find my way myself,' she tried, walking a little faster. 'Please, you've done more than enough.'

He gave her a slanted look that cut off her protests. As they rounded the corner to a deserted street, something changed in Ilan's step. Csilla's heart skipped, reacting to some instinct a half-second before he grabbed her and yanked her into an alley so quickly she couldn't scream. He jammed his cane against her chest, the pricks of the ears on the silver wolf-head handle biting through her shift dress and into her sternum.

'Now that we are alone, tell me the truth. What were you looking for?' His eyes were icier than the midwinter wind.

Her heart hammered, but the rest of her was frozen, torn between the pain that would come from both lies and the truth. He tilted the cane slightly.

'You're hurting me,' she spat, but her words died as she realised that was the point. He was no longer the Head of Justice, but he'd have the interrogation.

His eyes narrowed. The pressure grew until she was sure there would be spots of blood beneath her chemise and the imprint of brick on her back as she tried to shy away.

'We want to find the killer,' she forced out, and he withdrew the cane, a sweet relief. 'He's helping me save the city.'

She'd caught him by surprise. An awkward sense of pride cut her fear at the open confusion on his face. She had to take advantage of it.

'I know the Church wanted him dead. If it's willing to break its own laws, things must be dire.' She couldn't read what Ilan was thinking, but the fact that he clearly was thinking was a good sign. 'I was looking at your things because I needed names to know where to start. And you showed me the demons, and I just talked to refugees from Ruze, and . . .' Her rushing voice caught, remembering the fear in the woman's eyes. 'And I think you might be right.'

Ilan's posture eased a fraction.

'And I'm not going to say Mihály is perfect.' She wasn't entirely sure she would even say he was good. 'But he is blessed. And he knows things.'

'Does he have any leads?' There was something new in his gaze now. Curiosity.

'He has ideas.' Terrible ideas, yes, but at least that was true. 'And power. With the Incarnate gone, Mihály is the most blessed thing our city has.'

Ilan hesitated a moment, then stepped back. 'I'd like to talk to him.'

Csilla stiffened. She'd meant to save herself, not set the idea out as bait. More time with Ilan was the last thing she wanted.

'I'll tell him, and we'll send a message . . .' That would give her a little time to confer with him at least.

'Now will do.'

The stranger and his soft request for names came back to her. He'd been wearing the uniform that had once been Ilan's.

'And why didn't you bring this up in front of the new inquisitor?'

He tapped his cane against the ground sharply next to her foot, and she winced, though it only hit stone. She shouldn't have spoken, even if it was to remind him of what he should already know.

The ice in his eyes had turned to fire.

'I'm sworn to follow Asten. There have been missteps in the past. I'm making sure Sandor isn't another one.'

The passion in his words reminded her of Mihály, when he was lecturing her about his theories, but the name was unfamiliar.

'Sandor? Which church did he come from?' She hadn't heard of any priests on the way to Silgard from other territory basilicas or smaller houses of worship.

'Directly from the Incarnate's warfront.'

She gave a disbelieving cough, then smothered it. Directly from the warfront, and Ilan was questioning it. There was having a suspicious nature, and then there was wounded pride making more than there was of a situation. She'd always respected Ilan's role, if not liked it, but being bullied over what amounted to a *professional rivalry* . . .

She shook her head. 'If your position has been taken from you, I'm sorry for that. But we don't get to choose how we serve, and—'

'The fact that Sandor let you go is proof enough he doesn't understand our city and should return those reins to me.'

Let her go. A new thought dawned.

'You didn't tell him what . . . who . . . I am.'

For all his anger and suspicion, Ilan hadn't said a thing about her soulless nature or shown the man her crossed palm.

Ilan blinked, face shifting in surprise, as if he hadn't realised it himself. 'No. I didn't.'

Csilla let out a soft breath, twisting her hands together. Perhaps it wouldn't be so bad to hear him out. Ilan was the striking hand of the same Church that wanted Mihály gone, but he also had details they needed.

'If you let me take you to Mihály, he can explain things better than I can. But you have to listen. Regardless of what heresy you hear, you have to remember that we are trying to save the city. Like you.'

Ilan's jaw tightened, weighing the choice. Finally, he gave a little nod.

Csilla swallowed hard and motioned for him to follow her. He was no demon, but angels had once been equally terrifying in their justice – perhaps all the more so because the punishments they dealt were deserved.

15

Csilla

CSILLA SLUNK into the foyer, cringing at the scrape of door over jamb that echoed over-loudly in the early morning silence. Ilan clucked his tongue as his gaze swept the walls papered in striped pink and gilt and the stained cherry wood of the stairs.

'So this is the Varga house.'

His tone was dry, unimpressed. No doubt it was too ostentatious for his tastes. Ágnes had been right to look at her with such concern. In these clothes, in this place, it would be hard for anyone to believe she hadn't abandoned everything she'd been brought up to value. Or trust how dearly she wished to go back to it.

Where should she take him? Csilla bit her lip. This wasn't the cathedral, and she didn't know the household's rhythms. If she left Ilan while fetching Mihály, some servant might stumble across him and set off a panic before she even had time to come up with a plausible explanation.

'This way, please' she said, leading him past stone-eyed portraits of ancestors to the room she stayed in, though having him near where she slept shifted her stomach.

The bed had been made with an invitingly fresh quilt sometime in her unwilling absence, and the plumped pillows set off an aching desire to lie down and be warm. There were new dresses draped across a chair as well, piled embroidered rose and gold and summer-sky blue, a layered cake of luxury waiting for her. She held her head up, imagining this was her normal routine and she didn't stink of cellar dirt. With stiff arms she transferred the pile to the bed, resisted the plush call once more, and gestured to the chair.

'Please sit. I'll go get Mihály.'

Surely he could hear her heart hammer as she left. What had she done, bringing him here? If this was some kind of ruse, they'd face worse than jail with what she'd admitted. Mihály thought they had been brought together for a purpose, but there was only so long even Asten's grace would stall.

Mihály's room was empty.

Csilla groaned. Was he trying to find her? Perhaps he didn't know that she'd been let go and was looking for him.

The thought unspooled a little of the frustration. It was warming to imagine someone bothering to check after her when she'd spent so long ignored in the cathedral's corners.

And it was better than imagining he'd forgotten about her and traipsed home with someone adoring as soon as she was out of sight, not even realising there had been any fuss at all.

She shut the door and leaned back against it with a heavy breath, letting the wood take the full weight of her exhaustion for precious stolen seconds. But that was all she could allow herself with the wolf waiting.

When she returned to the room, apologies already on her dry lips, Ilan was standing over the pile of dresses, examining the lace on the sleeves of a delicate goldenrod day dress accented with fawn-brown velvet leaves. She couldn't read his expression – disapproval at the styles, some of which were not modest enough for Silgard's tastes, or surprise such things would be given to someone like her?

‘They belonged to Madame Varga’s daughter,’ she explained as he smoothed out a crease in a rose-pink skirt.

‘The dead one?’

Well, he wasn’t known for tact. Csilla nodded.

He tilted his head. ‘Must be strange for her to see them on you.’

Csilla scowled, though he was right. ‘It would be a waste if no one used them.’

Ilan looked doubtful but made no further comment, so Csilla continued. ‘It seems Mihály is still out.’

Ilan returned to the chair and leaned back, seeming perfectly content to wait in silence. He was not overly large in height or breadth, but the drape of his black cassock and the dreadful stillness of his presence was like one of the statues that peered from the cathedral facade. They didn’t have to move to make one feel watched and small.

Unsettled panic fluttered in Csilla’s ribcage. It could be hours before Mihály returned, and Ilan was apparently just going to sit and stare at her. It would have been too much to hope that he could sit ten minutes without judging someone. She’d always tried not to think about those who were drawn to Mercy’s opposite, knowing that the sick and helpless guilt she felt at seeing people split open for the Faith was her own weakness. After all, the Church had deemed his service far more acceptable than hers.

Seconds crawled by. Csilla folded the dresses, then refolded them. She sat on one side of the bed, then the other, then finally moved to the window and pretended to be absorbed in watching the nightsoil carts making their morning stops.

Ilan continued to sit, an occasional foot-tap the only sign of any impatience.

‘Are you thirsty?’ she finally asked in desperation. The gnawing in her stomach and scratching weight of the silence trumped the awkwardness of possibly explaining to the madame why she'd brought Ilan into her home. 'I'm sure I can find something.'

He inclined his head slightly, and she jumped on it as agreement, motioning for him to follow her. Down in the sitting parlour, Csilla stared at the tarnished bell chains, her hand half-raised to pull. It was so early that even though there were likely servants up, they were also likely busy.

'That one should call the kitchen,' Ilan said, pointing to the right-most chain, 'if it's like most other houses.' He didn't meet her eyes as he said it.

There was no reason for embarrassment; it wasn't surprising he spent time in well-off homes. Everyone sinned; it was just a matter of which sins you could afford and how you bought back your Brilliance.

Csilla grimaced and pulled. Within a few minutes, a maid came to the door, her breath huffing and kitchen cap askew. A smudge of white flour on her chin and egg yolk on her sleeve showed how they'd interrupted the breakfast preparation.

'Yes?' She caught her breath and bowed slightly, though there was well-deserved annoyance in her eyes.

'Could you bring us something?' Ilan interrupted before the woman could ask why she was being called. 'Water, at least.'

The woman gestured to her dusted state. 'I've just got to baking, but I can find something I'm sure . . .'

'Please do,' Ilan said, turning to the low lounge.

'Thank you!' Csilla called after.

Ilan was already sitting, one foot resting on his knee and looking strangely at home despite the incongruity of his plain cassock against wine-dark velvet. Csilla settled across from him, arranging her skirts.

'Did you grow up with servants?' she asked. He did have a certain commanding air.

His narrowed eyes told her he wasn't going to answer. She sighed.

'Inquisitor,' she squared her shoulders, trying to appear like the lady she wasn't, 'if we can't speak to each other, we won't be able to work together.' He'd seemed, if not kind, at least tolerant when he'd come to her rescue, and when they'd spoken in the library. But clearly that had only been a measure of professional respect when he still thought her a fellow servant of the Church.

'We can certainly speak to each other,' he said, 'about things that matter.'

She swallowed down another attempt to be conciliatory. No one could say she hadn't attempted to show him graciousness.

The door opened again and the servant reappeared with a tray with two cups of tea steeped to burnt umber, day-old hard bread with crumbling cheese and brown-speckled potato she hadn't bothered slicing evenly.

'This is all I could manage. Breakfast won't be for hours, I really apologise—'

'It's fine.' Ilan picked up the teacup and inspected the dark tea, tilting the cup so the liquid rested just under the lip.

'Thank you,' Csilla said again on behalf of both of them. Regardless of what the maid had said about the food, the tea was hot, and that was what mattered. Csilla took an encouraging sip; if he was drinking, he would have to stop staring at her so frankly.

He set it back in his saucer. 'I still have questions.'

'I can't tell you much about the murders.' Her voice dropped away from any chance-listening ears. 'We haven't gotten much ourselves.'

And if it was other information he was after, at least the Izir might be able to explain his ideas in a way that wouldn't get them both thrown out of the city with lash-marked backs.

He uncrossed his legs and leaned forward, and Csilla stiffened as the distance between them closed.

'I want to know why *you're* working with a heretic. You're strange, but never trouble. Ágnes spoke highly of you. Your work was commendable. That's why I was surprised when you seemed to be straying.'

And why he'd defended her to Prelate Abe. 'You asked about me?'

Few in the Church thought of her at all unless they needed extra hands for something particularly unappealing.

'I didn't have to. You were one of the first things they told me about when I took my post in Silgard. A soulless girl is quite the theological question.'

He was studying her now, as if there were some sign he'd missed that manifested the reason for her difference. She bit her lip at the idea that he'd been watching her all along.

'And you didn't do anything?' Surely any consideration merited a personal discussion of the very soulless girl involved. 'You could have spoken to me yourself.'

He took a slow sip of tea. 'By the time I came the question had already been debated to death and they'd judged you no threat to the Faith. Unlike the Izir.'

'No threat' must have been the kindest thing the Prelate had ever thought about her. 'He's no longer preaching heresy.'

'And I'm to believe he's dropped it? Or that you believe that? Why is it so important that you be the one to save the city?'

Csilla hesitated, searching for the right words as she cradled a teacup in her hands. Ilan was the embodiment of the rule of Asten. He would hurt her in line with those principles, but if he thought helping them was the divine will, he would do that, too. 'We want the same thing: home. Safe in the Church. You want to restore your position. I need a miracle to stay.'

Because whether it came from Asten or Mihály or the gracious leave of the Faith, that was what staying would be. A miracle.

Droplets of tea dribbled over the lip of the cup, a line of burnt brown down white porcelain as her hands shook.

'If catching sinners earned you miracles, I'd be the most blessed man in the Union,' Ilan said, but his voice was softer.

Was that compassion? She looked up to the quietness in his gaze. It was certainly the least fearsome look she had seen on him, and she wondered what hope kept him praying in the dark.

'If you do want to work with us, it may mean accepting a certain amount of . . .' She didn't want to call it heresy. '. . . unconventional doctrine. He's done a lot of research, you know. Everything we have isn't everything there is.' She paused. 'Please don't hurt him.'

Ilan was quiet for a long moment, tightness in his jaw. 'I will not act against the Izir unless absolutely necessary, regardless of how I feel.'

That promise was a small relief, though she had only her trust in his honour that it wasn't a lie. 'You probably won't like him—'

'I already don't like him,' Ilan cut her off. 'He's obnoxious.'

That startled a laugh from her, and she smothered it. Ilan had meant it as fact, not jest.

'I'm sorry about what's happened. I was always afraid of you, but I didn't mean for you to lose your position.'

'You were afraid of me?' Ilan let out a disbelieving breath. 'What did I ever do to you?'

What had he ever needed to do to anyone? The sure violence of his bootsteps in the corridors had been enough to have even the Prelate stand a little straighter.

'Well now you've arrested me, and not very nicely.' Her chest still hurt from where he shoved her. 'But it wasn't what you did to me.' She'd been close enough to his interrogation halls to hear every cadence of scream, and mercy work was often the tail end of delivered justice. 'It was what you did to others. Ordinary men don't take such joy in punishment.'

His eyes glittered, blue as the sapphires she'd given away. 'Ordinary men have not been called.'

From down the hallways came voices, one of them distinctly Mihály's forceful baritone. Csilla let out a quiet sigh of relief. She didn't want to argue with Ilan about the Church's stance on pain.

He threw the door to the room open. His skin was damp with a light sheen of sweat, his pupils dark and wide. Tamas's warnings about spells came back to her.

'Csilla, you're alright, aren't you?'

His words were half-lost in panting breaths as he charged forward, and she barely had time to set her cup on the table as he came at her in a storm of worry, kneeling and grabbing her by the shoulders. He was partially undressed, shirt untucked, pants creased, and the scent of tobacco clung to his hair.

'I was absolutely panicked.' He turned and looked at Ilan, face half a snarl. 'And apparently I have a good reason to be.'

Were you? It was an uncharitable thought, but by the wrinkled state of his clothes and the smell, he'd been somewhere in the house smoking and dozing.

'I'm *fine*.' She gave a small, reassuring smile and removed his hands, though the flush lingered. It *was* nice to be worried about, even with the sobering knowledge that she wasn't really the one he was panicked over. 'The inquisitor brought me back.' She paused. The least ridiculous way was just to say it. 'He wants to work with us.'

' "Want" is a strong term,' Ilan said, standing.

Mihály's flustered worry turned slate. 'Last time we spoke, you all but threatened to have me flayed.'

Ilan scowled. 'You deserve it.'

Csilla looked between them, exhausted shoulders sagging further. This was wonderful. If the two of them couldn't speak civilly for five minutes, they were all damned.

'Goodbye, Inquisitor.' Mihály gestured to the door. 'If that's all you have to say, you can leave.'

Ilan made no motion to do so. 'Csilla tells me you have delusions of saving the city. Why do you think you'll be able to do what I couldn't? We've been hunting the killer for weeks.'

'Other than the fact that Asten clearly likes me more? That has to count for something.'

Ilan's fists clenched, and Csilla had a sudden vision of scrubbing blood of various degrees of holiness out of the rug. She put a hand on Mihály's arm, but he wasn't in the mood to be pacified.

'Go back to the cathedral. This doesn't concern you.'

Ilan's frown deepened. 'It's in my city, under my charge; it most certainly does. Hopefully before Silgard rots even more.' There was something grave and unsettling in his gaze, and Csilla rubbed her scars. Ever since she'd touched the body, they'd prickled like an ivy rash.

Mihály raised an eyebrow, looking him up and down. 'You know, I seem to remember more decoration on that cassock of yours. So, you're acting on your faith, but the Church has lost faith in you. Don't come here looking down your nose when you're asking for our help, as selfish as the rest of us. Say we help you. When you do get your position back, what of us? The killer's trail is lined with heresy. When you're back in charge, will you remember what you saw and bring your justice down on us? We're trying to clear my name, not ruin it.'

Ilan opened his mouth, but Csilla cut him off, even as it pained her to do so. 'You promised you'd listen.'

He shifted, looking to her. 'And I did. Now I'm starting to feel like I made a mistake. This is no path to Asten's return.'

'Then we don't need your help,' Mihály said. 'No doubt there are plenty of people breathing a sigh of relief you're not in charge of their souls anymore.'

'I don't trust the man they've placed in charge.' Ilan's voice was level, but there was murder in his gaze.

Csilla edged her way in front of Mihály. The Church had wanted him dead once. Ilan could probably get away with trying it again.

'Of course you don't. He stole your job.' Mihály's words were strained with incredulity. 'Coming to us is a bit extreme, don't you think? If you truly believe we're evil, you're risking your own eternity being here.'

It was true. Of the three of them, Ilan was the only one with something left to lose.

'You were at the club too, weren't you?' Ilan asked, looking Mihály in the eyes. 'Maybe I should bring you in . . .'

He shot Csilla a look that set off fresh guilt. He didn't know what had happened. 'Why? I left right after Csilla. Lost my appetite. You can ask anyone there.'

'Mihály,' Csilla started. 'Someone was killed there. In the exact same way.' She'd assumed he'd heard the commotion if nothing else. But if he'd come home to sulk, he'd been gone before the alarm was raised.

Mihály's eyes widened. 'But we were just there. I didn't see anything.'

'No one ever sees anything,' Ilan said, voice clipped. 'That's the trouble. You're very sure you didn't see anything? No one with a darkness on them?'

'I don't know that I would have been able to tell. I don't carry Church glass.'

'I would have thought you could sense a demon.'

At that, Mihály sat back. 'The Church thinks it's a demon now? Open-minded of them to consider a failure.'

Ilan drew himself up. '*I* think it is.'

'And that's why they aren't letting you be in charge anymore, is that it?' Mihály's grin was the closing teeth of a bear trap.

A muscle in Ilan's cheek twitched, a clear fight for composure. 'Yes. And their attempt at fixing things is only going to make it worse.' Ilan turned back to Csilla. 'You heard Sandor's new policy. He's promising indulgence for turning neighbour on neighbour.'

Mihály cocked his head and gave half a shrug. 'Not that I'm endorsing the method, but if they have information, maybe it will help.'

'Anyone who has actual information would have already brought it to us,' Ilan said. 'Now they're just trying to shove someone else in front of them to avoid suspicion, and our time is going to be wasted squeezing stones for blood.'

'Torturing innocent people, you mean,' Csilla said as her heart skipped. Mihály settled close beside her and put his hand on her leg for reassurance, and Ilan raised an eyebrow. Csilla didn't shift. She wasn't entirely comfortable, but it was rare to be offered comfort, even if it did lessen whatever opinion Ilan had of her.

Ilan nodded slowly. 'And they'll hate the Church for it.'

'What does it matter to you if you're whipping one citizen or ten, for sins you've catalogued or ones he's trying to find?' Mihály prodded, his fingers tightening on Csilla's thigh in his passion. 'They call you the wolf, but you're really the Church's dog, and the second they give word you'll snap to heel.'

Ilan snarled in a way that did little to disprove Mihály's assessment, but the Izir continued to stare him down. 'So you don't like the new man in charge. So the Church doesn't believe your theory. Doesn't mean we should help you.'

Ilan was going to walk out and take all his information with him. Whatever his feelings, he still knew more about the murders than they did. This was their chance to get help from someone on the inside.

She put her hand over Mihály's, his fingers loosening to allow hers to slide through.

'Mihály, he's right. We don't know what we're doing.' Regardless of what Ilan would say about what they planned to do with the killer, they didn't have much hope of finding him alone. Ilan would be useful.

Mihály's glare had a hint of betrayal, but he didn't contradict her. He sighed, then moved his arm to slip around her shoulders. It was uncomfortably warm, but she forced a smile.

'Fine,' the Izir said finally, continuing to hold Csilla so she couldn't even squirm. 'But if you want to work with us, you see all of it.'

16

Ilan

IN THE sharp light of full day, agreeing to leave Silgard for whatever the Izir deemed necessary seemed like a terrible plan. The sun-dappled greens and lichen greys of the woods were soothing, and the scent of pine and dank leaf mulch called just as strongly as they had when he was a half-feral child galloping his parents' lands, but he was far from the city that needed him.

Ilan was loathe to admit to mistakes, but that didn't mean he didn't make them.

Ilan unhitched Vihar beside the run-down farmhouse as Mihály helped Csilla down from the cart with care. Her gaze didn't leave the Izir, but it wasn't quite a look of devotion. It was concern.

Csilla trailed them to the barn, hands twisting in her skirts and pursed lips that spoke to questions. Her nerves needled his curiosity.

'With all you're willing to say in the city,' he said to Mihály, 'I can't wait to see what you think you need to hide from us.'

Mihály merely unlocked the weathered door and pushed it open, letting dusted light slant over the carnage.

Whatever his opinion of the Izir, Ilan hadn't imagined so much scattered fur and rot in his homestead. Dead animals, some dry and withered, some still bloated, littered the ground, and a rabbit hung by its hind leg from a rafter, half-torn by yanking jaws that left the drying meat in dank strips. The whole thing stank of curdled blood.

So this rancid display was what the angel did when no one held him accountable. Ilan slid his gaze to Csilla, her lips pressed thin, but no surprise in her eyes. She had known about this. He never would have expected her to be so sunken into heresy already. Nothing in this macabre scene was mercy.

'Shit. Something got in.' Mihály lit a lantern and swung it in an arc of cast orange, but there was no scurrying in the shadows.

Ilan picked the ripped head of a fox from the ground, lifting its black lip with a thumb to examine the frozen fangs. If the Izir had been a hunter, he could respect it. But these weren't food, and weren't trophies. They were corpses, laid out without the care even animals deserved.

'What is this?'

'This is . . .' The Izir paused, mouth working for the word. 'Research.'

'Research.' Ilan tilted a prone squirrel upright. Its black eyes shone as if it were about to break the spell that held it and scamper away. 'And what have you learned from all this *research*?'

A distance clouded Mihály's eyes. 'Not enough. I can touch their souls, keep or even draw them back here momentarily. I can give them a new . . . container as it were, but they don't have enough fire to stay.' His voice bit on the last word.

Ilan hummed a prayer as he moved down the line of unfortunate creatures. 'What in Asten's holy name made you want to mess around with souls?'

His eyes went to Csilla on the word as she crouched, gathering up the mess and speaking softly to animals long past hearing her. No wonder she'd been taken in by him. The difference between immortal saints and the forgotten Faithful was often a measure of divinely sanctioned violence: Wise Angyalka, hanging with bulging eyes, Ladislaj the bounty, feeding his village in the starving season with strips of his own regenerating flesh. To someone so desperate, this massacre would look holy.

Mihály smiled, a grim contrast to the wretched surroundings.

'Surely you wouldn't want me to turn away a gift? Knowledge is a virtue, and how do we get more of it if we don't experiment once in a while? Miracles are proof of the transformative nature of the divine. I'm doing nothing more.'

Knowledge. A fine summation of chewed-on birds and crusted feathers and tufts of matted fur.

'You're divine, but you're no god. Knowledge without obedience is heresy.'

Csilla seemed to have glossed over the details with his promise of miracles, but the tiny broken bodies should have made her afraid. Being raised in the Church had given her too much trust in the appearance of the holiness, without a soul to understand it. If she'd never experienced the ecstasy, she couldn't understand the horror.

But Ilan knew that she had lived her own kind of horror, one that had led her to kneel in old sawdust on a barn floor with a lap full of dry dead things.

'It's a very old kind of power,' Mihály continued. 'From before the Severing.'

'People weren't moving souls before the Severing,' Ilan countered.

Angels and demons had lived among humans and added their magic to their territories, swayed them one way or the other, but the basics of souls never changed. Everyone had two aspects, Brilliance and Shadow, and the side you nurtured during life determined your eternity. You couldn't touch them or redirect them. That power belonged to Asten alone.

'People weren't. Angels were. Sometimes a soul could be held for a day or two. Sometimes it could be brought back; Lajol did his best for

Graced Rozalia. But in this corrupted world, it needs something to cling to. Something fresh, almost like life.' Mihály pushed the hanging rabbit lightly, and it danced on its rope, a grim and slow waltz.

'Blood.' Ilan knew how easily the body gave it up.

Mihály nodded. 'Still warm. Enough to give it a physical tether while Csilla accepts it. And the killer has spilled enough to forfeit theirs.'

The image of Csilla, chestnut ringlets matted and pale skin smeared crimson, was unholy intoxication. In the dusty light coming through the wood cracks, she was splattered in golden sunlight that could all too easily be running red.

'That's madness. Not a miracle. And Graced Rozalia herself remained a corpse, no matter how perfect.' How could this man be one Asten Themself had marked as holy?

'If your faith is that weak,' Mihály's voice held needles, 'then I'll show you.'

Ilan's lip curled. Faith didn't mean believing every heresy that crossed an Izir's mind or giving witness to it. But the part of him that had been a child shaken by stories of miracles, who'd lived his life in pursuit of that unknowable perfection, still craved.

'Please do.'

Mihály stretched and cracked his knuckles. 'There's a cat around here somewhere, if she hasn't died . . .'

'No!' Csilla jumped upright, gathered feathers and wood-stiff mice falling around her feet. 'I fed her. You're not killing her.'

Her protests were comical and brave.

Mihály put a hand on her head, a mocking benediction. 'One meal wouldn't have made much difference to the poor thing. It was kind of you, but not helpful.'

'Well the cat isn't here,' Ilan said as Csilla's lip trembled, 'but there are a fair number of rabbits in the woods.'

The snow was half-gone after the brighter past few days, so much so that it was impossible to tell tracks from melt holes, but there would be plenty of game out to nibble on the green poking through. Twigs snapped and leaves rustled as small things had jumped away from their approach. The forest was alive and waking.

Mihály scratched his beard. 'True enough, but I'm not very good at hunting unless the thing is already half-dead.'

No surprise, as he wasn't even good at being quiet. Ilan made a quick inventory of what was strewn about. The mess of stained cloth looked the most promising, and he picked up enough to construct a sling.

'Luckily, I am.'

The brush at the boundaries of the farm property was clearly flush with rabbits by the gnawed bark around the lower parts of the trees and bushes and the dark pebbles of scat. He reached into his pocket, where he'd tucked a few crusts of bread as a treat for Vihar – not the most appetising snack, but the horse wasn't picky. He crumbled the crust into smaller pieces and scattered them among the dead grass. Hopefully half-starved animals were equally as undiscerning.

He settled beside a tree in the lacy shadow of its branches, waiting in stillness for quarry to come. It didn't take long for a crunch and flutter to reach his ears. A grey-plumed grouse, her white neck-ruff puffed with concern, stepped forward and gave a cautious peck. Ilan held his breath and readied his weapon.

He was good but out of practice. His first shot scattered dirt and roots, the bird taking off with a shriek that made him groan. The second struck too true, the rabbit who had come to investigate dead before it could try to run. He took a few test swings and said a prayer to guide his aim as scrubby leaves shook. The heft of the rock and the rhythm were a rare nostalgia. His mother had taught him when he was old enough to crave the excitement of a hunt, too young to be trusted with a bow, and for years he and his littlest sister had taken the place of their hounds as the champions of the gardens. The cooks and furrier had always indulged them by making their catch useful.

He stretched out his legs, a twinge in his lower back. Crouching for hours hadn't felt this bad when he was eleven.

Dry dead vines shook as something approached. Rabbit or grouse or vole – hopefully whatever appeared was something he could leave alive enough to see what the Izir would do with it. Three chances was more than most hunts offered.

A rabbit, its nose and muscles twitching as it weighed safety against nourishment. Ilan swung. The next launch hit true. The rock cracked the creature's back and it cried out with a stomach-churning bleat, its front legs grasping for useless purchase against the dirt as it realised it couldn't run. He picked it up by its scruff, still screaming, and carried it inside where Mihály had turned his examination table into an altar, laying his own coat down and putting a small dish on it. Csilla gasped and reached out for the struggling creature, but he elbowed her away. He'd offered up his own hands for this stain.

'Took you long enough,' Mihály said, propping a hand on the table. Ilan squeezed the slingshot. The Izir's skin would look quite nice with a few round bruises.

The creature had begun trembling and turned glassy-eyed in shock. Ilan set it on the table, and Mihály looked between the pair of them. 'Who wants to give me blood?'

'You do it,' Ilan said, before Csilla could volunteer. Her palms were together, fingertips against her lips.

'Hurry up,' she said, voice stiff. 'Don't let him suffer.'

Mihály made a quick slice on the pad of his finger with a small, scalpel-like blade, hissing and cursing all the while. He squeezed out three fat beads of red onto the clay surface of the dish.

Then he pressed the rabbit down and cut its throat, its legs kicking weakly against the wood. Fresh blood pooled on his jacket, but he held his hand cupped around something Ilan couldn't see.

'Come close,' Mihály whispered, his voice urgent and deep. He placed his hand over the dish, then let it fall back to his side.

Csilla's face was white, as bloodless as the creature dying before them, her chest still with held breath. Ilan stepped forward, looking between the drops of human blood and the dark trickle slipping down the matted fur of the rabbit's neck. The air had a humid, coppery tang that sat in his mouth.

There was a new tint to the Izir's blood, and for the briefest second it pulsed, struggling for fresh life as it reached for something invisible and holy. The droplets rolled then stilled, dying a second death. Ilan's mouth went dry. He hadn't blinked. He couldn't deny what he'd seen.

Mihály had moved a soul.

The bastard wasn't lying.

Csilla's lips were slightly parted, breath shallow, her large eyes lit with warring disgust and reverence. Ilan fought the urge to step in front of her and block the wretched sight, cutting off whatever hope it had ignited.

Mihály looked up, his perfect smile back. 'There, now you've seen it. A little bit of blood, a little bit of soul.'

Ilan made a gesture over the blood, warding it against dark uses. He wasn't entirely sure that what he'd just seen wasn't dark. 'That's . . .'

'Shadow work?' Mihály's tone was obnoxiously teasing. He was breathless, elated, intoxicated by his own success. 'You just saw a miracle, and you're going to complain?'

'I'm . . .' Not complaining. *Concerned.*

'I know you want to kill the man.' Mihály continued. 'Do you really care how much of his blood gets spilled if you're the one to do it? If it doesn't work, at least we'll have taken a murderer off the streets. And if it does, Csilla gets her blessing.'

The open hope in Csilla's eyes at that was painful in its sincerity, an ember to be smothered before the blaze took the whole house down. A part of him wanted to take her head and force it to look back at the raw mess of open vein and clot-covered fur that was the price of this mad power.

This holy power.

Was the violence here so different from what he wrought in his calling? The knowledge that he, too, had spilled blood in his work sat uneasily in his chest. But he'd only struck the deserving and used pain to remove their sins. Csilla saw this as salvation, but it could damn her.

'You'd give her a soul that stained? She'll have to work it off the rest of her life.'

Csilla only lit more brightly at that. Of course she wouldn't mind the thought of a life sworn back to service. He looked back to Mihály; far easier to maintain the proper disdain in his tone.

'No, I don't need the killer's soul; I've already got one of those. I just need enough of their blood to hold it while I do the work,' Mihály sniffed.

'You've got a soul.' Ilan repeated the words, eyes darting around the dim room. He wasn't a child grasping his mark against ghosts. He still wanted to.

'Not here,' Mihály said. 'But one close to me, one I know will welcome a second chance.' He smiled at Csilla in a way that could have been mistaken for warmth if Ilan weren't so used to looking for sin. There was avarice behind his gentle touches, and Ilan was sure that Csilla wasn't aware. Maybe even Mihály didn't realise. But it was always the worst sort of people who wanted nothing more than to think of themselves as good.

Csilla stiffened, tilting her head. Maybe she was more aware than he gave her credit for. He could push again if it would help wake her from whatever thrall Mihály held.

'Is this why you've been preaching that there can still be form beyond death? Trying to make yourself feel better about your own ghosts?'

The Izir's handsome face sharpened into something fierce.

'One ghost. But I think everyone has the right to know that what is dead is not necessarily lost. There's precedent. Angyalka. Rozalia.' He spoke with too much fire for it to be beautiful.

'Angyalka never fully died, and Rozalia was the lover of an actual angel. Your theology is rather self-serving.' Miracles were miracles because they were rare.

'And yours is far too narrow. Csilla will be quite comfortable, don't worry for her. I'm seeing to that.' He reached out, a finger gliding along the cream lace at her neckline.

She'd gone pale, and Ilan raised an eyebrow as her lips parted, closed, then tried again. She pulled at her collar where Mihály had touched like it choked her.

'Csilla? Are you alright?' Mihály ran a hand over her head, a master being gentle with a pet.

'I don't feel well,' she said, not looking at either of them. 'I'd like to go back.'

The first sensible thing that had been said here, really. And she still did look incredibly pale, trembling almost imperceptibly, alone as an untethered boat in a storm.

She just liked that he was divine.

The grieving father's words came back to him. Kovács Lili, who had trusted Mihály's power and the comfort it brought. And the man at the club, killed only a few feet from where Mihály had passed.

The Izir had death among his followers and death in his secret home. If he knew more, that thread of connection could lead back to the source.

Ilan stepped back from the table, resisting the urge to yank Csilla behind him. But she had made her own choice even after seeing all of this.

'Well, Inquisitor?' Mihály asked. 'You can see I've only told you the truth about the power the divine has granted me. No lies. No heresy. Will you help us?'

He should ask to pray on it, to take it to a higher power. But it was a struggle to conjure images of righteous saints and not shaking blood and screaming rabbits. The draft on the back of his neck felt too much like ghostly fingers, the settling sighs of old wood like something unseen breathing in the room. The Izir didn't even seem to understand the horror of what he was saying. A soul stuck to this plane wasn't some academic curiosity: it was a person's very essence being tortured.

The only answer to all of it was to find the killer as quickly as possible and set everything back in order. He would save Silgard, both from the violence of the murders and, once all was done, this unsettling man.

He glanced at Csilla again, so clearly putting on a mask of acceptance, as if by wanting something to be normal badly enough she could make it so. Perhaps she was right, and the Church would accept her again after all this. When she had a soul.

'Yes,' he answered, the mark on him heavy. 'Damn me, but I will.'

17

Csilla

ILAN HAD asked that they come and look at the latest body in the morning before Matins and Prime prayers, when the fewest people would be up and about. That meant far too many hours for her to keep to her own troubled thoughts. She'd excused herself to a bath as soon as they returned, and Mihály had been happy enough to leave her to it; the trip back had been awkward enough with her feigning cramps and exhaustion, Ilan split between what seemed to be mild concern for her and less mild contempt for Mihály, and the Izir himself lost in some reverie with his ghost.

Evaline's ghost. She should have put it together more quickly. Csilla had been wearing her clothes, likely drinking from her cups, costuming herself in her jewellery, being made a puppet of what Mihály wanted in truth. She should have asked more questions, been more suspicious from the moment he was delighted to find a hollow girl among his admirers. An odd shame sat heavy in her stomach, twisting. She shouldn't have been so naive as to think his quick desire to help her, to coddle her and show her off, had had anything to do with her. In a way he was no different than Prelate Abe. She was made to be useful, not cared for.

There are worse things than being useful, she told herself.

It was scant comfort as she made her way to the room of the woman she might become; she'd guessed its location through Mihály's darting glances and the faint line of dirt in front of the door that suggested even servants left it alone. The draw was part curiosity, part masochism. Perhaps if she could see who Evie had been, she could understand why she'd been so dearly loved.

If Csilla had thought her guest room opulent, that was nothing compared to what was given to the cherished daughter of a wealthy house. She pulled back the sky-blue window curtains, quilted with tiny pearls, each one worth a day's portion of Church rations and still lovely despite the dust dulling their lustre. The view faced the cathedral, where the gilt of the towers turned what little light there was into haloed glow. Below were gardens of the house; beyond, public lawns that would be green come full spring. What had been designed to please Evaline also pleased Csilla. That was some comfort. Perhaps a part of her would feel at home.

But there was no ghost. She held her breath to see if anything stirred the air, but it was silent as a snowfall. Where was she?

Had Mihály even told Evie what he thought about souls? Csilla dragged her fingers over the spiralled mahogany bedposts, Evie's marble-topped writing desk, nicked with careless pen-knife strokes, the small bottles of perfume gone rancid. Little things untouched by the grieving hands still in the world.

Perhaps she loved Mihály regardless. Love often stole sense and self-interest. At least, that's what Csilla had gathered from overheard confessions. And Mihály's looks and charisma likely made up for his . . . eccentricities.

But she grimaced when she thought of his workshop, blood and dust and feathers and raw, holy power. Had Evie put up with that, too?

Perhaps she'd approved. Csilla wasn't Mihály; she couldn't ask directly, and she wasn't entirely sure Mihály would give her an honest answer if she asked for his intervention.

She shut the door with reverence and walked back towards the guest wing, where lamplight glowed in a crack of pale orange under Mihály's door.

He didn't answer her knock at first, and she half turned away. It would be much easier to push the whole thing aside, to focus on the task and worry about the result later. But that result was going to be her soul.

She knocked louder and finally got a grunt in response.

Mihály was cross-legged on his bed, thin shirt half open and a light sheen of sweat on his brow. Empty bottles littered the sheets, and when he looked at her his eyes were only half-focused.

'Did you need something?'

She should just say it.

'It's Evaline.' Csilla paced around Mihály's bed, sure she would wear the rug to threads with her anxious feet. It was so clear now that this was the source of his wellspring of heresy – not hidden knowledge, but his own grief-fuelled hopes. 'You think you can make me be her.'

He blinked and dragged a hand down his face. 'I can't *make* you do anything.'

No. But he knew how few options she had. How few they both had. She should have guessed earlier. All his sweet words, his gifts, his care . . . They weren't for her. They were for the ghost she would become. It was a strange sort of disappointment; she hadn't wanted the attention, though it was still nice to have it after a lifetime of being something less than. The Church had only seen a use for her as a weapon. For Mihály, she was a toy at best. She was his means to a future with someone better.

'You did agree to help me,' he continued. 'Just as I agreed to help you.'

And he was holding up his end of the bargain. She couldn't be the one to back out. It wouldn't be truthful. It wouldn't be kind.

It would leave her right back where she was, outcast and hopeless. She had to learn to like this, or she was worse than damned.

She took a deep breath. 'Tell me about her, then. Tell me what happened. Tell me the truth.'

Everything she knew about Evie came from the things she'd borrowed, but lace and pearls couldn't summarise a person.

From the drawer by his bedside, he pulled a well-creased portrait of a young woman with thick black hair braided through with tiny white and red flowers and narrow-set green eyes. The curve of her lips suggested a coyness and joy in her own skin that was foreign to Csilla, and it gave her a vibrant beauty that radiated through her otherwise plain features.

'Evaline was my soulmate. I realised as soon as I met her.' He stared at the portrait with the adoration the Faithful reserved for worship.

'Okay.' Csilla could spare the talk of soulmates, which managed at once to seem like a childish fancy and to hit some place raw inside her. She swallowed down the lump and forced her face to remain passive. Her pains weren't his problem, and he needed someone to listen.

'We were happy. Engaged' – his voice caught on the word – 'but she became very ill shortly before I was set to graduate. Nothing I did, nothing anyone did, helped. She spent days on the edge of death, begging for deliverance. In the oldest stories, angels resurrect the dead.'

One had, at least. The angel Lajol had so loved a human he'd crossed the ether to bring her back.

'Graced Rozalia.' It was the kind of miracle that hadn't manifested since the Severing.

Rozalia had come back perfect after touching the divine and stayed perfect long after her death, but nothing more was written of Lajol.

Angels had been charged with loving the imperfect creation that was humanity, but it had rarely ended well for the angels. Some cults insisted the Severing was in part protection, a parent separating ill-suited playmates. It was only natural that Asten took the side of the better of Their projects.

Mihály's cheek twitched.

'Yes, Rozalia returned whole and alive suggesting the emulsion into glory is not instant. Tamas was the one who had read enough to know what was possible, and was brave enough to try it with me. We would let Evaline die, then bring her back before she could be joined with the greater Brilliance. My blood would provide the conduit between the physical and the divine.'

Blood was the price of creation.

'But something else came with her. At least, that's the best I can gather.' He pulled up his own sleeve, where a pale sliver of a scar bisected the blue vein. 'I wasn't quite conscious at the time. Turns out I don't have that much more blood than other men.'

'That's not possible,' Csilla said, brows furrowing. 'We're protected.'

'Silgard is protected.' The plainness of Mihály's words made her shiver. 'Outside the city, things can still be coaxed through. You saw the seal on the roads. Why else would we need priests to tend them?'

Her face must have betrayed her concern, because he gave a brittle laugh.

'Don't look so scared. The Servants of the Road do their work well. We were blastedly lucky Tamas knew the invocation to take care of it. And it didn't *not* work, exactly. She came back for me. Just as I knew she would. Only as a shade, not fully herself.'

He fished a flask out of his other pocket and took a long sip with a sudden waft of spiced liquorice, eyes closing as he stole a second of intoxicated bliss. No wonder Tamas worried for him. Trauma was its own form of illness.

'And you want me to be her.' Even she could hear the reverence evaporating in her voice.

'You'll still be you. Just . . . more.'

'How do you know? Are you just saying that to make me feel better?' It was a tasty sort of lie, sugar to make the medicine more palatable.

He startled, then deflated, his shoulders sinking. 'I guess I don't. And I guess I am.'

The honesty was sweeter.

Csilla was suddenly very aware of the damp hair curling against her neck, the night robes she wore – not that a single sinful sliver of flesh was showing. Standing before him dressed for the bedchamber was scandal enough. Mihály's lip curled up, and she realised she'd been wordlessly staring.

'Are you wishing you'd killed me now?' The words themselves were jagged.

Csilla's heart seized, the way it always did to see a thing in pain. She sat next to him so gently the bottles didn't shift or clank.

'No. But I wish you'd told me before.' A slight hitch in his breath told her he was listening. It was ridiculous to think anything she could say could help the great Izir. But he was still a man, a young man at that. And his grief was still so fresh.

'Would you have believed me? Would you have agreed? Wait, no, you would have, wouldn't you.'

She couldn't tell if there was admiration or censure in the tone. Maybe there was a measure of correctness in both.

'Yes,' she admitted. 'And I believe you now.' She drew her knees up, hugging them. 'Will you hate me if I'm not her?'

If I'm a disappointment to you, too?

Her answer was in the barest shake of his head. 'I know you won't be exactly the same; how could you be? Having a soul won't take your memories, your own dreams. But I will love you. So much.'

She held herself closer, unable to look at him.

'And if it doesn't work at all? You'll still help me save the city?'

'I said I would.' He reached over and tapped her lightly on the nose, forcing her to look up. 'I'm not perfect, but I'm no liar.'

Well. It depended on one's definition of lies by omission. But his pain was so raw she couldn't bear to agitate it more.

'You said you know she's still here. I'd like to . . .' Her voice faltered. She believed, she did, but calling ghosts was more of a prank, the kind of thing older children faked to scare the younger ones on new-moon nights. But they'd never had an actual ghost to try on. And there was more magic in the world than she knew. She'd seen it in those shivering drops of blood. In the fact that Mihály knew his lover was still in the world, even if all Csilla saw was dust kicked in the air of a too-empty house. 'I'd like to meet her.'

He shook his head. 'I don't think you can.'

'When do you see her?'

He closed his eyes, lips curved in a mocking smile. 'All the time. She's almost always there, in the corners, in the shadows. But I don't know how to make anyone else see.'

The loneliness there was drowning. She put a hand on his arm, though she knew the small anchor wouldn't help.

'What about when you sleep? Is that better?'

The slightest shake of his head, then a shiver down his body. 'Sleep is worse.'

She sighed and settled on the far side of the bed, propping herself on a pillow. They couldn't help each other in this. She should go.

But he looked so sad.

'Do you want me to tell you a story?' She'd told the younger children stories as best she could when they cried. She wasn't very creative, but it rarely mattered. Even saint tales, so overtold ears closed as soon as they started, could help when all someone wanted was a soft voice and the comfort of someone making time for them.

He stretched out and rolled over to half look at her, and some of the darkness in his eyes had lightened with actual amusement. Good.

'You're so bad at lies, I can't imagine you tell interesting stories.'

She scowled, but he wasn't wrong. 'Why don't you tell me one, then?'

His head was tilted so he was speaking into her shoulder, his arm moving to drape across her. Her breath caught, but it would be cruel to shake him off. She'd endured far worse in the name of help.

'Once, there was a boy who could turn his touch into gold.' His voice was languid with medicine. 'Once his powers manifested, his parents took him from place to place so he could repay their debts, but their debts were large, and he was small.' He yawned. 'But then when it turned out the gold he made turned to ash the next morning, they tossed him out again to the scholars.'

'That's not a very good story.' She tried to keep the pity out of her voice.

He chuckled. 'Well, it wasn't a very good childhood. I envy you a little, being an orphan.'

He caught her injured hand and brought it to his lips. She froze at the contact.

Then he rolled over. 'Good night, Csilla. I think I will get some sleep.'

She watched his back until his breathing was even and deep, then started to ease off the side.

Suddenly, he shuddered so hard it shook the bedframe, a cold sweat on his skin. Csilla started, feet slipping on the cold floor as he gave another thrash.

'Mihály?'

His eyes flashed open, the pupils wide and inky and unfocused. His lips and tongue were moving with the zeal of prayer, but no sound emerged.

She rose to her knees to turn him on his side – he didn't look nauseous, but there was no telling. If he was having a seizure . . .

He grabbed her wrist with such force that it felt like he could break it and she gasped at the bright stab of pain as he squeezed down to the bone.

'Mihály!'

She shook him as best she could even as her stomach turned and her panicked heart raced, but though his eyes fell shut again, his grip didn't ease. The pillow beneath his head was damp and darkening with sweat, the palm against her skin cool and slick as she twisted and pushed against his chest. This must have been what Tamas had been talking about with his spells, but among all the bottles, she didn't see any true medicine. Pinprick pain lanced her fingertips. Soon her hand would be numb.

'Let me go.'

She shook her arm again, but there was no change in his expression, no sign that he'd heard her. Swallowing, she raised her free hand and probed his mouth, grimacing at the wet saliva. Well, he hadn't swallowed his tongue in his fit, so he wasn't choked and dying. She thumped his chest again. His heart was beating far slower than hers. If he didn't let go soon she would have to scream.

His fingers finally softened, and the thumb that had been jammed onto her vein changed to sweet stroking, and he murmured something she couldn't make out. She froze, and his eyes opened again, lighting with surprise.

'Csilla . . .' He looked at where his hand still wrapped her wrist, as if it weren't part of him. 'What did I do to you?'

‘What you’re doing now, that’s all,’ she answered, but when he pulled away there was blooming red that would soon turn withering blue and black. ‘Are you alright?’

She kept her voice soft and even. Mercy workers who dealt with soldiers or other victims of violence spoke of similar visions, the way a mind tried to protect itself. A bruised wrist was nothing.

‘I’m so sorry.’ The whisper barely registered before he reached for her again, reverent as he brushed the pain.

There it was. Light. Purity. Her heart thrummed a divine cadence, and the ache in her skin eased.

‘There,’ he breathed, bending forward to rest his forehead against hers. ‘Better?’

Csilla cradled the tiny miracle of her newly uninjured arm.

‘Better,’ she lied, both in words and the way she forced herself still when he kissed her brow, his exhalation still sour with drink.

As soon as his breaths were regular again, she slipped away.

18

Csilla

'YOU'RE SURE about this?'

Mihály pried the wooden boards off the stable floor, broken flakes of hay now pushed all over the room as they cleared the space. While they'd tried to be stealthy, they hadn't entirely succeeded; Erzsébet had found them, and was perched on the highest hay bale, tail twitching.

'I know all the back ways into the cathedral,' Csilla replied, keeping an eye on the cat. She looked far too keen, and if they didn't flush out any mice she might just pounce on their heads.

Hopefully this was what Ilan had meant when he had asked them to come in quietly. If not, they were in for a dark, cold wander.

The tunnels under the cathedral ran fifteen metres deep along the foundations, coupled with wells and trenches washing waste out to the river and cesspools best avoided. Some passages stretched out under the eight districts of the city, quiet except for the occasional sinkhole. The diggers had thought that one day there may be an emergency that required quick removal of the most holy treasures or safe passage for the Incarnate. Now the tunnels were sealed off at their ends and nothing more than places for Church-raised children to scare each other with ever more outlandish stories of the ghosts of saints and mad anchorites chasing visions in the dark.

'And what's down there besides rats and the dead?' He heaved again, and Csilla winced as slivers of old wood shattered.

'I don't think there are any dead.'

She bit her lip. The other children used to whisper that even the mortar used to bind the foundation stones had been mixed with the ashes of the Faithful, their devoted bones given immortality as the cathedral's skeleton, and the occasional bones of an unlucky craftsman only fed the rumours. The true holy relics were nearer the Seal.

'A saint, maybe.'

'And the Seal.' Even Mihály's voice took on a dark note that verged on reverence.

Vihar and a cart pony paced and kept watch, keenly interested in what was happening to their food. Csilla tossed a few handfuls of hay to them, then winced at the ear-pinning and squeals. The pony won, and Csilla sighed as the large black horse sulked, head hanging inside the rough-cut window.

'You could defend yourself, you know. You're much bigger,' she clucked, but Vihar only lowered his dark head to lip at what little hay he could reach.

The floorboards gave way to reveal a covered entranceway. She pulled at the handle of the round cover set on top of dark inlaid stone just an inch high, barely moving as she tugged.

'A well?' Mihály asked, taking a step back and eyeing it suspiciously. 'I suppose you think we're going to swim our way down in holy water? Angels aren't fish.'

Csilla smiled and turned so he wouldn't see her roll her eyes. He likely wasn't trying to be difficult, but if he'd listen to her this would go more quickly.

'There hasn't been any water there for centuries. You could stop talking and help me move this,' Csilla said, with a tug that gained them another few groaning inches. Mihály grabbed the handle and, with a single pull, the entrance was open. Csilla rubbed her own strained fingers. At least he was useful for moving things.

'Go on.' She gestured to the hole, the floor below hidden by swallowing dark. 'I'll cause less damage if I fall on you than the other way around.'

Mihály looked doubtful but climbed down anyway. Csilla followed him.

The holds carved into rock were narrow and chipped towards the bottom, the grey stone weak from the years it held water. Csilla held her breath with every step down, the rock threatening to give way under her, but they both landed in the inky blackness. What light there was above was pale and dim, the narrow glow like a crescent moon. The air was thicker, with a cool and dewy humidity, the scent of mould and loam surrounding them.

'Now what?' Mihály's voice was only a trickle of his normal volume next to her, and she jumped as he grabbed her arm. For a heartbeat, she remembered being in his room, pressure on her wrist like it would break.

She moved his hand down to hers, her fingers dwarfed by his. It was merciful that the dark hid her expression at the slide of his smooth palm against her scabbed one, bringing a tingling awareness all over her skin.

'Follow me.'

As they walked down the sloping ramp the space became a pit, and the damp squeeze on her hand tightened. The echo of their steps made her startle, but it was only a trick of the sound in the dark. Knowing that didn't stop the feeling of being trapped, or watched, or even followed. Anything could – and did – happen in the dark.

'I didn't know these tunnels were here.'

Mihály's tone was light, but there was a choked note beneath it. Something skittered in the blackness, and Mihály stepped into Csilla so hard she was pushed a half-step forward and nearly lost his hand.

'Don't worry. I think we're almost there.' She paused, then led them further left, mentally trying to reconstruct the halls and stores above.

'Good,' he muttered, clinging to her hand. Sweat beaded where their palms touched.

Csilla sighed. Her angel was scared of the dark.

'Csilla? Mihály? Where are you?' Ilan's whisper echoed towards them, and they moved closer to the sound with stumbling steps until they found each other. A blaze of silver light lit the area and Csilla winced as her eyes protested.

When she opened them, the light revealed walls streaked with black dirt and rivulets of water stain, a few areas patched with a lighter chalky clay. Ilan had passed Mihály something holy to illuminate the path. It also showed the low ceiling, a handspan above Mihály's head, and layers of spiderwebs like dusty lace. By the look on his face, he'd been happier in the dark.

The silver burned spectral as they made their way across the tunnel. The depth meant the walls were still frozen, and every breath brought the taste of dirt. There were miles of similar passageways, all cold and indifferent to the souls walking over their heads. If someone died this far below, they'd never be found, never blessed, never burned. Every time they rounded a corner she scanned for forgotten bones.

Csilla squeezed Mihály's hand harder on instinct, regretting it when he pulled her closer.

After long minutes winding through corridors that were a kingdom of the holiest rats and spiders in the land, the floor began to slope upwards again, landing in front of a wall. A dead end. Mihály looked at her in confusion, but she had no answer.

Ilan pushed. The wall cracked and opened, and they were standing in the hall of cells.

'What . . .' Csilla ran her hands along the expanse of rock. Her fingertips caught the slight raise of the seam, but even the full pressure of her weight didn't move it. 'I didn't think blessed magic could do that.'

'Asten gives us the power we need to protect what must be protected,' Ilan said simply. 'But the Church also had clever architects.'

And one had left this pocket room, for prayer or protection.

As she stepped into the small space, she froze for another reason. The body, the one she'd last seen in the cells during her own imprisonment, was now here with them.

The days had not been kind to the victim. The white sheet drawn across him was stained with oils and excrement, and though a small forest of incense sticks surrounded him, the smoke only gave the putrid smell false notes of cloves. Csilla touched her chest and covered her mouth, bending close to the wounds.

Ilan's voice was steady.

'We haven't even gotten in contact with his family, and they're going to burn him. So look quick.'

She reached out and touched the cuts, now too old and clotted over to bloody her hands.

Her fingers burned like touching frozen metal. She snatched them back and tucked them into her palm, hoping they hadn't noticed. But Ilan was only looking at Mihály.

The scar on her palm began to itch. The Izir's face was pure horror as Ilan gestured to the mutilated body.

'I spoke to him that same night.' He knelt down and touched his face, a loving caress, as if not seeing the bloat and sunken eyes. 'He was a pilgrim, not from Silgard.'

'Was he one of your followers?' There was a new, sharper note in Ilan's voice. Csilla stepped to Mihály's side.

'A new one, but yes—'

'And Kovács Lili? Twenty. Long blonde braids. Wanted to join the Church. Here, this one.' He produced a sketch, one Csilla sighed to see was stamped with half a cat print.

Mihály was blinking rapidly now, his face paling to the colour of linen. Csilla put a hand on his back, but he didn't seem to notice.

'I noticed she'd stopped visiting, but I thought she'd taken her vows.'

Ilan raised an eyebrow.

'She died.'

He went through his record, every person listed bringing a new twisting grief to Mihály's face. Csilla clenched her teeth. Mihály, self-absorbed to the marrow, hadn't bothered to learn the names of the people who followed him. He only knew the accusing faces etched in dark charcoal.

Finally, Ilan stopped. Mihály's hands were on his knees, white knuckles clutching tight.

'They really are mine.'

Csilla's chest squeezed at the shake in his voice. In a way, the Church had been right, even more right than they'd known. Those people had also put their faith in Mihály. The hands that healed and bought them precious days of hope and ease had also painted a target on them. Comfort wasn't meant to have a price, let alone one so high.

Ilan nodded as if he'd already known as much.

'I don't suppose you have an explanation?' Mihály shook his head, wordless. 'I could try to get one out of you, I suppose. Why would you be the only connection?'

They weren't so far from the torture rooms, and as shocked and broken as he was, Mihály would probably volunteer. Csilla stepped between them.

'You can't possibly think he's involved,' Csilla said, keeping one hand behind her, on Mihály, as he trembled.

Ilan frowned. 'You saw his experiments. Would it be so large a leap to think he would practice on people?'

'He wouldn't.' He healed people and spent his nights sick himself. A flailing rabbit was one thing, a living person quite another.

'If I were going to practice on people,' Mihály said finally, 'I could do it with far less trouble away from here, and none of my followers would hesitate to leave the city with me. Did you see any bodies at the farm? Am I not trying to figure out the cause of this?'

A twisting ribbon of fear drew tight around Csilla's stomach. If the killer wanted victims, there was no one closer to Mihály than she was now.

'Sin outs itself in the end.' Ilan's voice had an edge. Csilla was suddenly aware that of the three of them, he was the only one armed.

'I wouldn't know,' Mihály countered, waving his hand. 'The closest we have to a killer here is Csilla, actually, and that was on Church orders.'

She hoped her flat look told him he really wasn't very funny.

Ilan seemed equally unamused. 'You're our only connection.'

'Me and every person who follows me. They all know each other.' Mihály's face was anguished, deep lines on his forehead and around his eyes twisting his beauty. 'I'm only trying to help people. What good is this divinity otherwise?'

But they'd seen the monstrous way he used his divinity, a blessing delivered with screaming and blood.

Ilan stepped forward, and Mihály grabbed him by the front of his cassock. Where the Izir's skin brushed his mark, it sparked white.

'There,' Mihály growled. 'You can see I'm innocent.'

Ilan glared, shoving him back hard enough that the Izir almost lost his footing.

'I can see you're *divine*. Nothing about innocent.'

Csilla looked between them, old and new faith warring in the glimmering light.

'But the marks,' she said finally. 'Whoever is doing the killing is also destroying the Seal. Mihály couldn't do that.' She turned. 'Could any of your followers have done this? Are any of them educated, trying to keep you for themselves, perhaps? Or maybe they're just taking the next step in heresy.'

The leap between the Church being wrong about one thing and a desire to destroy it was large, but some would make it.

'I doubt it. They aren't bad people, regardless of what the Church thinks.'

Ilan ignored the pointed look. 'And you're sure you can't read it?'

Mihály sighed and turned back to the papers, eyes sliding from the faces to their mutilation. His expression calmed with the distance of pondering an academic question, and then his eyes widened.

'This is the order, correct?' He folded the first drawing with neat creases, then the second, even as Ilan complained behind him, laying them over each other so all that was visible was the charcoal scrawl. 'I can't read it, but look.'

Csilla peered around him, unsure what she was looking at in the fanned sheets. Ilan pressed next to her, arms crossed.

'Look at . . .' His voice trailed off and he edged past Mihály to get closer. 'Wait, are you saying . . .'

'It looks like any ritual song, does it not? Even without knowing what it says, there's cadence. Repetition.'

Now that she was looking at them together, it was undeniable that the eyes danced across the symbols like a poem. Or a prayer.

'So not a message at all,' Ilan breathed, fists balling. 'It's actual Shadow work.'

Mihály nodded. 'I don't think any human, no matter how far they'd sunk, would have found this kind of knowledge. Someone has to have released one.'

There was a tiny measure of relief in knowing it wasn't the people themselves weakening the Seal, slipping faith or no. 'But why?'

'The Church has always had enemies,' Ilan said. 'I'm more concerned with how someone possessed got into town in the first place.'

Someone possessed. Csilla chewed the idea, choking and bitter. Demons were so corrupt they couldn't hold material form long and couldn't pass for part of the world when they did, but they could be invited in, welcomed, and nurtured by a soul feeding its Shadow appetites. Anyone like that would boil to walk around the holiness of Silgard. A demon couldn't parasite a person of true faith.

But there were dirtier ways in than walking through the gates. It would take a lot of work, but what was physical strain to someone happy to damn them all?

'The tunnels,' Csilla said, crossing her arms over herself with a claustrophobic constriction. 'If they dug out an old entrance, it's possible to get into the city from underground.'

Ilan nodded. 'There aren't that many potential entrances. We can go down and see if any seem freshly opened.'

Mihály gave a small grunt, clearly displeased with the idea of spending more time in claustrophobic holes.

It was a potential how. But it still didn't tell them who had broken the demon from its prison or who was giving it a home in their flesh, or why they'd chosen to hunt Mihály's flock.

'Think,' she pressed. 'Mihály, is there anyone who would have cause to hate you or be jealous of your followers? There has to be a reason they're the victims.'

His snort was derisive, echoing in the crypt-like cool. 'We're living with the worst of them, and she's no killer.'

No. Madame Varga might look askance at Csilla, point her words like needles, but her anger stopped at verbal barbs. Ilan spread his hand over the paper and then pushed the sheets back together.

'We'll gather your people, then. You can preach, and we'll watch for signs of someone possessed. If the killer knows your followers, they're likely among them.' Ilan's voice was clipped, sure, but Mihály stiffened.

'Why don't I just talk to them?' Mihály was pacing now, breath huffing, and Csilla watched for signs of illness. 'Find out if they've had strange experiences with any of their fellows. There's no reason to do what amounts to taking them to market.'

'And tip off the killer if he catches wind? Spread even more rumours through the streets? Besides, you've been quiet enough, for you, and yet here's another body. Do you want to wait until every person who had the misfortune of overhearing your foolishness is dead?'

Mihály put a hand on Csilla's shoulder, tight and searing with desperation.

'If you won't use them, use me. Whoever it is has likely seen me with you enough. I can go places alone. Make myself more conspicuous.' Though she wasn't exactly sure how she could become more of a sight than walking arm in arm with the Izir while wearing a fortune in borrowed fabric.

'Absolutely not!' The shock in Mihály's voice rang like the strike of a blacksmith's hammer on iron. 'If I lose you, I have . . .'

'Nothing?' Despairing tears sprang to her eyes. No one was about to let *him* go cold or hungry, and all he would lose was the lover he would have lost long ago if he'd been any other man. 'It's a good plan,' she assured him, putting her hand over his as a comfort. And even if it wasn't, it was the best they had.

He gave a tiny, terse nod. 'Fine. We'll bring them together. But, Ilan, you'd better be watching so nobody gets hurt.'

Ilan was still looking at the corpse, lips pressed thin and determined. 'Not nobody. Only those who deserve it.'

19

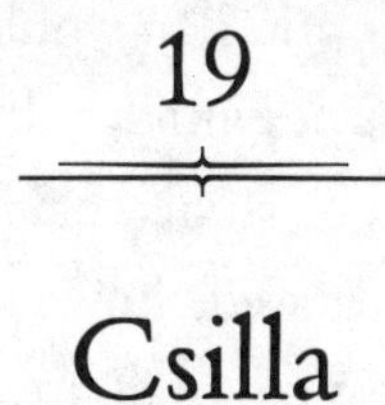

Csilla

Mihály's fingers twitched at his collar, pulling it from his sweat-dampened skin. He seemed to think the inn was overly warm, but Csilla's arms were covered in gooseflesh.

'Remember why we're doing this,' she whispered. The words half-choked her. People were crowding into the room, and she tried to take the measure of their faces. One might be the killer. One would be a victim.

But now we know, she told herself. *We can end the whole thing if we're quick and clever and blessed.* The words repeated themselves, building a wall between her mind and the tug of wrongness in her gut.

Mihály looked down at her, then put his hand on her head and smiled softly. She tried to smile back, like this was a perfect idea, like his touch was warming instead of a further pulse of worried ice down her spine. If this was what it took to get him to lead one of his lambs to the chopping block, so be it. She could swallow her doubts and pretend it pleased her.

'I'll be watching from the back.'

He started to bend closer, but she ducked and scattered toward the edge of the gathering crowd with an apologetic wave. They needed to focus on him, not the attention he was paying to the girl he arrived with, especially when she was bolting the door. She would watch, try to spot the most suspicious, and Ilan would wait outside to test their souls and find the vessel. They might all be grey with listening to heresy, but only one should be ruined black with Shadow.

What they hadn't anticipated, however, was how many would show up. There were people from all areas of the city, those whose clothes were mended with coarse thread and those with subtle gold on their ears and necks. Some were even pilgrims or refugees, wearing the kind of clothing that would be dear to import. Death made no distinctions, and so neither did the kind of person who feared it.

So many faces she knew, at least in passing; the ill were the first to search for a miracle.

A hand caught her arm.

'Csilla! I've missed you. I couldn't believe when they told me you'd left service.'

Elmere. She froze as he kissed her cheeks and fussed over her fine dress with a grandfather's teasing. He shouldn't be out here. She took his hands out of habit, frowning at his loose collar and the rash creeping down his neck. 'Elmere . . .'

'It seems you've been doing well for yourself, though, dear. And you went to the Izir, like I told you.' His eyes were nothing but kind, and she hoped he couldn't tell how forced her smile was.

'I'm well enough. But you shouldn't be here. Go home and rest.'

Mihály's curious gaze was hot on her back, waiting for her to get in place. She stepped aside, but the old man still had her hand. 'And miss his preaching? He hasn't been on the streets in days.'

Because of Csilla. No wonder everyone here was desperate to see Mihály again.

'What if I promise you he'll come visit you later? Personally?' She tilted her head, trying to look convincing. 'I'm working with him now. You don't have to stay in this crowd. It won't make you feel any better.'

'I've already come all this way.' But he was unsteady on his feet, and she squeezed his hand.

'Trust me. Please.'

He sighed, but the fondness in his gaze squeezed her chest. 'I always have, little girl. Well then.' They walked arm in arm to the door, Elmere leaning on her for balance. 'I suppose standing for hours wasn't going to be the most comfortable experience. But I expect to see you soon.'

'You will,' she promised, guiding him past the tight-pressed bodies. 'Please, rest.'

He patted her arm, pausing in the doorway. 'I am glad you're doing well for yourself, even if you couldn't join the church.'

Doing well. She tipped up and kissed his cheek again so he couldn't see how her face twisted.

The agitated crowd began to shift and caw.

'Where have you been, Izir? They've no right to stop you from speaking,' a dark-skinned man with deep furrows across his brow said. 'We need your council.'

So many voices chimed in that the individual words were smothered, but bits reached Csilla's ears.

'The deaths prove we've been abandoned. They're saying the bodies are putting the city under some kind of spell.'

'Who is "they"?' Mihály asked, but any answer was lost in yet more questions and accusations.

'Why hasn't the Incarnate come back? He should be here in his stronghold, not frittering with the governors or pushing our borders.'

'We came to Silgard because it was supposed to be safe. Asten isn't going to return if all of us are dead.'

Csilla's heartbeat picked up. No one should dare mutter the things they were saying, and here they were, speaking them in clear voices heard by more than just Asten. But a hard knot in her breast told her they were right. The Incarnate *should* be here. How could the people trust the Church if the voice of their god wouldn't come back to salve their wounded faith? The laws of the Church were supposed to be the armour that protected people from their own worst impulses and the leaders examples of what it looked like to live hand in hand with the will of the divine.

But the Incarnate's absence showed Asten cared more about war than bringing his most holy city to peace.

'Were the victims somehow touched by evil? Have we lost our protection?' The woman's voice was half-wail.

'We have,' another man spoke up. 'I heard what happened in Kis. The wards were broken, the demon found a host, and they burned the cathedral and everyone in it.'

Csilla glanced over the crowd at that, searching for a reaction at the mention of the possessed. There were grimaces and gritted teeth on every face, but less surprise than there should have been. Truth was leaking.

'Were you there in Kis?' Mihály spoke over the fearful murmurs, and the man seemed to shrink, pulling at the wooden mark hung around his neck.

'Well, no. But I heard from a pilgrim, who heard from a merchant . . .'

The adherents jostled and complained and reached out for Mihály, who soothed them as best he could but soon looked like he was up to his neck in water in a grasping sea.

'Peace, all of you.' Mihály raised his hand. 'This anger risks your souls. You shouldn't fear.'

They should have become soft at his words, pliant and meek. Instead, a palpable agitation rose. The room was sweltering.

One man kicked his chair, the sharp, angry rattle drawing a momentary silence.

'It doesn't matter if we're angry or not.' He pulled up his shirt, where the skin across his back was bruised in a lash line of mottled brown and yellow. The mark was human-made, and all the uglier for it. 'The Church isn't protecting us anymore. This is what they give us for keeping the Faith.'

Mihály flinched like he'd been struck, and Csilla pressed her hands to her heart. It was likely Ilan's work.

'I know. I'm only trying to provide comfort.' He offered them his glorious smile, but it was hazy around the edges.

'Comfort doesn't bring back the dead.' The man who spoke next was dressed in fresh mourning blacks. 'Comfort doesn't stop my children from panicking every time a rat scutters through the beams.'

'I'm sorry,' was all Mihály could say, over and over, until it became its own kind of intercessory prayer smoothing the edge of violence.

Csilla looked between the faces; blotchy, pained, and feral. She couldn't see anyone she would pin as a killer. This snap-jaw anger was only the instinctual reaction of the hunted, not intentional violence. It was all painfully human.

'Please. Listen,' Mihály pleaded.

'Listen to what, Izir?' A person in front of him hissed. 'We came because we thought you'd have answers. Why are things only getting worse? Are you going to tell us it doesn't matter, we should happily die and let our souls know peace? You're the one telling us ghost stories. Where is the peace in that?' A few people spat at the statement, the air growing rotten.

Csilla edged her way to the front of the room, dodging splayed feet and cocked elbows. Mihály caught her gaze, and she put her hands together. *Pray*, she mouthed. If his own words were failing him, the saints that had come before had left them plenty to use.

Mihály closed his eyes a moment, lashes falling over his cheeks, still and perfect. His voice deepened and took on a resonant tone like the bells chiming through the square.

He began to pray.

Csilla's lips moved along with the old words to the litany of peace Ágnes used to use in place of a lullaby, set down by Blessed Imre, said to have been whispered to him in Arany's arms. As Mihály spoke, he seemed to glow from within, holiness radiating. Everything around him seemed brighter, more perfect, and Csilla squashed an urge to go to him, to see if standing next to him would let her share the blessing.

The crowd softened as surely as if they'd taken a dose of Mihály's sweetest drug, violence charmed away by his beauty. Csilla looked over the gathered again, searching for any sign of a killer's appetite and claws. But all of them seemed ordinary people. Scared, hopeful, faithful people, now under the angel's sway.

Sweat glistened on Mihály's brow, and his words tripped, slurred with nerves.

Dismiss them, she mouthed. They'd done their job. But he wasn't looking at her now, and he continued to speak until his throat grew parched and the words became hoarse exhalations.

Even an angel's voice couldn't last forever. He coughed, shoulders wracking, and slumped forward.

One man stood in the broken pause, face flushed and eyes wild.

'We believed in you. I closed my ears to the rumours. But this city was safer before you showed up.'

His punch caught Mihály square in the stomach. The Izir doubled over, holding out an ineffective hand to try to protect himself.

Csilla scrambled as chairs were overturned, passionate faith turned into violent fear in an instant. Mihály brought up an arm to block a second punch, but other fists landed.

Not every hit fell on target, and there was another crash as someone brought an arm around a man's neck, and others tripped and set off new waves of flailing and retaliation.

Csilla squeezed through the bodies, tugging her skirts away from grasping hands, sucking down the pain as a booted heel crushed her toes. Others pushed around her, stealing the air as they went for the door, but tangling and tripping her as she tried to get to Mihály. Her head snapped back as her chin was cracked by a glancing elbow.

She shook off the dizziness and squeezed through and got there first, bracing herself in the doorframe against the shove at her back.

'Ilan!' He stepped out, sword in hand, and the pushing people behind her stilled. It didn't calm the chaos deeper inside.

From inside his cloak, Ilan pulled out a silver whistle and blew three shrill blasts, piercing the quiet of the night. She started to turn back, but Ilan grabbed her arm and pulled her firmly out. She jerked her arm, but he didn't let go. There was something dark and worried in his eyes, deeper than the worries of the moment, and it gnawed at her.

'You're just going to get yourself knocked out. Stay back.'

Inside there was another crack and shout, another heart-straining moment of Mihály's pleading. Two people pushed past, shoving Csilla to the dirty stone, and Ilan cursed and kicked at a third trying to escape.

Csilla picked herself up, her palms now scraped by the gravel. This was supposed to be the way they made sure no one got hurt. She was achingly glad Elmere had left before he could see Mihály turned into a scapegoat for his people's fear.

It took too many minutes for three inquisitorial priests to appear running towards them and calling questions in breathless voices.

'Bring out every one of the heretic's flock,' Ilan ordered, and the men obeyed as if he still had the right to order them. Within moments the brawlers had been ushered to the street. Red swelling was already visible on split lips and punched-in eyes, and one man's sleeve had been torn half away.

Mihály came up last, bleary-eyed and shivering. His lip was bruised, and the imprint of a hand stained his cheek.

Csilla ran to him.

'Are you alright?' She glanced behind at the agitated crowd, fuming with accusations as the priests tied them for questioning.

'I think so,' he said through chattering teeth. Csilla slid her arm around his back and braced her shoulder against his ribs, though his weight was almost enough to knock her over. The people were watching the priests with even more suspicion than the eyes they turned on each other.

Ilan approached. Csilla opened her mouth to say something, but there was no recognition on his face. It was a cold, judgemental mask, and for a heartbeat she worried it wasn't acting. Maybe he'd seen all he needed to, and was ready to take them to the rack.

'Izir. You've been warned multiple times about your heresy.'

'He wasn't preaching heresy,' Csilla spoke for both of them, Mihály still shivering against her. 'He was praying, proper prayers, and trying to soothe them.' Csilla looked over Mihály again, gentle apologies in her touch. He hadn't wanted this. 'He tried to help.'

'Tried to help how?' Sandor came from behind and pushed Ilan aside, taking charge and no doubt ready to take credit.

'Nothing but the honest word,' Mihály managed. 'The people are scared.' His words were muffled by the blood in his mouth, and when he cringed she could see a tooth sitting crooked in his gum.

Csilla's heart clenched. He hadn't even tried to defend himself. Guilt stabbed for every moment she'd doubted him. He loved the people, just as she did.

Sandor looked him over with a disbelieving glare, but it was clear he lacked the will to say it to the Izir's face.

'Bring everyone in for questioning.' He looked back at Mihály. 'Your kind only answers to a higher jurisdiction. You can go. But we may want answers later.'

'It's not their fault,' Mihály said, stepping forward and dragging Csilla with him. 'I don't want them hurt. They're innocent.' He directed the last statement to Ilan, who gave the smallest nod of acknowledgement that the plan had failed. They hadn't turned up anything worse than people bested by fear.

But he didn't step in to defend them.

Sandor pushed one of the staggering witnesses out of the way.

'That's not for you to decide. Bring them all in.'

'But they didn't do—'

'But they may know something,' Ilan cut her off, and an unfamiliar anger sparked in her belly as Sandor gestured to the crowd, approving.

This was always just an exchange of information, of tools. It wasn't like he agreed to be kind.

There was none of the consideration she'd seen from him before as he watched the arms of the gathered be looped with hemp rope, lip curled, no longer looking at her at all.

Relief and sorrow collided in her. There was still a chance one of these people knew something that could help. It might all be over, but every one of these people was going to pay for the crime of wanting answers. For wanting peace.

She turned back to Mihály, but he spoke before she could.

'Go back to Madame Varga's,' Mihály said, gaze darting towards the mausoleums, his breath fast.

Csilla looked up at his swelling lip.

'No. You need care, not a ghost.' She reached up to try to check the damage, and he slapped her hand away so hard it stung.

Their faces mirrored each other in shock, and she turned away before he could offer an apology. He'd rather run away to a ghost than face the problems with her, even though she had her own bruises from trying to help him.

Csilla pressed close against the wall as the group marched towards the cathedral at Sandor's barked order. But Sandor wasn't going with them. He watched them, hands broad on his hips, a picture of the Church's authority. But as they moved on, he turned heel and walked in the other direction.

In the shadowed overhangs, Csilla followed.

20

Csilla

CSILLA KNEW the doorway Sandor stopped in front of and the worn and thoughtful face of the man who opened it: Tamas.

What business could Tamas have with Sandor? He wasn't at the riots; Mihály hadn't even mentioned his name.

'Inquisitor?'

Surprise coloured Tamas's voice. Csilla didn't have the luxury of moving closer to read the nuances of his expression, and the glint of his glasses shadowed his eyes. Sandor looked back at the road, quick glances left and right before stepping close.

'About your Izir . . .'

Their words faded as they stepped inside, and the door closed with a thud. Csilla slipped close and pressed her ear to the wood, the cracked red paint scratching her cheek. But it was a thick door built to block both heavy snows and the clatter of street traffic, and all she heard was the quick thud of her own pulse, strong under her skin.

She walked around the house, dragging her fingertips against the brick walls, searching for a crack or vent leaking whispers. It was no use. The shutters were already tight against the approaching night. The only sound was a creeping cold air and the shriek of a distant crow. Csilla crossed her arms against a shiver. The last slanting sunlight was disappearing into violet dark behind the rooftops, a few scattered stars peeking overhead.

After long minutes, Sandor emerged. The door slammed behind him, and neither spoke a parting blessing.

Csilla counted to one hundred and combed her hair forward so brown waves fell over the tender spot on her jaw. Then she knocked.

'I don't want to. Oh, Csilla.' Tamas stepped back and looked down at her, lips pursed. 'You're here now? It's late, and I hear there's been trouble.' He glanced over her shoulder, but Sandor was gone. 'Where's Misi?'

'He wanted to be alone. May I come in?' She forced her voice to sound small and respectful. Suspicion would get the door slammed.

'Of course. I thought you'd been ignoring me completely.' He ushered her in and shut the door after a final glance at the streets.

Inside, the room smelled like pipe smoke laced with cloves and a strange, sharp tinge she couldn't place. She furrowed her brow.

'Ignoring you?'

He waved her over to the small table in the middle of the room where stubby candles were burning and gestured for her to sit. Yellowed wax dripped onto stale crumbs and what looked like spilled sugar, oddly rich in the humble surroundings.

'I'd sent a note to Mihály asking about you. Perhaps with all the trouble he's causing he didn't have time to pass the message along. Is he well?' The urgency in his voice worried at her.

'Well enough.' She didn't want to tell Tamas she'd gotten his precious student punched if Sandor hadn't mentioned it. Tamas arched an eyebrow.

'And his spells? Have you seen anything?'

'Mmm. He drinks a lot – I'm sure it doesn't help.' Her mind darkened, remembering the salt-sharp fever in him as he slept, long fingers crushing her wrist. 'But it's not his fault.'

Tamas sighed.

'So he keeps his own faith and drowns himself in a weak man's baptism. Well. I can't say I haven't had a part in that, though I wasn't expecting him to be in the well so long. And I wasn't expecting you to stay with him.' The accusatory note in his tone was the sting of a lash. 'I did warn you to leave.'

Csilla laced her hands and rested them on the table in front of her. She wasn't here to talk about Mihály.

'What did the new High Inquisitor want? I saw him.'

'He thinks I can take responsibility for Mihály. As if anyone could.' He tapped his fingers against his lips, the creases in his forehead deepening. 'How is he treating you?'

'Mihály? Fine.' Better than fine when he forgot she was Csilla and not Evie. The echoes of his desperate touches lingered on her shoulders and in her hair, the clinging remains of love with nowhere to go.

'And has he managed to get you a soul?' Tamas gave her a pointed look. 'Or save the city, or whatever it was you thought would save you in turn?'

She shook her head, pulling her hope around her. She wouldn't let his needling hurt.

'We haven't had any luck at all.' Whatever evil was lurking, it was well hidden.

Tamas sighed, then picked up his pipe and lit it. He took a deep drag as a thicker smoke haze danced above them.

'Are you certain you never had a soul?' he asked. 'The mercy priests didn't take you wet from between your mother's legs.'

His eyes locked with hers, and she flinched. It was like being stripped bare all over again.

'If I'd had a soul and lost it, I'd be dead. Do I look dead?' Anxious prickling made her throat thick, his gentle questioning jabbing her most sensitive spot. At least when she had a soul, even if it was Evie's, no one would question her right to exist.

He clucked his tongue.

'Not at all, poor thing. You could still leave. Why do all this work if there's no reward in it for you?'

Csilla pursed her lips.

'I want to rejoin the Church.' The words were a good reminder to herself. She had to believe it was still worthwhile, even as the anger at Ilan's coldness in bringing in the citizens churned.

'A faith for a god who ignores you. In some ways you're the luckiest girl in the Union. You don't have to waste a second of worry on any of it.'

'How can I not?' The words came out in a snap. 'If I'm ignored, I'm ignored, but how can you look at people, look at creation, and not try and help?' There was such responsibility that came with opening your eyes.

A sadness passed over his face.

'Sometimes help doesn't look like help on the surface. When you set a child's broken bone, they wail all the louder. The healing takes far longer than the injury.'

'That's what the Church does.' It was why the road to Asten's return was so long. Tamas only snorted, and she clenched her teeth to try to quell the sting of his disdain. 'I'll tell Mihály to come by.'

Tamas pushed his glasses further up on his nose.

'You shouldn't care for him so much.'

The words weren't an insult, but she took them as one.

'Are you going to tell me to leave him again? I care for everyone.'

Tamas clucked his tongue. 'I know. Anyone can see you're raw, lighting yourself on fire to keep strangers warm.'

She frowned but held her argument. If he couldn't understand caring for someone meant their pain was yours, it was better he'd left the priesthood.

Tamas took another long drag of smoke, the grey haze of his exhale surrounding them.

'Has he even told you what she was like, other than perfection or grace incarnate or any of the other ridiculous images lovers create? Don't try to lie, I can guess what he's planning. I know the boy too well.'

Evie. Mihály had promised she wouldn't change, and she clung to those words like a life raft. But Tamas's tone was full of jagged stones to sink her with worry.

'Did you know her well?' He'd been there the night she'd died, and everything had gone so devilishly wrong.

He nodded. 'Not well, but I knew her.'

'And?' she pressed.

'She was loud,' he said after a pause to think. 'Always chattering about this or that, asking questions, laughing. Smart but not wise, and selfish as sin. They were well-suited to each other.' He snorted at some private memory. 'If you want to serve the Church, you won't be able to do it as Varga Evaline.'

She stared into the candle flame, the crumbling black wick burning up into pale fire like Asten's eternal Eye.

'Nothing will change. I love the Church.' But even though it wasn't exactly a lie, guilt weighed on her heart. She loved service, and duty, and the pure worship of helping Asten's flawed creation. But seeing innocents cower from it, its own leader refusing to protect it . . . that she hated.

'And they never even gave you a choice in that, did they?' His smile was grim.

'I'm choosing now,' she answered, and a strange look passed his face again.

'Choosing Mihály.'

'Yes.' That wasn't the whole of it, but it couldn't be denied. 'He told me a little about his past. Told me he was jealous of my being an orphan, in fact.'

Tamas snorted. 'That doesn't surprise me; from what I understand of his parents they nursed bottles more than their children. He comes by his vices honestly. Though if divine will made any sense it would have stopped any power from manifesting again in that line.'

'It was kind of you to mentor him.' Even if it came late in life, she knew the influence that just one caring figure could have.

'Well maybe I didn't have a choice in that, in the grand scheme of things. And now that he's told you his sad tale, you feel like you don't either.'

She pursed her lips and rose before he could criticise her empathy again. 'I should go.'

'Then let me give you something against the night.' He stood and went to a shelf of tins and bottles, picking up one that lit under his touch. Consecrated glass, but old.

Csilla kept her hands in her lap, fingers tightly laced.

'What is it?' She'd nearly had enough of holy touches; they never seemed to work out like she wanted.

'Old habits in places from when the angels and demons were around to teach us. They say the well it came from was blessed.' He gave a little chuckle. 'Maybe it will do you a little good, anyway.' He pushed his glasses further up the bridge of his nose. 'If nothing else, the liquor in it will warm you.'

'But you're not a priest anymore.'

He waved his hand at her. 'I was when I blessed this bottle. That is good enough. Humour an old man, will you?'

There was hardly enough in it for more than a few drops to be put into the tea he was making. His hand moved over the cup, then reached for a small jar of honey. He added more than would be sensible for a guest, even as she protested that he shouldn't waste it.

'It's no waste, I don't have many visitors and don't like the stuff myself. Now, drink.' His voice was even but heavy with the weight of years of decisions.

'Where did you go when you travelled?' she asked, picking up a cup for a sip. Servants of the Road were nomadic by calling, tending to the spidery cracks that had been settled but not blessed.

'I spent a lot of time in Sol.' He gestured to the window where strings of shells from the southern coast hung, waiting for the weather to be warm enough for open shutters and music-calling breeze.

On the borders, then. 'In the war?' The western territory of Seda was one that broke away from the Union nearly fifty years back.

He laughed. 'Do I look like someone who went to war? Shall I tell you shiver tales of heretic generals and their demons?'

Csilla shook her head. She'd cared for veterans in her mercy work, and they didn't speak of war so lightly. Seda had once been two territories, under the care of Arany and Ezüst, respectively, before Arany had settled herself fully in Silgard and Ezüst agreed to look after her people as his own. Perhaps that early abandonment was why they didn't accept the Union, and soldiers claimed they had dark forces in their army. It was ridiculous – even before Seda had broken off, the demons had been sealed and the bloodlines that could spawn Sotir wiped clean. It was nothing but their powder weapons that made demons out of ordinary men.

Or so she would have thought before Shadow had leaked into their city. She knew everything about the creation of the world, very little about how it was actually run.

She took a deeper drink, the honey not quite covering the herbs, as if it could wash down her discomfort. Tamas watched her closely, chin propped on laced hands, as if studying every bob of her throat. She forced down a cough.

'Thank you for that, and for speaking with me.'

He paused, still watching her with a curious expression. Then he shook his head slightly, whatever reverie had taken him dissipating. 'Shouldn't you have an escort? I'll go with you if you like.'

She started to say it was kind of him, then shook her head. There was no guarantee their little trap had caught the person they were after, and if the killer was still looking for someone involved with Mihály, there was no better target than Csilla. It could also put Tamas in danger, and she didn't want to draw that onto him.

But there were no footsteps trailing her, not even a prickle of unease as she walked towards the cemetery through grey streets and the scant moonlight. Curfew was soon, and though her hand and jaw still ached, Mihály needed her. It was enough to make her go on.

When she found him, he was asleep against the tomb, medicine bottle loose in hand. Sighing, she took his shoulders and propped him up a little straighter, then wiped the drool from his lips. Even that didn't cause him to stir.

'Mihály.'

His eyelids fluttered. She pressed a palm to his cheek in case her hands would stir his blood. He turned his face and closed his eyes firmly.

'You're going to let yourself freeze out here? You're practically setting yourself up as bait.'

And if she thought that would work, maybe she'd let him. But the killer only seemed interested in those who listened to him, and might even be with the inquisitors now with everything gone so toppled over.

He didn't respond. She looked around the cemetery. There was no one else save a dim figure wiping down a grave on the far side and a few ash-coloured pigeons claiming the highest points of the domed stone to roost on.

'Mihály!' Perhaps she should kick him while she didn't have a soul to blacken.

The person across the way was looking at them now. Csilla swallowed hard and crouched down close. 'Come on. We have to go.'

'She's not here yet.' Mihály's words were brittle in their frustration. 'She's always here, but I can't see her.' He curled his fingers around the side of the crypt as if he could shake the ghost from the stone.

'Do you think she'll come at all? The Seal has weakened. Maybe . . . maybe ghosts went with it.' It felt cruel to say, but Tamas had been right that sometimes treatment looked like torture from the outside.

'Asten lives in my blood, diluted as it is,' he said simply. 'The Church's power doesn't matter, gone or not.'

Not to you, she thought with a frown, though there was comfort in the reminder. The divine meant hope. Csilla tugged on his arm, but she'd have had better luck moving the stone. Perhaps a different tactic would be more persuasive.

'I'm sure she doesn't want you to freeze.'

He half-lifted his shoulder in what could have been a shrug. 'I've stayed out in worse.'

Csilla sat down next to him, deftly removing the bottle and pouring the pungent remains on the ground, just in case he decided to self-medicate further back to where he couldn't even listen to reason. It wouldn't affect the sleep of the dead.

He opened his eyes to glare. 'That was not easy to brew.'

She let the bottle drop on the brown and trampled grass. 'I don't care.'

‘Well, that’s a first.’ There was a depth in his eyes like the river on days it was exceptionally still and dark. How could he be so educated and handsome and yet so completely, bafflingly self-destructive? The charming man he’d shown her the first night they’d met had all but disappeared.

‘I care about you,’ she said finally, ‘which is why I am here in this cemetery and not somewhere warmer. Why don’t you go see Tamas? He wants to help you, you know. He tried to help me.’

She might not have welcomed his attempts to push her away, but that didn’t make them not a kindness.

A few late-season snowflakes drifted to kiss her hair, sharp white crystals on the breath of the night air to remind them that while it might already be third month, the weather made no promises. Csilla stared at the clouded sky in despair. Men who drank froze quickly, and she had no way to move him. She unfastened her cloak and spread it across the pair of them, settling herself in beside him. He was barely warm.

‘What are you doing?’ The touch of concern in his voice softened the brittleness of her irritation.

‘I want to meet this soul.’ She had to face the girl he wanted her to become.

Mihály sighed. ‘I don’t know if you’ll be able to sense her, even if she’s here, even with my power. Have you ever seen a ghost?’

Some of the novitiates whispered of things haunting the halls of the cathedral, rites gone wrong and angry spirits, people who had loved too much to even give it up for eternal joy, those who feared eternal cold. Some of the braver ones tried to summon them and had their ears boxed for it.

Any ‘ghosts’ were the cats, with their quick feet and ability to appear and disappear like spirits.

‘No,’ she admitted. ‘I looked for them, though.’ For a while, imagining her family had died had seemed a more pleasant fantasy than the idea that they'd left her. 'No one came and asked for me, so I thought . . .'

She'd checked and wiped every monument in the cemetery, offered candles and wine and endless tears. The spirits hadn't seemed to notice, though the mercy priests praised her secretly selfish dedication to the dead.

Her chest squeezed with the shame of it.

Mihály rubbed his eyes as if trying for sobriety. Then he shifted and put an arm around her, pulling her to his chest with an awkward thump. It was like being embraced by a drunk but friendly bear, and she squirmed, but he held fast. Finally, she sighed and relaxed, letting her cheek settle on the coarse wool of his coat.

His breath slowed. He was falling asleep again.

More snowflakes landed on her makeshift blanket, sparkling crystals glittering for a moment before melting into dark spots on the fabric.

Where were the ghosts? And where in this cemetery did she belong?

The sounds of the city beyond the walls grew fainter with people making their way in for the night. Her nostrils burned with every frosted breath as the snowfall picked up.

'What would it take to get you to leave?' she asked finally. Waiting for ghosts was all well and good, but his split lip needed cleaning.

He muttered something that sounded enough like 'nothing' to make her roll her eyes.

'Come on. You miss her all day. Let her miss you one night. And Madame Varga will worry if you don't come back.'

'We have plenty of time.' He lolled his head to rest it on her, and she sighed at the extra weight.

Did he not realise the early dark was already here? Finally she hit upon the one thing she could offer.

'Come back and I'll stay with you all night. You won't be alone, and you won't be cold.'

He hummed interest against her skin and his hand slid from her shoulder to skate down her arm. She flushed, but at least she had his attention.

'Last time, you left.'

She turned her head to look into his eyes, their faces so close he was all she could see, his breath warming her cold-nipped skin. She hadn't known he'd realised when she'd slipped away.

'This time I won't.' She reached up and brushed the cut on his mouth, crusted with darkening blood, before he leaned further in. 'Can't you heal yourself?'

'I could,' he conceded, turning to kiss her fingertips and smiling at her shiver. 'But I like being tended to.'

She stifled a groan and closed her free hand around the cloth on his coat. 'Come on. We've had a bad day, but . . .'

He caught her by the chin, and she flinched where his thumb jabbed the blooming bruise.

'And you want to make it better?' He reeked of potent wormwood, his honey-brown eyes liquid dark. 'Did you see them? They don't trust me anymore. And do you think any one of them was possessed?'

She softened at his pain. No matter his faults, he loved his followers.

'They're scared.'

His hand slid to her neck, the pressure of each finger a blade against the skin, cutting her voice to a choking whisper.

'We're *all* scared. But staying out here won't help. It's time to go . . .' She faltered, tongue heavy. The Varga estate wasn't home, and never would be. 'Back.'

He paused, face lit with desperation and moonlight. 'And you won't leave?'

She regretted the offer now that his hands were hot in her hair and against her waist, but she knew the rawness in his voice – she had the same painful spot, well-coated as it was with faith.

'No.' She stopped pulling and leaned into him instead. This cheek pressed to his woollen coat, the guilty ache gnawing at her . . . they were just another way of showing mercy.

'I won't leave.'

21

Csilla

A SCREAM ECHOED in the dark cathedral hallway, bouncing off stone and into Csilla's ears.

She shuddered, stomach clenching, offering a small and useless prayer of solace as she rubbed her fingers together, nails stained with traces of Arany's gold that she'd brushed as she passed the statue. No one had given her a second look as she entered. Wrapped in a wool cloak dyed a dear robin's egg blue, brown hair uncovered and curled loose around her shoulders, she looked like any other citizen come to beg something of the Church, not belong to it.

It was a part to be played, but it fit worse than the dress. As she hurried through the cloister walkways towards the rooms where the Church's justice was dealt, she kept her head down, pulling her hood up whenever she heard footsteps. It wasn't only that she couldn't risk being seen. She wasn't sure she could bear it.

Perhaps she should have waited for Mihály to fully wake, but it had been enough of a challenge to get him in motion and into a proper bed before sunrise. At least he'd slept; with him breathing in her hair and kicking her in the throes of sweat-soaked nightmares, she'd barely had a chance to close her eyes. She'd kept her promise, but what sleep she had gotten felt haunted. All she could see was the cracked eyelids of corpses and her ears were full with the whispers of a dead girl, urgent and rattling.

When she'd tried to rouse him in the morning, even over-steeped tea and thick liver paste on thicker toast with enough paprika to make her sneeze hadn't been enough to chase away his hangover, and he waved her off with a groan and promised to join her later.

When she arrived outside the chambers, tucking herself beside a painted wood icon of Ignaz and her many-tailed lash, the sounds of pain leaking from beneath the door made her wish she had waited. While she wanted to know if there had been any pay-off to their gamble, she wasn't sure she wanted to face Ilan. Or if he'd even talk to her – he certainly seemed to have gotten what he wanted last night. No matter what small favours Ilan did for her, she shouldn't forget where his loyalties lay. The muffled cries of his victims were as much her fault as if she'd been the one flogging them.

When the man limped out, cradling his shirt to his chest as red welts swelled on his back, Csilla's stomach lurched. She stepped forward, wanting to offer something, but her hands and pockets were empty, and he wouldn't meet her eyes to let her soothe him with words.

Ilan followed minutes later, starting at her but recovering quickly. He didn't look put out in the slightest, save a light sheen of sweat from the exertion. She swallowed back an admonishment, knowing her anger should be turned in at herself. Ilan had never claimed to be anything but what he was, and she was the one who had put Mihály's followers into his hands. Justice was a virtue. If this could be called justice.

'Did any of them tell you anything helpful?' That would at least make this worth it.

Ilan's gaze slid across the empty hall, silently chiding her for recklessness. He gestured for her to follow him.

Ilan's room wasn't any different from the small rooms used by the other clergy members privileged enough to be granted privacy, everything simple and serviceable. As he shut the door, though, he reached up and slid an extra chain lock on the inside. The untarnished iron was stark against the centuries of wear around it.

'You shouldn't be here. What if it hadn't been me in there? What excuse would you have given then?'

She didn't have an answer, and her shoulders sank.

'Well I could hardly *not* come. You don't have to beat them, you know.' They hadn't punished Mihály's followers before, merely warned them, and surely just being dragged into the cathedral was enough to make them honest in their answers. 'They'll think themselves martyrs and hate us even more.'

'Consider it a blessing. The riot means I was able to interrogate them for something they actually *did*. Everyone in the city is going to end up on the rack at some point if Sandor keeps on, and at least this might be useful.'

Fair enough point. But something in it rankled her. These people weren't just part of a puzzle to be solved or a collection of clues. They were alive, and they hurt.

'But did they actually know anything?' She crossed her arms, bracing for the answer she'd come for.

Ilan paused, an annoyed twitch on his cheek. 'No. Not yet. But we're not done.'

Her stomach dropped.

'So we've got nothing.' Yanking their single thread had pulled the piecemeal cloth to tatters. 'None of them are guilty at all? What do their souls say?'

The cold anger she'd seen in Ilan's eyes as he pulled her away from fists and curses returned.

'Nothing so dark as murder. Certainly not possession. And none of them have seen any sign of demons here, though the stories the refugees tell are horrors.'

Csilla turned away from the window and sunk down on his bed. She spread her hand on the grey blanket, imagining the Seal beneath her fingers, the faint glow on the stone and dirt and bone below. Mihály would be sick over putting his followers under Ilan's striking hand for nothing, and she would be sick over bringing him the news.

She was sick now with how she'd only made everything worse for the people she wanted to help. And Ilan didn't seem to think anything of it beyond how it affected progress in their case. She studied his face and the calm there, nothing sweet in it, but not even the slightest touch of guilt.

He turned, a thoughtful tilt to his head, and she pulled her gaze away and pretended she was studying the wall behind him instead.

'Would you like to pray? You do still do that, don't you?' Ilan asked, kneeling in front of his altar.

He lit a stick of incense, and her nose twitched at the note of fir resin under the warm spice of myrrh. It called up the forest more than the worship hall. She eyed his icons with curiosity. Beside the Eye of Asten was an image of shadowy Ignaz, aloof in her justice, and Sainted Vasya with her wolves. There was even a rendition of Gellért's forest, beautifully translucent. All were as detailed as the most expensive of illuminated manuscripts, and the style had a certain ring of familiarity.

'Did you do these?' Apparently he was skilled at more than just sketching the dead. She had an urge to pick them up and study, but his look stopped her.

'I asked if you prayed.'

'Not enough.' She couldn't remember the last time she'd tried to properly speak to the divine. It didn't seem to matter as much when she had Mihály beside her. She gathered her skirts and got to her knees, self-conscious as she tried to maintain some semblance of grace.

'I'll pray for the people you've got in there. And Mihály, I suppose.' She could pray that he would rouse and be well and that he wouldn't need her quite so close tonight.

Ilan's eyes swept over her as she fidgeted with her layers. When they stopped, there was a new crease in his brow and a curl to his lip.

'Are you in love with him?'

Oh.

'No.' Unfortunately. That, at least, would be something other people could understand. 'I just think he could use it.'

'You worry for him an awful lot.'

An exasperated laugh bubbled up in her throat. If that were the criteria, she was in love with the whole world.

'By all the saints, I wish I *were* in love with him; it would certainly make things easier. But I'm not. And I worry about you too, you know.'

Ilan looked abashed, a slight redness rising on his pale cheeks. 'I don't need you to worry about me.'

As if not needing to worry had ever stopped a single worrier. 'I suppose you don't, with the new inquisitor so pleased with you.'

His eyebrows raised, and she flinched, placation rising in her throat. She really hadn't meant for that to come out. 'Excuse me?'

She shifted, looking everywhere but his narrowed blue eyes.

'I'm . . .' *Sorry* was the first word on her tongue, but she didn't want to apologise. 'I thought you didn't like him. But you still took everyone in when he ordered it.'

'That was always the plan, Csilla. He only thinks it was his own idea. I still loathe him, but he was momentarily useful. You don't have to like the people you work with, especially in such vital matters.'

It felt like a direct dig, and she stared into her lap. Well, she'd never planned to be liked. It didn't matter.

'The result is what's important, not the means,' Ilan continued. 'I'm loyal to the principles of the Church. I know my place. As I thought you did.'

She raised her eyes to meet his, unable to answer.

They never gave you a choice, came Tamas's mocking voice again. But she'd made a choice anyway. She'd chosen the Church. She'd chosen to help.

Sometimes it seemed like those things weren't the same, a worry always just out of sight in the dusty corners of her mind.

But Ilan would never understand that. He was already turning to his prayers, lips moving silently. With no one to glare at, his face was calm and assured, and she would have traded anything for a moment of that peace. She used to find it so easily here, taking comfort in ritual so old it left physical marks; stone worn down by praying knees and ceilings stained to smudge with candle smoke. Now everything was jagged.

He opened his eyes, and she flinched at being caught. 'Yes?'

'I . . .' She held out her hand. 'Ágnes always said that it might help Them listen. To me.' Her words grew small with flustered embarrassment. No one else in the Union needed a conduit. Least of all Ilan.

If he did take her hand, she could at least absorb a touch of his confidence, if not his blessing. She would give anything for even a fraction of that self-assurance.

He pushed her hand into her lap. 'You're not a child. You can pray for yourself.'

She shouldn't have expected better. But her face must have shown her disappointment because he beckoned her to kneel closer to him. Together they leaned against his altar, and if she wasn't entirely comforted, at least she wasn't alone. Shared weariness was still companionable.

Please help us. Please come back. We've messed everything up, but we're trying.

The prayer was hollow. She didn't want to deliver empty thoughts to equally empty air. All her cold fingers wanted was Ágnes, her body hungry for the safety of sitting with someone who loved her. She sucked back what might have been a sob.

'You can go to her if you like.' Ilan opened his eyes again, though they flickered with hesitation. 'She's been worse lately.' Csilla pressed her lips.

'How did you know I was thinking . . .'

'You're easy to read. And I do also have a mother.'

She supposed he must, though she couldn't picture him as a child. The idea of his sharp expression on a small, rounded face was vaguely unsettling.

'Ágnes no longer goes on mercy rounds, and I wouldn't be surprised if she goes into anchorage soon,' he continued.

The ill and elderly went into anchorage when they were ready for deliverance, spending their time in solitary prayer and writing their reflections to guide the future members of the Church. It was meant to be a joyous time, the culmination of a life lived in Brilliance. But when Csilla thought of Ágnes spending her last days alone, with no visitors or care, her chest seized so strongly she lost her breath.

'I don't know if she'd even want to see me,' she said after a moment. Ágnes had been so disappointed in her when she found her in the cell. She could only be more so to find that Csilla hadn't taken any of her advice.

'It's up to you. But it might be your last chance.'

She opened her mouth to protest again, but the soft determination in his eyes stopped her.

'For her sake, Csilla.'

The words were another Church-sanctioned kindness that felt like pain. She nodded, trying to reconcile the priest who caused the agony that still rang in her ears with the man before her, urging her to do what she was made for: comfort. Regardless of his personal feelings, he understood her. She would try to offer the same.

'Thank you.'

Ágnes was in her room, lap draped in fur and a copy of the writ, and she was sleeping. It was relief and pain in one. If she was too ill to tend to others and take mercy missions, she'd be sick in heart as well as in body.

'Ágnes?' Csilla crouched before her, placing a gentle hand upon her knee. The older woman's thin lashes fluttered, and she looked down with rheumy eyes.

'If I wasn't still so cold, I'd say this was a vision. A welcome one,' she added at Csilla's worried frown. 'Why are you here?'

'You,' Csilla answered, achingly aware that wasn't the whole of it. 'I hope they've been helping you.' It didn't look like it.

'I help myself, and Erzsébet keeps my lap warm. I'm glad to see you,' Ágnes said, and Csilla lit with guilt. 'But you're still only in Silgard because of the heretic, aren't you?'

Ágnes always had been able to see right through to the truth of Csilla. It didn't take blood to know a daughter.

'Yes.' But only until I can come back, she added silently. It was one of a thousand little darknesses that would be swept away in greater glory once they saved the city. 'I can't leave Silgard. I don't want to leave you.'

Ágnes touched her cheek. Sitting at her feet was like being young again, being read to on long, lazy afternoons, told it was because she was bright and loved the word best. She'd only learned much later those afternoons had been when families were coming to take other children. Ágnes had tried to spare her the pain of being passed over by making her feel chosen, darkening her own soul with the lie. Just like she was doing now, allowing Csilla to sit where she didn't belong and take up her precious seconds, soft tokens of affection worth more than any gift.

'I'll be gone soon, Csilla. I've worked with illness too long not to recognise it in myself. I'm not hastening it, trust me,' she soothed Csilla's small noise of distress. 'But there's nothing to be done.' She swallowed back a shaking cough. 'Here, I'll read to you. Asten hasn't taken my eyes yet, so there's that blessing.'

'No, let me.' Csilla took the book from her lap and settled back. She leaned her head against Ágnes's legs, in tears at the gentle pressure of a hand on her head. 'If it gets worse, you will tell me before you go into anchorage, right? You can send word through Ilan. He knows where to find me.'

A person's final days were between them and Asten. But Ágnes stroked her hair gently and nodded.

'I will, dearest.'

Csilla nodded and opened the book to a saint story, one of the first she'd memorised when she was small: St. Ferdek's miracle that brought a springing well to a parched town and saved thousands overnight. The angel Orsolya had given him a running crown of her tears, and the illustration had always reminded Csilla of her dozen unlucky baptisms. The madder and azure were more faded than she remembered, years of finger pressure eroding the crispness of the pages.

She used to love to think about the miracles and how wonderful it was that divine magic came to save.

Now what lay on her heart was how terrible it was that people needed saving. People could find meaning in suffering but that didn't mean it meant anything on its own. If Asten were here, and just, Their creation wouldn't have to hurt. They wouldn't have let it break, leaving Shadow and pain.

'Do you think,' she asked carefully, forming the delicate words like they were bubbles of spun glass, 'Asten intends to come back at all?'

Among the questionable games a pack of orphans with little supervision played was one of holding their heads underwater in a trough to see who could hold their breath the longest. In the end, everyone came up, but whoever won the game had a headache and sore chest for their prize.

What was happening now didn't feel like worship. It felt like that standoff, and the world on the edge of drowning.

'That doesn't sound like you,' Ágnes frowned, leaning forward slightly. 'I know your road is hard, but don't make it harder with doubt.'

How? she wanted to ask.

From far below came the shrill whistle of alarm, quick blasts that could only mean death. She stood so quickly her knee popped.

'Csilla?' Ágnes reached a hand out. 'That was the alarm. Stay here.'

'I know,' she said, leaning forward to kiss the old woman's cheek, catching the scent of the mint oils used on sore bodies in a last effort to soothe aches.

'That's why I have to go.'

22

Ilan

THE WOODEN cart clacked as it was rolled into the churchyard, the faces of the young inquisitorial priests drawing it grim. There were already other priests and curious novices darkening the courtyard, and from the corner of his eye he could see Csilla skirting the edges, no doubt summoned by the bells. She didn't look any more settled for having been to see Ágnes. This certainly wasn't going to help.

'Where was the body found?'

He pulled back the millet-stained tablecloth that had been draped over the old man, not even bothering to feign surprise at the marks on his wrinkled and pocked skin, another line in the cruel prayer. The corpse's mouth was open in a frozen gape, revealing holes where rotted teeth had fallen, and from the body came a stench of fetid rot. The man's eyeballs had already begun to shrink, the skin around them purpling and falling loose. He reached to tug the veiny eyelids down out of respect and habit.

The young priest who had pulled the cart was explaining, still half-panting with exertion.

'By the southern wall. He was at home. A mercy worker found the body when they were taking treatments.'

'Are they here? Where is his family?'

'No family that we could locate, and the one who found him went with the High Inquisitor. I don't know . . .'

'I know him.' Csilla's voice was clear as she stepped forward, far more steady than it had any right to be. Her hazel eyes were watery, but her mouth resigned, and Ilan gestured for the priests to move back and let her through.

'Svoboda Elmere.' She walked close to the cart and brushed the wisps of white hair on his forehead, on skin that was still warm. 'He didn't have any family here.'

The small, sad smile on her face pinched something inside him.

'Did he . . .' If he was one of the Izir's, at least it was confirmation.

'Yes.' Csilla tenderly put the cloth back around the corpse, smoothing it with the care of a mother putting down a baby. 'I'd promised him . . .'

The other priests looked at her, confused, but it seemed they hadn't made the connection between the mercy girl everyone tried to ignore and this noble daughter dressed in wool and fur, and one put his hand on her shoulder.

'Step back, girl. You can't help him. We'll take him to those who can, now.'

Csilla's eyes widened, a struck expression as she was guided away from the body. He almost wanted to tell them to let her stay, but they still had parts to play. She was a wealthy woman of Silgard who let the Faith deal with the rawness of life and death. He was the Church's impeccable servant, with no connection to heresy.

Any worry for Csilla was chased away by the thrum of footfalls. A young inquisitorial priest, just sworn at the end of the year, ran through the gate, her breath heaving.

'Is the High Inquisitor here?' Her dark eyes darted between faces, landing nowhere like a fly unsure of its footing.

Ilan raised his hand. 'No. But we have the body. Sandor is with the mercy priest who found it.' Or so Ilan was told.

'Oh, you've got the body then, that's—' The woman glanced at the man and drew back. 'But he's got both his hands?'

There was an intake of breath that had to be Csilla, and the hair on the back of Ilan's neck prickled.

'Should he not?' The bodies had never been mutilated in that way before. 'Why are you here?'

Her throat bobbed in a heavy swallow. 'Because I found something worse.'

'Worse than a body?' Two bodies, perhaps? Either the killer was growing bolder, or they had accomplices.

The woman swallowed, grim. 'Depends. What do you think of part of one?'

He spared a last glance at Csilla, who was still looking only at the dead man in the cart, her fingers worrying at the cape knot at her throat. Then he turned and followed the priest to see what new trouble had arisen.

A ribby, fawn-coloured dog trotted back and forth in the circle of horrified onlookers just inside the western gate, a bloated hand covered in dirt and blackening bite marks in its mouth.

'Why did they let it in?' one said, his face paling as the dog shook his prize and a jaundiced nail fell from a sausage-swollen finger.

'It must have startled the guard.' Another was repeatedly touching his mark, oily fingerprints marring the metal.

The hand was unsightly but hardly more than the other bodies they had been dealing with. Ilan pushed his way in front, to the dog whose wary look didn't stop him from a slow wag of his tail and coming to sit.

Ilan put a gentle hand out to allow a sniff of introduction, then rubbed the dog's floppy ears. They were still puppy-soft, and the dog's tail thumped in the dirt, rump wiggling with pleasure that at least someone was acknowledging his good deed. He must have belonged to one of the pilgrims or refugees and run off after game. Or perhaps he was the loyal friend of whoever owned the hand.

'Well done. Drop it.'

The dog's tail wagged harder, and he dropped the hand. Ilan continued his ministrations as he inspected the pale bone, gristle, and what wrinkled skin was left. The wrist was jagged, mottled with dozens of small abrasions. This had been chewed off, not sliced, and there were no scraps of clothing to help identify who it was. There was only so much he could do with a lump of greying flesh.

He gave the dog another appraising look, glad the pup wasn't trying to lick him.

'Have there been any reports of missing persons on the road?' He turned and looked at the gathered crowd, most of them not wanting to meet his eyes.

Everyone shook their heads in turn.

If it were a citizen of the Immaculate Union, it was their duty to find the body and ensure it had rites. The last thing they needed was someone using the body for a Shadow ritual. The flesh there would be a bounty for the damned. The deaths had breached the city's borders, and they had to take responsibility.

'Bring me something to wrap this,' he said, and after flustered hesitation one of the men ran down to a baker and grabbed a bread bag. Ilan shook off what he could of the dusting of flour and wrapped the hand.

The dog was still wagging his tail, and Ilan offered him another bit of praise. He didn't know how well he'd done.

'Ilan. Does your . . . dog need a blessing?'

Prelate Abe raised an eyebrow as they approached the altar of the sanctuary hall. The dog trotted along at Ilan's heels, though whether it was from having decided on a new master or worry over what would happen to his prize, he couldn't say. The creature's nails clipped on the marble tile of the floor as they passed by the dark benches of the nave, his footfalls echoing in the vaulted ceiling in quick staccato.

'Sit,' Ilan said as they reached the altar and its burning Eye, and the pup sank down on his haunches. At least he seemed trained and not inclined to pee on the pews.

'He brought us something.' Ilan unwrapped the hand, now smeared chalky and spectral. The curled fingers grimly beckoned to the Prelate.

'Is this related to the murders?' Abe gestured blessing over the hand, then another to be sure.

'Unclear. I'd like to go look,' Ilan continued. 'Perhaps the dog will lead us back to the body.'

'It's beyond your jurisdiction,' Sandor said, coming in from behind. As large as the sanctuary was, it became suffocating with his presence. 'Is there any sign of dark magic on the bones?'

The dog tensed beside Ilan with a low whine.

'No,' Ilan answered. The hand was just a hand. But the fact that it was *just* a hand was a problem in itself.

Sandor huffed. 'Then that body can sit until we've dealt with the latest one here. It's dangerous out there now. You've seen how we've weakened. Every priest is needed in our walls.'

Ilan seethed, reaching down to touch the dog to diffuse his anger. 'Every soul is sacred.'

'Chase down one of the bard-priests. They're the ones who handle such things.' Sandor gestured to the hand. 'It could even be a deserter, damned anyway. Burn the hand or throw it out – something will eat it.'

'The Servants of the Road do holy work,' Abe chided. Sandor at least looked abashed. One didn't insult the other branches of clergy, even if their work was mostly travel and stories and the occasional rite. Not everyone was called to work in Silgard or serve the Incarnate.

'And you yourself told me how busy they are,' Ilan interjected. 'What with us having to burn our own bodies.'

Sandor stiffened, though Ilan couldn't read if it were anger or surprise.

'Say rites over the hand and burn it if you must, and I'll send word that if anyone sees anything suspicious, they should report it. It's unfortunate, but we have to remember the greater danger.'

Leaving a soul was unfortunate? Caring for souls was the least of Asten's commands. Suspicion crawled through him again, a dozen quiet notes that couldn't be silenced. He thought of Csilla and her last terrible hope that hadn't been extinguished. She was being offered bloody rebirth and salvation, and though the admission was a dank rot, he wanted her to have it. This was part of that.

Perhaps his own sheen had dulled. He reflexively reached for the glass in his pocket.

'A dark thought cross your mind?' Sandor asked as the glass lit in Ilan's palm. He stared, looking for the judgement his lie of omission would bring.

The surface glowed pale, no smoke-shadows creeping through the opalescent sheen. If anything, it was brighter.

'You look surprised by your own virtue.' There was a cut to Sandor's words.

'It's simply nice to have my virtue confirmed.' He held it out, still luminous. 'If your methods are so righteous, let me see.'

The older man hesitated, then took it. There was a sheen on the surface, but in the centre, drops of blackened sin. Ilan let out a chuff.

'And you lecture *me* about obedience? You require penance.' Whatever it was looked too dark to be a simple lie or stray lustful thought.

Abe raised a hand.

'Ilan. Not everyone is as assured of their blessing as you. You'll find darkness on every soul here. You'll find darkness on the Incarnate himself. That is why we serve; because we understand what it is to sin.'

'He needs—'

'Allow me to speak plainly, Ilan.' Sandor looked ready to throw the glass, but clutched it instead. 'I know who you are and that you think having given up every luxury possible to play hero to the Church makes you self-sacrificing, special, when the position you took was one you dearly wanted anyway. I know you think you earned your former title when it's your father's gold that paid for last year's repairs.'

The rage that rose was like the snap signalling an avalanche. He was going to punch the other man in the face.

'Sandor.'

It was Abe who stepped inbetween them, and Ilan felt a bolt of shame at resorting to being handled like children brawling in the street.

'We do not bring up our servants' pasts. They come to us as they are, for what reason they do.'

That was true, and Sandor would know it. The ire ebbed, leaving more suspicion. The low blow was a tactic to knock him from his course.

'Prelate. The Incarnate is returning and pilgrims along with him; the roads need to be pristine. There will be merchants, celebrations. We can't have bodies on the road.'

It wasn't celebrants crowding the city now. It was terrified refugees.

'We've seen no sign of bodies on the *road*,' Sandor said. 'And the people coming to the city are all the more reason we need everyone to stay here and protect them. This could be old, and from anywhere in the woods.'

'Not that old,' Ilan said. He'd become quite an expert in the ageing of dead flesh.

'And what of the latest murder? You'd put that aside for something that might not be murder at all?'

'I'm not putting it aside. I'm being thorough. We all should be.' It was on the tip of his tongue to point out the latest marks and their bloody poetry, to beg them to consider the stories refugees were telling more carefully.

Instinct won out, barely. Sandor had already rebuffed him once. If Abe also refused to accept that the weakened Seal was actual dark magic and not just a matter of faith, Ilan would find himself branded a heretic and no longer in any place to do anything at all.

'Very well,' Sandor said after a moment of standoff. 'If you're so concerned, you can go. You're excused from our rounds if the Prelate thinks it wise.'

Abe nodded. 'We shouldn't abandon those seeking refuge here. They are ours, in the gates or out of it.'

Ilan tried not to let the surprise show on his face. 'Thank you. I'll take—'

'You'll go alone.' Sandor followed.

They never went out alone.

'That doesn't seem safe.' Ilan was confident in himself, but extra eyes were always helpful.

'Walking around in a forest scares you?' Sandor's smirk galled. 'Still on about your demon tales? Well, if you don't think it's safe, stay here. I'm not sending more priests who are needed to defend a place more holy.'

Ilan weighed the options and took a quieting breath. Instinct rarely led him wrong, and instinct told him to go. And to take Mihály. Finally the Izir could be useful for something.

'Fine,' he said. 'I'll report what I find. Come,' he told the dog.

'And throw that cur out of the city while you're there. It's likely diseased if it's been feasting on corpses.' Disgust dripped from Sandor's words.

Well, the dog was thin, his yellow-brown coat patchy, and he was in bad need of a delousing, but his eyes were clear, his temperament good. Ilan had grown up sneaking his father's hunting pack into his rooms on cold nights, and this pup would be an equally pleasant addition to their staff.

Sandor's annoyed scowl didn't fade as Ilan considered. That was the best argument for keeping the dog.

'He's my dog now, and he will stay with me.'

The dog seemed to understand, stopping when his new master did and thumping his tail in confused happiness. Hopefully he continued to behave and didn't chase the cats.

Abe shrugged. 'It may prove useful to have a hound about. As long as he stays clean and you feed him, he's welcome to live out with your horse. Besides, he's likely to know where he found the corpse. Makes for quick work.'

Ilan smiled, but it was the smallest of victories.

It would be a blessing if the owner of the hand was the only body outside.

23

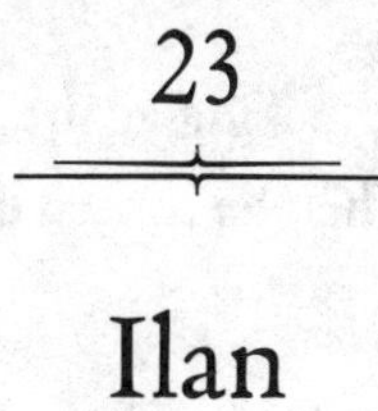

Ilan

THE DOG pulled at the leash, nose alternating between the ground and the air. As he dragged Ilan and Mihály off the road and through brown brush tangle, his ears were pricked and his steps quick and sure.

At least one of them knew where they were going.

The Izir was uncharacteristically silent, trudging behind without a single comment about the ridiculousness of Ilan being forced to rely on him for protection. He should be grateful that the man wasn't picking over the scabs of their failed plan or Ilan's treatment of his followers, but the tense quiet was fertile ground for stewing over thoughts of being sent out here alone, as if his very rational plan was something Sandor was only humouring. At least Csilla had agreed to stay in the city, writing to Elmere's family. The Church wouldn't let her do anything else for him, and it meant one less person and her feelings to worry about.

The dog stopped, the short fur of his ruff raising. His barks echoed off the trees as he paced at the base of a knobby oak.

The ground was like any other part of the forest, grey and brown leaf litter with curls of hopeful vines springing through in spots, but there were broken branches, the pale and stringy roots of bushes knocked over. Signs of a struggle that were more than damage from old snowfall or passing badgers.

Mihály moved in front, kicking at the underbrush, then bending over to pull some aside. When he turned back, his face was pale.

'He's here. Partially.'

Ilan breathed a prayer.

The woods hadn't been kind to the body. Fresh meat was hard to come by before litters were born, and the animals, possibly even humans, had left the man in scraps. His eyes had been picked out to hollows, the meat of his cheek shredded to bone and the cords of his throat sharp and pale. A few early flies crawled over the blackening gash where the hand had been attached.

There was no clothing, not even tatters. A human had to have been involved somehow, if only to rob the man and leave him for dead. Animals wouldn't have stripped him.

Ilan pulled the straining dog to heel and offered the lead to Mihály.

'Well, we shouldn't leave him. Let's take him to your barn. It will be easier to examine him there.'

Carrion birds cast slow scythe-winged shadows, waiting for a chance to steal a few more bites. Bigger, hungrier things might be pacing out of sight. Ilan glanced over at Mihály. The pair of them would be no match for a winter-starved wolf pack or a ravenous bear just out of hibernation.

One good thing about travelling with Mihály: he was big enough to carry the man's body and barely look winded, and he'd held his tongue about the smell. Within the hour they'd gotten an old tablecloth from the farmstead, one moulded with disuse, and wrapped the body. They pulled it onto the table, scattering the stiff animal corpses like so many children's game tiles. Mihály straightened the corpse, laying him out with scientific precision. If he didn't look pleased, neither did he look sick, and that was all Ilan required.

Most of the damage had been done by nature, which was, if cruel, at least not evil. The person was of average height and what was left of the hair was mussed and dirty blond over the patches of scalp. The breadth of him, though . . . He'd had plenty of weight on him before he was attacked. Not like someone living on the outskirts of society or who would be begging for a spot in the Brilliant City. A man who had wealth enough to eat like that was a man who would be missed.

And yet there had been no reports.

'You can see souls,' he said, looking at Mihály. 'Allegedly.'

The Izir paused from where he was straightening the corpse's legs. 'If they're here. This one is long gone, may it rest wherever it is now. There weren't any ghosts in the woods.'

That was only to be expected. It would have been all too convenient if Mihály could simply tell them who the man had been, or if a ghost was lingering to answer their questions.

He wanted to snap bones. A frustrated scream lived in his throat, pushed deep, but always waiting.

Perhaps Sandor had been right. What did it matter if the man was in the woods or in the grave? There were bites on his chest, the print of carrion birds and opportunistic things, but no marks.

'Do you have incense?' he asked. Mihály nodded and went to collect it as Ilan probed the corpse.

It was likely the man had been robbed and left, not just murdered. He rolled him enough to check the back, the skull. No bruising or fractures. But the neck was gruesome.

He tilted up the jaw, ignoring the exposed bone. The majority of the soft tissues had been torn away, but the lines along the edges were crisp. Clean.

His arm instinctively drew over, mimicking the motion of the killer. A swift slice from behind.

How had the man not heard it coming? Perhaps it was a drunk after all.

'Killing him all over again?' Mihály asked, his tone mild. In addition to the incense, he had paper, a pitcher of water and a reasonably clean linen towel. Good to see he had some basic knowledge.

'Did they teach you rites at University?' It wasn't a part of the general student curriculum, but Izir were rare enough to be special cases in a number of circumstances. He'd only met one before Mihály, a tall woman who visited his mother after his eldest brother's death. She hadn't been terribly good comfort either, though she'd been kind enough to take all of Ilan's questions with perfect seriousness.

'No, I never took much education in doctrine. Maybe I should have.'

Ilan gave a little laugh. Of course he wouldn't have had to study for any part of his blessing. He pulled a flint, lit the incense, and handed it to Ilan.

Sweet sandalwood filled the room. Ilan breathed deep as rotten wood and old dust turned as hallowed as any gilded sanctuary.

He dribbled water onto the shrivelled remains of the man's lips, his single hand, his feet, though no toes had been spared by the cold. Mihály followed behind with the cloth, solemn.

'Asten, we deliver this man to You. We trust You will weigh his soul, find the balance of Justice and Mercy. His time in this world is done. As You will.'

The words should have held weight, but he wasn't practiced at saying them and didn't know who he was saying them for. Even as a Curate he'd rarely been asked to join rites of comfort.

He took the incense and held it to where the man's nostrils would have been, clearing out any remnants of life. If this were a funeral, friends would speak for him, his family would plead intercessions, excusing any last wrongs he had done in life so he could go clear into the next. They would watch the body for three days, letting anyone who knew him come and offer a goodbye. But neither Ilan or Mihály had any right, and this man's sitting days were long past.

'Do you really believe you could bring him back?'

'If I knew anything about him.' Mihály looked down at the body, his eyes dark. 'Otherwise, everything across the ether is as hard to grasp as smoke.'

'So you know the soul you're providing for Csilla, then?'

Mihály's smile was inscrutable.

He picked up the cloth and put it over the body. He wished he could promise he'd give the man justice. Even the writ was perfunctory with no way to know which saint watched him, and Silgard's Blessed Imre a mile too far to claim him. He finally selected Angyalka. The hanged saint was a strange choice for a death writ, but her choking and pain had been in hopes of getting answers. Answers were what they needed now.

At least this man didn't seem to be related to their other victims. The ritual murders were being confined to the city. Ilan drummed his fingers on the table, turning that over. Confined to the city, but affecting the entire Union.

Mihály was already at the barn door, shrugging off the horror as easily as an ill-fitting jacket. 'Would you like a drink? I have tea and whisky and am more than happy to combine them. Or dispense with the tea altogether.'

Ilan was about to protest, but there was that lump of a body, the ragged flesh beneath, and the rare pain of helplessness stabbing.

'If I drink with you, are you going to tell me more about what you intend?'

Mihály grinned. 'Get me drunk enough, and why not.'

There was a gleam in his eye that was distinctly disturbing, in both the way it lit his face and how the silver-bright hook of it caught Ilan's curiosity.

'Fine.'

He took one cup to Mihály's two, and sipped it slowly, savouring the bitterness and burning. Either the Izir or someone who had gifted this to him knew quality. The dog's head was on his knee, warm and welcome.

It would be nice to be so easily pleased, Ilan thought, scratching behind the dog's ears. The satisfaction of a job well done was something he understood.

Mihály poured another cup, more whisky than tea. Ilan raised an eyebrow but didn't comment. Everyone had their way of coping when faced with mortality. He'd allow it for the moment.

'You perform all rites? You've sworn vows.' Mihály's words were slightly slurred.

Ilan put his drink aside. 'I've sworn vows, yes. I know all the rites, but I only do those related to my duties.' People didn't want someone known for torture handling their children or blessing their marriage.

'Can I confess to you?' He leaned forward and it turned into a lurch, hands clamped.

Ilan's lips parted slightly. 'Is this about the soul? I don't see why you need to make it a confession. You're above my pardon, as you so like to remind me.'

'But you've taken vows. You can't refuse.' Something dark and writhing flashed in his eyes.

'I'm not refusing to shrive you.' Refusal would be a very dark mark against him indeed. 'I'm saying it's stupid. No one ever thought I'd be a good choice for manning a confessional. And to be frank, your sins aren't the type that can be forgiven just by airing them out.' Confession was a first step, not a final one. The final one left scars.

'That's why I want to tell you.' He leaned back, rolling his head to stare at the ceiling and bare his throat. 'I don't want the dull comforts of the congregational priests.'

'This is hardly the place for a proper confession.'

Mihály shrugged. 'Asten the almighty is as present in a beetle's asshole as in the blessed hereafter. Why not here?'

Ilan found himself scratching the dog's ears harder in discomfort, so much so that the dog shook Ilan's hand away with a soft whine.

'Very well. It would be . . . amiss in my duties if I turned you away. But you could also just say whatever it is you want. You've never held back before.' He could quietly seethe, but vows were vows.

There was an awkward pause, and they stared at each other. Ilan waved at him to turn and at least create some illusion of private confession.

'I'm not supposed to be looking at you, you know.' People's tongues were freer when they weren't eye to eye with their judge.

Mihály's cheeks were red with drink, his movements slow as he turned his chair. Ilan straightened his collar. This probably had something to do with Csilla, and the idea needled him. Mihály should know to be careful with someone who'd been starved of affection and was so desperate to make everyone happy. Csilla was as open as the sanctuary, just as vulnerable.

Ilan rubbed his forehead, trying to stave off a headache.

'Power greater than us, hear this man's confession and grant me the power to cleanse him from his sins. Let the darkness be cast out with each word that leaves his lips, and the confession will be met with . . . mercy.' The invocation rang false with every syllable. Mihály was already saved, and Ilan was no comfort.

'Now . . .' Typically they would address a seeker as child, or cousin. He didn't particularly want to call Mihály either of those things. 'Izir. Confess your sins and be forgiven.'

But the other man was quiet.

'Mihály?'

Ilan didn't particularly want to hear his confession, but he'd steeled himself to hear whatever lurid things were going to leave the Izir's lips, and he was ready to get it over with and get to judgement. Even if he couldn't actually do anything, explaining to the Izir what he deserved would be a delight.

Mihály tilted his head, chin upturned. 'Did you really not know I was engaged to Madame Varga's daughter?'

'Madame . . . What in creation has ever given you the impression that I would care about a socialite's engagement?' There was enough of that in letters from his family, as if he had time to care about which cousin had married up or down or whose baby had inherited what title. 'And that's a fact, not a confession.'

Mihály swirled his drink. 'So pedantic.'

'Do you need prompting? There are any number of sins literally in this very farmstead we could start with.' He clenched his teeth to stop further complaints. Mihály wasn't wrong; he had sworn to do this. But listening to an Izir's confession was a farce.

'Never mind.' Mihály stood, and there was sweat around his collar and on his forehead. His eyes were wild. Troubled.

'If you need to talk about something and don't want to confess, talk to Csilla. She's spent enough time with the mercy crews; she's probably as good at listening.' She couldn't offer forgiveness, but perhaps shared tears would be enough. She had plenty of those.

'No.' Mihály's headshake was quick, sure.

'You don't give her enough credit,' Ilan said, but Mihály only glowered. Ilan sighed. Fine, he'd ask. 'What have you done that's worse than everything I already know?' It must be something lurid, to have the Izir looking so guilty. A small part of his curiosity was titillated. He was rarely privy to gossip, only the result when sinners and masochists came to his chamber to have their faults and shame beaten out of them. There were some things that had to come to light before they burst like a boil. Confession was a lancet.

Mihály topped up his cup again as if liquor could burn away the guilt coating his tongue.

'You're right, I don't need forgiveness, nor must I answer to the Church.' He swallowed the rest of the drink in a gulp.

A more compassionate man would try to get the secret out of him, take some measure to share the pain and in doing so lessen it.

Ilan was merely grateful the conversation seemed to be over.

'We'll have to leave the body here until I can bring a cart at least. I'm sure even if they won't let him back in you won't want him burned on your property?'

The stink of crematoriums soaked into the wood, and the place was wretched enough already without the char of burned fat and flesh in the walls.

'It doesn't matter to me. If the Servants of the Road can't come and claim him, do it here,' Mihály said. He reached for the bottle again, and Ilan snatched it before he could.

'If you get so drunk I have to carry you back to Silgard . . .'

It was the emptiest of threats. Mihály had ten inches and who knew how many pounds on him and would be impossible to move. Facts were facts even if admitting it was a slight bruise to the ego. But Mihály shrugged.

'It takes more than alcohol to put me out, unfortunately. But I do enjoy it. What do you enjoy, besides hurting people?'

'I enjoy when annoying people are quiet.' Ilan tamped down his nerves and set down his glass. There was something about Mihály that was dangerously enticing, the way a moth would fly to a candle even if it singed.

Mihály laughed, and of all the things Ilan disliked about him, the fact that his laugh was so inviting was somewhere near the top.

'I've been called many things, but rarely annoying. You don't find me charming? Attractive? So holy you want to lick my boots? I'd let you.' He raised his glass, then downed the contents again.

Ilan rubbed his forehead.

'Don't make me puke all this up. You *must* be drunk if you're fishing for compliments from me.'

But it was clear enough that Mihály didn't want the compliments. He just didn't want to be questioned or think more about what had led him to ask for confession in the first place.

Which meant he probably should talk.

'Whatever you tell me in confession is held in confidence,' he reminded Mihály, who was busily trying to shake the last amber drops from the bottle. His hand stilled, and he set the bottle down.

When he turned his gaze back on Ilan, the look in his eyes was so fierce Ilan was struck. Old records said angels could only show a fraction of their true forms while on the human plane, lest they shatter the mind of the flawed creation that could only have second-hand knowledge of the fullness of the divine. Mihály had never looked to him like anything more than an exceptionally well-formed, exceptionally awful example of humanity.

But now Ilan could feel the phantoms of wings and eyes and celestial fire he carried in his flesh.

'What if I tell you that sometimes I think I killed Evie, that I don't remember if she was breathing or not before I split my veins? Or that when I look at Csilla, I wish there was a way I really could exchange them, body and soul?' His breath was ragged, a new and oily note in his voice that hurt Ilan's ears like nails on glass.

'You want Csilla to die?'

Ilan was half on his feet. It was part of why he would have made a poor congregational priest – the moment he heard something awful, his first instinct was to punish it.

'I don't want her to die. I just want Evie to live. I can call the ghost, but I don't know how much she'll change.' His eyes were darting now, no doubt looking for another bottle, and Ilan wasn't sure which woman Mihály was referring to.

'Csilla thinks you care about her.' Ilan couldn't keep the disgust out of his voice. Csilla looked at Mihály with eyes luminous as a saint's image, trusting and sure. 'She's ruining herself to help you, and you don't even want her.'

'I don't have to want her; I need her to want me. And I know she's trying to help herself. She wants a soul. It's as selfish as anything else.' He moved to a cabinet, looking through leftover bottles for something still drinkable.

It wasn't; it was far worse than any petty greed he'd beaten out of the citizenry. But people often saw others as a reflection of themselves. People often mistook Ilan for callous, not understanding that what he did came from deep care and devotion. *This* was callous.

'It'll be fine once she's Evie, I'm sure I won't be able to help but love her then. If you want to tell me how awful I am, that's fine. I tell myself every day.'

The hair on the back of Ilan's neck stood up.

'If you just want to whine and self-flagellate you might as well let me grab a horsewhip and do it for you.'

If that's what he wanted absolution from, he wasn't going to get it. The self-loathing rant made him want to shove Mihály's face in an icy well, possibly not let him come up, and place Csilla in the nearest cloistered order.

Mihály raised an interested eyebrow, then took another long sip.

The darkness was suddenly gone, replaced by troubled confusion. He set the bottle down, though the glass rattled with his unsteady hands, went back to the chair, and put his head in his hands.

'I want to be better. But I'm not. And you can't tell her that.'

It made him itch to get back to the city, and he sincerely regretted not bringing the cart. The entire walk back was probably going to be keeping the damned drunk Izir from tripping into a ditch. If it wouldn't have made Csilla sad, Ilan would let him break his neck.

What would make Csilla sad shouldn't matter.

There was sharp electricity in the air as they left, grey clouds that promised violent rain and couldn't be outrun.

Ilan watched the landmarks as they passed, using them as a way to take his mind off how he would have to tell Sandor that he had been right, they had found nothing that would help the city, and the body itself was another mystery, a black splotch of a dot he couldn't make connect. So instead, he stomped and counted. A fallen tree, roots overturned and tangled, a shattered wagon axle tossed aside, the sealed demon . . .

What should have been a black mark on the road was only dirt.

'Mihály,' he said quietly, looking at the trampled mud, long ruts that looked like claws digging in the earth. The dog trotted around the furrow with a low whine in his throat, the fur of his ruff prickled. 'Tell me I'm misremembering where we are.'

Judging by the Izir's pale face, he wasn't.

Darkness danced in the air, coming together like a swarm of flies, coming together, then breaking again.

Demons could take temporary physical forms but they couldn't hold those shapes for long. And they enjoyed crawling into human shells, stealing closeness to the splintered Brilliance they were denied.

'Mihály,' Ilan hissed. 'Are you going to do something about this?'

A divine touch should dispel the Shadow. But Mihály was frozen.

Ilan stepped forward, prayers racing through his mind. If the demon had gotten free, it meant the holy magic had weakened even more, here and everywhere. The Servants of the Road were useless without the Church's power behind their prayers.

The Shadow condensed further, undulating before them, beckoning. Within Ilan, something tugged toward it, though the part was small. Humans were part corruption, too, and his very flesh knew it. While in Silgard, while behind cathedral walls, priests could pretend they'd conquered all the baseness of their natures and were close to divine. But this was the darkness he saw in every sinner he'd cleansed, the darkness each person had to settle in themselves to achieve perfection.

And there was something so tempting in the smooth whisper of blackness before him. It was all hunger, all greed, every impulse it would be so easy to give in to. The creature came together, piece by joined piece: thin arms, a birdlike head, ropy tendons and visible ribs. All pieces it had no doubt seen in its long life, cobbled together in an attempt to appeal to the corporeal.

'Mihály,' he tried again, not even sure his voice, edged with terror that it was, had reached the other man. Ilan swallowed. He might not even have the strength to contain it, much less banish it. He touched his mark and reached for faith. Asten guided him, but the distance between dirt and the divine had never felt so far. Ilan stretched his shaking hand out, asking for power he didn't have.

'Leave,' Ilan said, and the creature tilted its head and clacked its beak, a sharp sound he felt in his skin like a shallow slice. But it slunk towards him, light catching scales in ripples of hide stretched over too many bones and joints, alluringly grotesque. A memory of fishing flashed in his mind, putting a knife to the soft belly of a trout and gutting it to the jawbone.

He had his sword, but this thing couldn't be fought with blades.

It won't work. You're just going to get possessed yourself.

That was the insidious nature of demons, the most corrupted version of everything the divine had tried to create. Just being near them brought every Shadow impulse out to smother Brilliant purity. Fear and doubt were easy to drag out, but if he gave the creature time, rage and lust and all their kin would surface until he welcomed the Shadow and begged it to take him. A demon couldn't possess the unwilling, but they had so many ways to make you want to open yourself.

It came closer, stretching out a clawed hand to meet Ilan's outstretched one.

'Mihály!'

There was no answer, and he couldn't risk looking away. He shoved his palm against the creature's chest, groaning at a sudden paralysing fear that turned his vision grey. The demon pressed its sharp beak against the soft meat of his cheek, the gentle nuzzle of a lover matched with knives. Ilan gritted his teeth as his body tingled, darkness pulling as the demon tried to fight its way in. But it was shaking. Holding this form was taking all its strength even as holding it off was taking all of Ilan's.

And he prayed harder than he ever had before, begging for power. The muffled sound in his ear became a roar as he spoke in an ancient tongue, a language brought from Asten to command the broken parts of the world and repair the cracks with what caulking faith could do. His fingertips sunk into softening gelatinous flesh, the darkness in the demon's eye sockets writhing like so many worms. The smell that soaked the air was the cold ashiness of an extinguished hearth. It was a smell of nothingness, of doused potential.

It would be easy to welcome the darkness. All he would have to do was let it claw him enough to offer his own blood and an entryway. Humans had dual souls, and if the demon was horrifying, it was also familiar. Ilan had long starved his Shadow soul, but it was gorging itself by the second, and the cold dredge was as comforting as any moment of Brilliant worship. Souls found home in both.

It was up to the person to choose. And he would, before his faith deserted him.

The creature stilled against the fervour in his touch but didn't dissipate.

'*Mihály.*'

If he died gasping the fucking angel's name he was going to forgo his blessed eternity to haunt him.

It seemed to shake the other man, and as Ilan's vision dimmed with Shadow-born images, Mihály touched the demon from behind.

That should have been enough. Ilan stumbled backwards, cursing a litany that tasted of sulphur and poison, as the creature turned and took Mihály's own face in its hands.

It cooed a question in a language that sounded like the scrape of rocks rolling down a dry mountainside, and Mihály's answering prayer was an avalanche wind. The Izir spat on the ground, and under the touch of the demon, his saliva steamed on the dirt.

'What are you doing?' Ilan asked between fervent prayers. 'Get rid of it.'

Unless even Mihály wasn't holy enough. His blood still had magic, but it was old and weak. He couldn't even heal someone properly.

A snap of his shoulders, and his posture changed. This time, his prayers were in language Ilan understood but were spoken with a resonance that raised bumps along his skin. The Izir was lit with a glow of divinity, tall and handsome and effortlessly righteous, and in his deepest heart Ilan knew it wasn't the demon's presence stirring the jealous hatred he couldn't smother.

The creature hissed more clacking words as it clawed down Mihály's leg, ripping fabric and flesh as it disappeared into an inky black. Mihály stamped on the last of it, and it disappeared into a dull mica shimmer, then plain and honest dirt.

'Mihály—'

The Izir fell to his knees and promptly vomited, a yellow-brown stream of bile puddling on the ground.

Ilan continued to stare at the ground, no trace of darkness remaining. There were similar corrupted creatures bound all over the Immaculate Union, and not every territory was lucky enough to have an Izir.

Every territory. Rumours and evidence knitted together in his mind. The refugees who claimed there had been a demon in Ruze, others who claimed it was Outer Inosko that was being cursed. They'd been so overwhelmed with the how and the who of the murders inside the city, he hadn't given more than a passing thought to the wheres.

But each district of Silgard was once the seat of a territory angel. Arany's sacrificed divinity had kept the Church's faith and power, with her blood and city dirt taken as relics. He wasn't sure anyone realised how well that had kept the divine link between the far-flung municipalities and the holy capital. Links set by holy blood and erased by corrupted death.

It wasn't an attack against the city. That was only blowback. The real strike was at the entire Union. From the coastal east to the warfront of the west, nowhere would be safe once the ritual was complete.

'We've been so stupid.' His fist clenched with a need to punch the ground.

Far down the road he could hear the steady march and low voices of another caravan, lucky pilgrims who had no idea of the danger they'd just been saved from, or unlucky refugees who knew it all too well.

They needed a safe place, but Silgard couldn't offer it. After his report, the Prelate would want to close off the city and lock down the citizens, at least until they confirmed the gate wards held. Better a handful of people sleep rough than risk bringing more demons through.

24

Csilla

'THEY CAN'T shut the city.'

Csilla's shoulders shook as she looked at Mihály's drawn face, Ilan's stoic one. 'People need to come in. They'll be safer here.'

Not fully safe. A strange, dank odour on Mihály's skin lingered even under his clothes, a smell that was half-storm and half-burned sugar wafting off him. His fingers were stained charcoal dark where they had touched the creature.

Those blackened fingers twirled a few chestnut strands of her loose hair in soft connection and Csilla couldn't bring herself to push him away even as her skin crawled. Ilan's frown only deepened.

'We can't risk more traffic in or out.'

Her stomach clenched at the very idea. This was a pilgrimage city where people came for hope. No believer should be denied that.

But if Mihály looked bad, Ilan looked worse, and that was only after one brief encounter.

'I should have been there.' She'd let them go alone, convinced it was better, and they might not have come back at all.

'There's nothing you could have done, and you're the most vulnerable of us,' Mihály said, a plain truth that still ached. The honeyed affection in his tone was meant as a balm over her worry, but it only made it sting. 'We made it back.'

'Does it mean we're already too late?' But they had managed to banish the demon. They weren't totally powerless.

'Frankly, it doesn't matter to me.' Mihály brushed the backs of his fingers over her cheek, an exhausted tremor in the gesture. '*My* power is fine. Certainly still effective enough for our plan.' He slid his arms around her and pulled her to him, delicate fetters around her waist. Ilan coughed and Csilla turned, an elbow wedged against Mihály's side to give herself air.

'Mihály. It matters to *me*.'

Whatever the demon had brought out in him was ugly and raw. Maybe it had always been there, and the scab had only just been pulled away to reveal the wound beneath.

'We're likely too late for most of the continent,' Ilan said quietly. 'Even if the Incarnate returns now.'

Csilla shook her head, the words refusing to sink in like oil sliding over water.

'I don't understand. The Church's magic still works, you banished the demon . . .'

'That was Mihály. I was useless.' The words came with a flash of self-loathing even she could see. 'I don't think you understand the Seal, Csilla. In fact, I'm starting to suspect none of us did, not really.'

Mihály opened his mouth to speak, but Csilla stopped him with a raised hand.

'What do you mean?'

'You know Silgard was founded to be a central gathering point for the angels; that's where the city's districts came from. Each territory got a seat, a district, a place for their citizens to stay when they came to the grand Church to gather and celebrate.'

'Yes, Silgard in glory, and?' That was the most basic point of Church history, next to the Severing. A significant part of her early lessons had been reciting the territories, their angels and saints, and learning where they'd made their home in the capital.

'And after Arany's sacrifice, we wanted people to know. Priests from all the territories took Silgard's dirt for their mock seals in their home territories and placed them in their home churches.'

'Of course they did. Not everyone can travel to Silgard. It was a kindness to have reminders all over the Union.' The mock seals weren't powerful except in the way that any visual representation of the Faith was.

'It's a kindness we still bleed over with our vows. But those seals and centuries of blood connected us to this city and our angels, feeding the original Seal in loop. And with each polluted district, the connection is severed, the power weakened.' Ilan flexed his scarred hand. 'I was confirmed in Saika.'

Whose seat had been in the southernmost part of the city. Where Elmere had been slain.

That district had fallen and taken Ilan's blessing with it. What was it the woman she had helped said about Ruze? Csilla closed her eyes tightly. She'd said they'd gone through several priests before finding one who could still banish. It must have been one whose home was still tethered. And as each fell, the number of priests who could stand against Shadow shrank.

There were very few confirmed in Silgard itself. The clergy here were more often given the position as a reward.

'So whoever, whatever it is, they have to kill here next.' Csilla kept her eyes down, not wanting to see the confirmation. 'And then what? Even if you catch them . . .' The damage had been done. There wouldn't be any way to strengthen the Seal again. They no longer had any divinity to sacrifice.

'As long as we can keep faith alive, there's hope.' Ilan's voice was strangely quiet. 'I'm working on it. But I'd like to speak to you first. In private.'

Csilla blinked, mind still on the horror she'd just been told. 'About what?'

Ilan's eyes slid to Mihály, and his hands tightened around her.

'I'm not going to let you rake me over when I can't even defend myself.' Mihály turned her to more firmly look at him. 'Please assure him that you know all about what I intend to do with Evie's soul and that it doesn't bother you.'

He had an awful lot of confidence in her being unbothered.

Ilan tilted his head. 'Is that true? Are you happy to be his lover?'

The direct question, addressed as she rested in Mihály's arms, sent a bolt of hot shame through her. She'd told Ilan she didn't love the Izir, but it would look like a lie.

The inquisitor stepped closer. 'You know he doesn't even . . .'

Mihály's eyes went white-wild and betrayed. 'We were in *confession*.'

Ilan's breath was a hiss sucked through clenched teeth.

'He doesn't even what?' Csilla broke from the suddenly loosened grip, stepping closer to Ilan. The stink of Shadow was worse on him. Her hands ached to touch him and brush away the darkness she'd brought him to.

Ilan stepped closer, then back.

'Don't go through with what he wants, Csilla. Don't become someone else. It's not worth it.'

Not worth it. When her other option was to live a life never being accepted, never serving? Her hands clenched at her sides. It was the easiest thing for him to sit and give judgements about what should be done. The consequences would be entirely on her.

'If I don't get a soul, I can't join the Church . . .'

'Then don't join the Church,' he snapped, and she jerked back, thumping against Mihály's over-warm chest. 'There might not even *be* a Church if this continues. If you walk away, at least you won't be damned. At least you'll stay *yourself*.'

'I think you should go.' Go, before she started crying. Though it didn't seem she could lose any more of his respect.

'Csilla.' His face was near to pleading.

She wanted to imagine there was an apology on his tongue, but the odds of that were slim. She raised her chin before he could speak again.

'Do you know what I was doing when the two of you were out?'

'Writing letters, no?' Ilan said, and Mihály nodded behind her. She looked between them, frustration rising. They really didn't understand.

'Writing letters to the family of a man who was brutally killed, a man I've known since I was six. Someone I'd promised to take care of, in life and in death.' She held up her cross-marked palm. 'Someone I won't be allowed to sit with, or wash, or speak for. The only family I have are the people I've cared for.'

Ilan's expression sharpened. 'When you're Varga Evaline, do you think you're going to care?'

Tamas had said the same thing. It was like a flexing grip around her heart, doing its best to squeeze out every stubborn hope. She couldn't allow that.

'I have all the information I need, anyway,' he continued, no longer meeting her eyes. 'The pair of you stay inside. The city will be locked down by tonight.'

'But don't you still need our . . .' She was drowning, grasping for a buoy and finding only water passing through her fingers.

'Help? I know what we're facing. And now I know where to look next. Your cooperation is no longer needed.'

He was going to take everything from her. 'But you know we need the killer. We need the blood of whoever is directing this to . . .' *To complete the ritual. To get me a soul.* He'd seen the way Mihály had used the dead rabbit to make shed blood dance with spirit. He knew it was possible. Did he not care for her at all?

'You're really not going to help . . .'

'Csilla, I *am* helping you. I'm telling you to stay inside; this district is the most dangerous at the moment. And I'm telling you to forget everything the fucking Izir has ever told you.'

She stepped further back against Mihály, curling against him like a wounded animal. She wanted to snarl, but the only thing that came out was a whimper.

'Fine. Go.'

The streets quickly became filthy with the lockdown; people threw waste out windows that no nightsoil men were out to collect, and bored children screamed just to hear the echo. But there hadn't been any new bells tolling death, and even though Ilan had said this district was a target, there was no sign of anyone out. Csilla would know; she spent the nights walking from window to window, watching for candlefire or shadows where they shouldn't be.

All it left her was ever more despairing and exhausted, and now she was being put to work.

Mihály sat across from Csilla in the parlour, pretending to be absorbed in a book, occasionally glowering at the mess of brocade and thread in her lap. That was fine. She was frustrated, too. Ilan hadn't returned, not that she'd expected it, but even Mihály was quiet. Which meant he didn't have any better ideas than she did.

It shouldn't matter. Ilan had solved his puzzle and would likely find whoever had orchestrated the deaths, and barring a miracle that was the best they could hope for. It was selfish to resent that she wasn't getting anything out of it.

She stabbed the fabric and nearly pricked her thumb. The task was mostly busywork. Madame Varga had seen her wandering and deemed it aimless, then set her to altering a vest, one fitted for Mihály that could be hidden under a coat if it ended up a mess.

She didn't sew badly. Pride and a need to think about anything other than her own misery had her focused on the little stitches, the golden fabric smooth on her palms. It caught the lamplight with the sheen of a sunrise.

He was still in mourning blacks and their host would have him dressed in forest green and gold. She bit the inside of her cheek.

'Come here, and let me check this,' she said, motioning for him to stand so she could hold the fabric up to him.

He did so, slow and quiet. She found herself missing his easy smiles and sweet words, even as Ilan's angry warning heated her blood every time she remembered it.

'You sew well,' Mihály praised, forced lightness in his tone.

'I had a lot of practice growing up.'

Sewing habits, altar cloths, and skin had made her fingers dexterous. Another task she wouldn't be going back to. She placed two more pins, clamped another between her teeth, then set back to work.

But he was staring, and her stitches were suffering for it. She tied off the last thread with a flourishing loop. 'There.'

He put it on, and she sighed. 'I know you don't like it, and I think this is uneven.'

Mihály caught her hand before she could take it off to go back to work, skimming his thumb over her skin.

'It's beautiful, Csilla. My not liking it has nothing to do with your handiwork.'

That was fair enough, though her sore fingers would have liked more appreciation. 'What's wrong with it then?'

He slipped it off and handed it back to her. She held it up again. It *was* uneven, but the flaw was slight enough that maybe no one would notice.

'The only thing wrong with it is where I'm going to wear it to.'

'Hm? We can't go anywhere.' She'd assumed the woman had just wanted to dress him up like a fine horse or carefully crafted doll.

He snorted. 'Tell the rich about your rules. Those lucky enough to have made it in before closing consider themselves deserving of a distraction. I'm to go with the madame and be quite a centrepiece.'

What kind of people couldn't stand a few days of austerity when it might mean saving their lives? They had everything they needed on hand.

Unlike Elmere, dying alone.

The fabric suddenly seemed a gleaming shroud.

'You should come with us,' Mihály continued, as if it was his decision, as if the frivolity were something that mattered. 'You have a whole wardrobe of things you can wear.'

Evie's things. She recoiled, though there was a tiny part of her that was tempted. Church wards didn't get chances to attend things like balls.

And they shouldn't want to. She could dress up and go, but it would be another game of pretend. She'd seen other girls on their way to parties, her arms laden with bandages and pungent with herbs instead of perfume. They didn't look like their skirts were heavy, or oil made their hair itch. They didn't look like they had anything to lose.

A small, terrible part of her wished she could take that easiness.

'Even if Ilan doesn't want to help us, you can find out more about what's been happening in the other territories. Maybe they know something that can help.' Probably a lie, but a comforting one.

'I'd be useless, I don't even dance.' The closest she'd ever gotten was twirling Erzsébet, and that fancy had left her with a ripped frock and claw marks in her chest.

'Dancing is easy,' Mihály said. 'Let me teach you.'

She raised a sceptical eyebrow, but he was already pushing away the low table and chairs, creating a dance floor on the pansy-patterned rug.

'But we don't have any music—' She broke off. He looked cheerful again, a little more like the man he pretended to be when others were around. Anything that took the morose look out of his eyes after his wretched experience with the demon was worth indulging in a little.

'It's no matter. Come here.' He held out his hand with a posture that said not to argue.

With a sigh she stood in front of him, holding out her arms. It felt ridiculous. 'Like this?'

He took one hand in his own and placed the other on his upper arm.

'You're very short.' He jostled his arm a bit, trying to get her to reach and get his hand closer to her waist than her ribs, and she drew herself up to the very top of her height. The crown of her head still barely came up to his shoulder.

'You're very tall.' Her neck ached from looking up at him at this distance.

If she focused on what was uncomfortable, she wouldn't focus on anything else, like the warm pressure of his hand enclosing her fingers, the fact that if she took a half-step forward she would be laying her head on his chest.

He really was all she had now.

'Come now, as I count. Right foot back, left foot back, step together . . . One, two, three, one, two, three . . .'

Mihály gave her a quick twirl, her skirts lifting, before pulling her into him. Too close. He smelled like sweet tobacco, and the thrum of his quickening heartbeat echoed beneath the shirt scratching against her cheek. She wasn't sure what she was supposed to feel when dancing with a handsome man, but it probably wasn't this twist like a stomach full of sour milk.

Or perhaps it was. A lot of what she'd heard made love sound terrible.

Ilan would be yelling – well, speaking strongly – at her right now. She pushed that thought out of her head. His opinions didn't matter.

'How did you know?' she asked. She tried to turn to look back up, but he had her locked to him, too close to even turn her head.

'Hm?' His hand had slipped to her lower back.

'With Evie. How did you know you loved her?' Maybe there was something she was missing.

Mihály laughed softly and ran his fingertips along her back, the light pressure enough to set her heart racing with fear that he would misunderstand.

'Let me start at the beginning. With Anica.' He swallowed, drawing her to the sofa. 'My sister. We were twins, actually.'

Csilla nodded slightly, not sure what to say. Tamas had mentioned children, plural, though it hadn't seemed right to pry. Mihály didn't seem to need her encouragement and continued.

'We were almost four when she died, it was just after they'd realised what I could do,' he said. 'I don't have many memories of her. I remember her more by her absence if that makes any sense. My family wasn't wealthy until I came along, and Anica and I shared everything.' He was staring into the distance, no longer even in the room. 'I don't think I even knew we were separate people until she was gone.'

His fingers worried at the fabric of his trousers, nails picking at a catch in the cloth, rubbing the ripped threads until a little hole appeared. It was a good thing she already had thread.

'What's your first memory?' he asked, and she blinked at the change of subject. 'Was it when you realised you were different?'

'I always knew that.' It was as much her as her name, mentioned so often it was never not a part of her. She tilted her head, sorting through hazy glimpses of the tumbles and joys of childhood.

'I was hungry.'

The smell of the pie was the clearest thing. She must have been visiting a home, toddling after the Faithful who cared for her, and there had been a pie, cool enough that baby hands had felt comfortable grabbing for it. And a woman laughed and told her she was a pretty thing and cut her a piece, a few of the cooked apples falling through to the floor. Then, luxury of luxuries, she gave her a second slice when she cried for more.

'You're smiling over being hungry?' Mihály was looking at her now, brows raised.

She blushed at how he laughed at her, harder when she realised how silly it was.

'No. Someone gave me a piece of pie. I don't think anyone had ever given me anything like that before. I don't remember who it was or even where I was, but it was delicious.'

Even now her mouth watered, and her heart ached. It was a lovely thing to be fully satisfied by something as simple as pie.

'That's sweet.' But he sounded more disapproving than charmed, and she flinched with embarrassment again. She should have picked something more important to share.

'Why ask?'

He gave a half-shrug.

'It's interesting to me. I don't remember how much I loved Anica. My first memory is my mother screaming at me to save her. I told you I didn't have a terribly nice childhood, though I suppose I'm thankful now. That was the first time I realised I could touch something beyond our world. That it wasn't just life and death and nothing, though I didn't realise the importance until later. Not that it mattered to anyone.' His words were quick, his eyes glassy with too much white around them, on the edge of panic.

Csilla's breath caught. 'You were a baby.'

Before they'd moved her to the cathedral, she'd taken care of the toddlers at the orphanage, wiping up messes and making sure they always had someone to nap on. They were blameless.

He continued as if she hadn't spoken. 'When I met Evie, from the first second I saw her it was like I wasn't alone anymore. Every day I was with her, everything was brighter.'

And losing her must have been like being ripped in half again.

'We don't have to wait, you know.' Mihály's voice was low, rolling. 'She's close. We can do it now.'

Csilla started, heart skipping. 'Now? But you said you didn't want to use your own blood again.'

He brought her hands to his lips. They were cold, not even warmed by his breath.

'Powers we don't understand are being unleashed. What if our killer isn't even human at all? There might not be any blood to use, even if we do somehow find him before Ilan.'

The idea that a demon could hold its form long enough to kill was absurd; there would certainly be blood.

'It will hurt you.' Her own scars itched at the memory of his. He chuckled, grim, and there was so much pain there that she couldn't help but put her arms around him. She knew well enough that physical hurts were nothing compared to those of the heart. She'd seen him sweat with traumatised fever; she'd seen him cry. Maybe he was the only person who would let her help him anymore.

His fingertips combed through her hair, soft like petting a kitten.

'I'll be more careful this time. And if Ilan's right, perhaps you can still help. You were raised here, confirmed here.'

'Expelled from the Church here.' Her hand twitched.

'Your blood is still on the Seal.'

And having a soul could give her whatever spark it was that borrowed the presence of the divine. She tilted her chin to look up at him, taking in all his grief and glory.

'Please.' The word was the plea of a burning man needing water.

She had agreed to this. And she didn't want to die and be nothing. But . . .

'You won't care about saving the city anymore. And I might not either.' Tamas's warnings and Ilan's threats rang in her ears, loud as any death bell.

He flinched, caught, and she took both his hands in hers.

'Promise me we won't leave Silgard until it's safe,' she said. 'Promise me we will keep trying.'

'And if you don't—'

Her smile tightened.

'If I don't want to? If I tell you I want to run away to the last safe province, marry and have your babies?' Each word was salt in her mouth. 'Then you'll know that that is *not me*. And you'll have to say no. Not until this is over. Can you be that strong?'

After a long second, he squeezed her hands. 'I swear.'

She nodded, knowing she shouldn't believe him. It was always going to come to this.

The thin curve of the moon barely gave enough light to see the sharp lines of concentration on Mihály's face. The knife in his hand was freshly polished, looking shop-front new.

All life began and ended with blood, be it gushing or cooling. A rebirth was no different.

'We should both sit.'

They were behind the house, where dark garden soil would absorb any spill and make it innocent, and the thin weaving branches of dead rosebushes would hide most eyes. Night wind pulled at Csilla's hair and eyelashes, the sting teasing her to close her eyes. Mihály settled himself in the dirt. Csilla started to follow, sitting across to face him, but Mihály reached out. The moonlight outlined him in silver, every inch divine.

'Against me. The closer we are, the less chance of a mishap.'

She settled in the V of his legs, half turned so her shoulder met his chest. Cold from the ground leeched through her skirts and the thin leather of her shoes, and when she shivered against him, he smiled.

'Trust me, Csilla. This will be good for you, too.'

Good was starting to seem like such a relative concept. Every nerve in her body was alight, jumping at the slightest brush of his body against hers, twisting at the whisper of his voice against her neck.

'She's here now?' There was nothing hanging in the clear night air that she could see. The only thing spectral was the faint white of their breath.

He hummed assent as he rolled his sleeve up, then tugged on hers. The material had less give and ripped under his hand. He turned her arm so the pale underside rested upwards, showing this blasphemy to the heavens.

She squirmed, all instinct telling her to double forward and protect everything vital. His steady breaths pushed against her back, the rise and fall of his broad chest lulling. If he was so calm, there couldn't be anything to worry about.

'Don't worry, Csilla,' he whispered against her ear. She could hear the smile in his voice, soft and hopeful. 'And don't move.'

Carefully he traced the old scars on his forearm with the blade, blood rushing up to meet it. The urge to take her skirts and staunch it was like a sudden itch. This was good blood, she told herself, like letting out poison. It didn't make it easier to watch.

He took his bleeding cut and smeared it over her arm like he was washing down a board for chopping meat. There were so many notes in the streaking red, crimson glisten and thinned rust.

The rabbits had been clinical, no different than a surgery or stitching. Neat. Planned.

This was birth.

His fingernails scraped a pattern over her stained skin, and the whispers were an invocation. With each syllable the smell of old ash rose around them, and her body froze as if bound by invisible rope.

'Mihály . . .' Even her jaw felt the pressure. Nothing about this was holy, and as the dead scent crawled down her throat and stopped her protests, she gagged.

The knife on her forearm drew a sharp slice. It was like pledging herself to the Church, she told herself as her fingers dug into his thigh. Ceremony and faith, real stars above instead of dying magic below. It only felt wrong because she was scared, and that was her own weakness.

'Steady now.' He jammed his thumb against the cut, opening it wide, as white pain sent her shuddering. 'You have to be open to her. Let her in. Otherwise, she can't stay. Say yes, my dear.'

The pressure on her head released to allow for the tiniest nod.

A buzz like locusts vibrated in her ears, under her skin, shaking her to the teeth with unnatural, discordant notes. Something cold moved on her exposed skin and hooked, more like the slide of slick leather than delicate spectral hands.

Her chest jerked upwards outside her own power and she groaned. His free hand slapped over her mouth, stifling any sounds, and the panic of drowning set in, her gasps against his palm like the desperation for air. This was wrong. This was no ghost. This was a thing she'd seen in old books and nightmares, and . . .

The darkness set on her wound like a suckling babe on a breast, ice filling her veins. Every scream was stoppered in her throat as the Shadow found a home. It laced itself inside, thin as a razor blade, cutting as a garrotte. And everywhere it settled, she felt its hunger. Notes of bile and copper filled her mouth, and her heartbeat felt sluggish. The sound of each pulse was far away, like it was beating from the bottom of a pit.

'There,' Mihály whispered, freeing her mouth and pushing the raw edges of the wound together. 'There, my sweet. I've saved you now.' There was wonder in his voice. He bent close, lips on her bruised ones, his breath and falling tears the warmest thing on her.

She jerked away from the kiss, legs bracing with an urge to stand. 'Mihály,' she managed through chattering teeth and what felt like a hand on her mouth, 'what did you do?'

'It might be uncomfortable for a moment.' His breath had a faraway hiss as she pushed herself up, balance coltish. She felt heavy and dissolving at once, and the pressure of the ground under her feet was unnerving.

'Mihály . . .'

'Hush, Evie.' He struggled to his own feet, right hand clamped to his forearm. She couldn't quite stop the blood dripping down her arm, watering the grass with rich rain.

Do I sound like Evie? she wanted to say, but there was too much pressure in her head, under her skin, in her lungs. She pitched forward and he caught her, her back becoming a compress as he locked his arms around her. She forced herself to push away enough to raise her head and meet his eyes. 'Mihály. I'm not . . .'

She had just enough consciousness to watch his expression change before her eyes rolled back and everything went dark.

She woke in front of a fire, wrapped in furs. Dimly, she recognized the small and bare space as Tamas' house, and the angry voices behind her as Mihály and his mentor. She raised her hand to look at it in the red-tinged glow. It looked as it always did, scars and all. When she put it against her cheek, it was warm. Everything seemed as it should be, though her dress was filthy with dirt and her arm throbbed.

'You didn't do anything except send her into shock, which even you should have known enough to recognise, and cut yourself and her in a garden likely filled with fertilising pig shit. What were you even thinking?'

'I did *something*. Evie is gone—'

'If she was ever there, you delusional, arrogant—'

Csilla pulled herself up, the movement cutting off the argument. There was hope in Mihály's indrawn breath, worry in Tamas's. They were in the house, but she couldn't tell how many hours had passed. She'd been unconscious long enough for Mihály to call for a second opinion.

'I'd like some water,' she said, voice cracking with the words. Her throat was raw, strange since she remembered not screaming. Her old scars ached in a way they hadn't since she was very young.

'Evie,' Mihály tried, but she shrunk back before he could reach for her.

'Csilla.' She meant the word as a slap, and by his recoil, it hit. But it wasn't entirely enough to deter him; he knelt by her side and after a moment she leaned against him, grateful for the firm support.

'You don't feel any different?' He *looked* different. His skin was sallow, dull, but his eyes were clearer than they had been.

She shook her head. She couldn't even say it wasn't the outcome she'd hoped for. Maybe it was her fault; Evie had sensed her doubts and refused to make a home in Csilla.

'I feel ill, but not different.' She ran an experimental hand down her torso. The strange cold and hunger were gone, a nightmare evaporating in the dawn light.

There was something sweet about the guilt on Mihály's face.

'Well, there is one way to check.' Tamas procured a small, wrapped bundle, the embroidered yellow and red flowers far too cheerful for the atmosphere. He unwrapped the cloth and tumbled the glass piece onto her palm.

She held her breath, waiting for the shimmer of a soul.

There was still nothing save shadows cast by firelight.

None of them should have expected any better. She squeezed her eyes shut. It didn't matter – she still had things to do, a slice of hope thin as her new cuts that they would perform some great good for the city.

Her stomach rolled at the thought, and she slumped against Mihály. Surely she hadn't lost enough blood for this level of exhaustion. Even her thoughts were slow.

Tamas set the glass down hard enough to rattle. 'Let her rest.' The words were more an order than request.

'Well I won't be able to look after her, I'm escorting that woman to her party.' Mihály gave an irritated inhale. 'And if I don't go . . .'

'You'll piss that old woman off and lose what home you have managed to give the girl. Go with her. I'll take care of Csilla.'

'You're right,' Mihály said, and there was a softness in his voice, in his hands as he stroked her shoulder. 'I'm sorry, Csilla. I'm so sorry.'

The apology wasn't much, but it was genuine.

'I'll be fine,' she said, bracing herself to stave off the dizziness. If she just said it enough, even to herself, it had to be true.

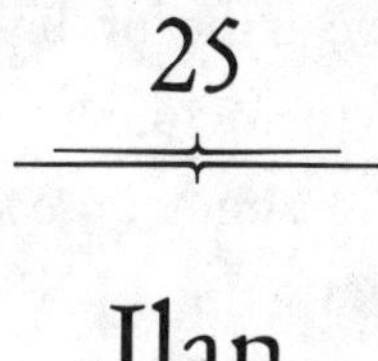

25

Ilan

SAVING THE city was well and good, but there was nothing better than being right.

Ilan drank deep of the satisfaction as the elders and Sandor looked at him with alarmed expressions. Ágnes was seated, wrapped in a grey shawl and murmuring prayers between hollow coughs. Abe's face was unreadable, but he was listening. Frozen in stained glass, the angels seemed to be listening, too.

'Look at the evidence, the history. We can't deny the connections.'

He gestured again to his notes, the paper still creased where it had been folded by Mihály's hands; he pressed his lips at the reminder of the Izir. 'I assume the completion of the ritual will cut the continent from Arany's protection entirely.'

'And erase the Seal?' Prelate Abe asked, pale.

'I don't think that's possible,' a congregational elder interjected. 'Not unless they pollute it directly. And it's protected.'

We were protected, too.

'If they complete their ritual, it will hardly matter. A heart can barely beat if the body is so broken. Maybe those lucky enough to have been confirmed here will still be effective, but there are hardly many. And it's not as if the angels show a sign of coming back and bleeding for us again.' He looked up to the image of Arany. The gold on her wings was dull orange in the low light, but the red-stained glass at her feet had darkened to the richness of wine.

'Then, forgive my language, but we are already fucked, are we not?' Sandor's hands slapped his thighs, and a few jumped at the sudden echo. 'There's only one place that's left uncorrupted, even if the Church guards the Seal.'

Ilan frowned. 'That's no reason to give up. We can still find whoever did this now that we know where they'll be hunting. There are priests here who can still banish.' Abe nodded at that, clearly grasping at the slim thread on offer. 'We can get the demon out of whoever it's possessing to do this dark work and see if they know how to reverse their spell.'

He'd pull the details from their killer himself – the killers, if need be. There was always a possibility the demon was using more than one body. Anyone greedy or foolish enough to let a monster in deserved their bones smashed to powder in their skin.

'Reasonable.' Abe stood, smoothing down his robes. 'We will send out small patrols, inconspicuous, with a Silgard-sworn priest in each. Keep the people inside. Don't trust anyone you speak to, save each other.' He touched his mark, the glow faint as the last slip of sunset. 'And pray.'

'I also would like a word.' Ágnes stood before the members could depart. 'I've decided to take my anchorage. I'm too tired for mercy work, and my priests' hands and attention are far more needed by others now.' She smiled weakly, spiderweb-fine wrinkle lines around her eyes crumpling. 'I should like to spend my last days praying for the safety of the Union.' The soft acceptance of pain reminded him of Csilla.

The air sank with the intake of breaths. Abe moved first, placing a hand on the woman's shoulder. 'You've more than earned your rest. We will make you comfortable.'

Csilla. She'd been heartsick enough over not being able to tend to the old man. She'd never get over this.

The other priests touched Ágnes's hands in blessings and reverence. The touch of those about to enter anchorage was also sacred, close to Brilliance as they were.

The old woman's grey-eyed gaze was sharp even now as he bent before her to offer his respects. 'Your prayers will strengthen us. Go peacefully, Elder.'

Her eyes fell shut, her lashes thin across veiny lids. 'I don't know that I can. But I thank you.'

Mentions of Csilla hung in the air, an unspoken ghost. Ágnes wasn't going to ask him to go. He didn't need to go. Mihály would comfort Csilla well enough when she found out, or at least distract her with his own melancholy.

The thought turned his stomach. He was going to have to anyway, or it would be more salt in a self-inflicted wound. She'd told him to leave, and he had. She might tell him again. But at least she'd have some say. She had so little in this world. And perhaps Ágnes could get through where he couldn't.

Ilan slipped out the back of the chapel and to the stables, Vihar nickering at his sudden appearance, hopeful for early dinner.

'Alas, more work,' he apologised as he tacked the horse up.

But when he showed up at the Varga house to ask for Csilla, the person who answered the door wasn't the maid he'd seen before. It was an older man, his face tired and clothing equally creased. His homespun trousers weren't what a butler serving as the face of the house would wear, but they also weren't what the woman would provide a family member or lover.

Ilan ran his tongue across the roof of his mouth. It likely wasn't important, but it was another thing out of place as he listened to the old man's explanation.

'They've all gone, off to stick their heads in the sand at the Vasvari estate. Won't be back till past midnight I assume, what with all the drinking.'

Gone? He could see the Varga woman and even Mihály electing to cloak themselves in the false safety of carriages and walls and money, but Csilla should have known to ignore it.

But why would she want to listen to him when he'd become just another voice of the Faith denying her what she so rightly wanted? She'd told him to go with the last snarling gasp of a trapped animal.

And, despite her protests, she was besotted with the Izir, or at least by his neediness. But he recognised the chasm behind Mihály's gaze. The Izir would swallow every drop of sympathy Csilla could offer, and it would never sate him. He would never even love her for it, and their natures would complement each other in perfect misery.

He rubbed the bridge of his nose, reins in his free hand, head already aching with regret at the dozen small hypocrisies adding up to this very bad decision. It shouldn't matter to him if Mihály drew Csilla further into his thrall or if one elderly servant passed to Asten without acknowledgement. It had nothing to do with saving the city, wouldn't stop the killer's knife or reseal the broken magic across the Union.

All it would do was stall the breaking of an unfortunate girl's heart, and the fact that it ate at him was disgusting.

And yet he still found himself riding towards the western edge of the city, away from the cathedral spires.

The estate hosting the gathering had once been the city residence of Lajol, still owned by the governing family of Inner Inosko, his territory and the one most directly bordering the city's property. With curtains pulled back on all the windows to let them sparkle in the sun, it was as alight as the cathedral.

The attendant at the front started at seeing him.

'Is there Church business here?'

He could say there was; they would not deny him entry, and they were breaking curfew. But there were softer ways that would cause less panic. No one was leaving Silgard; he'd get to the guests' sins soon enough. There was no need to bring open threat to a party.

'I'm a guest of the Baron Koriatovych,' he said instead. 'He will cover my revelry tax.'

It was nauseatingly easy to slide back into this life and these words. There were few things that felt worse than getting things based on who he was, not what he did. It was different when it was due to his position as a holy inquisitor; that was respect and obedience to the Church as a whole. But the Union's nobility were simply the rich who had been granted the privilege of taking local governance off the Church's hands and been rewarded, and they taxed the people to two coffers for it. His family weren't the worst of them, but the fact that they were here at all meant they'd been fine with joining them in black revelry.

The attendant blinked, taken aback. 'I . . . Just a moment.'

Ilan rubbed Vihar's neck perhaps a bit harder than was called for as the man disappeared into the dazzling house, swallowed by bodies and light. His father might say no. Ilan hadn't returned his last letter. Or the one before that. Or the one before that, come to think of it.

The man returned, relief on his face.

'Your sins are paid for. Welcome.'

The words rolled heavy in Ilan's stomach as he trotted to the entrance and passed Vihar to a waiting stable boy, with a few choice words about consequences if anything should happen to the horse while in his care.

Inside, the stately greys and gold of Silgard were replaced by blush pinks and powder-blues, trays of cakes baked hastily with what scant rations were available and over-iced to hide the flaws, and pale spirits passing briskly. The air was laced with perfumes, but also the odd note of incense. And there were far more people than he expected, elbows and draped fabrics brushing against each other in hurried conversations. Across the vast foyer doors were open to a courtyard garden, where a few younger guests played lawn games on still-yellow grass.

Ilan tugged at his collar, scanning faces. They'd all passed through the city gates and shown their souls; they shouldn't be corrupted. They clearly felt safe here. They shouldn't.

A cough echoed behind him.

He turned. A young man he couldn't quite place stood with fists clenched, the high collar of his braid-trimmed coat undone to reveal scalded red across his neck. The burns were like streaked finger marks against pale clay.

'Taking an interest in your family for once?' The man's voice was gravelly, like he had coals in his lungs, and after a moment Ilan placed him as a third cousin or some other equally distant and grasping relation. Though the last time they'd met, the man had been a foot shorter and dumped peas in his lap.

'Filip.' Ilan inclined his head, though his eyes didn't leave the other man's throat. He recognised those marks. He had their echo on his own demon-scalded skin.

'I thought you were supposed to be protecting the divine.' He gestured to the scalding, yellowed and brittle like a fall-touched leaf at the edges. 'Run away when you realised you couldn't?'

Ilan's fingertips tingled at the reminder. 'You were attacked by a demon?' Ilan tried to remember where Filip called home, how close it was.

'Possessed,' Filip spat. 'I lost myself for three days before they found a priest who could still work. And I'm not the only one. Why do you think we're all in Silgard?'

There were briars in the eyes and tangled voices that surrounded them, and he noticed now that between jewelled brooches and golden chains was the dull protection of consecrated metal.

'Ilan.' A deeper voice cut Filip off before Ilan could answer. Posture suddenly painfully stiff with the muscle memory of childhood lectures, he turned to face his father.

The Baron Koriatovych was not tall, and the breadth that had been military muscle and hunting prowess had softened as his taste for action declined but his appetite for other things remained. His face was hale, but his left arm hung limp in a greyed bandage sling. Ilan couldn't tear his eyes away even as his father extended his good hand.

'We haven't heard from you in over a year.' There was reproach there that made him feel ten years old again. But there was also relief. His father was glad to see him, and Ilan was shamefully glad for it. He was even more glad to seem them safe in the city away from the dangers on the road, though he shouldn't care for them more than any other citizen.

Maybe Sandor had been right to accuse him of clinging to the past.

'I'm here on official business,' he said, but guilt quickened his words.

'Clearly,' a lighter voice sighed, and Ilan suppressed a groan as his mother Olga grabbed him from behind with a squeeze. 'I was *hoping* you came because you worried about us, Ilya. You look like death.'

The possessive grasp of his waist was coloured by the long years of terror every time he was sick or injured, which had been often. She was never satisfied until she was practically absorbing her children back into the safety of her skin.

Losing them would do that to a mother.

'I'm just tired. I need to fetch the Izir and his guest. He is in attendance, yes?' There still wasn't a sign of Mihály's blasted head, much less Csilla.

The older man inclined his head towards the deeper parts of the house. 'They haven't let him off the dance floor all night. Your mother danced with him.'

She laughed, pearls on her ears and in her fine blonde hair catching the light.

'You can't blame us for wanting some intercession. We could all use more protection now. He even looked at your father's arm. Which you haven't asked about.' Her grip tightened with a prick of nails. 'They had him back on the front for six months.'

The baron nodded confirmation as Ilan swallowed hard, trying to choke down the pebble of resentment that a man who had already given years of service would be called back for more fighting.

'It's a mess, all of it. I'm lucky to have come out so lightly, starting to think the old boys are . . .'

'Hush.' Olga clucked her tongue to stop him from finishing. He didn't need to. Ilan knew well that there were plenty in Saika who thought the westmost territories had the right of it and independence would serve them better than the bonds of the Church.

'I'll find the Izir and his guest and take my leave.' He'd stolen enough seconds away from his mission, and if the escape was also an excuse to slip from his parents' pleading eyes and the strangle of his own feelings, there was no harm in it.

His father caught his arm.

'If you're going to use my name to enter parties, you could come home once in a while.' His father's words were true enough to hurt. 'The birds need shooting and the horses need riding. Asten lives within our borders too.'

Ilan raised his chin, green homesickness in his lungs. He'd sworn away attachments, wealth, and his family name. But saying you renounce a thing didn't mean not wanting it; he'd whipped many a priest for the same selfish desire he'd never fully managed to kill at the root.

It was easy to say you didn't love a thing when it wasn't right in front of you.

'There is more important work. Even you have to be careful in the city now.' He turned again to his mother, her lake-blue eyes a mirror of his own. 'Obey the lockdown orders, and stay away from the Izir.'

Ilan wove through the throng towards the grand room at the rear. He could already see Mihály, a head above most of the crowd, a woman dressed in wine-red in his arms with a drunken blush on her cheeks and decolletage to match. He looked around for any hint of chestnut curls; Csilla was short enough she'd likely sink into the crowd, but if he could grab her without directly talking to Mihály, so much the better.

But no such luck.

'Mihály.' Ilan strode towards him as the music died and grabbed him by the embroidered sleeve the second he let his partner go.

'Ilan?' His eyes darted as if unsure that this wasn't some prank.

A man pushed into Ilan's side as he jostled towards Mihály.

'Izir, I've been *waiting*.'

'I'll say a blessing for your family,' he said, waving him off and taking Ilan by the arm instead. 'What are you doing here?'

'Where is Csilla?' He'd keep the conversation as short as he could. From the corner of his eye he could see his mother waiting, poised with the perfect stillness of a hunter with quarry in sight. If he didn't hurry, he was going to be cornered and hugged again.

'She's at home. And I'm sure she doesn't want to see you.' Mihály's expression became a hairsbreadth more measured. Ilan knew it for what it was now – a quick calculation, gauging which version of himself would get the most favourable result. Ilan, however, hated every face he had.

'She left already?' He'd congratulate her for her good sense, but he also wanted to hit something.

Mihály frowned. 'She was never here. She wasn't feeling well.'

A prickle slid down Ilan's spine. 'I was told that everyone had gone. If she is here and you just want her to yourself, I need you to think beyond your own ego for a moment. Ágnes is going into anchorage. Csilla should know.'

'Told by who?'

The music was starting up again, and with it came people with outstretched hands, reaching for Mihály, asking to be granted the next turn. With a graceless tug, Mihály had Ilan on the dance floor.

'Talk here, otherwise people will keep interrupting. I'll let you lead.'

For fuck's sake. As if they needed this to be more ridiculous. He could smell the brandy on the other man's breath. 'Someone is dying, and you want to dance?'

'Someone's always dying,' Mihály countered. 'Why shouldn't we dance?'

'I know this might be hard to get through your head,' Ilan said as he yanked Mihály in rough steps that at least effectively kept them from getting run into, and prayed his parents weren't watching what he did with his years of dancing instruction, 'but you owe something to her. Whether you like her or not.'

'You don't know the first thing about what I owe her . . .'

Ilan's heel dug into Mihály's toes, and though he knew the crack was shoe leather, he dearly wished it was bone. The stumble sent them too close to another couple, and Ilan pushed Mihály out of the way, off the floor, with a palm in his ribs to match the verbal jab.

'For the virtues, the one redeeming trait you *have* is that you seemed to care about the people you served. Or was that a lie, too? You like the worship, not the good that would earn it? And when Csilla asks you to be the least bit accountable, you disappear?'

Mihály's eyes flashed dark. 'I told you, she's sick. I left my mentor with her.'

Well *that* was comforting.

'And you're here, drinking and swanning about like there's nothing else that could possibly require your attention. Is she not even worth the tiniest bit of the power you get your worship from? Whether you like her or not, you didn't have to leave her ill.' If there was anything that could crack Ilan's faith, it was this: that Asten had let such a selfish man wield divine power.

There was something stricken in Mihály's gaze, the look of a bird stunned by a sun-blinded collision with a window. The song ended, the last crying violin notes fading among a smattering of applause and rising chatter.

'What's this?' Madame Varga appeared at Mihály's shoulder. 'Come, Misi, it's my turn.'

Mihály looked between the woman and Ilan, jaw clamped tight. Ilan's lip curled.

'By all means, stay and dance, Izir. This is probably the best place for you. I'll figure out the miscommunication on my own.'

'No,' Mihály said. 'You're right. I'll go with you.'

The woman went a shade paler than her powder.

'Nemes Mihály, how dare you take my hospitality and repay it with this humiliation,' the woman hissed. 'You *cannot* leave me in front of everyone like this. I'll have to leave too, and I'm not—'

Mihály cringed, but when he spoke his voice was firm. 'I have to get Csilla.'

'It can wait—'

'It can't,' Ilan said. She would sigh, and the Church would lose her money, but the Varga fortunes were running thin already. It wasn't much of a loss. He grabbed Mihály by the hand, ears burning but not trusting him not to run back to the easy adoration and flowing drink. 'Come with us if you have to save face.'

He could breathe more easily when they were back out front, the night wind cool on his sweltering skin. At least the woman had the sense to stay quiet, though her eyes held myriad complaints and she held Mihály's sleeve.

'Call your carriage, Madame. I'll ride beside.'

In the shadows inside, Mihály was placating her, face as false as anything painted on the party guests as he raised her hand to his lips. By her answering frown, she wasn't believing him.

Ilan took a deep breath, about to lean over and say something, but there was something new on the wind: the sharp burn of smoke and distant screams. Vihar tensed beneath him, ears strained forward, and the carriage horse jigged as running people came into view.

Whistles and bells joined the cacophonous, bright sounds clawing the dark.

'What's going on?' Ilan shouted to one of the people running, a large empty milk pail swinging on his arm.

'The Church,' the man yelled back. 'The cathedral is on fire.'

26

Csilla

'CSILLA.'

The sound of her name barely passed through the foggy haze spinning in her head. She stood at the window, hands resting on the sill just to feel something cold. Orange sun dipped through the little cracks between close-crammed buildings, drawing night in as it slipped down.

Time moved strangely. Her breaths were no longer than they had been, but every time she looked at the sky, the light had shifted. Stars sprouted and moved like kicked-up sand, clouds melded into black and reappeared as if the divine had breathed them. A door opened somewhere below, and she heard a voice she knew she should answer, but it slipped away into deep whispers lulling her back into stillness.

She must be ill. It was strange. She had never been truly ill before. She'd never caught any of the outbreaks of scarlet rashes and spots that spread through the other children. Even the oldest fish never sent her running to the privy. None of her care had ever sent her to their own mercy wards. Ágnes always told her that her health must be proof that she was at least a little blessed.

And now that was gone, too. Her fingers curled, nails further cracking the web of tears in the old paint.

'*Csilla*.' Tamas's hand closed around her upper arm. 'Lie down.' At his touch something seemed to crawl under her skin.

'I'm doing better. I think.' She smiled, though the movement set off another small pounding in her head, and her mouth felt coated in metal, like she'd been licking one of the old snow-chilled spoons they gave teething babies. Whatever Tamas had fed her with in her lucid moments was certainly flavourful.

'Indeed.' Tamas came close and tilted her chin, pulling at her eyelids. His thumb only added to the pressure, and she flinched as he withdrew, black and purple spots blooming in her vision.

'Drink this,' he said, offering a bottle. 'It restores the blood.'

She frowned, but politely downed it. The thick wash of liver-flavoured tonic hit her empty stomach in a jolt. It was certainly potent medicine. As she lay back down, he took her newly cut arm, scabbing over and flaking.

'And he didn't even think to heal it properly.'

She wanted to say that they'd been well distracted with Csilla perhaps dying, but her tongue was heavy, and everything was just out of focus, like the altered reflections in shifting water. From behind Tamas, she thought she saw a glimpse of someone clad in grey, moving like dust in the air.

Was she seeing ghosts now? She shook her head. No ghosts would care enough to come for her.

Below, a door slammed hard enough to feel through the floor. Tamas's lips curved into a grim smile. 'And now I will help you further.'

Heavy-limbed and dizzy, she couldn't move as Tamas's finger traced something on her arm, just as Mihály had. The pressure behind her eyes increased, like there was something else aching to squirm out of her, thin fingers combing through her eyelashes, claws reaching behind her sockets. Burrowing in her like a new den.

His hand came to rest on her chest, the heel of his palm against her breastbone.

'This is the best place for you. This vessel is disposable.'

'What?' She forced herself to sit up, wrenching her arms behind her to push up, shaking his hand off her and swallowing away the crawling under her skin. Tamas froze, hand suspended midair.

'Csilla. You need rest.'

'Who were you talking to?' Because it didn't sound like he was talking to her, even as he touched her. Even though she was the only person here.

She looked beyond him, but even the grey spectre had faded.

'You, of course. Who else is here? You're not well. You might be hearing things.'

Her arms were already shaking from supporting her. *Something else.* The words sat on her lips, something stopping them. The more she pushed, the more something inside gripped her by the throat.

'Don't worry, little Csilla,' he soothed as she lay back down. 'You're fine. Rest.'

Rest. Whatever was inside her echoed the order. *You're serving your purpose.*

When she opened her eyes again, he was gone. But the knife on the bedside table was new. She picked it up, her sallow face a reflected ghost in the blade, and her blood went dark and slow like chilled syrup in the vein. Her skin prickled with gooseflesh and her vision dimmed around the edges. She slipped out of bed, each barefoot step cold on the floor. A deep thudding surrounded her; a heartbeat, pounding steadily against her skin. It wasn't hers.

There were three other heartbeats in the house, pushing on her from different sides. They kept time in her eardrums, pounded through her soles. Three hearts meant someone had returned.

Mihály? But he would have come to see her.

Stay in bed, she told herself as the walls echoed.

She was in bed. She was sleeping peacefully, drifting in the blissful hazy cocoon the syrup had provided. She adjusted her face on the pillow, smoothing out a crease.

Her palm ached around the knife she was clasping. She tried to set it down, but her hand was cramped around it, refusing to obey. A black moment, and she was at the door. Another, and she was at the top of the stairs.

But she was asleep. Perhaps she woke for a moment, wrinkling her nose at the intrusion of moonlight she hadn't shut the curtains against. Nothing a sheet over the head couldn't fix. She'd slept in far more uncomfortable circumstances at the cathedral.

Tamas's presence was heavy behind her. He reached out and brushed a hand through her hair, down her spine, to rest mid-back. Through the thin shift the imprint of his palm was as clear as if on naked skin.

'Finish this.'

He pushed, and she took a half-stumble onto the first step, heel hitting hard. One heartbeat in the house began to slow, falling more and more out of time with the others.

She followed it like a dog tracking scent. Step after step, anticipation bubbling in every breath.

A dream. Csilla nodded to herself, even as her feet didn't stop moving. Best to sink into it, let it run its course like a fever until a breaking point woke her. Because she was still in the bed. If she rolled her cheek, she could just feel the down, a hint of scratchy feather under the quilted cover.

She drifted down the stairs, where there was something other than cold wood under her feet. Deep, deep below, past dirt and hollow tunnels, there were traces of something gold and Brilliant. The last echo of holiness. She smeared her foot across the wood as if it could be rubbed out like a dropped cigar.

Such drenching satisfaction at the thought.

In the parlour, Madame Varga sat on the sofa, rubbing her forehead. Her shoes had been kicked off, her hair half-unpinned and falling in greying waves. All her finery was gathered on the table, golden rings and necklace chains in a careless tangle. The slump of her shoulders spoke to weakness. Good. That would make it easy.

Make what? There was a block between her movement and her thoughts, like the dark curtain hiding hands pulling strings from the audience being entertained.

You're dreaming, Csilla reminded herself as she approached. She couldn't see the woman's neck but a sudden image appeared, kissing it, whispering promises. A hand between her legs, saying not to worry, the girl is a child, show some charity. The voice speaking was deep and sweet and too familiar.

Her stomach turned. A nightmare, then.

The woman shifted, looking over her shoulder with tired eyes. The movement pushed the veins of her neck to the surface, the swell of a ripe fruit ready to burst under hungry teeth. Csilla's mouth watered, her tongue against her lips.

'If you're looking for Misi, he's not here.' Her powder was clumping and the wax was bitten off her lips, already done with its night. 'There's been a fire, and . . . you're ill?' She shifted, the wax further crumbling at the corner of her mouth with her frown. 'You should go back to bed. You look feverish. Didn't he leave you with some caretaker?'

But she was in bed. With every breath she took in the dried herbs Tamas had packed around her pillow. It was good of him to take such care of her.

The woman turned back to her discarded finery, muttering as she tried to unwind a knotted chain. Csilla stole closer.

She twisted in her sheets, pulling the quilt up against the sudden chill.

In the dim sitting room, she drew the knife across the woman's neck.

Her arm was stronger in this dream, pushing through the resistance of flesh and muscle, the windpipe cartilage thick even as the corded veins and arteries spurted blood. The woman turned with her last bit of strength, leaning into the knife but digging her nails into Csilla's face. There should be pain, but it was as if the woman were scraping clay as she spluttered through her sliced neck.

Flashes of other terrified eyes pulsed before her, and the settling knowledge all the others had been just as easy. They never really fought him.

So little time. She pushed the woman forward even as blood foamed at her lips, taking the knife and ripping down the back of her dress. She held her free hand to the neck and cupped blood from its fountain, smearing it across her canvas. In knifepoint, she began to write, whispering words she couldn't know in a voice like the steady grind and scrape of a millstone.

The sacred thrumming deep beneath her stilled, the gold on the edges of her vision receding like the tide. The icy sigh that escaped her lips was hedonistic pleasure, joy in taking some control. It was never going to let go. It hungered for this, and her feet tapped and danced as the power of the words carved in flesh released another few links in the chain that had them shackled.

The part of Csilla that was still herself screamed, but no sound escaped her lips. They were set in a splitting smile.

You can wake up now. Any time. Her inner voice was tiny, a candle in a cavern of darkness.

Everything was broken. That was what her gut had been anticipating.

Her scars burned. Csilla dropped the knife as her breath left in a dark exhale, fast as if she'd been punched. The discordant buzzing drowned her, pressing afresh at her eyes, her ears, pushing down her tongue, desperation seeking an opening.

She clamped her jaw even as her eyes widened in horror. She wasn't asleep.

And she was glowing. A sharp light, not the warmth of Arany's gold but the cold far-watching fire of starlight. The blackness clumped together, struggling to maintain form, unable to touch her. It pulsed and writhed, and she saw it for what it was: the corrupted essence of a demon.

But Madame Varga. She moved forward with tiny steps, each somehow feeling like crossing a mountain.

The body. So much blood, and a torn-out throat, the white of the trachea startlingly clean among the yellow fat and red and broken veins. Every jagged detail was outlined in the unforgiving light, the gruesome feast of human matter lent a measure of divinity by the shine.

This couldn't be real. The woman's pale face, the blood smeared on her own hands. It wouldn't be, it couldn't be. Her heart pounded as she swallowed down the last notes of metallic bile.

She wouldn't let it be.

It wasn't.

Csilla blinked as the last of the dark confusion in her shrank then fled. Madame Varga sat up in her soaked and shredded dress, her throat knitted back together, her back unblemished save a few spots and creased lines from where clothing wrinkles had set themselves into skin over the night of sweat and dancing.

Csilla looked down at her hands. They were ordinary hands, only sticky-wet and red.

'Madame?' she whispered, willing herself to wake. She had seen herself asleep the whole time.

You can't see yourself when you're asleep. Not unless that's the dream.

The woman clutched at the front of her dress, lifting a hand from the sodden couch. She touched her face, leaving a skeletal print in scarlet. But she was whole and alive.

'Csilla?'

A miracle. There was no other word for what she'd witnessed: it was the violent transformative nature of the divine. A perfect death and resurrection in as much blood as a birthing bed.

There had been no official miracles since the Severing. There especially shouldn't be one now. She'd felt the light die underneath her.

'Just . . . stay still,' she told the twisting woman, trying to collect her thoughts in some sort of order. 'I'll get . . .'

Tamas. Leading her to bed. Pushing her down the stairs.

Talking to someone in the room who wasn't her. And then nothing until she was faced with a corpse, in a blankness of stolen dream time. That rejuvenated corpse, now talking to her.

Csilla choked back a cry, a hand slapping her mouth. She tasted salt and copper.

'I feel lightheaded,' Madame Varga was saying, voice slipping in the way of someone in the midst of hallucination. 'Get me some water, please?' At that her eyes slipped shut, and she slumped over, the red on her face an accusing badge.

Csilla slapped her own cheek, stinging against scratches she didn't remember getting and drawing tears. There was no sudden jolt into waking, and when she looked down the dropped knife between her feet pointed back at her in accusation.

This was how the demon had been hiding, directed by Tamas's knowledge from his years of walking the Union. Neither she nor Mihály would have knowingly said yes to Shadow. But Shadow was always willing to lie.

Asten Themself had intervened. They'd saved Madame Varga. It was worthy of praise. She'd felt the light herself, beautiful and far colder than anything she'd ever imagined.

When she touched the back of her neck, all her old scars were gone.

27

Ilan

VIOLENT ORANGE and red advanced on the outer buildings in a hot and ashen wind that stole all the chill of the night, demolishing boards and licking heavy against stone. Panicked people crammed the courtyard, shouting, carts coming from all quarters with over-full buckets of water and muck from the river to try to smother the flames. Someone had spread a large quilt over the stones beneath the statue of Arany, and a few injured souls sheltered beneath her many wings, her presence shadowing their puckered and blistered skin as dripping gold painted their wounds.

The Church had been attacked, and he hadn't been there to stop it. He was the one who deserved to be scoured over this, and when the flames died he would kneel in what was left of holiness until his knees bled, whip himself until the pain matched his loathsome lapse in judgement.

'What happened?' Mihály ran up behind him, panting.

Ilan's eyebrows rose; he would have thought the Izir would have stayed in his carriage, going to what was important to him.

'You followed me?'

'Of course. If people are hurt, I can do something.'

That was uncharacteristically thoughtful, but no reason to question small miracles. Everyone's hands were helpful in a crisis.

'Go find the injured, then. Help them if you can.'

Ilan's eyes swept the building, trying to piece together the origins of the fire. The smoke had a strange sting – not the clean burn of wood or even the sooty one of oil, but something chemical, a smell he associated with feverish childhood days trapped indoors – sharp medicine and spilled paints and wood finish. As buckets of water were dumped, the heated wood and nails sizzled and the gagging scent intensified.

Heavy steps echoed behind him. The Prelate.

'You know how weak we are.' He lowered his voice. 'And you bring the heretic here.' Rhythmic shouts and splashes from buckets of hauled-in water sounded behind them, regular as bells.

'He can heal the burned. This isn't a time to question what little of the angel's gifts remain in the world.' Fuck, he was defending the Izir. Small miracles indeed. 'What happened? This was clearly no cooking fire.'

'One of ours said he saw a flash like dark deliverance.' Abe touched his mark.

Ilan's heated blood went ice. 'The demon?'

Or the killer with some other dark magic. Perhaps the Seal could be washed by more than corrupted blood, and the ashes of the Faithful would scour it useless all the same.

But demons didn't feel like this, as he now knew. The loathing and guilt in his throat were a meal he made for himself, the burning well-deserved as it went down, and Arany's flowing tears told him there was still something blessed on this land.

'We haven't let anyone else in the city,' Abe replied, which wasn't an answer.

'And the Seal?' Ilan sucked in a breath at the same moment the priest sighed.

'Still hidden. I don't want to risk going down there while this is going on.'

Wise. More than rats and cats might follow.

'Is there something I can do?' He fumbled for the knife sheathed quiet and patient in his boot, pulse strong and worried. He would open a vein over the dying divinity, punishment and penance in one.

'It won't help.' Abe curled his weathered hand over Ilan's fingers. His skin was a mass of nicks and fresh scabs. 'Nothing helps, but as long as Arany weeps, there's hope. Talk to the witnesses. I'm going to count the dead.'

Ilan touched his mark as he headed towards the makeshift coalescence in the courtyard. It would be a good thing for the victims to die under Asten's bright and eternal Eye. Better if it happened quickly.

One man was sitting up. Mattias, one of the Inquisitorial priests who'd served under him till everything shifted. The man's right cheek was splotched in fetid purple-black, his eyelid bugling and swollen shut, lashes gone to cinders. If anyone had had a good view, it was him.

'Can you speak?' Ilan asked, and Mattias nodded slowly, shifting so his uninjured eye could catch Ilan.

'It hurts, but I can.' His voice was gravelled with pain.

'Were you there when the fire started? Where was it?' Everyone had a different story, when they noticed, what had burned first. Mattias was the worst off, the most likely to have seen something.

It still galled that if he'd been there, he might have been able to stop it. Mattias' eye would have been the least of what he could have saved.

Guilt was a terrible emotion; how could sinners stand it? Perhaps that's why confession worked so well. The demon's touch still boiled on him. If he could stand to be less honest with himself, he would blame that lingering stroke of Shadow for his doubts.

For all his faults, he wasn't weak enough for the comfort of self-delusion.

'I was washing out the drains. There was a violet flash and smoke. I thought I was being delivered that instant.' His face tightened on the last word, his curled hand stretching towards Arany. 'But it was fire.'

'No one else was there?'

Mattias shook his head, single eye wide. 'I would have sworn it was a demon. It skipped like lightning, wasn't natural.'

A demon. Just as they'd feared.

In Saika they said demons smelled of cut ice; here they said tar. But the demon on the road had been old fireplace ash, and the smoke here was rancid linseed.

'Did you notice or smell anything? Powder or spilled oil?' When he was twelve a cousin had brought little tubes of black grains from Mitlosk that exploded green and violet when lit and singed the silverberry leaves. Chemistry could mimic a miracle for a time.

Mattias groaned. 'The drains always stink. How was I supposed to smell anything else?'

Fair point. Ilan left to walk around the remnants of the outbuilding to the drains Mattias had claimed lit with unnatural fire. He pulled off the cover, suppressing revulsion at the thin film that coated his finger. Along with cold sludge came traces of white filament.

He traced the path of the fires, where flames caught like ball lightning before running up in smoke. Someone had known just where to strike, where there would be dry wood and not stone.

It wasn't an accident, or the result of restless violence, or even a demon. It was sabotage.

And it couldn't have come from outside the Church ranks.

Mihály knelt among the injured beneath Arany, touching burns and speaking softly as his finery was ruined. Of course now they welcomed the blessed touch of the heretic – a hypocrisy, but an understandable one. One prone figure, however, slapped his hand away.

Elder Ágnes, taken from anchorage, grey but still alive.

'I can ease your breathing, at least momentarily, if you let me,' Mihály was saying, and though the woman's answer was lost in coughs, the shake of her head was emphatic. She hadn't wanted any hands spared for her before, she wouldn't want any now. That was the point of anchorage.

Ilan walked to them, gesturing for Mihály to rise, but still mildly surprised when he did so.

'Mihály. Get Csilla. This is why I was trying to bring her.'

Ágnes shifted, eyes cracking to look at him. A smear of ash had fallen over her hairline and streaked her face like a dried tear.

'Csilla?'

Ilan nodded, gaze still flicking to catch anything that might tell him why this happened.

'She'll want to see you.'

Ágnes reached out and touched his hand, barely the weight of feather brush behind it.

'Please watch her.'

The memory of the despair in Csilla's eyes as he told her to go stung like a nettle whip. She wouldn't want him to be the one who watched her.

'You're not going to let her see you like this, are you?' Mihály spoke softly. 'You took in a lot of smoke. Your lungs are already damaged. At least let me make you comfortable before she gets here.'

'I'm comfortable.' She held out a shaking hand as a ward. 'I'm safe under the gold.'

The old woman turned her palm up to catch a blessing.

Nothing came. The running gold was dry.

28

Csilla

THE DOOR creaked opened. Footsteps approached, and Csilla couldn't bear to turn towards them. Punishment or salvation – either would be welcome. Either might loosen the scream that was stuck in her throat.

How could she explain all the blood? Madame Varga was still unconscious, resting but alive, on the splattered couch. Every one of her breaths was over-loud in the room, proclaiming the miracle.

And Csilla, nightgown stained, feet red and face scratched, crouched and shook. All of her mind was clouded grey until the golden moment the woman had sat up with a gasping breath. She'd brought her back, but when she tried to remember why she'd had to, everything fell apart. Her clarity had returned, but the memories were a pile of shattered glass, no way to reconstruct the original shape.

Don't panic. Try to smile. She'd told those in dire situations to have heart over and over – she shouldn't ignore her own very good advice.

Tamas. Syrup in her mouth, syrup in her veins, and a cold hand on her back.

And now a miracle, stinking up the room like an open carcass.

She touched her knucklebones, now starting to chafe under the dry and flaking brown. Rubbed them over and over again, until the friction hurt.

Breathe. Remember. Panicking isn't going to help.

As if saying that ever helped anyone.

'Csilla.'

Mihály approached with careful steps, avoiding the worst of the floor. 'Are you alright?'

He knelt next to her, and she studied his face for any hint of understanding of the horror she'd been through. All she could see was concern, and exhaustion. And for some reason he smelled like smoke.

Csilla shook her head, tracing her bones again. How had there been starlight where now there was only blood?

'You're both fine? Where is Tamas?'

'I don't know.'

She forced herself to stand. The sodden night dress clung to her thighs, the hair around her face matted. She dropped her gaze at Mihály's horror.

'What happened?' He reached to touch her, but stopped short at the crimson smears. 'Madame Varga . . .'

He walked around the couch, putting his fingers to the woman's neck then holding up his palm for her breath to warm her skin. 'Who did this? Did you see the killer? Your face . . .'

Even her cheek was stained. *I did. I think it was me.*

She squeezed her eyes shut.

'I was standing at the top of the stairs.' Saying the words brought the memory back. 'Tamas was there.'

There and pushing. Insistent. Her body itched all over with grit like ashes.

'I had a knife. I think it's still on the floor.'

By Mihály's sound of assent, it was, and she nodded.

'I thought I was asleep, but I wasn't. I was . . .'

Standing, feet in a puddle of blood and hands stained.

Breaking, something breaking deep below, clean as a snapped wishbone.

Watching, a carved woman's skin stitched back together, crackled clay smoothed back by an invisible finger.

For a moment another hand had held her heart and worked through her, and she was complete.

There were no words for the horror and fewer for the ecstasy, and the sharp salt of tears stung the abrasions on her face.

I think I did a miracle.

Bells. Her clarity had returned enough to hear the bells. Of course someone would be coming. It was right that monstrosity be immediately met with punishment. No one would look at all this blood and think that she was innocent. 'They're coming for me.'

'They're not. The Church was burning.'

'Burning?' Her breath hooked in her throat. It couldn't be an accident. Not when she'd felt the light go out.

He nodded. 'And I have to tell you Ágnes was caught up in it. Ilan felt you should see her before . . .'

Before it was too late. Csilla's heart clenched.

'Scrub off the blood and change.' Mihály stood and gestured to the stairs with an air of crisp finality. 'Be quick about it.'

Csilla's head snapped up at the coolness in the order.

'But you should stay. What if she . . .' What if she woke up and remembered? 'She's going to need someone here.'

What if she never woke up at all?

Mihály's expression softened into something painfully tender. 'I can only help one of you at the moment. I'll pick you. There's nothing worse than being too late.'

Csilla shook her head, heavy as it was. 'I can't leave her. It's my fault. I did this.' The hollow in her was back, and stained.

'Did what, exactly?' Mihály's lips thinned. 'You look a sight, but there's not a single scratch on either of you that I can see. Surely Tamas wasn't trying something after yelling my ear off about how stupid it was?'

'I . . .' He had been there, talking to her. Talking to something in her. A dark understanding dawned. 'Oh no.'

'Oh no, what? Csilla?'

She ran a hand through a curl of hair, sticky with drying blood. 'Yes. Let's go back to the cathedral.' She didn't know if Mihály would believe what she now knew about Tamas, and if he started to argue it would take up time she didn't have.' But we can't just leave her. Find the maid. Tell her we're getting help.'

She turned up the stairs, back to her room, and stripped off her dress. The bright stains on her skin looked all the more stark against pale, uncovered flesh, and she poured water quickly into the wash-basin, sticking her hands in until the water turned pink.

It was wrong that her reflection looked no different than it always had as she rinsed her hair as best she could, careless splashes puddling on the dresser wood. She'd held evil, given it her heart and hands.

But you also held light.

She tried to pick up a comb, her hand shaking too much to hold it.

A high scream echoed from downstairs, followed by the muffled cadence of Mihály's comfort. For now they had to get back to the cathedral.

She'd see to the breaking of her own heart, then worry about his.

The damaged sanctuary was a makeshift vigil, candles dripping beads of wax and incense that couldn't cover the bitter smell of powders sprinkled between corpses and those near to, keeping insects away. Those well enough to be moved had been taken to nearby homes. Ágnes wasn't among them. Wrapped in blankets, she looked like a baby born too early. Fragile. Grey. Strange how Asten brought everyone back to infancy at the end of life.

The fresh linen lying across her stained body was a lie, making everything seem peaceful as it rose and fell too slowly. Csilla knelt beside her, folding her hands and looking back up at Mihály.

'Did you heal her?'

He shook his head. Fear rose in Csilla's throat at the hopelessness of the gesture. 'Her lungs were already damaged. The smoke ruined what was left. She is suffocating.'

A slow and nasty death. She deserved so much better. Better than this end, better than a wayward orphan to comfort her.

Ágnes opened her rheumy eyes. 'Csilla.'

'You have to let Mihály help you.' She wiped the woman's forehead with a damp rag, the cloth already rank.

Ágnes's voice was weak, but firm. 'Stay away from him.'

The movement set off a spasming cough. Csilla grabbed for water that had been left for later mercy and tried to force some between her lips, but it dribbled down her chin and wet the blankets.

The helplessness of not being able to care for the person she loved was worse than the loneliness of no care at all. She stroked the woman's thin hair and hummed softly, a lullaby she'd been sung as a child, not trusting herself to get the words out. The comfort was short-lived. Ágnes's dry lips were flecked with blood.

'He's an Izir,' Csilla reminded her. 'I've seen him heal.' *For me, if not for you.* It was pure selfishness, and she grasped it. What was one more sin for the night?

'No, my dearest, no. I'm ready. I was ready before he took me out of there.' She closed her eyes. 'Promise me before I go.'

'No, please let him buy you time. I'm . . .'

But there was no honest way to finish the sentence. She was never going to be welcomed back. She clutched her skirt in bone-white fingers, hating the richly dyed wool. It was no help at all.

'I'm sorry. I tried very hard to be good. And I did one thing.' She wanted Ágnes to know. 'I think I felt Them. It was so much more than you ever . . .'

Ágnes was still. Csilla wiped the woman's forehead again, but the woman's skin was no longer twitching under her touch, and when she put her palm to the sunken cheek there was no response. Her chest was unmoving. No breath. No pulse.

Impotent horror seized Csilla, denial thrumming with her heartbeat.

She'd seen this moment dozens of times, offered comfort. Why had no one ever told her there was no comfort to be had? Ágnes was with the eternal now, her work done. Her face had lost all its tension; there was clear peace. It was supposed to be a joyful time.

When Madame Varga died, a flood of divinity had healed her and brought her back, unblemished and as whole as Graced Rozalia. Csilla raised a hand, waiting for the shine.

Nothing.

Mihály reached for her, but she shifted away.

'Csilla.' His voice was tinged with hurt, but there wasn't enough free in her to care.

'She died, and my last words to her were defending you.'

She should have been thanking her, telling her how much she loved her, not filling her last moments with worry. She put her hand to Ágnes's cheek, still warm, and stroked the thin hair that was straw-brittle under her fingers, until the woman's chest was wet with drops of dark dampness on the mercy grey. The faithful spoke of turning their pain over to Asten, no burden too great for Them. It would be such a comfort to have that option. Csilla would have to keep everything alone. Whatever had touched her was gone.

'Thank you for bringing me.' She forced the grief down into numbness. It wasn't easy; the grief was very large, and the heart that needed to hold it was broken. 'We should go back. Madame Varga will wake up. She'll want you there, and she'll have questions.' They wouldn't have answers, but they could be there.

'I don't want to be there, so stay here as long as you need.'

Csilla frowned at the dismissal in his voice. The woman wasn't overly kind, but she was still a person who shouldn't have to come to in that horrible scene alone. 'That's cruel.'

Mihály recoiled.

'Cruel? Do you even know what I'm doing for you? Do you think I like being surrounded by Evie's things? Do you think I like sharing the old woman's bed? Virtues and vices, the things I've done to her to keep her eyes off you, and you can't even stay put and be grateful.'

'You what?' Csilla spun, fists clenching. Something flashed back in her mind, a diluted memory of being choked by the scent of goat's milk and roses, a dark pleasure at the novelty of slitting the woman's throat instead of kissing it.

Mihály's laugh was bitter. 'You think she lets me stay for old times' sake? Because you're such a dear? Darling, that's why I didn't want to go to her house in the first place. She's wanted me ever since Evie first brought me home, and letting her have me was the quickest way to shut her up.'

'That's . . .' It was more than a sin. It was cruelty itself. 'She shouldn't be allowed to live here.' She shouldn't be the one Asten chose to live. If Csilla had one miracle in her, it was wasted.

'It's not much of a sin. I agreed to it. Why I agreed doesn't really matter.'

Horror and empathy warred in her chest. 'You shouldn't have . . .'

He smiled, but it was the hollow grin of a skull. There was no beauty to it. 'It doesn't matter what I do, I'm blessed.'

That dissolved her bitterness. She was only blaming him because he made himself a target. He hadn't asked to be what he was any more than she had.

'It's for Evie.' There was a bite to his last word, a hint of sheathed claws. No wonder he hadn't cared when he saw the woman soaked in blood. 'I never wanted it.'

He'd only wanted Evie. And that was what had damned them all. She tried to find the words to break him, but she wasn't Ilan. She wasn't made to hurt people.

But she had. The both of them had.

And the Church needed to know.

'Find Ilan,' she said quietly. 'Bring him here.'

He would deal with them fairly if nothing else. He would know what to do next. And it would give her a moment to think of how she was going to tell Mihály that not only had he been the one to place the targets on the victims' backs, he'd put the knives there as well.

'Please.' She reached out to touch his hand, just to show she forgave him. She always would.

At the brush of skin on skin, the air around them lit, silver and cold.

Her breath caught at the shine and a rolling whisper surrounded her.

Once a visiting priest from a coastal parish had brought a shell and let Csilla hold it to her ear. They told her it contained the voice of the sea, something so vast you couldn't see the end of it, or hope to know its depths. The metaphor had been blatant, even to a twelve-year-old.

But this sound was like that.

Csilla drew her hand back, and the light and gentle roar dimmed.

'What in creation . . .' Mihály took a strand of her hair and curled it around his finger, where it became a shining cord. 'How?'

The word was half whisper, half prayer. He touched her hair, her lips, her neck, leaving a ghostly trail of starshine as she shook.

'Find Ilan,' she whispered again, staring at the silver glowing in her fingernails. 'Quickly.'

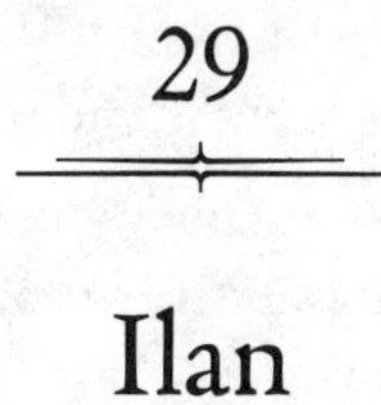

29

Ilan

THE FIRE had been smothered save for a few smouldering heaps still being beaten out. The majority of the clergy had moved from the broken cathedral to other homes opened to them by the citizens. It gave him room to hunt.

The stone buildings and the stable were fine, though Vihar had kicked a wall in panic and his coat was soaked through, and the dog whined with strained barks. It seemed a smart choice to take the hound while wandering an empty cathedral. There were traces of chemicals in the smouldering remains of the granary, on the stone outside the chapter house, in the garden beds that had yet to be prepared and would now grow poison in the upcoming year. Whoever had done this had known where there were cracks in the Church – the building and its Faithful. A cuckoo in the nest of sparrows.

He rubbed a further spill of snow-white grains between his fingers. This was someone's violent science, not magic.

Faces of novitiates, priests and elders flitted through his mind, each a potential enemy. Even when they had the glass, it could only tell them who had sinned, not the nature of the crime. Priests gave in to Shadow like anyone else, were punished by him like anyone else. But of all the ones he'd ever struck, none seemed to hate the Church this much. Even those who only turned to Asten's house to escape abuse or poverty were grateful for what they'd received. They still attended service days, painted themselves in Arany's gold.

No one watched them now. If the Union she died to bless was now corrupted, the eyes of the Church dark, there were no more blessings on the gates. Another Shadow war would come on them as things woke from long sleep.

The Church itself was empty. Ilan's thoughts seemed to echo in the space meant for hundreds, now only him and his dog and a few corpses outside. If their enemies had wanted them weak, they'd gotten it; the glass was dark. Arany's statue was nothing but decoration, no more miraculous than the human-wrought iron of the gates.

They hadn't just wanted them weak. They wanted them out. And the smell of dead ash would more than cover any demons. The realisation clicked with a hyper-awareness, every creaking beam and gust blowing through cracked windows possibly an enemy.

The dog stopped his sniffling hunt, a low whine in his throat as he bristled.

'What is it?'

There were no footsteps echoing, no voices. They were alone, not even ghosts. Anyone who died here would have immediately passed to Brilliance.

The dog scratched at the wall and whined again.

'Hm?' He put a hand on the stone, searching for any irregularities that would speak to hidden passages. 'I hope you aren't smelling one of the cats.'

They hadn't seen a single cat, fortunately. Cats knew to get out at the first hint of trouble. Csilla would have been pleased.

He didn't need to think about her right now.

His fingertips caught a small indention, shallow for fingertips to grip. To the eye it didn't look any different than the pattern of weathering across the rest of the wall.

The door retracted and slid scant inches into the section of stone behind it, wide enough for him to squeeze into if he pressed himself flat and put his back to the wall. The dog stuck his nose in expectantly, squirming around Ilan's legs.

'Back.'

He didn't have a candle on him, but far down was pale wavering yellow, tiny flames in a cavernous dark. The angle suggested stairs, and the dark meant being unable to see if any were broken or missing altogether, perhaps intentionally. The Church protected what belonged to it, but if their arsonist was one of them, they might know enough to use one of these secret pockets of stone.

'Stay.'

He held a hand out to the dog, who didn't seem to understand and whined at the chiding tone, then whined louder when Ilan shoved the door back to no more than a crack with a little black nose pushed into it. He wouldn't risk more than his own neck. Besides, if he died down there the dog could show where his own corpse had ended up.

With a hand on the wall, he moved towards the tiny glow, enveloped by stale air and incense.

Incense would be a strange addition to a room for plotting treason unless one was trying to cover up the scent of something dangerous or rotten. With every step closer the light intensified until he came to the source: a smaller room, painted in gold, with two half-used-up candles on either side of a bed of tattered white silk.

In that bed, a corpse in shambles. Bones burst from darkened and leathery skin, a caved-in mouth gave her the look of choking on her own teeth. Bits of still-bright blonde hair clung to a mottled skull and twisted around a crown of square-cut jewels, and a cramped hand clutched the dusty brown stalks of what were no doubt once flowers.

Graced Rozalia.

He had never doubted her miracle or the power of Lajol to deliver what he had felt was just, but had always privately thought the tale of her entombment was fanciful. And yet here was a tomb.

Rozalia was said to be proof of the perfection past the ether, the saint who came back unmarred and lived a hundred years never ageing a day more. When she finally passed, she continued to exist as beautifully as she had in life, only put into hiding when worshipers couldn't resist taking bits of her hair and dress and, in one case, several toes and part of her ear. The saint that helped Mihály feel like there was some truth to the idea that he could have his lover back.

He lifted the edge of the whisper of old fabric hanging across her legs. Her toes were gone, and the old wound was blackening with mottled gangrene.

Another miracle collapsed. Rozalia decaying, Arany dry. They really had been abandoned.

He'd given it his best effort, kept what he still regarded as a perfect balance of virtues, given the Church everything, and it hadn't been enough. Even being right hadn't been enough. They were all as inconsequential to the divine as Csilla now.

Ilan sank beside the body's altar and rested his head against the faded and dusty rose silk of her draping shroud, torn between curses and wild laughter. His entire life and purpose had come to nothing but mangled bodies and failure, and he was still thinking about Csilla, still stinging that she'd clung to the Izir. The hurt was embarrassing, even if the only witness was a rotting saint.

A loud bark echoed down the steps and then the air shivered with a growl. Ilan ran upstairs without care for the broken steps, cursing every time he missed one, cursing louder as his shoulders ached to pull the stone enough to slip back out.

It was a strange relief to see Mihály there, and not some further horror.

'Ilan.'

Mihály's deep voice echoed in the dim and filtered light, a soft note to it. Awe.

The Izir had never seemed awed by anything but himself. Certainly not a burned Church whose holiness had been stripped. More certainly not Ilan.

He tried to call up a sharp tone, but his nose was still full of the stink of incense and decay, the fight in him torn away like the peeling flesh left by Rozalia's venerated toes. There was little else the Izir could do to hurt or save the Church now.

'What do you want?'

'It's not what I want. It's Csilla.'

'She's here?' The want to see her hit like an unexpected breeze on a burning day. He tamped it down. 'For Ágnes?'

'Yes, but . . .' He gestured, the gesture loose and helpless. 'Come to the sanctuary. She wants to see you.'

'She's sick of you, then?'

The Izir snorted. 'Come and see, and I think even you will be out of snide commentary.'

He swallowed. He wanted to see her too, but that had to be set aside.

'Mihály, we've lost the miracles.'

There would be no more banishing demons, no matter what they did. Shadow would crawl through the population soul by soul, corrupting them. When the physical vessels finally gave up, they wouldn't be allowed to join to greater peace. They would be in anguish for eternity.

Their only chance now was to catch the conspirators and hope they knew a way to reverse the magic, or trust that the Incarnate would arrive in time to guide them back to the light. Neither of those things had panned out terribly well so far.

'We've lost the old miracles,' Mihály said, reverence still illuminating his voice. 'Let me introduce you to a new one.'

The pews were filled, but those in them were dead or dying. Even the few candles that had been set out in hasty respect had blown out in the wind cutting through broken windows.

Csilla was on the floor next to where Ágnes's body lay, head pillowed on her arms, pale and still like a corpse herself in the moonlight. For a moment his heart stopped, only starting again when she took a deep breath that ended in a small snore.

If she were dead, it would be sad, but it wouldn't matter, he tried to remind himself as his steps quickened.

At least now there was no glass to show how he lied to himself.

'Csilla.'

He crouched down next to her, frowning at the pink scrapes marring her cheek. She opened her hazel eyes slowly, lips curving into a soft and relieved smile, and the dog lunged forward to lick her and receive a pat.

He couldn't help but smile back, even surrounded by detritus and the bodies of people they knew. All of this around them was his failure, and yet he was still happy to see her breathing. If she hadn't been, none of the rest of it would matter. She was safe, and he was desperate to touch her, to feel that she was fine. He clenched his hands instead.

The feelings were as natural as any other illness. He could starve or slice them out the same way and be quietly jealous of the dog.

'Ilan. You're alright?'

Of course she would ask him, when she was the one sleeping in a makeshift crypt.

He nodded. 'But you don't seem to be.'

He gestured to her face, and her hand flew up to touch her cheek as her eyes darted to Mihály.

'It's . . .' Her eyes darkened. 'I have so much to tell you.'

'In here?' It was far too open, indefensible, and his skin was still crawling from a brush with an ancient corpse.

Csilla looked down at Ágnes. The woman's face had taken on a grey cast, and her mouth hung wide in the loose-jawed gasp of the dead. Csilla touched the sunken cheek. 'I'm fine here.'

She was grieving and loyal, not fine.

'Off the floor, at least. Not every pew has a body.'

Csilla rose then stilled, the perfect pause of a bird about to take flight.

'Watch.' She approached the altar as if entranced, broken glass crunching under her feet.

The flame in front of the ever-seeing Eye still burned, licking yellow and orange across her skin. Perhaps that was where their saboteur took their own fire from. The light ringed her in gold, blending the shadows on her face into something soft and sacred.

'Mihály. Come here.'

The angel surprisingly said nothing, hurrying at the quiet command. Csilla offered her hand to him with a small nod.

He took it and raised it to his lips, and the holy firelight was eclipsed by white and shining Brilliance, Csilla in the centre of it all. She slanted her head towards him, the slightest hopeful smile on her pale lips as silver kissed every inch of her. Holiness and beauty incarnate.

Ilan fell to his knees.

30

Csilla

EMBARRASSMENT YANKED her hand away from Mihály.

'Please stand up,' she said, hand fluttering as the light faded. She wanted Ilan to tell her what he thought, like he always did, not this worshipful silence as he knelt, eyes turned down from her. She wanted answers, and his reaction seemed to mean he didn't have any. The only thing reflected in his gaze was a shocked awe and yearning.

He finally stood, looking between them, eyes wide and lips parted. 'What was that?' Then, softer: 'What did the two of you *do*?'

Csilla swallowed. There couldn't be any more stalling.

'We tried the ritual to give me Evie's soul.' Her mouth was sour at the memory of lying against Mihály and bleeding under the stars. 'But it didn't work.'

And she had to tell them why. Csilla took both Mihály's hands in hers, pressing her palms around his fingers as they glowed in silver comfort. Devastation was a consequence of the hopeful human condition. And she could be gentle, though he hadn't been gentle with her. Perhaps the numb shock of her grief would be a blessing at the moment.

'It didn't work because that wasn't her. She's gone.'

That expression . . . the kind, bemused look he'd given her the first moment they'd met, but more genuine now. She squeezed tighter, heart cracking at his smile, and dropped her gaze.

'You were tricked.' She braced herself for the denial and anger to come, like readying for the first thundercrack of a storm. 'We both were.'

He clucked his tongue with a pitying look and Csilla's blood rose. She was being better to him than he deserved. This was a moment she should be taking for herself, and he would mock her for it?

'Just because I failed in a ritual . . .'

'No.' Csilla's skin crawled, pieces of the evening coming back. The softness of her bed. The weight of the knife. 'Do you even know what it was you were doing? Or did you just take Tamas's word for it?'

'I . . .' He gulped air, words lost as he jerked away.

'Think.' Her head pounded. Blood and magic. They'd used for themselves what the killer was using now. And the only person they had claiming it was holy was the grief-stricken boy who'd have done anything to get his soulmate back. 'Who was it who told you how to do it? Who knew about the blood and the magic, about Evie. About your holiness and how it could blind us?'

Mihály grabbed her wrist. Light flared, but the shadows it cast were sinister. Ilan leaped forward, but Csilla raised a hand to stop him. She had to see this through.

'It was a miracle. You don't question miracles. And I'm blessed.'

'I've seen miracles.' Her voice choked. 'You're just a *man*. Whatever you and Tamas did didn't save her, and it may have damned us all.'

'You're mistaken . . .' He tensed like a wild creature newly caged. But she couldn't let him edge away, no matter what a slippery thing he was.

'The mistake was what you did. They used you, you're not to blame, but *think*.'

He sank down onto the steps and put his head in his hands. Was he praying?

Crying.

'He brought me here because I needed looking after,' he whispered into his hands. 'That's what he told me.'

A part of her wanted to scream at him over the audacity of his acting as if he were the only person here grieving. Ágnes's body was next to them and not yet cold.

But that wasn't a pain she wished on anyone else.

'He used you to hold something evil. You put it in me.'

Mihály's laugh into his palms was wormwood bitter. 'Well, it's all gone now, isn't it?'

If she couldn't be Evie, did he really not care at all? A helpless laugh rose in Csilla's throat. 'It happened before, Mihály. I killed Madame Varga. And I brought her back. And you killed the others. You were never ill. You were possessed.'

'But I—'

'Don't remember? Or remember doing other things? I was sure I was in bed. And I think if I hadn't come to, that thing in me would have made sure I knew nothing about it.' She dragged her hand across her chest, as if she could rake out the memories of darkness.

'And you say it's gone?' Ilan shook his head. 'Did you see a mark? Demons are pure corruption. They can't stay in form long and they leave traces when they're banished.'

He was dissecting her with his eyes now. All soft worship was gone, leaving only steel, and she was glad for it.

Csilla ran a hand over her arm. 'There wasn't a mark . . .'

Ilan shook his head, cutting her off. 'So it found another host.'

Another host. She'd damned someone else, adding to her pile of guilty sins.

Mihály let out a long breath. 'Look. The Seal is ruined. There isn't going to be a Church for you to join, Evie's gone, so fuck it all. Let's just leave. Whatever you are, we will figure it out later. It's not safe here.'

There wasn't anywhere safe, not anymore. Perhaps they could find somewhere to hide from Shadow, but it wouldn't save them. Running would be a disgrace.

'You should earn that blessing you were born with.' The words came from somewhere deep and boiling. 'Even if you don't care about me, you should care about the people who put their faith in you. They're still here.'

This time, when Mihály met her eyes, there was no endearment.

Fine. Let him resent her for who she was. Better than being loved for the ghost she wasn't.

'I do ca—'

She put her fingers over his lips, silencing him with pressure and light.

'I don't want to hear another lie out of your mouth. You owe me more than that.'

He exhaled against her hand, bowing his head. 'Then what would you have me do? Find Tamas, bring him here to be punished?'

'And us as well, I suppose.'

She would stay here as everything horrible and miraculous faded into a dull and sunken quiet. Even if no one else knew, she had the memory of the knife in her hands and the sick knowledge that when asked if she would accept darkness, she'd said yes. Why she'd said yes didn't matter.

'I could have stopped it, too. I just wanted to believe you.'

She met Mihály's gaze, a new quiet on his face. Resignation, without pretension or defence.

'Csilla.' Mihály reached out to graze her cheek, silver on his fingertips. 'All my life, people – including you – have offered me very undeserved grace. Try extending it to yourself.'

She took a deep breath and gave the smallest nod. Ágnes would have wanted that, too.

'Go get Tamas.'

Mihály's smile went grim. 'We don't have to waste time dragging him here. I've killed before.' The paleness in his face undercut the words.

'No!' Csilla shook her head, grabbing his sleeve. 'I don't care what you think about your divinity, you're not staining yourself.'

Ilan made a *hmm* of agreement, a sharp light in his eyes. 'He can't talk if he's dead. But go fast. If this was all they were after, he'll likely have run.'

'Ilan, you'll keep her somewhere, won't you?' Mihály said. 'At least now we don't have to worry about anyone getting killed on the streets.'

It was a poor attempt at levity, but she let him get away with it, and Ilan hummed an affirmation.

Csilla sagged in relief, suddenly desperate for quiet, to sit with Ágnes in the dark. This was where they'd found her at the beginning of her life. It was right she be in the same spot to see the woman through the end, no matter how it hurt.

Her tears finally fell, as steady as a shower of blessed gold.

31

Csilla

Ilan hadn't asked her to move, and for that she was grateful. There was something primal about sitting with a body, appeasing the inner animal that had to see a thing with its senses to know that it was true. Ágnes was stiff, but so was she, shoulders curled and legs drawn up, back cracking every time she shifted.

And Ilan, sitting on an empty bench with his dog at his feet, eyes never leaving her. His face was gaunt, eyes rimmed with exhaustion. She likely didn't look any better. It would be smarter to go and rest. Things were always clearer in the morning.

She didn't want to face that clarity. The bone-ache of sleeplessness and the fog of grief were a welcome cushion, no matter how much they hurt.

'Do you hear Their voice?' Ilan asked, the words echoing in the midnight still. His tone was measured, but she could hear the hope behind it.

She brushed a fingertip across the metal pin on Ágnes's still chest, the light dancing across it no longer pleasing. Saints didn't get to pick their miracles, and the truth of that left her sour.

'No. It wasn't me doing anything or being told to do anything. I couldn't control it. If I could . . .'

She still would have saved Madame Varga. She would have just done *more*. The horror of it all still squeezed her chest. She wanted someone to hold her and tell her it would be fine, but the only person willing to was cold.

Well – and Mihály. Perhaps she should have asked him to give her some of that drink he used to forget his own pain. She could forgive him the vice more easily now that she knew what it was to have your heart smashed to ground glass, tearing bits of you from the inside with every beat.

'If anything it felt like I was being used,' she admitted. 'I wanted her to come back to life, truly I did, but it wasn't me making it happen. It was like They came through me.' Like she was a pane of glass, refracting the power of the sun.

'Isn't that prayer?' he countered. 'We direct our wants, not the power that answers them.'

The fact that only the Incarnate should be able to even hear the direct answer to a prayer hung between them, as present and effervescent as the lingering smoke.

Ilan was no doubt thinking how glad he was that she had been sent out from the Church – no one this embarrassingly distraught deserved to serve the divine. Grief was for laypeople who hadn't fully surrendered their lives to a greater plan.

'Come on.' Ilan stood and gestured for her to follow him. 'You need to rest. You've done your sitting. You can tell me whatever stories you like. And in the morning we'll start her rites. I fear that things are going to get lost.'

It was a short mourning. Whatever family Ágnes still had should be told, and Csilla didn't even know who her family might be, only that she'd been raised in a lakeside village near the city of Kis that she didn't often speak of. Csilla had loved the woman with the simple selfish innocence of a child, never taking the time to understand her as a person. It was cruel that this was what it took to realise that.

'Thank you.' She rubbed the scratch of drying tears from her face, then placed her palm against Ágnes's cheek in a silent goodbye. 'For doing this for her. For me. Even though . . .'

'Even though?' He ushered her out of the sanctuary, blocking her from turning back.

That was kind; everything in her wanted to stay.

'Even though you don't like me. And I'm a murderer.' It was by manipulation and circumstance, erased by something strange and holy, but there was blood crusting under her fingernails all the same.

His hand pressed harder against her lower back.

'I never said I didn't like you, Csilla. And there wasn't any sin on you.' He turned her down a corridor she dimly remembered as leading to his room. This far in the stone interior was untouched by the fire, but the char flavoured every breath.

'There was never any visible sin on Mihály, either. And he did awful things.'

Perhaps she was trying to goad him into punishing her. Burned skin or broken thumbs had to be better than this.

'I wish I'd been stronger, like you. If I'd just *obeyed* . . .' But if she'd had the choice to make again, she would have chosen the same, and she hated herself for it. 'You would have killed him.'

'Without a second thought,' Ilan agreed. 'And we wouldn't be any better off for it. They would have found another way.'

He pushed open his door, nose wrinkling at the stale air. The odour of the fire had permeated even here. 'You can recite for her in the morning.'

'I'm no priest.' Nothing she could say would help Ágnes, and there was no one around who needed soothing through grief except her.

'No.' His voice was low, a half-whispered caress. 'But you are something holy.'

'Shouldn't you take me to the Prelate, then?' To anyone who had knowledge of why a girl without a soul would be worked through for a miracle. A small part of her hoped he'd be pleased to see her shine.

There was a long pause, then his voice quieted even more.

'I don't know that we can trust the Prelate.'

Csilla stiffened in surprise. 'What?'

Ilan locked the door and stepped away from it but still kept his voice near a whisper.

'Whoever tried to burn the cathedral did it from the inside. It was someone with intimate knowledge of the architecture, of our schedules. I don't think we can trust anyone until the Incarnate gets back to put things right. Or we settle this ourselves.'

Her hand pressed her mouth. There was no one to trust.

'Whatever happened, I'm going to protect you. And I'm going to get you down to the Seal, whatever is left of it. You might be able to save us.'

She sank down on the bed, gripping the edge as her head fell forward, all energy drained. She dearly missed her cat and had half a mind to get up again and try to find her and steal a moment of normalcy.

'I'm afraid I might be one miracle and done.'

'Be that as it may, right now we have a demon in our city, others across the continent. Even if we find Tamas and banish this one, it's not going to help the other territories. We might not even be able to banish this one. The glass is dead. I saw Rozalia, decaying like any other corpse. I don't know where the Seal is to see if there's still anything there.'

'So there might not be anything to save.' The hollows beneath the cathedral might be nothing but mud and bones. But more than knowing the physical heart of the Church was empty, it hurt to know the people might be, too.

Ilan touched his fingers to his mark, where the metal stayed dull. Then he took it off and placed it in her hand, his own resting beneath. It glowed in misty silver. She could have laughed. Now she was the only one who could see the divine, and it was at the doom of Their creation.

'There might not be,' Ilan said quietly as the little star burned cold in her palm and his skin warmed the back of her hand beneath. 'But you're our best hope.'

When he said it like that, she could breathe again and almost believe she was.

They'd searched the cracked eastern walls, turned over what was left in the library – all the most important papers had been moved out with the clergy for safekeeping – until the both of them were voiceless with exhaustion. There was no way to know what was happening on the streets while wrapped in the walls of the cathedral, not with the demon or Mihály. Sound was muffled, the sky still dark, and it was very like being the only people left alive.

She cupped Ilan's mark like a child holding fireflies, the glow hazy against the folds of her palms. When she closed her eyes, she could feel the filaments of divinity still woven through the glass and stone, a web tattered to the centre. They whispered to her like the call of water washing over rock, cleansing and wearing it down at once. She glanced to mention it to Ilan, and saw him leaning against the wall. His head had dropped forward, a fan of blonde hair obscuring his face. She had half a mind to find a cushion and attempt to make him comfortable; it wasn't like anyone else would get any more use out of it. But he'd only wake up and be cross with her.

The thought was strangely tender. He could be cross with her all he liked as long as he stayed honest.

He opened his eyes, and she flushed to be caught staring.

'Did you find something?' he asked, wincing at the crack of a joint as he straightened his neck.

She shook her head. Maybe they should both go to sleep, but trying to sleep only meant thinking of death and loss. In the liminal space before drifting off it would be easy for her mind to forget everything but the familiar walls of the cathedral buildings and make her think Ágnes was alive, only for the crash of reality seconds later.

'It's almost morning. I don't know how much time we'll have before they start sending novitiates to collect the bodies.'

Ilan nodded. 'That's not the only thing. Whoever set the fire wanted everyone out for a reason. Mihály might get Tamas, but I doubt he was working alone. There could already be an infestation.'

They both paused at his words, but the air was empty of other breaths or footfalls. The sanctuary might as well have been a crypt.

'You think they'll go after the Seal themselves? They've already ruined the city.'

'If they can find it?' His lips thinned. 'I have no doubt. We keep going.'

But the western walls seemed equally unwilling to give up any secrets, with no catches for searching fingers.

'Can't you sense it?' Ilan complained as she slapped her palms flat against stone in frustration.

He certainly thought a lot of this supposed new divinity.

'I'm sorry, I can feel it's *there*, but I don't have the ability to dissolve layers of rock. Perhaps ask your dog.'

He raised an eyebrow at her testiness, and she forced back another apology. She deserved to be cranky for a moment.

‘If he were as good at scenting holiness as he is corpses, we’d be set. But he doesn’t even seem to like Mihály.’

Mihály. The fact that the Izir wasn’t back was worrying in itself. They didn’t know where the demon was or what else Tamas might have planned.

This wasn’t how the cathedral was meant to be. Stripped of the human element, it was cold, only stone and wood and glass. Csilla swallowed a lump in her throat. Maybe she’d been alone in finding it a place of hope. Maybe there had never been more to it at all.

‘Did you hear that?’ Ilan asked, catching her arm and pulling her behind him. She hadn’t, too wrapped up in her own thoughts.

Ordinarily the footsteps would have been covered by voices and song, but in the silence they were clear. A door at the end of the hall creaked open, and two long shadows fell across the aisle.

Sandor. And Madame Varga behind him. The woman’s eyes were triumphant, but there was a tiny note of fear.

‘That’s the girl,’ the woman said. ‘The one who attacked me.’

Csilla’s mouth fell open. ‘But you’re fine, and we said . . .’

Sandor shook his head. ‘You said you were going to the cathedral to get help, and then you actually came here. Stupid. She had to find me herself and tell the story.’

‘There is no story,’ Ilan spat.

‘No story in a woman waking up surrounded by blood? A knife in the room?’ Sandor stepped closer. ‘Show me your hands, girl.’

Csilla clenched her fists. She’d washed, but she couldn’t have caught every drop. There would still be signs of blood in her nailbeds or in her hair.

‘The woman is alive.’ Ilan didn’t move from his place between Csilla and Sandor. ‘She clearly drank too much. Perhaps she cut herself, or maybe she’s yet to have her courses stopped. Blood alone is not evidence.’

Sandor's snap of teeth was the grin of a trap closed on a fox's leg.

'Still, we have some questions. How can we not, with the killer we've been searching for no closer to being found, and here we have blood. Come, Ilan. If you're so concerned with the truth, you can help. I wouldn't have put you as one to ignore a potential lead.'

Csilla's voice caught. Any truth would be punishment, a lie unacceptable. Sandor examined her face, her hands that weren't quite clean enough. At least her cheek was better, only faint whitish lines where there had been inflamed scarlet.

The man rubbed the pad of his thumb against a suspicious crust on her nail.

'And you say you had nothing to do with this? The woman was soaked in blood. The prints around her body were little feet.'

And if they removed Csilla's boots they'd see the stains between her toes.

Ilan stepped in front of her.

'The woman was able to call for help and tell you about it herself. There was clearly some accident, but not a crime.'

I did it. The confession was hot in her mouth. She could tell Sandor everything, about the demon, why the glass went dark, the murders and her own hand in them. She could touch his mark right now and show the lingering miracle.

But her confession would only make things worse, at least until they had Tamas. And if Ilan was right, she couldn't trust anyone who claimed to belong to the Church.

'Mihály came to get me. Madame Varga was sleeping when I left. She seemed fine.' Not a confession, but still the truth, or part of it.

'But you must have seen the blood. What did you think of that? And our local heretic? You seem closer to him than anyone.'

'Suspiciously so,' Madame Varga interjected, and hot anger bolted through Csilla. To have her of all people making accusations.

‘He stopped preaching heresy. At my request.’ She thought the admission would emphasise how good she’d been. Sandor only grimaced.

‘I was wrong to let you go the first time. Ilan, see if she’ll give you a better answer after twenty lashes.’

Csilla’s head swam, her breath freezing in anticipation of the pain.

‘That’s excessive,’ Ilan snapped. ‘She’s tiny. Ten would be sufficient.’

Csilla glared. *None* would be sufficient.

‘Inquisitor.’ Ilan gave the title like a curse. ‘If Csilla says she doesn’t know anything, I believe her. Just talking to a former heretic is not a crime.’

Sandor gave him a measured look. ‘Lucky for you.’

The blood drained from Ilan’s face as the man continued.

‘You enjoyed hurting his other followers well enough. She’s no more innocent than they were. And if she won’t talk, you either make her or make her wish she had.’

Csilla shuddered. Her bones were close enough to the skin as it was; he’d whip her to ribbons.

‘That is ridiculous,’ Ilan spat, voice rising. ‘She doesn’t have a soul. It doesn’t matter what she does.’

To her surprise, Sandor didn’t even look askance at that. She narrowed her eyes. Someone had told him about her history, even though she’d left the Church before he came.

Pray that Sandor didn’t see fit to test whether she was still soulless after all.

‘Even if she can’t sin, attempted murder is a crime. She’s our only witness, and you know what to do with witnesses who won’t talk.’ Sandor grinned, flecks of spittle on his teeth as he held out the whip from his belt, a coiled and braided lash that would make a nasty crack. ‘Even the best hound can’t have two masters. If you won’t do it, perhaps the Prelate would also like to know how you have been leaving the city with the heretic, spending time you should have been with me chasing fancies and this girl. Is she the reason you wanted the whole place to yourself? Certainly clever, though I don't think the Prelate will think much of you whoring in the cathedral.'

Ilan turned a sick shade of pale, breath short like he'd been punched. Csilla took a deep breath and thought of Arany laying herself out for the world and pouring her blood into the earth. This wouldn't even kill her. She'd seen Ilan's kindness, she could bear his cruelty.

'You're right. I have listened to heresy. Perhaps I don't belong here. But you're not going to get anything out of me but the truth.'

Whatever was done to her wouldn't be any worse than what she'd already been through, and they still needed Ilan to be above suspicion. They had to stay in the cathedral a little longer. She still needed to touch the Seal. Raising her chin, she glanced at Ilan and prayed he could read her gaze.

'Beat me, then, if you think it will set this right.'

Sandor looked surprised, a look that deepened as Ilan snatched the whip from his hand, took Csilla's, and pulled her down the hall.

The inside of the torture chamber was as awful as Csilla had always pictured it, dark and claustrophobic, with a lingering reek of copper and old leather. There were tables and instruments of twisted metal whose purpose she didn't desire to know. While prayer halls and places of shelter had burned, this room was pristine. What that said about Asten's inscrutable will was nothing good.

Ilan tossed the whip on a table, and for a moment the fear that had stolen Csilla's moment of bravery dissolved. He wasn't going to harm her. Then Sandor walked in, shutting the door like the closing of a tomb.

Ilan took a light wooden cane from the wall, swinging it with easy grace. It whistled as it stung the air.

Csilla clamped her fingers together, trying to press all her shaking into her hands. There were those who put themselves here willingly to cleanse even minor sins. Maybe it would make her feel better. Lighter. Clean.

'You're being soft on her,' Sandor chided.

Ilan brought the cane down in another measured arc. 'Shall I show you how soft it is?'

Csilla's eyes darted to the strung ropes and shackles, the short lead he'd used to drag her in when she'd cost him his position in the first place. Then she set her shoulders and breathed the leather-scented air like sacrament. Saints and martyrs had endured far worse than a little beating.

But she wasn't being punished for her faith. She wasn't even the point of this. Her body was to be the battleground on which they fought, and Sandor had rigged it to come out the winner whether Ilan obeyed or not.

'Where would you like me to stand?' The words came from a dissociated place of calm, untouched by the dread ribboning down her spine.

The only real blessing was that Ágnes would never know about this.

He gestured to the iron bar set out from the wall. She stepped to it and offered him her back, and put her hands up without prompting. The cold metal chafed, and her fingers settled into worn grooves where countless others had stood and accepted gloried pain.

'Take off her dress.' Sandor waved down the length of her body. 'She's not going to remember it if you hit her through wool.'

She thought Ilan would argue, but he nodded as she clutched the cloth of her overdress.

'You can leave your linens on if you like.' He raised a hand at Sandor's protest. 'We don't need to take her modesty, do we? They're thin enough the blows will feel the same.'

Csilla's hands shook so hard she fumbled with the buttons, and the cloth fell in a pool of ivory around her ankles as cold covered her in goose-flesh. Ilan pulled her hair off her neck and over her shoulder, and she shivered at the brush of his fingers on her throat as he bared her. His thumb scraped a place behind her ear; a dried fleck of blood she'd missed?

Run, every instinct screamed.

You deserve this, another voice said.

Before she could obey the primal pulse, Sandor seized her wrists and tied them to the bar with worn leather straps.

'Tighter,' Ilan said, leaning over her shoulder close enough his breath warmed her neck. 'If she faints, I don't want her to fall.'

'So I dislocate my shoulders?' Her dead weight would wrench bone from socket. She'd seen that kind of injury before, grotesque bulging beneath bruised skin and screams as mercy workers tried to push everything back into place.

'Better than accidentally striking you across the neck,' Ilan replied, but the tension in his voice undercut the calm words. His fear stoked hers.

Sandor's second attempt still wasn't to Ilan's liking, and he redid them with quick and practiced knots, then ran his hand down her forearm. The gentleness was a small comfort against the scratch of rope on wrists.

Sandor stepped back, only visible as a shadow in the side crack of her vision. Further than he had stood before.

Ilan spread his palm between her shoulder blades, then skimmed it further down.

He drew his index finger across her shoulder blades, rubbing the skin through the cloth of her under dress.

'This is where I'm going to hit you.' He paused, tracing another line beneath the first. 'It is going to hurt.'

She winced at the whistle of the cane, but it was another practice blow. The actual pain couldn't be worse than the anticipation burrowing in her stomach.

'Get on with it.' Sandor's voice was tight. His gaze darted between them, trying to watch both at once.

Ilan bent close to her. 'I need you to scream.'

'What?' Csilla's heart was lodged in her throat. She'd heard what came out of this room and seen Ilan's face when he finished a session. Screaming was not going to be a problem.

He pressed his palm against her back, warm and solid. 'Trust me.'

She nodded. Despite the squeeze of leather on her wrists and blows she knew were coming, she did. He'd never been anything but honest with her, even when she was hurting.

He stepped back. 'One.'

She shrieked and dug her palms into the bar as the cane whipped down on her back, a white-hot line of cracking pain.

But not unbearable.

She turned to look at Ilan again. His jaw was set, his arm trembling. And Sandor was still behind, watching for any sign that Ilan wasn't doing his duty.

'Two. Is there anything we should know?'

Nothing you don't know already. 'No.'

The wood came down again. Csilla screamed through another set of strokes, the sharp sting sending her rigid and tears squeezing out of the corner of her eyes as he continued, blow by blow. He was unfailing in his warnings, followed by pauses to let her gasping cries turn back to easier breaths.

Three more, with questions she couldn't answer accompanying each blow. She was shivering, sinking into the surrender. Her mouth was dry, her ears hurt with the sound of her own moans echoing off the unflinching stone, but she was still standing. There was pride in bearing the pain and comfort in the confidence with which he applied it. She'd done a miracle worthy of any saint. She could be a martyr.

He touched her side as if to adjust her, but she could feel the assurance behind it. A smile ghosted over her cracked lips, and she readied herself to be struck again.

32

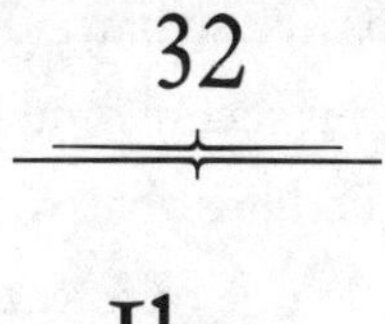

Ilan

ILAN CLENCHED his teeth as he rolled Csilla onto his bed. She whimpered and buried her face in his pillow. At least she wouldn't see the sick guilt mixing with his gratitude. She shouldn't have offered to submit. He shouldn't have accepted. There hadn't been a choice.

His inner clothes were soaked with sweat, chilling with the fading adrenaline.

'Csilla.'

There was no answer. He instinctively reached out to touch her, then hesitated. Perhaps he'd lost the right to touch her kindly.

'I know it hurts, but it's over.' He replayed the past minutes, wrist flexing in memory. 'You did well. He believes that you don't know anything.'

She turned her head slightly with a quiet murmur, an eye and part of her face visible from her curtain of dark hair. She had the look of a deer with an arrow through the throat, awaiting the last seconds before the inevitable.

He sat next to her and brushed the hair away from her face so he could see her better. She tilted her head slightly, a hint of forgiving pressure against his palm that went straight to his traitorous heart.

The part of him that ached to see her desolation was infuriating. He'd never met anyone who tried so hard to be good for so little reward. It was what faith required, but seeing it taken to conclusion was unsettling more than inspiring. Perhaps that was what made Sandor relent and not throw Csilla directly out onto the empty streets in a city too afraid of shadows to open a door of charity to a stranger. Even Justice and Obedience had to acknowledge the role of Mercy in the Faith.

Perhaps he simply wanted Ilan to stew and suffer. If so, that was also fine. Resentment might not nourish, but it was invigorating in its own way.

'Can I look at your back? I'll put something on it.'

He'd had to poultice Vihar when he'd busted his leg on a fence, and he kept a few things for headaches and monthly pains and the like. With the servants now spread through the city and the remaining mercy priests busy with the burned, there was no one to call for her. There was no one else he'd want to tend to her. It was his responsibility to fix what his hands had done.

She shifted, hand clenching at his blanket as she seemed to weigh the relative pain and modesty. Finally she nodded, and he gently lifted her shift.

He'd struck well, the thought bringing a possessive sense of pride as he sat next to her. There were sharp welts across her upper back, purple blooming out of the red and pale islands of skin between them, but he hadn't broken her, hadn't risked any organs. It was beautifully done, and she'd been brave.

'Well?' The misery in her voice tamped down his admiration of his own handiwork.

'You're fine. Or will be.' He rubbed his finger in the mixture until it warmed with his skin and soaked strips of linen. He lay a strip across the first of the marks, the line of flesh hot and swollen. She flinched but didn't ask him to stop.

When he was small, his family chapel held a painting of Vasya, hung so she caught the sunlight in the layers of paint and gesso, and he'd kept it dusted and lit candles beneath, and tried and failed to recreate its entirety for his own altar. Her image was still the first thing that came to mind when asked to think on the beauty of holiness.

It was nothing compared to Csilla.

'If we can't find the Seal, or if we fail, I need you to leave,' Ilan said finally. 'My parents are in the city. They can pay enough to get out of lockdown, take you to Saika, away from all this.'

They would if he asked. For all the trouble he'd made for them, they had always done everything he asked. Too much so, perhaps. Here he was, still expecting to be spoiled, relying on them again.

She turned with a wince, body going momentarily rigid and sheets falling off her bare shoulder.

'What will going to Saika do? All I'll see if I leave is the refugees at the gates, reminding us of how we failed them, and Shadow will come to every remote corner eventually. If I'm needed anywhere, it's here.'

'Doing what?' She was holy, yes, but they didn't know how to use her power. He wasn't even sure she could use her power when it was all at the discretion of the divine. 'What if it doesn't work?'

There was passion in her eyes but no violence. It was the warmth of a hearth fire, just as alive and comforting.

'Then I can still help. It's better than running away.' She smoothed her hair and shifted, moving gingerly with lingering pain. 'They can hardly do anything worse to me than everything they've already done. And I have so much to make up for.'

She couldn't possibly believe that. 'None of it was your fault.'

'Of course it was.' Her eyes met his, clouding with quiet despair that cracked his heart. 'I said yes.'

There was nothing he could say that would take that knowledge from her.

She shifted to cover herself again, tugging her shift over pale thighs and bony knees.

Then she moved to stand.

'What are you doing?' He reached for her arm, but she caught his hand instead, fingers closing around his in a gentle grip as arresting as a vise.

'We can't just stop.' The pained set of her jaw undercut the determination in the words, and Ilan pressed his palm more firmly against hers, shifting her back to the bed.

'You're not in the shape to go anywhere.'

She frowned but didn't shake him off. Or pull her hand away.

'That doesn't matt—'

'That's the only thing that matters.' The divine might be waiting, but they had very human concerns at the moment. Csilla's pain. His own exhaustion. Hunger and filth.

'We can't just give up.' But as she tried to get her feet under her, her shoulder twisted forward and she gasped, soft lips pulling back to show teeth.

'If you keep going, you're going to be cold. Tired. In more pain than you are now.'

She deflated, sinking into the stuffed mattress. 'No good to anyone at all, you mean.'

'Not what I said.' She was so much more than what she could do for others. 'But if that's what gets you to stay here, then yes.'

She squeezed his hand, and though there was no shine, the warmth of her fingers kindled a heat. He pulled away, and she looked down, hands bunching in his sheets.

'Fine.'

'Good. I'll lock the door.' She'd be safe while he robbed the dead.

'Where are you going?' Panic coloured her voice as she reached for him again, and he forced himself to step out of the grasp of her stretched fingers. There would be no further contamination of her holiness.

'To get things for you. Clothes. Food.'

She brightened at that, the first spark he'd seen in far too long. Then she settled on her side, taking his pillow and cradling it against her. He turned to stop looking at the sight she made.

'Be quick then, will you?'

'As quick as I can.'

'Did you know she was special?'

The corpse didn't answer; of course she didn't. It was a struggle to get the robes over stiff arms, and he apologised silently as a rough tug sent her neck lolling. Church dead were never sent out with even their clothing; cloth was far too dear to waste. That didn't mean Csilla would have appreciated seeing this.

'You must have known something.' He'd never had much cause to speak with Ágnes, save at clergy meetings; he preferred to take care of himself and leave the mercy crews out of it. 'Otherwise you wouldn't have spent so much time on her.'

But maybe Ágnes had just been better than the rest of them.

There wasn't much in the kitchen, either; they'd taken what was good to the families housing the displaced clergy. The onions and potatoes that had been left were spongy with rot, and the bread that had been missed was stale. It was still better than nothing.

He opened the door quietly when he returned, in case Csilla was sleeping. By her quiet, even breaths, she was, but there were damp spots on the pillow. Ilan folded up the robe and placed it by her head when he caught sight of her splayed hand. The chaffing on her wrist, the angry red where he'd tied the leather, was gone. Sucking in a breath, he leaned forward, combing back a thick hank of her hair and tugging down the neckline of her shift enough to see what had just been bruise-mottled skin.

She looked untouched. Freshly born.

A prayer rested on his lips as he knelt beside her in silent worship as she slept on the altar of his bed. It wasn't miracle enough to be worth waking her for, but it was a miracle all the same.

33

Csilla

Ágnes's robes were heavy, the hood drawn so far down she had to turn her whole head to see anything but the shade of the cloth. She traced the embroidered poppies on the rough fabric, loose threads she had sewn back herself for practice, the hem worn ragged from walking the streets in service. They had been well-filled in their life and even now kept her safe, knowledge that was an ache in her heart with each whisper of fabric on rubble. If anyone looked, they would see a mercy worker sweeping up ash and stone, persevering in caring for what had already been lost. She wouldn't give them a chance to see her face or cross-marked hand. She wouldn't let them see what she was really looking for.

And Mihály still hadn't returned, though she glanced at the open gates time and time again. It had only been a day and some hours, but it took mere moments for things to go wrong.

She pushed another chunk of broken rock, bringing a puff of pale dust with it. A small, annoyed meow echoed from the hollow in the wall.

'There you are!'

Csilla grabbed the cat despite the claws catching her arm, dropping a kiss on the dirty fur of her head. Erzsébet squirmed, jumping from

Csilla's arms and then twining against her legs as if to say there was no harm done.

A catch rubbed in her throat at the normalcy in this broken place. The cat didn't know what had happened, save that Csilla was no longer around to slip her dinner. And even that she forgave. Csilla reached to give her another scratch, for a moment absorbed by the illusion of the life she had wanted: meaningful service and her cat.

Bells sang across the city, calling joy in the blue sky. A quick tolling pattern she hadn't heard in far too long – not horror, but celebration.

Finally.

Asten spoke in whispers, but the Incarnate came with a gale. The gold of his carriage caught the shafts of sun breaking through billowing clouds, tossing off light that people leaning out windows raised their hands to like coin. The hooves of his horses, a gleaming team six strong, cracked against the cobblestone with hammer-strike precision as they approached the cathedral courtyard, and he was followed by a half-dozen of his militant guard, the oddly cheerful jostle of their armour joining the ringing bell choir. It was enough to make anyone believe in a coming judgement.

Csilla stepped back against the stone, watching from behind an outcropping. Prelate Abe was in front of the sanctuary, in his High Day vestments, the billowing robe embroidered with silver thread marks of four and Arany's golden hands and wings. The picture he made was marred by the dark shadows under his eyes and the weighted slump of his shoulders.

Ilan stood at his right, lips pressed in a thin line. Sandor was on the left, slightly back, equally grim. The horses pulled so close to the stairs Csilla's breath caught.

The Incarnate stepped from the carriage onto ground that seemed too filthy for his feet. Prelates and Elders were allowed a white on their robes to show how close they were to Brilliance, but the Incarnate dressed in white so bright it hurt to look at, embroidered with silver words of holiness, such a contrast to the scattered dirt stone that he almost appeared to hover. The head above the robes was wizened but strong, grey hair closely cropped and the warm brown shade of his eyes not matched in the judging look in them. He was an image of Church authority that could have easily joined the ranks of painted angels in the cathedral's heart, and Csilla dipped in a habit-born pointless genuflection.

'It's a joyous thing to have you back in the city,' Abe said, but the Incarnate was eyeing the damage to the Cathedral and Arany's dry gold. A shamed pang grabbed her chest at the contrast of his gilded splendour and the sorry state of the grounds.

'A necessary thing, by the look of it.' His disapproval radiated. 'Why was I not informed of how much damage there was directly? I had to hear from pilgrims and lay priests from our stops. What is there left for us now?'

Abe and Ilan exchanged a glance, and Csilla bit her lip at the simmering anger there. He would leave them, too, and then there would be nothing. She wrapped her arms around herself, a metallic taste filling her mouth as the nameless ocean washed her again. It was the same sensation of being passed through.

A metal splash echoed, followed by another and another. Abe gave a soft cry of praise as dripping gold beaded on the courtyard, falling from each of Arany's dozen eyes.

'She weeps again. Your presence gives us hope, Incarnate. A sign not all has been lost.'

The drops condensed to a puddling sheen on the stone, the clear sky and spires above reflected in perfect gold.

Sandor coughed, and the Incarnate glanced at him, looking between him and Ilan in puzzlement as if seeing for the first time. 'Who is this new High Inquisitor?'

Abe stilled. 'You sent him to us, Your Divinity.'

Csilla pressed her hand harder against the wall, leaning forward to hear.

'I can understand his confusion,' Sandor said. His voice was placid, no stress on his face. 'The man I replaced broke his leg near Mitlosk. Word was sent to you, but we decided it was better if someone went than no one at all and far better than waiting the months it would take him to recover, if he did. Was the message missed?'

'He had your writ, stamped with your mark,' Abe confirmed.

'I thought you said you came from the front,' Ilan said, a trap-hook look in his eyes.

'It's certainly near enough the mountains to be considered a front, and one of the most precarious spots at the moment.' Sandor offered his hand to the Incarnate who inspected the signet ring, twisting it with narrowed eyes. 'I was on the pressing front two years ago trying to reclaim the southwest, yes. After spending time with the Servants of the Road.'

At this, the Incarnate stepped back with a slight nod.

'Your face does look familiar.' It seemed like a lie, if a polite one.

'It would be an honour if you remember, Your Divinity. There were many of us there.'

Ilan's gaze found Csilla's even in the shadows, and she could read the suspicion, though there was nothing to be done for it at the moment. If the Incarnate was satisfied, they could hardly argue.

The Incarnate gave a slow nod.

'Then let me see the sanctuary. I can pray for your dead while I look over this disaster.'

He entered alone, his faithful guard with their backs to the door as it shut. What would he make of it? Perhaps Asten's voice would soften the horrors for him, though they wouldn't for her. Perhaps he had enough experience that he could make sense of the dim nausea that came with enlightenment of the eternal.

She couldn't get past the guards, but that wasn't the only way in. She sprinted around the side, to the smaller door where novices carried in the boxes of candles and incense for the altar, an unobtrusive door for the endless menial work that kept the fires of holiness burning.

There were luckily a few older boxes, half-cracked and dirty, that could be pushed around in a show of cleaning. It would be less suspicious to be caught than to confront. As far as she knew he hadn't laid direct eyes on her since she was a small and confounding thing, unlikely to recognise the young woman in grey fruitlessly trying to repair what was better thrown out. With a quiet apology to whoever had carried over the box in the first place, she picked it up and let it drop.

The wood splintered with a sharp crack and crash, and she braced herself as quick footsteps marched toward her. There was a startled violence in his eyes – she hadn't considered the reaction a man newly back from war would have to a crash. But it softened.

'Ah, a mercy girl. I didn't think anyone was here.'

Csilla smiled, clenching her hand so there was no chance of him seeing the crossed cut.

'Your Divinity.' She took a deep breath, ready to confess, even if she couldn't readily explain. With all of Asten's grace behind him, he would know what she was, and what could be done. It would be wonderful to pass over some responsibility and feel less burdened. 'I—'

He continued as if she hadn't spoken.

'There's no work for you here. I need to survey the damage, not have it repaired. I have asked to be alone.'

The voice should be telling him to go to the Seal. They should be telling him who she was and why she was here. She waited for the light of recognition in his face, but all that came were further creases of impatience between his brows. He was a hair's breadth from calling his guards, and there would be no hiding then.

'I'm sorry, Your Divinity, but I have to show you.' She reached out, but when small hands touched weathered ones, the Incarnate pulled back like she was something noxious. There was no spark of acknowledgement, much less divine fire. Her mouth only tasted of old spit, her skin only warm with the layers of wool.

He didn't know her at all.

'If you want a blessing, there are other ways to get it. Do you not understand what a dire situation we are in? If I took time for every single person's individual prayers, I'd be here a thousand years and we'd be no closer to glory.'

Explanation of her miracles, already stuttering, died on her tongue. Csilla swallowed, hiding her expression with a bow. She wanted to say nothing, but it would be a lie. She was alight with everything, painful as it was. She couldn't say it was nothing.

'I can tell you're new to this, so have faith. The city is suffering, but there is meaning behind it. We will overcome this, and be stronger.'

Her mouth twisted. That was what people always said when there was nothing they could do.

The platitude was another piece of dry kindling in her newly formed kiln of deep anger, and she opened her mouth when fresh commotion outside caused them both to turn.

Mihály. And Tamas beside him, not fighting, not speaking. He looked frighteningly calm for a man being brought for a trial he would never be able to defend himself in, looking at his pupil as proud as a father at his child's first recitations.

Csilla's heart skipped at the wrongness. Of everyone here, she was the only one who seemed afraid.

'Who are you? Who let you in?'

Mihály's smile was cutting as he placed a single hand on the plated door frame. There was no shift at first, but a shiver passed over and through Csilla, deep and cool and picking at the oldest-laid blessings of the Church. An answering glow ringed him in silver, pure as morning light and a painful contrast to his grim expression.

The Incarnate sucked in a breath.

'You're the Izir who has been causing so much trouble. I thought you were dead.'

'Well, it's a very good thing I'm not,' Mihály said, pushing Tamas to stumble over the threshold. 'I've just answered your prayers. This is the man who organised the fall of the city.'

Csilla waited for Tamas to speak up and say that Mihály was the man whose hands did the dirty work. He remained quiet, which was worse.

'And you think this buys you pardon?' The Incarnate shook his head and raised his hand.

Freshly drawn blades gleamed behind their backs as the guards strode in and surrounded them.

Mihály's eyes found hers, widened and wild, but there was nothing she could do. She couldn't let herself be seen by Abe, or defend Mihály and condemn herself. Guilty and sick, she turned and fled back through the small door as the Incarnate's order echoed.

'Arrest them both.'

34

Ilan

THE IZIR had accepted his imprisonment with uncharacteristic quiet. Ilan could see the weight of the truth Csilla had dragged out in the press of shadows on his cheeks and the sag of his shoulders. Wilting didn't suit him.

Night brought with it a fresh fall of silence as Ilan escorted Csilla to the cells holding the prisoners. She'd said that when the Incarnate touched her, he hadn't known her. It didn't seem possible that whatever Tamas had done could silence the voice of Asten, but either Csilla was lying, or the Incarnate was. One of those seemed more likely than the other.

Tamas sat cross-legged on the floor of his cell, unbothered by his lack of over clothing or the dingy surroundings. Perhaps his long association with evil burned him from the inside, for he didn't even shiver at the cold that seeped up through Ilan's boots. For so many nights the image of their enemy had just been a wisp of candle smoke in the dark, and now he was here. The placidity of the man's lined face unnerved him. He should be begging. He would beg.

'The inquisitor.' Tamas's mouth worked awkwardly as he spoke, jaw swollen and yellowing with a bruise in the shape of Mihály's fist.

Csilla stepped right to the bars of the cell, an odd note of pity on her face. Of course she could dredge up sympathy for an enemy.

‘Ah,’ Tamas continued, tilting his chin. ‘And the mercy girl. Here to stand for me? I tried to save you, you know. How many times did I ask you to leave?’

Only Ilan could see her tremble. ‘You did, and at least three. And for that I’ll bring you water and a blanket, so you don’t suffer before you die. I’ll pray; death is not the worst thing that can happen if you confess and accept your punishment. But I can’t defend you.’

His eyes narrowed, but he nodded, approving. ‘Perhaps you’ll survive the coming Shadow after all.’

Ilan stepped to her side, resisting the urge to put a steadying hand on her back.

‘Is that what you wanted, then? Demons can’t be controlled. You’ve only damned yourself.’

‘Perhaps I have. Perhaps I’m truly serving the divine, more than anyone else here in this overbuilt cage of stone and gold ever has.’ He dragged his knuckles over the rusted bars in emphasis.

‘How would death serve Them?’ Csilla’s voice was cut with anger.

‘Any chance we had at true faith was stolen when Arany left her mark on the world. Just a little bit of stolen divinity, vague enough that the Church could twist it to suit its own needs.’

‘You may have broken Silgard, but you didn’t win.’ She nodded, firm. ‘There are still priests who can fight.’

Not many, and not well. And not when they didn’t know where an enemy would turn up next. Not when the next body it took could be someone dear.

‘There’s nothing to *win*, child. Everything, the false safety you cling to, that warmonger on his throne, everything but that blood in the dirt is a lie. Go see what’s left for yourself.’

That was what they wanted to do. It sent a curl of wrongness to him that Tamas would want that too.

'You say I hate the Church,' he continued. 'I do hate the Church, but I love the Faith. Asten left us, and pretending They care how well we model piety and pray isn't going to bring Them back. They never wanted this, never wanted us. Humanity has to stand alone through the long darkness to prove ourselves worthy and come out purified on the other side. The Seal was holding us back, not saving us. Has there been a single miracle in all the time we've kept the doctrine? Anything at all to show that the Church is right to keep us in its service?'

'One,' Ilan spoke up before Csilla. 'There was one.'

Tamas sat back, mouth coy. 'Indeed.'

Now Ilan leaned heavy on the bars. 'Where did you send the demon?'

Tamas shrugged. 'What makes you think I didn't banish it now that our work is done?'

'If we can't, I know you can't. Who did you send it to? How many of your people are in Silgard?'

'A handful here, more elsewhere. Those of us who have seen enough to know how we've gone astray. Silgard's walls are a blindfold.'

'I don't want your reasons. I want names and numbers. I want to know how we can stop this.' Ilan reached forward but was stopped by Csilla's hand on his arm.

'We already have him here. You don't have to hurt him further. He's already going to die.' She should hate him for what he did to her and the blood his zealotry put on her hands.

'And I'll give you one part for free,' Tamas said, shifting so shadows fell across his face. 'You can't stop it.'

A dull clang of a foot hitting metal ricocheted, and Csilla stiffened.

'Mihály.' She gave another warning look at Ilan before hurrying to the other cell. He watched as she went to her knees and reached between the bars towards the angel tied in the dark and felt a dull, unwelcome ache.

Easier to think about hurting the man before him. He wrapped a hand around the bar and leaned forward again.

'You'll never be pardoned, but confessing now will save your soul.'

The answering laugh was hollow. 'And if I say my soul is fine, you have no way to verify.'

It was true and caustic.

'At least confess that the Izir had nothing to do with it, and they'll let him go. You can do that much.' That was almost a lie; Ilan wasn't sure of it at all.

Tamas shook his head. 'He didn't plan to kill, but he had everything to do with it.'

There was an answering slam of a heel against metal and a grunt from further down, Csilla jumping back with soothing words.

'Were you also the one who burned the cathedral? More ritual? Or was that simple distraction?' Tamas had known where they were and that Csilla had to be alone. The man inclined his head, a teacher's quiet praise of a clever student.

'Shall I confess something you don't know, Inquisitor? Something that might help you understand why I did what I did? Come closer. I'd like to see your face when you hear, and Misi broke my glasses.'

Good for him.

'There is nothing that would justify what you did.' He would know. Ilan had spent his whole life weighing one thing against another, finding the purest path. There was no justice that could balance the current suffering.

'I tried to kill Csilla to save her from all this,' he said. 'Tried to poison her as surely as your Church tried to kill Misi. But she walked away.'

Ilan didn't trust himself to speak as a slow rage spread, crimson licking the edges of his vision.

'Tried to save yourself so she wouldn't get close enough to figure out what you were doing.'

The man gave a little laugh.

'It was kill her or use her to kill. Two sides of a coin. Do you think she'll like remembering cutting that woman's throat? But it doesn't matter. She lived. And so did the Varga woman.'

'You made a mistake.' It was common enough for a physician to mix up one bottle with another, or not realise a herb had lost its potency. Even the most experienced mercy worker sometimes showed up with a confession that the mushroom they thought would nourish had turned out to be something fatal.

'I did indeed, but not the one you think. What does it mean, when a poison neutralises on the tongue?'

It was a question for first-year seminary.

'The miracle of Imre. A few Izir also share the gift, but we would have known if she were that blessed.' If only she had been from the outset. She would have served the world so much better than the man tied up scant feet from them. Her life would have been quiet, and happy.

'The incorruptible tongue, the miracle of Imre, and every Incarnate after him. Or so they say.' The man glanced aside, though from the angle there was no way he could see Csilla. 'I don't think they actually make them drink to prove themselves.'

'Impossible.' His head pounded with the idea. 'She would know.' The entire point of the Incarnate was as a conduit. There was something special about her, but she didn't hear Them.

'We succeeded in breaking every other ward. Including whatever was on her; I wasn't the one who made a mistake. I just wasn't open to the impossible.' He shut his eyes momentarily. 'I didn't expect my little angel to end up with a perfect saint in his ear.'

A saint. More than a saint, the true Incarnate, the one human hand allowed to brush the edge of the Severing and hear a part of the divine will. He turned his head to look at Csilla kneeling in the shadows, stroking Mihály's bound hands while silver danced around them.

'Now where did the demon go? You'll die soon enough. Telling me won't erase your victory.'

'As you will.' There was a dark glint in his eye. 'I've already been a far better servant than you.'

The man's fingers were callused, but no trace of burns or caustic oils. Ilan grabbed his smallest finger.

He hesitated. Tamas would scream, and Csilla would find a new reason to fuss.

But he had tried to kill her.

Now the man flailed, a fish caught on a barbed hook as Ilan twisted. The joint separated with a rewarding pop and an even more satisfying scream.

'You're going to say what you like regardless of what I do,' Tamas hissed as Ilan moved to his ring finger. 'I've told you all I will. I'll accept the rope around my neck.'

'Oh, this is just because I want to.' He twisted the second finger, bending it back and stretching skin and tendon as the man's eyes went glassy with pain. Leaning close, Ilan could see his reflection, sharp and well-justified.

'Ilan!' Csilla was beside him in an instant, a reprimand in her hazel eyes. 'You said you wouldn't hurt him.'

'No, you told me not to hurt him.' *And it's not like he extended you the same courtesy.*

Her eyebrows drew together in frustrated censure. 'I'm going to get them water,' she said simply, turning. 'You won't hurt him further. Especially not for your own enjoyment.'

He almost snorted at how simply she gave the order, expecting him to obey. But this care was her element, as surely as bones breaking under his hands was his.

Tamas's soft moans drowned in the slide of the door as she left with a final glance over her shoulder. Ilan gritted his teeth and turned from Tamas's cell to Mihály's, working the lock open with a bent key.

'Mihály.'

The Izir had been allowed to keep most of his clothing, though his pants were creased and filthy and his linen undershirt stained. Ilan worked the gag out of his mouth with quick fingers, nose wrinkling at the stale smell of it as Mihály rubbed sensation back into his face. Who would have ever imagined he'd be wanting the angel to talk.

'Took you long enough. Csilla couldn't get the door or that knot. Is she gone?'

Ilan resisted the urge to shove the gag back. 'Gone to get you water. How are you feeling?'

'Do you actually care? I'm fine considering I'm tied up and can't even piss except under guard. Which is quite unfair considering I brought you the man behind all this.' His nostrils flared in indignation.

'Your hands were the ones that held the knife.' But he did have a point.

Mihály went very still. 'And I was the one who gave him a chance to use his magic. Believe me, I know.' He swallowed. 'Csilla seems upset.'

That was an understatement. She was still sore, no doubt, and heartsick. Confused. Perfect.

'Did you hear what the man said about her?' He kept his voice low, though Tamas was unlikely to hear anything over his own laboured breathing.

Mihály's face lit with a strangely innocent illumination. 'It's all true. You've seen it. She lights brighter than the Eye itself at the touch of the divine. I wouldn't be shocked if the rest of her was incorruptible as well.'

Incorruptible. The quick healing of her flesh, how those red welts and plum bruises had faded to pale canvas within hours. The only marks that stayed on her were holy scars. No wonder poison turned to sugar on her tongue.

Another miracle from the yellowed pages of history that the current Incarnate had never shown.

'But there's no sign she hears the voice?' The craving for guidance hit with a pang of hunger. One word to show they were still being watched, that though perhaps some parts were misguided, their efforts were acknowledged, appreciated.

'Maybe They don't speak to her, but she can certainly speak to Them.'

'We still need to get her to the Seal.' They hadn't had any luck finding a true entrance. They were as likely to die in the labyrinth as find what they needed. 'With the Incarnate here there will be more clergy around. We're not going to be able to search.'

Mihály closed his eyes, lashes pale on his cheeks.

'I have an idea for that. She is going to hate it.'

35

Csilla

'NO. ABSOLUTELY not.'

Csilla's hands shook as she avoided Mihály's offered arms, not wanting to be swayed. She wouldn't stand here, wearing robes of mercy grey, and accept that he wanted to die.

'How do you know they'll even agree? Your death, or your request – the ethics of killing you were why they sent me in the first place.' Besides, the public wouldn't want to see him hang. She hoped.

'I still have some influence, and my death will be a bargaining chip,' Mihály assured her, voice far calmer than hers. Ilan had untied him, but the abrasions on his wrists were raw sores. 'Hang me, have them take my body to the Seal. You'll be my attendant. Then you'll do your work, with whatever holiness you have.'

Her work. She didn't even know what that was. 'I don't know how I brought Madame Varga back. I don't know if I can do the same for you.' It certainly hadn't worked for Ágnes. She'd been used to wield the power, but she hadn't been offered control.

'And I'm not asking you to. Let me do my penance.'

He leaned back against the cell wall, old dust shaking loose with the brush of his shirt. There were cleaner lines in the dirt on his face, where tears had washed tracks.

'Your penance would be better served with a long life lived well, in the service of others.' He could save ten lives for every one he'd taken if it made him feel better. It was selfish, but she didn't want to lose anyone else.

He gave her a measured look. 'I've never been very good at that. And what would you have me do instead? Escape? I promised I'd help you save the city, even if you told me you no longer wanted to. You can't go back on that now.'

He was right. She'd refused to run when Tamas had pressured, when Ilan had offered. She couldn't ask anything more of Mihály.

Desperation began to claw at the edges of her breath. She forced it down. There was a way. Saints had faced worse hardships.

Saints.

The beginnings of an idea whispered in her mind, twisted and holy.

'Ilan. Will you be the one to kill him?' She pressed her palms together, the scarred cuts raised between them, silently pleading for his trust.

Mihály laughed. 'Oh I bet he'll volunteer.'

Ilan rolled his eyes. 'I'm sure if I offered they would allow me the task. But what, you think we can pull him from the stage in front of everyone? That Mihály will grow wings and fly away? Me pulling the lever doesn't mean he won't die.' He turned back to the Izir. 'Are you sure there's nothing you can do?'

'You've seen everything I can do. Maybe that's why Asten allows so few of us.' Mihály's lip curled. 'People always want so much from Izir, and they're always disappointed.'

'Just give me a moment.' Images flashed through her head. Mihály's drink-tinged breath. Stiff blood on the bodies. Her wrists tied heavy to the wall, recitations of saint stories and miracles as she knelt on stone, her bony knees wearing through already old wool. 'You're right. We've got to let him hang.'

They stared at her.

'Let him hang,' she clarified, 'not let him die. Like Angyalka before her visions. She hung herself and lived.' She'd seen it illustrated in dozens of ways, some where she looked to be no more than sleeping, showing children the peace of suffering for a greater good, and some that showed that while it was good, it was still suffering. Angyalka's days of hanging, choked and barely conscious, had led to the naming of the first Incarnate and the promise of Asten's eventual return.

Mihály raised an eyebrow. 'She was blessed, and she only did it to show us the way forward. I'm not vain enough to compare myself to a saint.'

It wasn't false hope, if he trusted her. If she trusted herself. 'She's the best example but not the only one. I've read about executions years ago, before we found a better way. The hanged didn't always die at first.' Executioners always carried an extra blade, and even now the inquisitorial robes had an unused pocket for thin knives.

Well. Maybe not so unused in some cases. Csilla was fairly certain Ilan made sure there was always a quick way to dispense justice at hand.

Ilan nodded slowly. 'If the rope and the drop are calculated properly, the hanged would choke instead of snap. It's not that hard to strangle someone. And it's slower.' His lip quirked on the last words, almost like the thought was pleasant.

Csilla pushed that aside, and Mihály frowned, pulling at his own damp collar like it was a noose.

'We could make a harness, something to take some of the tension. Mihály, like you tied up the animals.' She traced her fingers against the floor, imagining what it could look like. Rope under ribs and arms. It might twist or pop a joint, but it was better than death.

Mihály stroked his beard. 'If you can get access to anything left in the mercy stores, I can teach you to make something to make me seem deader than I would look otherwise. We can thank Tamas for that.'

Of course she could. Even now she could smell the phantom aroma of crushed herbs. It was the same science of care she'd studied her whole life.

'But Mihály, if we're wrong . . .' She reached up, and he bowed to let her take his face in her hands. 'You'll be dead.'

'Then don't be wrong.' His lips brushed her forehead, and the air around them sparked like lightning.

Then it lit with something brighter, orange flame and dark shadow shapes slipping across the stone walls.

Sandor stood before the cell, a torch in hand. His eyebrows were drawn, his lips parted in shock. He had seen them. Csilla pulled herself tall. Her hood was down, and her face uncovered. He would know who she was. If he truly was a man of faith, he would know what that light meant.

He'd sent her to be whipped but thought he was in pursuit of some lead, doing what was right in questioning the girl with blood on her hands. And regardless of whether she could truly convince herself of that or not, there was no way to talk their way out of the truth written in the glow on her skin.

'Csilla,' Ilan warned, but she shook her head. It wasn't that she didn't want to hide and save herself. It was that now the only way out was to show everything.

She carefully took Mihály's hand, divine light illuminating her in outline, sparking along her skin with transformative fire.

Sandor flinched as if it were true lightning, a hand shielding his eyes.

'What is this?'

Csilla removed her hand and let the light die.

'Asten,' she said quietly.

He breathed what sounded like a prayer.

'You were right.' This was the only card she had now, and she'd play it even if it was played to lose. 'Madame Varga's blood was on me. It could have been a tragedy. But They saved her, through me.' She met his gaze. 'I don't know why or how. But I believe I can restore the Seal's power. It might be our only chance.' She reached for him in an offering of peace, but he shied away from her touch.

'And you haven't brought this to the Incarnate?' The words dripped with censure.

Csilla swallowed. It was a question, not a statement that he would tell. That was a good sign, but something in her shrunk back at the sight of him, the smudging scent of smoke from his oil lamp. The bruises may have faded quickly, but the memory of the cane strikes and the snide way he'd ordered them weren't so easily erased.

'No.' Ilan saved her from having to answer. 'We have reason to think he wouldn't agree.'

Sandor seemed to chew on that for a moment.

'Wouldn't agree to the restoration of the Church's power?'

Csilla didn't blame him for the suspicion in his voice. She swallowed. Two nooses could just as easily become four.

It was Mihály who spoke up this time.

'Not if it showed him to be powerless.'

'Powerless.' There was an odd note in Sandor's echo, like the dull splash of a stone sinking in still water.

Ilan's brows drew together. 'And you're hardly innocent. You lied about serving with him—'

'Out of convenience and for the sake of efficiency,' Sandor bit. 'Part of that darkness on my soul you saw, perhaps. And as I said, I did serve. Not recently. But not nearly long enough ago.'

'And while you were out there leading the Church to glory or whatever they tell you, did you see or hear of any miracle done at his hands? You were the one who brought the Varga woman back here. Did she tell you about the attack?'

Sandor looked Csilla down again. 'She remembered being stabbed and seeing a cloud of black. She didn't say anything about the . . .' He looked at as if the word didn't want to leave his throat. 'The miracle you describe.'

Ilan stepped in front of her. 'You saw how much blood there was, and you could see for yourself there was no wound. What's your explanation? From what you know of the Incarnate, if we told him this girl was a breathing miracle, that she brought someone back to life . . .'

I didn't. Csilla thought. She felt swept up as if caught in a river tide. She hadn't done anything except be there, but when she tried to explain, her mouth stayed closed.

'Do you think he would set aside everything else and let her try?' Ilan continued 'Do you serve the man or the Faith? If we're wrong and he legitimately serves the divine, he'll be nothing but pleased with our success. If we're wrong, he'll kill her before we have a chance.'

'You think he'll put his pride over the safety of . . .' Sandor paused for long seconds, flickering light creating doubtful expressions. 'Never mind. I saw him at war. I know he will. He's not a man who thinks he can lose.'

Csilla put all the pleading of a prayer into her voice. She didn't want to trust him, but with no way to deny what he'd seen, all she could do was hope for a miracle of conversion to their cause.

'There are a few priests who can still banish, but how many, and for how long? The blood will catch up sooner or later. Help us try. Or at least, please don't stand in our way. I know what a horror it is to lose yourself, to be forced to do things you would never.'

Something unreadable passed over his face, a purse of lips and half a sigh.

'And we've no hope, except for you.' The pointed note in his tone pricked her aching heart. She was exceptional and limited, and all they had.

‘Except for me.’ Her throat burned with swallowed tears. ‘And I can’t be enough. I can’t be everywhere. I can’t save everyone. Only those here.’

Sandor looked past her to Mihály, rubbing at his neck. ‘Including him?’

‘Including him,’ Csilla said firmly. ‘And myself.’ The second part was quieter.

‘And what of Tamas?’ Sandor turned towards the far cell. ‘Are you offering a blanket forgiveness with your miracle?’

‘If I could.’ The clarity in her voice, the strength of that truth, surprised even her. ‘I would not see a single person beyond Brilliance or damn any soul. But that isn’t my forgiveness to give.’ Her eyes met Mihály’s, a warmth diffusing through her at the sweetness there. ‘Only this.’

‘You’re very right, my dear.’ Mihály moved to the front of the cell and spoke, loud enough that the man down the hall could hear. ‘As for Tamas . . . the bastard will hang with me.’

36

Ilan

ILAN KNEW precision. It was the difference between a shattered rib and a pierced lung, a gouge that would serve as a lesson learned and a fatal arterial stab. It had never mattered as much as now.

The rope chafed his fingers, splintered straw scraping Mihály's chest and just strong enough to catch and stop him from his neck being snapped. Not enough to stop him from being strangled. But there would be a few minutes of graced time as he was cut, and the drink prepared would make his muscles lax. It was the same principle that made him not want to work on drunks; their bodies always took too pliantly to torture. At least this was a benefit.

'You don't look nearly as pleased as I thought you would.' Mihály winced as Ilan wrenched the rope more firmly, testing the hook that would take the pressure and keep his neck from snapping. 'I thought this was your idea of fun.'

Ilan tugged a knot into place, and gave it an extra pull for good measure, if only to see Mihály buckle and whine. 'You're not acting like a man who is about to die. A little respect, please.'

'Maybe die,' Mihály corrected as he righted himself.

'Hopefully not, but no one else knows that. Try to look afraid.' He held out the plain brown sackcloth robes of the condemned, the same ones Servants of the Road wore to keep knowledge of death in the forefront of the mind. 'Here, put this on.'

'Even if I do die,' Mihály said as Ilan turned and listened to the smooth rustle of clothing being discarded. 'I don't have to worry. You can look, you know, I'm not particularly modest.'

'Saints, you can't stand to not have attention on you for a moment?'

But when Ilan turned again, he had redressed. The robe barely hung past his knees, his bare feet knobby and oddly vulnerable.

'Before I go, is there anything you would like to confess? Properly this time. In case something goes wrong.' His voice scratched on the words. Perhaps he didn't actually want to see the other man die. A very small perhaps.

'Confess? You've heard all of it by this point. But I do want to apologise.' There was something like sincerity in those amber-brown eyes.

Ilan crossed his arms. 'I'm listening. Or was that the whole of the apology?' It would be rather like Mihály to sum the whole thing up in a vague hand-waved statement, let others fill in the absolving details.

'I could have been less annoying. I could have thought, for one blasted second, before jumping into dark magic. That's a big one. And I'm sorry for what I said about Csilla. You were right that she deserves better.'

'I'm glad you can see that now.' Ilan turned, eyes darting to the door. Without pretence or armour, too much of Mihály stirred sympathy. He and Csilla had both been badly used.

'Do I get a final request?' A teasing note had returned, and Ilan's irritation with it.

'A drink? I'm going to say no. You'll get put out hard enough with whatever Csilla is making. Be patient.' He certainly understood the desire; even he was tempted to blunt the knowledge of what they were doing. But the plan was risky enough without adding other intoxicants into the mix.

'A kiss.'

'A what now?'

So the man couldn't even be reasonable for the night before his supposed execution. Ilan looked back, and Mihály caught him by the shoulders. Before he could move, the Izir bent forward and kissed him lightly on his cheek, at the corner of his mouth.

Soft, and warm, and not nearly as terrible as he would have expected, even with the scratch of his beard. It had been a lifetime since his few awkward teenage romps, well before he'd taken vows, and though he knew he should want to bite, he didn't. Much. It had a feeling of finality, even more than his apology.

Ilan scrunched his nose, hoping the heat on his face wasn't visible in the low light. 'You're awfully pushy for someone whose life is in my hands.'

'I trust you. I'm showing you that.' Mihály's eyes turned distant. 'And if it does go wrong, you will take care of her, won't you?'

He's not planning on coming out of this, Ilan realised. No matter what he told Csilla. It was a stupid waste, noble and horrific all in one.

Still, Ilan nodded. 'I never intend to do anything else.'

Mihály gave a wry smile, one corner of his mouth turning up. 'You're in love with her.'

Ilan flinched at the accusation, far more than he had at the ridiculous kiss.

'I wouldn't go that far. But she is holy.' He still craved the order of the Church, with all its peace. If finding that peace meant following Csilla, it would be an easy path to walk.

'No, it's a good thing. Someone should be.'

Ilan snorted. 'Love is for people without a calling.'

'I had a calling. I still fell in love.'

'And look where it brought you. It's a feeling. It will pass.' Feelings changed. There was a reason why the Church demanded couples be wed before intimacy or asked that clergy make their brethren their new kin. People didn't take care of each other for life based on temporary affections. A lifetime demanded duty and sacrifice.

He had made a vow to defend everything holy, and if that was Csilla, he could do it until he no longer drew breath. It had nothing to do with something as flighty as love.

Mihály looked unconvinced and not a little smug. 'If she fixes the Seal, you can see for yourself how you're lying. I'm sure you kept your glass, yes?'

He had. Even now the weathered shard was heavy in his pocket.

'And if she doesn't?' He didn't want to think on it, but they had to confront the dark idea.

Mihály's expression faltered, his brow creasing. 'Then she'll need you more than ever.'

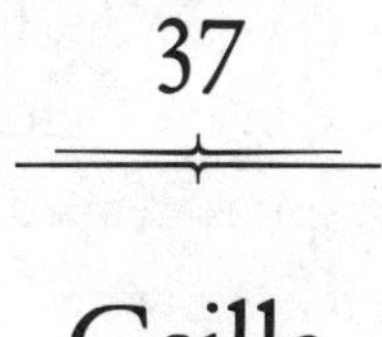

37

Csilla

THE TOLL of the cathedral bell shook her from toenails to teeth. It wasn't the quick call to prayers and service. These slow, deep peals were the dirge of a funeral.

The dull orange sun hung low in the sky as if not wanting to raise its face to the violence. The crowd pressed tight, their bloodlust reeking of sweat and hunger. Csilla's heart clenched to hear their words, their eagerness to see bulging eyes and a snapped neck. They wanted so badly to know that the creature who had been stalking their streets and haunting their nightmares was about to be put down. To see that the Incarnate had returned, their breach of faith was forgiven, and all was right with the world.

She tried in vain to turn a few children back. The parents scowled and herded them in front, away from Csilla's worrying hands and closer to the violence.

Around the courtyard, votives had been set up, holding incense to block smells and vials of holy water to purify those whose eyes were about to be sullied by death. Csilla passed a few coins to the priest and took a vial for herself, knowing it was likely from the river and not the broken holy founts. He didn't even look when she placed the coins in his open palm. His eyes were fixed on the fraying hemp nooses of the rickety platform, hastily built by too-eager carpenters and reluctant priests. It had been decades since anyone had been executed.

The pair of nooses wavered in the slight breeze.

From the long shadow of spires stepped the Incarnate, and an awe-struck murmur rose and fell in waves. His silver armour shone, polished as if he wore his Brilliant soul over his skin, but there were no dents to suggest it had ever been worn in battle. His gaze measured the crowd, and Csilla froze. It was as if he could read each person's worthiness without even touching their flesh, consecration given breath and form.

Tamas had called him a sham. She herself had touched his merely mortal flesh, but there was power there.

Topaz and diamond rings glittered like the many eyes of the angel hosts, vigilant in every direction, as he raised a hand.

Tamas was led forward, hands tied behind him. The crowd gasped at every stumbling step he took. A few shouted insults and flung splattering handfuls of dark refuse. Csilla pulled her kerchief down more fully over her forehead, shading her eyes as she made her way around the edges of the crowd. No one turned to look at the girl scurrying around them.

A fetid egg hit the front of the stage, splattering yolk and white down the front of the wood. It was followed by another and another, and Csilla winced at the crunch as shells hit wood.

Then there was Mihály. He looked smaller dressed in coarse brown robes, his beard and hair unkempt. But there was still something in his gaze that quieted the crowd, and a hiccupping sob from somewhere in the middle of the mass echoed.

The Incarnate stepped forward.

'Friends, I understand your fear and your rage. These men were behind the evil that haunted our streets, spilling blood on holy stone. They have damaged our connection to the divine. A sure death is the only fit punishment. We have the blessing of Asten today. This is the first step on the path that will lead us back to righteousness.'

Csilla shook at how he could stand there and lie. How had the Church not seen his deception? It should have Shadowed his soul like a thunderhead.

He turned to Tamas. 'Do you have anything to say on your own behalf?'

The older man shook his head. 'Nothing that won't be proved soon enough. I'm content with what I've done.'

The crowd hissed and shifted at that, a low tide of anger tugging them closer to the platform.

'And you, Izir?'

Csilla's breath caught at the quiet in his gaze. They hadn't discussed what he would say – if his pride would have his last words be in his own defence, or if he had a final prayer.

'Forgive me,' he said as he stepped forward. 'You trusted me, and I used you badly.' His voice was slightly slurred. Csilla wanted to touch her mark but she couldn't; the comfort would turn into a beacon. She'd done her part of stealing, mixing, and a little helpless praying. Prayers were still instinctive, even after everything.

The roar that erupted from the crowd was what Csilla had always imagined of the screams of demons at their creation; joy not from the beauty of the world, but sounds of relishing in its ugliness. Violence was an appetite not sated by its like. The more the Church offered, the more the damaged Faithful demanded in turn.

Csilla had to stand on tip-toe to see over the crowd, and even then, shoulders and hats and hair blocked her gaze. Ilan was in place, standing by as Tamas was first led to the centre. If he was perturbed at his role, there was no outward sign. He could have been at service. Attendant and at peace.

Sandor stood to the side, his expression harder to read. The white around his collar was starting to grey with sweat. He could still turn on them. She squeezed her fingers until her ragged nails cut her palms.

An egg hit Tamas square in the chest, a viscous smear dripping from his heart. He blinked and swayed as if the blow had force.

Another egg landed next to Ilan's shoe, and he looked out at the crowd. The gaze of the wolf was as effective a silencer as the Incarnate's voice, the curses and screams dying as if he'd grabbed their throats. He slid the noose over and tightened the knot, no tremble in his arms.

Tamas's knees half-buckled. Mihály bent for the rope, staggering slightly.

Ilan stepped in front of the man, pushing at Tamas's shoulder.

'The highest of holies has confirmed this writ sentencing you to death. You may still plead innocent and ask for mercy.'

A show, and the man knew it. There was no mercy for those crimes. He still managed to spit, the glob mixing with thrown rot at the toe of Ilan's boot.

'Very well.' He touched the man's eyes, not gently. 'May you see the clear path to your eternal rest.' His hand moved to the man's lips, a hard knuckle against his teeth. 'And may you speak only truth when brought before judgement.'

He pulled the lever.

There was a heartbeat second as the door held firm. Then it snapped and the man dropped, noose catching his neck as he gave a strangled groan. She held her breath for a moment until there was a sharp crack and he seized then went slack. The grim final jig of the hanged, all the more horrific for how the sound echoed the snapping of a chicken's neck. Even people were just meat and bone in the end.

And now for Mihály.

The blood pounding in Csilla's ears drowned Ilan's words, and the second lever went down with a sharp creak.

Angyalka had survived such a hanging and come out wiser. This could also be redemption. They couldn't have been more prepared. But she still wanted to vomit as he dropped. She watched his expression as he plunged, from resigned to pained. His hands clenched as if to scrabble at the noose, then they stilled.

Bile lurched in Csilla's stomach as the crowd shrank from the swinging body, giving her an even clearer vision as they parted. Her own breath stilled. His lips were turning blue, eyes bulging beneath the lids. There was no fight in his slack body.

He looked like every other corpse she had ever seen.

We were wrong.

Ilan sliced the rope.

It didn't give.

We were wrong. We were wrong. We were wrong. The line between success and a dead man was hair-thin as it was. With every second Mihály looked more certainly dead, and Ilan's slices against the fraying rope became more frantic.

Finally the Izir's body fell through with a thud, crumpling between beams of the framework. Csilla pressed her lips thin as two other inquisitorial priests pulled him out with no more care than they would handle a sack of garbage. Her heart thumped at the chalk-dullness of his face, the stiffness of his lips, but it was out of their hands now.

Tamas was hauled to a cart, Mihály laid on the side of the platform. Sandor stepped mercifully close, partially shielding his body from watching eyes, all the while appearing appropriately sombre.

The Incarnate raised his hand again, his weathered face a beacon of calm. Csilla wished she could have that confidence. Even the smallest pains to creation ground on her, and he could stand before death and smile.

'Holy judgement has been passed. Our terror has ended,' he announced. 'Take the body from our city as we celebrate Their ever-hastening return.'

As she tried to get close to the body cart, she found herself pushed away by others wanting to see him for themselves. *You've seen enough death*, she wanted to say. *Go home and hug your loved ones.*

But it wasn't enough. One person ripped off Tamas's boot, another grabbed at his hand, scratch marks streaking his palm as they pulled him grimly forward. One went for his hair, yanking a fistful of strands and waving them in the air like a thready banner. The guards made no move to stop the desecration as the fevered crowd stole talismans of safety.

A few moved towards Mihály, wanting bodily tokens or a sliver of their own vengeance, torn flesh for torn flesh.

The hanging was supposed to quell their violence. Csilla's heart fluttered like a hummingbird in her chest. She stepped back, foot finding a rotten potato peel and nearly coming out from under her.

Stop. She edged backward to the fringes of the crowd, pressing against the wall of the cathedral.

The air thickened, suddenly hot and humid, droplets beading on her skin. Violet-tinged clouds rolled across what had been perfect sky, and drenching rain came down as if buckets were being freshly dumped. Electricity like the sizzle before a lightning spark danced on her skin, transformative and keen.

The Incarnate bent for Mihály, and a flash cut through the air, sending him stepping back. The light didn't stop. It danced between the onlookers, not burning, only bouncing and sparking.

As she stepped away from the platform, her eyes caught on water pooling on the stone, glinting with rain-diluted gold. Arany was weeping, not just a few drops, but a stream of tears.

Good. She should weep to see what they were doing to her kin. What her Church had become.

Sandor gestured to Csilla, and she pulled her head covering further to shadow her eyes.

She could see the signs of life in Mihály. Or at least that's what she told herself. The eye twitch was life, not a final spasm. That his skin was not quite so pale, the bruises darkening to the colour of browning apple on his throat no sign of anything permanent.

Sandor wasn't looking at Mihály. He watched the cart with Tamas's body leave, ready to be dumped for the Servants he'd once found a home with. Maybe there would be someone he knew, and he could be sat for. That would be a mercy that even Csilla couldn't offer.

The Prelate and Incarnate stood before the body and Csilla bent forward, hoping to look awed. When she glanced up through her eyelashes, Abe's look was knowing.

The Incarnate bent forward, touching Mihály's forehead. Nothing happened.

She hadn't even known a little part of her still wished something would, to let her hold onto the last tatters of safe belief. All the people here had been deceived by what they'd believed in. But they'd also been fed by it. Brought joy from it. Found purpose in it. Nothing one man had done could make any of that less true. And she would still try to give them back their hope.

The Incarnate raised his hand, a vision of divine authority. 'Anyone, no matter how divine, can be misled. Burn him.'

Csilla's mouth dropped. That wasn't what they'd agreed to.

'Incarnate.' Sandor stepped forward. 'He asked to be laid with Arany's remains.'

He would be listened to. He had to be. She'd forgive the man every cruelty if he came through for them in this.

The Incarnate stared at the body, and this time the miracle she prayed for was for Mihály to remain as still as death, and for the Incarnate to agree.

‘He was still an Izir,’ Sandor continued. ‘Twisted as he was, it may help to have holy blood down there again. If you’ll allow me the knowledge, I’ll take him down. The mercy girl can clean, to save you for more important duties.’

‘There’s nothing sacred down there anymore. It’s dark.’ The Incarnate shook his head. ‘But very well. If he’d rather rot, leave him and lock the tomb.’

38

Csilla

THE SEAL had been a living thing, feeding on the holiness of the Union. Now it was starved.

Dark, light, then speckled like mica in a stone. Bright flecks turned black as seconds dragged into minutes. Perhaps the Incarnate hadn't been wrong in giving up the location. There didn't seem to be anything left here worth guarding.

Csilla's fingers itched to touch it, an impossible urge to heal the damage. She stretched out her scarred hand and something rippled in the magic. It was faint, a twist of flickering white undulating in the pale glow.

Mercy breeds good. That's what she'd always believed. And now she was in the belly of the cathedral, watching the holiest place in the world die.

But she could try to save it. She didn't know how, but if she were meant to be an instrument, let her be wielded here.

First Mihály. His body was stark on the dirt-smeared ground, his lips parted in a stiff gasp. He had given her the precise dosage to wear off within an hour of the hanging. It wouldn't work if his neck was already damaged beyond healing; repairing crushed cartilage took more than mercy skill. And she knew well enough that medicine was like a miracle – it could save, but it couldn't always be counted on. As Sandor lit rushlights to illuminate the tomb-like chamber, the red and raw abrasions on his neck only looked more gruesome. They echoed the cracks in the old stone, marring what should be perfect.

Under the watchful eyes of living clergy and false ones of the painted saints on the walls, she knelt next to Mihály, placing a hand on his chest, her palm rising with a shallow breath. A small knot of tension uncoiled as the thrum of his heartbeat echoed through her skin. She met Ilan's eyes, and he nodded.

Now to try.

Csilla shifted her attention to the cold dirt, spreading her fingers and pushing them down. It wasn't just Arany here. There were centuries of the lives of the Faithful on this spot, drops of their faith and pledge reaching for the hope of return. Spectral fingers by the thousands reached to twine with hers as old copper stung her nose. People across the Union had put part of themselves into this web. They would stand with her now.

Everything but that blood in the dirt is a lie.

Something caught within her, like a finger snagging a hole in cloth, unravelling everything stitched tight, and she gasped with a pinching pain. This wasn't the divinity Mihály had described. There was so much more here than simplistic joy, and her mouth filled with a film of metal, and dirt, and sharp salt. The blocks of creation: not nourishing, but foundational.

But nothing she felt was transferring to the Seal. She swallowed the choking flavour, pushing harder, tears pricking her eyes. She reached for Mihály's cramped hand, a silver glow connecting them, ignored by the earth.

The air was thick with the stink of dying embers. They were failing.

Sandor kicked Ilan from behind as the other man whirled to strike, knocking him to his knees with a heavy thud that sounded enough like cracking bone to strike her heart.

Csilla jumped, pulling away from Mihály with a cry.

'Ilan!'

Ilan brought his knife up in a wide, artless arc, slicing the man's outer coat, but not more. There was no way to get a good strike from that angle, and the larger man stepped heavy on Ilan's hand with a sickening crunch. Ilan hissed, pinned.

'What are you doing?' Csilla choked out through the pain of helpless shock.

Sandor cocked his head, darkness bubbling over his lips. It slipped around his face in a slide of oily caress and slithered back up his nose with a sickening slurp.

The demon had had to go somewhere. And with the Church's magic broken, there had been no way to see the home it had found.

They couldn't fight, she realised as a smoky film leaked from his pores, rising like steam. This wasn't a room of weapons, only struggling holiness.

'I told you to stay out of this, didn't I?' Sandor spat at Ilan, whose face went feral in response, white teeth showing despite the boot digging into thin finger bones. 'Or you could have at least gone out alone when I told you to and had a softer death next to the fool who gave me these robes.' He kicked Ilan in the chest with a cleaver-on-bone crack.

Understanding chilled Csilla. The man who was supposed to have been here was the body they'd found in the woods. Sandor wasn't just a poor member of the Church; he was no member at all.

'You were working with Tamas, then?' She tried to stall. If Mihály would wake, at least he would be a weapon. 'You'd rather lose your humanity than trust the Church? You served with them.'

When Sandor grinned, he had an extra row of teeth, sharp and pushing against his lips. 'Which only convinced me further. You'd be surprised how many of the Servants have come to see the truth. How many soldiers resent their sanctified conscription. How many know the only righteous path is the broken one.'

The next sound that came out of his mouth was inhuman and corrupt, and at it Mihály stiffened, then began to stir. It was a second resurrection. In the quiet of her shock, grief for Ágnes claimed another moment.

She'd be proud that Csilla was still down here fighting. The seeds of faith and goodness that she'd planted in rocky soil had bloomed into weedy strength.

'I should thank you.' The thing that was Sandor screeched. 'You finished our work well and broke all the remaining protections, took the Church's sight. I'm not as blessed as Mihály. No one could see past his shine.'

Her knees trembled. 'What?'

'It's a dangerous thing to play with souls,' Sandor whispered, cold like a new-moon winter night. 'They're tricky things, finding the cracks and pieces to cling to, letting themselves seep into awkward places. And angel blood is a lovely conduit when all they want is to touch the divine.' He looked at Mihály, whose eyes were laced with inky threads. 'I can feel how much it wanted to stay in you. Any mere human would be a poor substitute.'

He grabbed Ilan by the hair and pulled him back, knife point resting on his forehead. For a moment Csilla was back in the room with Madame Varga, her own hand carving darkness.

'We thought breaking the city would be enough, but you made a good point, little saint. We have to pollute this room so thoroughly no one will feel the divine again.' Ilan jerked, then winced as the blade skimmed his skin.

Mihály groaned and shifted, eyes fluttering.

'Tamas said it's for our own good,' Csilla said. If she could speak, she could stall. Every second was a beat of hope, even as no miracle came. 'That we need to face demons without our armour before Asten is willing to return. We have to prove we're worthy of perfection.'

'We aren't the only ones who think so.' Sandor rolled his head, as if his neck suddenly had an excess of vertebrae. 'And we aren't the first to try it.'

'Stay back, Csilla,' Ilan said, and at the words the knife slipped, slicing through his brow nearly to his eye. The cuts were starting to take shape, smoke curling from split skin.

Sandor turned slightly. 'Should I deal with her first?'

He leaped with inhuman speed that should have been impossible for his size and then his skin was branding hers, and beneath that, the dark corruption. He moved to scratch over the healing scabs of her face and she shuddered. Blood streaked down the peeled skin of her cheek in a sticky, crimson tear. There was darkness, probing the opening in the flesh, asking the question again. This time she knew better than to answer.

Sandor tilted his head and wrapped his free hand around her throat. She pulled away and gagged, then doubled over at the sickening woosh and thud of a fist in her stomach. The snap of her small ribs made her gasp.

Ilan was shouting something, but she couldn't hear through the blood-pounding nausea. Sandor grabbed her wrist and jerked her back upright. The Seal flared brighter for a moment in reaction, long enough for Csilla to half-form a prayer, a habit she was sure now she wouldn't live long enough to break.

Sandor's grin – the grin of whatever had him – widened, with large teeth and an outstretched tongue. The demon leeched from his skin, reaching for Csilla.

Behind him Ilan approached, eyes blood-smeared yet wild, alight with pain and anticipation. He had his own knife. It came down between Sandor's shoulder blades with a crack, resistance as metal hit muscle and back ribs, a twist and push as he aimed for a lung. Sandor fell forward as Ilan stabbed again, quick and lethal. Merciful. If there was no longer a willing host, the demon would struggle.

A buzzing rose in the air, released by the pain of the host, twisting and darting between her and Mihály, seeking familiar skin.

Mihály was still weak. She stepped between as the cloud began to solidify, hovering and writhing. She outstretched a hand, and it buzzed over her skin like a tight swarm of gnats with wings made of cutting glass.

'Leave him.'

The Shadow clumped more tightly. The air around her stung with needlepoints, and she could see the outline of some other creature, face masked by small, dark wings with trembling, oil-clumped feathers, and triplet eyes resting in the hollows of its collarbones. Pieces of a broken creation desperate to feel whole.

Darkness unfurled, and a hard pressure sucked at her lips as she went dizzy. To the side, Ilan wavered on his feet, and her own vision was dim. She wanted to scream for him to run, but her mouth was choked with tarry magic biting at her gums and tongue. It would take any opening it could find.

The thing smelled dead. Not in the rotting way of former life, but a nothingness. Clawed hands reached for her face. It wanted, and it wanted, and it wanted.

I didn't do a miracle for this.

She stretched her hands, only to have them sink into the corruption trying to take shape.

A crisp frostbite pain shot through her, and Csilla screamed with her freed voice, sudden and piercing enough that the demon stepped back with a shocked snarl. The lightning-white agony leeched into her pores, her lungs, even her teeth, every inch of her trembling. Something in her was waking with the fierceness of a sleeping creature jolted from its winter cave.

The blue of her veins, the pink under her fingernails, they glowed brighter than they ever had for Mihály, and the hovering creature in front of her reached to grasp.

'*Csilla!*' Before anyone else could move, Ilan had his arms around her waist to pull her back, but she shook her head.

'It's alright,' she whispered. Inside she was painfully alive, her skin thin with the brittleness of a cicada shell waiting to be shed. She'd felt the crackle of divinity when Mihály had healed her, the sizzle of darkness on the bodies, her own erasure when she'd done her miracle, but this radiance was consuming. This was a power that had taken the unknowable and turned it into the physical world in an act of reckless yearning.

The darkness began to die on her skin, flaking into dry powder, consumed.

A presence surrounded her, vast and ancient and alive, lodging in her bones to root. The tears that came to her eyes were sharp like splinters of glass.

Sandor gurgled and lay twitching, hand clasped to his throat. Csilla stepped to help him, but her touch didn't heal. Ilan was still bleeding.

'Mihály.'

He froze from where he was struggling to his feet as if she'd spoken a word of magic and not merely his name. The whites around his eyes were visible, staring down at her as if she were a thing freshly consecrated.

She was.

The demon whispered a line of twisted creation, cutting through the raw power singing over her skin. She reached forward. Around her she could feel the pure energy of life, the people with her, the breath of the soil and the small things that crawled through it, the ageless crush of minerals that had led to the rocks that built their walls, the strength of her own bones.

The creature before her was none of that. It was a mistake, a corruption, nothing but endless need to be more than empty, and no means of making it so save stealing the lives of others and dragging them into Shadow with it.

A prick of pity, one fully Csilla and none of the greatness that filled her, lanced the dizziness of power. This thing, dead and hungry as it was, was equally close to humanity as the pure Brilliance around them. It had been created by the same hands, even unintentionally. There was a stain of it in every soul.

'I understand. But you're nothing meant to live. Here.' She stretched out her glowing hand to the lumping darkness. 'It's alright.' She gestured to the wound on her cheek in welcome. 'I'm ready now. Please come in.'

Once again the creature slipped inside. The pure connection to creation echoed in a trillion invocations, stronger than every combined voice of the Union. A darkened haze surrounded her, smoke on her skin, her mind echoing with angry confusion.

All she felt inside was sorrow as it struggled to latch onto her and manipulate her flesh. It was only obeying its nature, and it wasn't its fault its nature was antithetical to the divine. She brushed a finger over her lips as her mouth filled with tar.

I'm sorry.

She exhaled, and it fell to powder at her feet. One mistake of creation corrected.

When she opened her eyes, Ilan was on his knees before her, eyes alight with reverence.

'Csilla.'

He breathed her name like a prayer and looked near to kissing her hands. She did have a second miracle to her name now. But not the most important one.

The seal was still dark. She'd extinguished one creature of Shadow, but there would be dozens more, finding hosts, and none of the priests would be able to seal them again, much less banish them.

Csilla knelt in the dirt, willing the magic back. Fierce power rolled inside her, but nothing manifested. Arany's remaining blood was ordinary loam.

You had me fix one life. They'd used her to bring Madame Varga back, out of everything broken. Why was that the one thing They fixed? Not Ágnes, who could have lived another twenty years doing good in the world. Not this, the remains of Arany's rebellion that had ensured people still had a chance to save themselves.

She slammed her hands on the ground, wincing at the helpless smack. She was going to be just a conduit for the divine will.

Everything but that blood in the dirt is a lie. The words echoed and hit home.

There was still something there. Everyone who had taken vows in the Union had lent a drop of Brilliance in their blood, save her. Now it was her turn to do it properly.

If she were to be a conduit, she would be a conduit for them all. If Arany could bleed and weep, so could she. She picked up the dropped knife.

'Csilla, what are you doing?' Ilan asked as she slipped off Ágnes's robes. There was no need for them to be stained with the rest of her. She folded them, and held the knife to her breast.

If Asten wanted to stop this, They could. Inside there was only endless quiet. She was being watched, not helped.

Was Tamas right? Do You truly want us to suffer?

But *want* seemed a distant and far too human concept. There was something alien in the quiet that answered her.

‘Csilla, stop. The Church isn’t worth this. We’ll find another way,’ Ilan said, but Csilla shook her head, everything in her far too old and heavy.

‘This isn’t for the Church.’ This was to give the people hope that a power beyond them still paid attention and cared, and to save them from immediate threat. To give her hope that all of this wouldn’t end in a second Severing, one even more disastrous than the last.

Mihály crouched next to her, his hand closing over hers on the blade. For a second her heart skipped, wondering if he was going to push it in.

‘Don’t,’ he said, eyes filled with a measure of the sweet affection she used to see when he would pretend she was what he wanted. Her fingers loosened on the hilt, and he pried it from her sweating hands.

Then he placed it against his own neck. ‘If a divine sacrifice must be made, let it be my legacy.’ His eyes were bright now, traces of the medicinal haze faded. He was beautifully, terribly awake.

‘No!’ Csilla reached for him again. Mihály’s sins were born from love and grief; he didn’t deserve death for them. ‘No.’

Her voice could barely rise above a whisper, and she forced a smile, though the stretch of her cheek was agony. ‘You can still leave. Go somewhere far away, and do good. This must be what I was born for.’

She’d always quietly hoped her strange life would have purpose. If this was the purpose, she would accept it.

He shook his head, calm and resigned. ‘You have to let others burn sometimes. You’re too important to die. You can’t help anyone if you’re throwing yourself on every blade offered to you. And you’re not the kind of girl to take an easy out.’

He was using the same smooth voice he did to persuade her of other things, so calm and soothing it seemed the most natural thing in the world. She still hadn’t developed perfect immunity to it. She shifted to look at Ilan, standing above them as if in looming benediction.

'Ilan, tell him not to do this,' she said, as if that would do any good. But Ilan only shook his head, his lips moving in a silent no. She swallowed a growing lump in her throat and turned back to Mihály. 'And what if it doesn't work? You've told me all along you're no real angel.'

'Divinity freely sacrificed will always be a powerful thing.' He reached out to cup her cheek, where their touch glowed and her open scrapes knit back together. 'This started with me. Let me end it.'

Ilan held out his hand to Mihály. 'Give me the knife. If you shake while you do it you'll make it worse on yourself.'

Mihály lifted his chin, pressing the knife more firmly against the skin. But not enough to cut, yet. He was trembling, a sheen of sweat on his forehead.

It had to be done. But she couldn't let him do it to himself. Csilla put her hand over the handle again, shifting his fingers from it. 'No. If someone is going to die for me, I'll be the one to do it. Because he's right.' She was nauseous and her heart might fail itself, but she had to. Ilan's jaw clenched, but he didn't protest.

And still the power in her didn't speak, didn't stir.

Wouldn't save him.

Mihály shifted, laying back to place his head in her lap, the position of a trusting lover, and closed his eyes. 'Make it quick for me, dearest.'

She looked to Ilan, to the painted eyes of the saints, waiting for an intercession that in the deepest parts of her heart she knew wouldn't come. He offered his hand again, but she shook her head. She slid a palm across Mihály's cheek so the last touch he knew would be soft. She cupped his chin, and tilted his head, blinking back her tears so no drops would fall and cause him to flinch. Then she drew the knife, as hard and fast as she could.

Ilan and Csilla flinched at the sudden shock of light pouring forward, brighter than anything Mihály had ever conjured.

Asten, she prayed, hands wet and shining. *I know You can hear me now. Whatever power I have, whatever love you had for him, let it work for this. Don't let this be in vain.*

The answer was an impossible swirl of breeze against her skin. The smoke-stained saints on the wall seemed to brighten, a new lustre in the dusted gold and ochre.

Mihály gurgled from the wound as he shifted and slumped against the dark ground. She was too slow to catch his head as he fell off her lap. From the cut poured lines of gold, the echo of the blessings in the courtyard, flowing into rivulets in the stone.

And the Seal began to awaken.

A shimmer blossomed above the body and she put her hand out, letting it come to rest on the open altar of her palm. It was dazzling, strange and spider-silk ether. In this state his soul was stardust. She let out a breath, the pain and hope equally terrible. It felt like Mihály's gentlest moments and softest words, a soul-deep beauty even his pain didn't tarnish.

'Csilla?' Ilan was behind her again.

'It's beautiful,' she breathed. This holiness was what all the light and glass and shine of the cathedral had been trying to capture. It was the poorest imitation, the wavering reflection of the moon on brackish water and not the resplendence of a night sky. This was the purest stuff of creation, a reminder that once they had all been infinite.

'What is?'

If she'd thought she was alone before, it was nothing compared to this. No one else would understand what it was to see the stuff of souls. Her face softened. Except, perhaps, Mihály, his body already stiffening before her.

The little bit of spun ether fluttered like a broken-winged moth. She pushed it towards the flickering Brilliance.

If You must take him, make it glorious.

From the Seal came a golden host of wings and radiance, long-fingered hands reaching to claim him with a hum like wind on water. The light illuminating her faded as the presence and his soul dispersed into hundreds of starry motes. The lines of it, so faint and delicate, glowed sunlit gold with the infusion of spirit. They filled the room from end to end. Inlaid between were points like tiny flickering sparks. All the souls of the Union, under her feet. Everyone connected and protected again.

Csilla pressed her fingertips to her lips, tears threatening to spill over her lashes.

Mihály had managed to do something lasting and good after all. But even he'd left her in the end.

She collapsed, forehead against the ground, adding its dirt to the mess of her face. The people would have their faith and hope, and the Church would have its laws and power.

But the blankness of Mihály's face, the gaping wound in his throat, made it hollow. Ilan caught her as she rose and stumbled forward.

He ran his hand through her tangled hair and let his fingers linger on the back of her neck. He touched her cheek, the healed flesh that was the last of Mihály's power.

'You're hurt.'

It was a silly thing to focus on now. 'So are you.'

She should go. Something insistent and old pushed through her power-drenched limbs, but instead she sank down by Mihály's body, tilting his head to rest against her leg, stroking his hair as he bled out for the world.

She once promised him she would stay, and that was a mercy she could offer to the last.

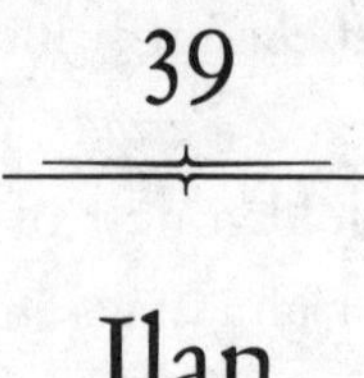

39

Ilan

The Incarnate's chamber was white marble and gold leaf, shining with what was meant to be all the immaculate beauty of the blessed hereafter. Ilan bowed deeply as he entered. Now it looked like the pale bone colour of teeth and fear, and the air in it was stale from months locked away.

Csilla had heard the divine, in some form at least. The thought pounded with Ilan's steps as he paced outside the Incarnate's chamber, trying to reason his way through the blasphemy. He'd seen Csilla deliver a soul. He'd seen her twisted face, the pain as she spoke to someone he couldn't hear, the way she lit with creative fire. He'd felt the peace of praying against her fevered skin as Mihály turned from Brilliant to cold.

Blasphemy or madness.

Her sobs echoed in fresh memory with every breath, even the tolling of the bells faint to his ears.

They'd saved the Seal in a fashion, though now it was Mihály's blood flowing within the sacred spaces. That was what he would have to focus on when he gave his report. The Church still had its divinity, though how this new magic could be used remained to be seen.

Even if Csilla's ecstatic power proved something about it was wrong. The Incarnate wasn't who had been called to save them.

'Welcome.' The Incarnate rose in greeting, serene and haloed by the cast of light off the diamonds and gold he wore. If he really spoke to Asten, it didn't weigh on him.

It should weigh on him. Csilla had looked as stricken before the Seal as she had in the torture room, like it was no gift to be a conduit. The Incarnate had the same aura as his father or any of the other governing cats prowling with as much attention on their physical wares as their souls. The Incarnate knew his power, clearly, but no more than any mortal man of privilege.

Csilla had *burned* with holy fire. She'd had a fever-sweat on her and skin that shone like porcelain as he'd pulled her up the stairs, her shivers rocking them both as he held her in the dim corridor until she calmed enough to walk. Calmed . . . more a shock-induced tranquillised state . . . enough to where the screaming at the blood upon their emergence hadn't broken through her haze. All she'd wanted to look at was Arany, her gold now running like a rock-cutting mountain stream, the people gathering with joy and splashing in the proof of their righteousness like children finding a puddle on a scorching day.

Mercies, how his head ached.

'Ilan.' Prelate Abe stood behind the Incarnate, even the deep angel-embroidered red of his robes austere in comparison to the lustre on Asten's chosen. 'We're waiting for the truth of what happened.'

He had to tell them. It was his duty. He wouldn't forswear his vows.

And yet when he took a breath to speak, he found himself still. He was always careful with his punishments. He would be equally careful with his words.

'We've been the victims of a group of Apostate infiltrators.'

'Not soldiers from Seda?'

Of course his mind was still on his war.

'Not ones aligned with their beliefs, though they've borrowed some of their techniques.' The explosive sabotage, for one. 'They are part of a group that believes the key to the return is forcing humanity to confront its darkness. They summoned a demon. The demon used the Izir to kill, destroying the territory tethers, and ended up in Sandor. A conspirator.' The recitation of facts was barely any explanation at all. 'Their goal was to destroy the Seal so that the Church could no longer banish Shadow, and let things play out as they would. It would have pleased Seda, but they weren't their soldiers.'

'So I've been told. And is that all they believed?' There was a knowing glitter in the man's eyes.

'I'm not aware.' He'd left a life of politics, but it wasn't that he couldn't see the pieces of the game. Accusing the Incarnate now, with nothing but assumptions and dead bodies behind him, would take him from a lauded place of strength into somewhere with much weaker footing. 'There is nothing more I can say.'

The Incarnate's lips pressed into a satisfied smile. So, silence was the answer he'd wanted.

'And you banished the demon, even with your power taken? And then had the idea to use the Izir's blood.'

The warm approval in the tone chafed. Ilan wasn't entirely sorry to see Mihály gone, but the death of an Izir deserved respect.

He shifted, looking down at the aisle cloth leading to the Incarnate's seat. It was barely worn, the fabric still white. A reminder of how privileged this audience was, and how it demanded the truth. And with the Seal restored, they could see lies.

'I didn't.'

The Incarnate pursed his lips. 'But the only other person down there was that mercy girl. The one who was cast out, if I'm not mistaken.'

Ilan didn't say anything.

'How?' Now it was Abe who looked concerned. 'Csilla has no soul. She shouldn't have any access to power. I cut her, but it was just for her own sake . . .'

'Asten worked through her, and the Izir's blood saved us. A miracle.' Let them think it was a singular event. Let them let her go. It was the threat to power, not the heresy, that had put the first target on Mihály.

'That's a large claim.' The Incarnate's eyes glittered in a way that set Ilan's lip to curling. 'How do you know it was Asten? Perhaps more than one demon was present. We know there is only one Incarnate.'

And would you prove it? Would you let us test it with your lips to a bottle of poison? Csilla would.

Ilan swallowed. 'She was able to touch his soul. She was the one who saved us.' He hadn't been able to see it, but he'd seen her. Righteous and broken and brave.

'She says she spoke for Asten, when that is a power reserved for me and mine. To allow others to lie about holy matters is to risk our perfection.' The disapproval in his tone was one step from an execution order, and Abe's face was grim agreement.

If Ilan said it wasn't a lie, he'd be branded a liar himself. So he remained silent, to see what path the Incarnate's words would lay.

'Then clearly you, one of mine, were the one who did the banishing, and the girl is a blasphemer.' The Incarnate inclined his head in praise. 'The miracle was your presence, not hers. Such devotion is commendable.'

Ilan's back was damp under his gaze.

'Perhaps even sainted.' The Incarnate's smile was a lure. Ilan had never wanted anything more than the power that came with enacting the will of the divine. The idea that he had worked a miracle and would wear a saint's crown, be allowed to dispense justice across the Union as he saw fit . . .

It was a mouth-watering temptation, his desire offered up on a holy altar. Had he not seen the glory in Csilla, he wouldn't have even recognised its darkness.

He spoke quickly, trying to create a shield of excuses to cover Csilla's power.

'I believe it was a miracle, but not mine. And not blasphemy. This is the city of miracles—'

The Incarnate raised his hand. 'Your humility is a credit to you, but this glory is not yours to claim or deny. You are Sainted, Ilan.'

Abe uplifted praise as bitterness filled Ilan's mouth.

'You will be lauded,' the Incarnate continued, and Ilan made a noncommittal noise he hoped sounded pleased. 'But in such a turbulent time, blasphemy will not be tolerated. You saw what heresy did to our city. And I will have to leave again soon, to make sure every territory is secure. We've been given the grace of a second chance.'

They wanted it all over, quickly. Ilan respected few things like he did order, but order was a home. If it were rebuilt on a rotten foundation, they'd find themselves in the same broken pit again. The Church was just wrong about the source of the rot. It wasn't the people below that were the problem. It was decaying up to the roof.

'Take her out to the wastes as close to the burning garden as you can, though take care not to get too close – we do want you back. Tell her to make her pilgrimage there and plead what she will. If she does miracles, one will save her.' The Incarnate stood, looming. 'We've seen the power our enemy holds. We can't allow them any more toeholds, or for any other groups to make cracks in our defenses. When you return, I'll have you at my side, bringing justice to the entire Union.'

Ilan started. It would have been exactly what he would have had hoped for, long weeks ago. Before he'd found something else to believe in.

'Incarnate, that's . . . generous. Abandoning the girl, though . . .'

Csilla had done what she set out to, save them all, and this was what they gave her. No one condemned had ever come back from that supposed end of the world, and no escort had ever ventured far enough to confirm or deny its existence. Ilan could see it for what it was: a slow execution in starvation, frostbite, and likely the teeth of hungry creatures coming out of their winter dens. Csilla would be a bounty in a place the snow wouldn't thaw for weeks yet.

Hints of purple anger bloomed on the Incarnate's cheeks.

'Are you hesitating? Do you still serve Asten?'

The slap of the question drew Ilan's shoulders straight.

'Of course.'

It was only that Asten wasn't here.

40

Csilla

The pressure of Erzsébet on her chest only exacerbated the ache in Csilla's back as she lay in the cramped room. She'd heard the whispers of those who'd come in to check on her, ones who prayed and ones who cursed, none of whom had dared touch her while she squeezed her eyes and pretended her heart was light enough to rest. The feel of Mihály's soul on her palm lingered like smears of altar oil, staining and sacred.

One thing had been clear in all the voices. The Incarnate had sentenced her to death. That's what this banishment was.

The low angle of the sun told her she'd been out for hours, lying in hot-skinned wait. Strength was coming back to her limbs, her parched throat cracking. Soon it would be dark enough to move. She had to, whether or not she was ready.

She shifted the cat and sat up enough to look out across the cathedral's steep slanted roofs, wondering what parts of the wood were still good, what could have been damaged. How she could get out without plunging through and ending up a broken body speared on a blessed statue. She wished she could call it a mercy that they put her here where she could look over her dear city, not in the bowels, but it was only because there were fewer ways to escape with a guarded door and a sure fall outside.

A sharp knock rattled the door, and Erzsébet stopped her kneading to raise her head.

Ilan entered, face grave. He wore white and gold, and there was a line of gold across his brow.

The signs of a saint.

It might have been her imagination, but she would have sworn his cheeks coloured as he caught her noticing.

Of course he would be the one to carry out the sentence. She'd claimed to speak for Asten, taken power that wasn't hers. The best she could have hoped for would have been to have her tongue cut out and another whipping, but now no one was inclined to mercy. She'd saved the Church, and he was the Church. It was too much to hope he'd choose her. She didn't have the right to want it.

If I was right to act, tell me. Better yet, tell them.

The silence ate at her bones.

Ilan turned the lock, then sat on the end of the bed. Csilla winced as Erzsébet stood to greet him, each paw a dig into her bruised flesh as she walked down Csilla's body to sniff his hand and say her hellos. As if this were a social visit.

Oh, for the innocent self-assurance of a cat.

'How are you feeling?'

She shrugged, trying uselessly to smooth her tangled hair. 'As well as anyone sentenced to die.'

She'd never been so aware of the fragility of flesh and bone, the thinness that separated every soul from the ether. She didn't know how it was to be done; a blade, a noose, being dragged to the end of the world and boiling in the dark, but she knew the order had been given.

Mihály had looked peaceful at the end, even with his life draining out. She would take comfort in that. Now she knew death wasn't the worst thing in the world.

'Do you think I'm going to let that happen?'

A small smile ghosted her face, bringing with it an ache as newly healed skin stretched. He thought he had a plan. Maybe he did.

'What kind of servant would I be if I let the Incarnate die?'

The worship in his voice made her shiver even as she wanted to laugh. The Incarnate sat on a throne of marble and passed judgements sung to him from above, didn't lie on sweat and blood-stained sheets, waiting to run in the dark.

But she'd saved the city, in a stumbling, terrified way. She'd taken two lives, given one back, and saved the faith of thousands.

A timid calm lapped through her, gentle waves on a softly worn shore.

On the day she'd willingly gone to bleed for the Church, the Prelate said that Asten didn't ask how she wanted to serve, but how she would serve. She closed her eyes so tightly tears squeezed out, clinging to the fading echoes of holy strength.

I don't understand what You want me to do.

The answer didn't come from the ether but from herself. It was the same calling she'd always felt, a fierce love threatening to pull her apart. Perhaps she'd never hear Them in the way that she wanted.

Perhaps it didn't matter. She'd done good work before, and she would continue, even if she had to do it alone.

'Csilla?'

Ilan's urgency drew her back to her present misery. She may have found a calling, but it was as an enemy of the Church.

'You offered to help me leave once.' She pressed her hands together. He reached out and covered her clasped hands with his own, warm and sure. Her breath deepened with the steady anchor.

'I never rescinded it.'

She nodded, spreading her hands slightly to let their fingers lace together, her throat full of acceptance and gratitude and other things she couldn't voice. The relief on his face hurt all the more knowing he wasn't going to like what was coming. Saika would be wild and beautiful, and safe for a time. But if word got out that she was there, the false Incarnate would see it burned and call the blaze redemption. She could rest there, plan and pray, but not stay.

And she couldn't tell him that.

'Are you ready?' His voice cracked like he wasn't.

This wasn't a thing one could be ready for. If she had time, there was still so much she would do. Ask, one last time, if anyone knew anything about her family or who she was. Who it was who had known she needed to be hidden. Pray over Ágnes's ashes, sit longer with Mihály while all his beauty turned grey and cold deep below them. Someone should.

For a moment, her ears echoed with the Izir's laughter, warming and drowning her at once, and she pressed her hand to her heart. For all the bitter things he'd taught her, there would always be a small crack there that was his.

Csilla bent down and rubbed Erzsébet's head, and the cat stretched into the touch with an appreciative purr. Maybe Ilan would let her share his pillow while he was there.

'I hope you've gotten better at mousing,' she told her sternly, and the rough tongue lapping the ends of her fingers in answer brought a smile to her sore face.

It was as much of a goodbye as she was going to get from the only one in the Church who would care. She offered Ilan her wrists.

They rode for a week, Csilla on Vihar, who seemed more put out at the work by the mile and relied on stolen nibbles of greenery to brighten his mood, and Ilan on the spitfire mare the Church had conscripted for Csilla to ride, likely hoping she'd break her neck on the trip and save everyone trouble. Csilla wore the hood of someone condemned, and in every settlement they passed through, people bowed to Ilan and offered him the best of their larder, and they hissed at her.

I saved you, but I understand, she thought, keeping her eyes on Vihar beneath her. Whatever rumours had escaped the city had painted the prisoner being escorted as the problem. They no doubt thought cursing her was an act of grace.

They were far enough north that the trees were thick with dark green needles and morning exhalations were frosted. Ilan paused at a crossroad and dismounted. He untied Vihar from where Csilla was being ponied, and helped her down, her leather boots landing gently on the ground, though after unpractised days in the saddle, her balance was coltish.

'Here?'

He'd told her he was leading her away, but the names of where they were passing were meaningless to her.

Ilan nodded as she shivered.

'My mother will be here soon, by Asten's grace. If she got the messages.' His face was regal in the filtered forest light, his pale hair and white cloak a beacon itself, and the air was suddenly no longer so cold. 'I haven't told her much, so you should probably just agree with whatever she . . . assumes.'

He didn't meet her eyes, and she sighed. Sending a disgraced lover away was at least a heard-of occurrence, and a little embarrassment was worth the convenient excuse.

They didn't have long to wait. A carriage pulled up beside them, dark-panelled wood with silver inlay, a wolf's head topping each corner and decorating the breastplates of the pair of horses, each midnight-coloured and Vihar's twin. Even after all she'd felt, Csilla had too much of a pauper in her not to stare. This was the kind of life Ilan had left for sanctity and blood.

Olga emerged, her red travelling cloak embroidered with amber-eyed hares and pale green winter sage; it was the colour of Mercy celebration, though Csilla knew she was the only one thinking of Ágnes.

'Hello, my dears,' she greeted. Csilla tried to bow, but a fresh bloom of pain in her thighs forced her to sag on Ilan.

Olga rushed forward, an extra pair of hands to steady her. Her blue eyes were kinder than her son's, but she held herself with the same unquestioned confidence.

'Is she sick?' Olga's voice was equal parts reproach and concern as she pulled Csilla to her. With a spare hand she reached for the clasp of her cloak.

'I'm just tired,' Csilla explained, flushing. 'I'm not used to riding.' A muscle in her hip spasmed in agreement.

'She's well enough to travel.' Ilan's hand was warm on her lower back, not quite around her waist. 'We'll get some food and more water in her.'

'We?' A hope as sharp as any knife sunk into her as she realised he hadn't intended to send her away alone. Ilan gave a small nod. 'I'll be riding beside.'

But she had to smother that, sheathe the blade and be brave.

'No.' She turned and ushered him back towards the trees, to privacy and violet shadows seemingly designed to soften terrible news. 'You need to stay. Find out what you can about the man who sits on that throne. That's one thing I can't do.'

He parted his lips to speak, and she shook her head.

'You're a saint now. He'll take you with him when he travels.'

'But what about you?' He wasn't even trying to disguise the raw fear in his voice. 'My parents can't know who you are. And the Incarnate will take me to war.'

He was right to be afraid. There were many ways to die between here and Saika, and thousands more across to the border. And even if they were both alive, they'd have the whole of the country between them.

But that didn't matter now.

'It's alright.' She shook her head and breathed deep, a precious and hollow memory of all creation nestled deep within her ribs. 'I'll find you again.'

'Will you?' The wind whistled between them, sharp and calling as the horses stamped with impatience.

'I promise.' Csilla reached out and put her palm over his mark. The dazzling flare of it was a lightning storm, every crack and hollow place within her flooding with purpose. She saw everything. She *was* everything.

And then it was gone, and all she was left with was Ilan's awe and a growing cold and the ache of leaving something dear. Still, she smiled, savouring the pain. It was only there because of tenderness, another thing to be protected.

'Have faith in me.'

Acknowledgements

I began *The Faithful Dark* in 2018. From there, it had a long journey, through Pitch Wars, indie publishing and finally to the version you have today. None of this would have been possible without many, many talented and generous people lending their hands and eyes.

First thanks to my agent, Julie Gourinchas, who loved the book so much she queried me and has been an absolute champion. May this book be the first of many!

To the team who kept the book on track and made my dreams come true, I couldn't ask for a better publisher. Huge thanks to my editor, Kate Norman, who was always down for making things even more disturbing, as well as to Victoria Denne, Saxon Bullock, Claudette Morris, Dewi Hargreaves, Robyn Bowler and George Biggs.

I owe massive gratitude and everything I know about revision to my Pitch Wars mentors Hayley Stone and Erin Tidwell, as well as my AMM mentor Liz Parker. And to my mentee sibling Maiga Doocy, I'm so excited our books will be on the same shelf!

Tara Christofes-Bell, you poetic and noble land mermaid, you always have the correct opinions. Leanne Schwartz and Heidi Christopher, I love being in the trash with you.

To the slack: Amanda Helander, Angel Di Zhang, Anita Kelly, Anna Sortino, Avione Lee, A.Y. Chao, Briana Johnson, Briana Miano, Brighton Rose, Chandra Fisher, Gabe, Elora Ditton, Emily Varga, Gigi Griffis, Hugh Blackthorne, Kaitlyn Hill, Kat Hillis, Kate Dylan, Katie Bohn, Lani Frank, LC Milburn, Maiga Doocy (again), Mercy Blackburn, Molly Steen, Piper Vossy, Sami Ellis, Sarah Mughal Rana, Siana LaForest, Sophia Mortensen, Tanvi Berwah, Vaishnavi Patel and Victor Manibo. I would literally be unable to survive publishing without you, please never leave me.

I don't think I could list all the wonderful people who looked at various drafts over the years, just know that if you read, commented, liked on socials or just said the book sounded cool, that's what kept me going over the eight years it took to get this book to its final form.

I have to express my deep appreciation for Ava Reid, K.M. Enright and Lyndall Clipstone, who supported *The Faithful Dark* from its earliest publication as an indie book, and Therese Andreasen, the trad edition's fairy godmother.

Of course I owe my mom who, in addition to giving me life, also gave me space to write my weird books without judgement.

And finally, to my beautiful cat Halle, who deleted this whole document halfway through. You really were no help at all.

Are you ready
to meet your god?

THE RUTHLESS LIGHT

CATE BAUMER

is coming in 2027

Good luck under
Asten's holy gaze . . .

HODDERSCAPE

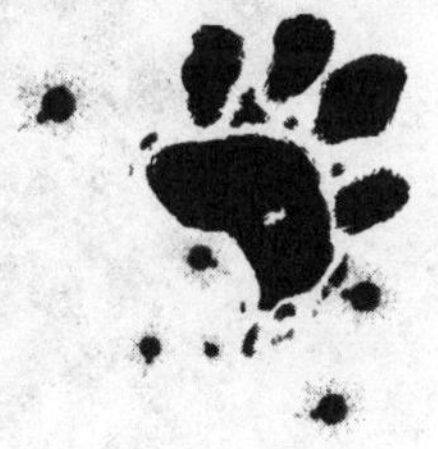

WANT MORE?

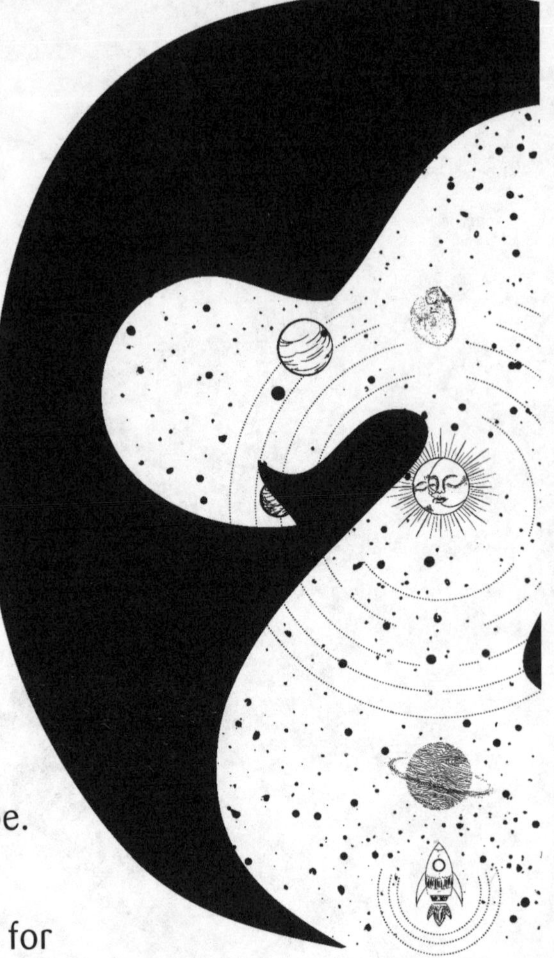

If you enjoyed this and would like to find out about similar books we publish, we'd love you to join our online Sci-Fi, Fantasy and Horror community, Hodderscape.

Visit hodderscape.co.uk for exclusive content from our authors, news, competitions and general musings, and feel free to comment, contribute or just keep an eye on what we are up to.

See you there!

@HODDERSCAPE HODDERSCAPE.CO.UK